MARIANNE
Napoleon's Star

MARIANNE
Napoleon's Star

JULIETTE BENZONI

Book 1: Marianne Series

First published in English as *Marianne* in 1969 by Heinnman.
Also published in English in two parts as *Marianne: The Bride of Selton
Hall*, 1971 and *Marianne: The Eagle and the Nightingale*, 1971.

This edition: Telos Publishing
139 Whitstable Road, Canterbury, Kent CT2 8EQ,
United Kingdom.

www.telos.co.uk

ISBN: 978-1-84583-213-1

Telos Publishing Ltd values feedback. Please e-mail any comments
you might have about this book to: feedback@telos.co.uk

British Library Cataloguing in Publication Data.
A catalogue record for this book is available from the British Library.

CONTENTS

PROLOGUE
1793, A Lonely Heart

Ellis Selton stirred the smouldering logs with the end of her cane. A long tongue of flame leapt up, curled like a glowing snake about the logs and floated up into the dark expanse of the chimney. She leaned back in her chair with a sigh. Tonight, she hated the whole world and herself more than anything. It was always so when the weight of loneliness became unbearable.

Outside, sharp gusts of wind were bending the tops of the great trees in the park, whirling round the house and howling mournfully down the chimneys. To the lonely old maid who was the last remaining Selton, the storm seemed to draw out of the ground all the age-old ancestral voices of the place. There were no men now to inherit the great estate, no proud joyous young men with loud voices and strong backs who would make light of such a burden. There was only Ellis, lame and thirty-eight years old, to whom no one had ever spoken words of love. Not that she would have had any difficulty in finding a husband, but those who were attracted by her fortune and the splendours of Selton Hall filled her with such contempt that she could never bring herself to make the choice. And so, rejecting one suitor after another, she had turned by degrees into this grey-clad recluse, entrenched in her pride and her memories.

The wind dropped for a moment and from across the park came the muffled clanging of a bell. The huge dog which slept, nose pillowed on its paws, at the woman's feet, opened one eye and cocked it at his mistress. He gave a low growl.

'Quiet,' Ellis murmured, laying a hand on the animal's head. It was probably a servant returning late or some tenant farmer come to see old Jim.

Idly scratching the dog's silky head, she tried to recapture her train of thought but the animal was still uneasy. His hackles had risen and he seemed to be listening intently, as though following by instinct the progress of the caller across the wind-swept park. At last, intrigued by his behaviour, his mistress muttered:

'Can it be a caller? Who would come at this hour?'

But the noiseless entrance of her butler, Parry, a few moments later, brought the answer. For once, Parry, usually the picture of dignified calm, looked flustered.

'There is a man outside, my lady. A traveller who insists on speaking with your ladyship.'

'Who is he? What does he want. What is the matter, Parry?'

'He's not at all our usual style of visitor, my lady, not at all. In fact, it was only at his strong insistence that I consented to disturb your ladyship —'

'Get to the point!' Ellis cried, tapping her stick on the ground impatiently, 'if you go on like this, I shall never find out what it is all about. And since you have consented to disturb me, I may as well know why.'

Somewhat disconcerted, the butler allowed his features to relapse momentarily into an expression of disgust. Then, his lips pursed in suitable disdain, he answered:

'It is a Frenchman, my lady, a catholic priest. He appears to be carrying an infant —'

'What! Have you gone mad, Parry — ?'

Ellis had risen to her feet. Her face was as grey as her dress and the blue eyes under her heavy, gingery eyebrows were bright with anger.

'A priest? And with a child? Some fugitive from justice, I daresay, with the evidence of his misdeeds! And a Frenchman, into the bargain! One of those wretches who have slaughtered their nobility and murdered their sovereign! And you imagine I will take in such — ?'

As a devout protestant, Ellis Selton had no love for Catholics and regarded their priests with abhorrence deeply tinged with mistrust. Her voice, as she spoke, had risen from her normal, well-modulated tones to a shrill and penetrating scream. She was on the point of ordering Parry to send the intruder packing when the library door, which the butler had left ajar, opened to admit a small, black-clad figure carrying something in his arms.

'This I think you will take in, however,' he said in a gentle voice. 'One does not reject what God sends —'

The newcomer was thin, almost frail. The dirty stubble which covered his cheeks added a touch of strangeness to an otherwise undistinguished face. There was something unexpected, also, about the rather comical turned up nose although its possessor's evident wretchedness made this more tragic than funny. At all events, the stranger was redeemed from being either ugly or commonplace by the beauty of his great, luminous grey eyes, eyes of great depth and candour which gave his intelligent face a definite charm. In spite of her anger, Lady Selton also took note of the slenderness of his hands and feet, infallible signs of breeding. However, this was not enough to calm her fury. Her face turned from white to dark red.

'Indeed,' she said with some sarcasm, 'so God has sent you. I admire your impudence, my good man! Parry, call the servants and have them throw this heavenly messenger out – and the bastard he's hiding under his cloak!'

She expected the stranger to be worried but he showed no signs of it. The little man did not stir. He merely nodded; his fine, honest eyes fixed steadily on the angry woman.

'You may throw me out if you please, my lady,' he said putting aside the folds of his cloak to reveal the child, apparently asleep. 'But take, at least, the thing that God sends you. For it was not of myself I spoke but of her –'

'Your protégées are no concern of mine. I have my own poor!'

'Of her,' the stranger went on inexorably, and his voice had taken on a solemn note, 'whose name is Marianne- Élisabeth d'Asselnat – your niece.'

Ellis Selton was thunderstruck. The stick on which she had been leaning clattered to the polished floor but she made no effort to retrieve it. As he spoke, the little man had thrown back the great, greenish-black cloak, shabby and rain-sodden, which enveloped him and moved closer to the fire. The firelight fell on the face of a baby some few months old, lying fast asleep wrapped in a tattered shawl.

Ellis opened her mouth to speak but no words came. Her eyes moved wildly from the sleeping child to the stranger's face and came to rest at last on Parry, deferentially holding out her stick. She seized it like a drowning man, clenching her hand upon the knob until the knuckles whitened.

'Leave us, Parry,' she murmured in a voice that was strangely low and hoarse.

When the door had closed on the butler, Lady Selton asked: 'Who are you?'

'I am a cousin of the Marquis d'Asselnat – and also, Marianne's godfather. My name is Gauthier de Chazay, the Abbé Gauthier de Chazay. His voice held no trace of defiance.

'If that is so, forgive me for this welcome, I could not have guessed. But,' she spoke more sharply, 'you said this child was my niece –'

'Marianne is the daughter of your sister, Anne Selton and the Marquis Pierre d'Asselnat, her husband. And the reason I have come to ask your care and protection for her is that there is now no one to whom she can turn for affection but you, my lady – and myself.'

Ellis drew back slowly, never taking her eyes off the priest, until her groping hand met the wooden arm of her chair and she dropped into it heavily.

'What has happened? Where is my sister – my brother-in-law? If you have brought me their child, then they must –'

She could not go on but the Abbé knew from the agonized break in her voice that she had already guessed. There were tears in the grey eyes that studied the old maid and an infinite pity. With her grey dress and the preposterous white cap with green ribbons which crowned her thick head of flaming red hair, she presented a picture that was at once bizarre and imposing. Instinctively, she tucked her crippled leg back under her seat. A fall on the hunting field, five years previously, had left her incurably lame. But the Abbe's knowledge of people was enough to show him the proud and painful loneliness of this woman. It grieved him to have to add to her sorrows.

'I am sorry to be the bringer of bad news,' he said softly. 'You must know that, a month past, Queen Marie-Antoinette mounted the scaffold already stained with her royal husband's blood, and this despite the efforts of some of her faithful servants led by the Baron de Batz, to snatch her from the jaws of death. They failed – and two days later some of them paid with their lives for their loyalty to the Queen's cause. The Marquis d'Asselnat was among them –'

'My sister?'

'She would not be parted from her husband in his death and they were arrested together. Life without Pierre meant nothing to her. You know the deep and passionate love which united them. They went to the guillotine as they had gone to the altar in the chapel at Versailles, hand in hand and smiling.'

He was cut short by a sob. Great tears which she made no attempt to hide were rolling down Ellis's face. The tears came so naturally, as though, without realizing it, she had been preparing for a long time to shed them. Preparing, in fact, ever since the day when her young and lovely sister Anne had fallen in love with a French diplomat and had renounced her own land, her religion, and everything that had been dear to her to follow Pierre d'Asselnat. Anne might have been a duchess in England, she had chosen to be a marquise in France, and in so doing had broken the heart of the sister, fifteen years older than herself, who had watched over her ever since the death of their mother. Even then, Ellis had felt that her little Anne was going to meet a tragic fate, although she could not have said what gave her the idea. Yet what the Abbé de Chazay had told her was, after all, no more than the fulfilment of her nightmares.

Moved by her silent grief, the little man in the rusty black stood before her his arms mechanically cradling the sleeping child. But then, Ellis straightened herself. She held out eager, trembling arms to the baby and taking her gently, laid her against her own flat chest, peering with a kind of terror into the tiny face crowned with a mist of brown curls. She touched the tight little fists with a timid, exploring finger. The tears dried and a look of gentleness came over her face.

The Abbé's legs, trembling under the accumulated weariness of weeks, seemed to give way and he subsided into a chair and watched the last of the Seltons discovering the maternal instinct. There, in the firelight, the long face in its frame of red hair presented an indefinable picture of mingled love and pain.

'Who is she like?' Ellis asked softly. 'Anne was so fair and this child's hair is almost black.'

'She is like her father, but she will have her mother's eyes. You will see when she wakes—'

As if she had only been waiting for the words, Marianne opened a pair of eyes as green as young grass and looked at her aunt. The tiny nose screwed up, the small mouth turned down woefully and the baby began to howl. Ellis started with surprise and almost dropped her. Her eyes flew to the Abbé with an expression of near panic.

'Good God! What is it? Is she ill? Have I hurt her?'

Gauthier de Chazay smiled broadly, showing firm white teeth.

'I think she is merely hungry. She has had nothing but a little spring water since this morning.'

'And nor, I daresay, have you! What am I thinking of, sitting here with my grief while you and this little angel perish of hunger and fatigue—'

Within seconds, the silence in the house was a thing of the past. Servants came running. One was ordered to fetch a person named Mrs Jenkins, the others to produce upon the instant a hot supper, tea and brandy. Finally, Parry was commanded to make ready a room for the guest from France. Everything happened at astonishing speed. Parry disappeared, the servants brought a lavish repast and Mrs Jenkins made the solemn entry suited to her position as housekeeper, her ample person and considerable years. But this majesty melted like butter in the sun when Lady Selton placed the baby in her arms.

'Take her, my good Jenkins – she is all that remains to us of Lady Anne. Those bloodthirsty scoundrels have killed her for trying to save the unhappy queen. We must take care of her for we are all she has – and I have no one but her.'

When they were all gone, she turned to the Abbé de Chazay and he saw that tears were still running down her cheeks but she made an effort to smile and indicated the laden table.

'Sit down – eat, then you shall tell me all.'

The Abbé talked for a long time, describing his flight from Paris with the baby after he had found her, alone and abandoned, in the d'Asselnat's town house after it had been looted by the mob.

Meanwhile, upstairs, Marianne, well washed and full of warm milk, was sleeping peacefully in a big room with hangings of blue velvet, watched over by the elderly Mrs Jenkins. The worthy housekeeper had dressed the fragile little body tenderly in lace and cambric that had once been her mother's and now, she was rocking her gently and lovingly and singing an old song conjured up from the recesses of her memory:

'Oh mistress mine! where are you roaming?
Oh mistress mine! where are you roaming?
O! stay and hear; your true love's coming,
That can sing both high and low...'

Whether Shakespeare's old song was addressed to the fleeting shade of Anne Selton or to the child come to find a refuge in the heart of the English countryside, there were tears in Mrs Jenkin's eyes as she smiled at the baby.

And so, Marianne d'Asselnat came to spend her childhood in the old home of her ancestors and grow up in old England ...

PART I

1809, The Bride Of Selton Hall

CHAPTER ONE
The Wedding Night

The priest's hand was raised in blessing and as he uttered the ritual words, all heads were bowed. Marianne realized that she was married. A wave of joy swept over her, almost savage in its intensity, and at the same time she had a sense of absolute irrevocability. From this moment, she ceased to belong to herself and became, body and soul, one with the man who had been chosen for her. Yet, though the choice might not have been her own, not for anything in the world would she have wished him other than he was. From the first moment, when he had bowed to her, Marianne had known that she loved him. And from then on, she gave herself to him with a passionate devotion which she brought to everything she did, with all the ardour of first love.

Her hand, with the brand-new ring, trembled a little in Francis's. She gazed up at him wonderingly.

'Forever,' she said softly. 'Until death do us part—'

He smiled, the kindly, rather condescending smile of an adult for an over-enthusiastic child, and pressed the slender fingers lightly before releasing them to hand Marianne to her seat. The mass was about to begin.

The new bride listened meekly to the first words but very soon her mind slipped away from the familiar ritual and returned, irresistibly, to Francis. Her eyes slid out from under the enveloping cloud of and fastened with satisfaction on her husband's clean-cut profile. Francis Cranmere, at thirty, was a magnificent human specimen. He was very tall and carried himself with a languid, aristocratic grace which, but for his muscular athletic frame, might have been thought feminine. Similarly, the stubborn brow and the powerful chin resting on the high muslin cravat, counteracted the rather too perfect beauty of features that, for all their nobility, seemed fixed in an expression of perpetual boredom. The white of the hands emerging from lace cuffs, would have done credit to a cardinal but the chest and shoulders moulded by the dark blue coat were those of a boxer.

Lord Cranmere was a man of contradictions, an angel's head on the body of an adventurer. But the whole had an undoubted charm to which few women were impervious. Certainly, for Marianne at seventeen he was pure perfection.

She closed her eyes for a second in order to savour her happiness, then opened them on the altar, decorated with autumn leaves and one or two late blooms amongst which a few candles burned. It had been erected in the great gallery of Selton Hall because there was no catholic church for several miles around and even fewer priests. The England of King George III was going through one of its periodical violent bursts of anti-papist feeling and nothing less than the protection of the Prince of Wales had been required to enable this marriage between a catholic and a protestant to take place according to the rites of both churches. An hour before, the priest of the Church of England had blessed the couple and now the Abbé Gauthier de Chazay was officiating by special favour. No power on earth could have kept him from blessing his goddaughter's marriage.

It was, moreover, a strange marriage, with no other pomp but these few flowers and candles, the one concession to the solemnity of the day. Around this makeshift altar, the familiar surroundings remained, as ever: the high white and gold ceiling with its hexagonal mouldings, the purple and white Genoa velvet hangings, the heavily gilded furniture and, last of all, the great canvases depicting the imposing figures of past Seltons. All this gave to the ceremony an impression of unreality and timelessness that was strengthened by the gown worn by the bride.

Marianne's mother had worn these things at Versailles, in the presence of King Louis XVI and Marie-Antoinette on the day of her marriage to Pierre-Louis d'Asselnat, Marquis de Villeneuve. There was a full gown of white satin oversewn with lace and rosebuds, worn over the wide cloth of silver underskirt swollen with panniers and a host of petticoats. The tight, constricting bodice with its square neck line was cut low, revealing a girlish bosom below the necklace made of many rows of pearls, while from the high powdered wig, frosted with diamonds, a great lace veil cascaded like the tail of a comet. This dress, with all its outmoded magnificence, Anne Selton had sent home as a keepsake to her sister Ellis who had treasured it ever since.

Many times, when Marianne was little, Aunt Ellis had shown her that dress. Each time, she had to hold back her tears as she drew it from its cedar wood chest but she loved to see the wonder on the child's face.

'One day,' she would tell her, 'you too will wear this dress. And that will be a happy day for you. Yes, by God, you shall be happy!' As she spoke, she would thump her stick on the ground as though challenging fate to contradict her. And it was true, Marianne was happy.

But now, the thumping with which Ellis Selton had been in the habit of punctuating her commands echoed no longer, except in her niece's memory.

For a week now, the generous, domineering old spinster had rested in the Palladian mausoleum across the park among her ancestors. This marriage had been her doing. It was her last wish and as such not to be denied.

Ever since that autumn evening when a weary man had deposited in her arms a baby only a few months old, crying with hunger, Ellis Selton had discovered a new meaning in her lonely life. Without effort, the ageing, arrogant spinster had transformed herself into a perfect mother for the orphan. Sometimes she would be overwhelmed by fierce waves of tenderness that woke her in the middle of the night, panting and sweating at the mere thought of the dangers through which the little girl had passed.

When this happened, she would get up, driven by an uncontrollable impulse, and fumbling for her cane, make her way barefoot, her red plaits dangling down her back, into the big room near her own where Marianne lay sleeping. She would stand for a long while by the cot, looking down at the baby girl who had become her one reason for living. Then, as the nightmare fears abated and her heart beat normally again, Ellis Selton would go back to her bed, not to sleep but instead to offer up endless prayers of thankfulness to God for granting an old maid this miracle, a child of her own to care for.

Marianne knew the story of her escape by heart, she had heard it so many times from her aunt. Ellis Selton, although fiercely protestant and anchored firmly in her religious beliefs, could value courage when she saw it. The Abbé de Chazay's exploit had earned him the Englishwoman's sincere esteem.

'He's a man, that little papist priest!' was her invariable conclusion to the story. 'I couldn't have done better myself.'

She herself was, in fact, a woman of consuming activity and tireless energy. She was passionately fond of horses and, before her accident had spent the best part of her time in the saddle, riding the length and breadth of her vast estates, inspecting everything with her keen blue eyes which very little was allowed to escape.

As a result, almost as soon as she was able to walk, Marianne was hoisted on to a pony and learned to accustom herself to cold water whether at her washstand or in the river where she learned to swim. Wearing little more in winter than in summer, going out bareheaded in all weathers, hunting her first fox at the age of eight, Marianne's education would have done credit to any boy but, for a girl and more particularly for a girl of her times it was more than a little unorthodox. Old Dobbs, the head groom, had himself taught her to handle weapons and at fifteen Marianne could wield a sword with the very best and shoot the pips out of a playing card at twenty paces.

Yet, with all this her mind had not been neglected. She spoke several languages and had been well taught in history, geography, literature, music and dancing and, above all, in singing, nature having endowed her with a voice whose warmth and clarity was by no means the least of its charms. Far better educated than the majority of her contemporaries, Marianne had become her aunt's pride and joy, and this in spite of a regrettable propensity for devouring every novel that came within her reach.

'She might take her place without shame on any throne!' the old woman was fond of saying, emphasizing her words with vigorous thumps on the ground with her stick.

'Thrones are never very comfortable things,' the Abbé de Chazay, to whom these glorious visions of Lady Ellis's were usually confided, would answer, 'but of recent years they have become perfectly untenable.'

His relationship with Ellis had always been violently unpredictable and now that it was all over, Marianne could not help looking back on it with a nostalgia touched with amusement. Lady Selton had been a protestant to her very soul and regarded Catholics with invincible mistrust and their priests with a kind of superstitious terror. To her, they still carried with them the slight but unmistakable smell of burning flesh associated with the worst horrors of the Inquisition. Between her and the Abbé Gauthier there was an endless and enthusiastic verbal duel in which each did his best to convince the other without the faintest hope of ever succeeding. Ellis flaunted the green banner of Torquemada, while Gauthier fulminated against the cruelties of Henry VIII, the fanatical furies of John Knox and recalling the martyrdom of the Catholic Mary Queen of Scotts, launched a virulent attack on the whole Anglican citadel. More often than not, the battle was ended by sheer exhaustion. Lady Ellis would ring for tea which came accompanied, in honour of the visitor, by a decanter of rare brandy. Then, peace restored, the two adversaries would confront one another again in a calmer frame of mind over the card table, each thoroughly pleased with the other and themselves, their mutual esteem intact, if not actually strengthened. And the child would go back to her play with the feeling that all was for the best in the best of all worlds, because the people she loved were at peace with one another.

Despite her aunt's convictions, Marianne had been brought up in her father's faith. If the truth were told, this religious instruction, like those interludes nicknamed by the child 'the wars of religion', did not take place very often. The Abbé Gauthier de Chazay's appearances at Selton Hall were brief and infrequent. They did not know how he occupied his time but one thing they did know, that he travelled a great deal in Germany, Poland and even as far as Russia where he stayed for long periods at a time. He was also to be found, from time to time, at the various residences of the Count of Provence who, since 1795 and the death of the Dauphin in the Temple, had become King Louis XVIII. The Abbé had lived for a while in Verona, at Mittau and in Sweden. Every now and then, he would make his appearance in England, only to vanish again, always in a hurry, always secretive, without ever saying where he was going. And no one ever asked questions.

With the establishment of the fat king without a kingdom at Hartwell

House, the preceding spring, the Abbé had seemed to be settled in England for a while. Since then, he made only one short journey abroad. Marianne and her aunt could not help being intrigued by all this coming and going. Lady Selton remarked more than once that it would not surprise her if the little priest turned out to be a secret agent for Rome.

Even so, it had been the Abbé she summoned to her bedside as she lay dying rather than the Reverend Mr Harris whom she heartily detested and referred to as a 'damned pompous idiot'. A bad cold, treated by the invalid with her customary supreme contempt, had brought her to death's door within a week. Ellis contemplated the approach of death without flinching, calm and lucid as ever, her only regret that it had come too soon.

'I still had so much to do,' she sighed. 'But whatever happens, I am determined that my little Marianne shall be married a week after I am underground.'

'So soon? I am here to take care of her,' the Abbé objected.

'You? My poor friend, I might as well trust her to a puff of wind! One day or other you will be off again on one of your mysterious journeys and the child will be all alone. No, she is betrothed, so get her married. A week, I said. Do you promise?'

The Abbé Gauthier had promised. And that was why on this wet November evening in the year 1809, true to his word, he had married Marianne d'Asselnat to Francis Cranmere.

Standing before the altar, wearing a white silk chasuble with gold embroidered lilies lent to him by Louis XVIII's chaplain, Alexandre de Talleyrand-Périgord,[1] the Abbé Gauthier de Chazay performed his function solemnly. His tiny, fragile figure in the priestly vestments acquired a kind of dignity enhanced by the slow, impressive gestures. At forty-five, his appearance remained obstinately youthful and only the streaks of white in his thick, dark hair below the tonsure betrayed the passing of time. But Marianne looked at these signs of age with love, dimly aware that they were earned by years of hard labour in the service of others. She loved him dearly, both for what she knew of him and the rest that she guessed and because of this her present happiness was a little spoiled because her dear godfather did not seem to share it. She knew he disapproved of her marriage to an English protestant. He himself would have preferred one of the young émigrés in the entourage of the Duc de Barry for her and he was simply conforming to the dead woman's wish. The Abbé de Chazay appeared to dislike Francis Cranmere as a man, and he was performing his sacred duty as a priest joylessly.

The ceremony over, he came towards the couple and Marianne smiled as

---

[1] The uncle of Napoleon I's famous minister, who had remained loyal to the crown.

though inviting him to smooth the frown from between his brows and share her happiness. Her own look seemed to say: 'I am happy and I know you love me. Why won't you be happy too?' There was anxiety in the mute inquiry. Now that Aunt Ellis was gone, he was all she had left and she wanted him to enter wholeheartedly into her love.

But the frown did not leave the Abbe's brow. He was looking at the young couple thoughtfully and Marianne could have sworn that there was in his eyes a curious mixture of pity, anger and anxiety. There was a silence which rapidly became so oppressive that Gauthier de Chazay became aware of it. His set lips curved into a joyless smile as he took the bride's hand.

'I wish you every happiness, my child. In so far as God wills us to be happy in this world. Only He knows when we shall meet again –'

'You are going away?' the girl asked in sudden alarm. 'But you said nothing to me?'

'I feared to add yet another disturbance to the household and to throw even a slight shadow on your happiness. Yes, I am going to Rome. Our Holy Father has summoned me. But now, I leave you in your husband's hands – I trust they will deal gently with you.'

The last words were directed to the young man. Lord Cranmere jerked up his chin and straightened his elegant back as he met the Abbe's eyes.

'I hope you do not doubt it, Abbé.' There was the hint of a challenge in his voice. 'Marianne is very young; I am sure she will prove biddable. Why should she not be happy?'

'To be obedient is not everything. There is also affection, indulgence, understanding – love.'

There was in both men's voices a note of barely controlled anger which frightened Marianne. Surely her husband and the priest who had just blessed their union were not going to quarrel right in front of the altar? She could not understand her godfather's scarcely concealed hostility towards the man chosen for her by Lady Ellis. She realized obscurely that this hostility was not religious in origin, that it was directed against Francis himself. But why? What could the Abbé have against him? Surely, Lord Cranmere was the most brilliant, brave, attractive, intelligent – whenever Marianne embarked on the attempt to catalogue her new husband's virtues, she generally found herself at a loss for superlatives. However, in this instance, she was not called upon to intervene. The Abbé de Chazay closed the subject by saying simply: 'I entrust her to you.'

'You may rest easy,' was the dry response.

The Abbé turned quickly back to the altar and, taking up the chalice, made his way back to Lady Ellis's old boudoir which had been turned into a temporary vestry. Not that the previous owner had ever had much use for the room as a boudoir, it was usually full of riding crops and hunting gear rather than dainty chairs and cushions.

As though suddenly relieved of some constraint, Francis smiled at his wife and, bending his tall figure slightly, offered her his hand.

'Will you come, my dear?'

Side by side, they began to walk slowly down the length of the big room. As befitted a wedding following so close upon a funeral, there were few people present, apart from the small knot of servants gathered just inside the double doors. But those few guests made up in quality for what they lacked in numbers.

With a firm hand, Francis led his young wife up to the Prince of Wales who, with a few friends, had insisted on honouring the marriage of one of his intimate circle. As she made her deep curtsey to the prince, Marianne found herself wondering that she was not more impressed. The future king had a considerable presence, even a certain majesty, but with the approach of his fiftieth year and the effects of a naturally voracious appetite he was lapsing more and more into obesity while a vinous flush was spreading inexorably over the august features. An aristocratic nose, commanding gaze and sensual lips could not preserve his royal highness from a somewhat comical appearance. Everyone in England, even the innocent Marianne, knew that the prince led a life of debauchery and that he was quite openly a bigamist, having been married first, by inclination, to his mistress, Mary Fitzherbert and afterwards, by necessity, to Princess Caroline of Brunswick whom he heartily loathed.

Such as he was, 'Prinny' smiled benevolently upon the young bride and condescended to incline his ample person to assist her to rise.

'Ravishing!' he pronounced. 'Positively ravishing, Lady Cranmere. By George, if I were not already quite sufficiently well provided for in the way of wives, I do believe I might have stolen you from my friend Francis myself. All my felicitations.'

'I thank your Highness,' Marianne stammered, her ears still full of the delicious sound of her new name. The prince however was already bellowing with laughter at his little joke and this laughter was dutifully taken up by Francis and the three gentlemen clustered round the heir to the throne. These three, Marianne had seen several times before. They were all three boon companions of the prince and Francis was often in their company. They were Lord Moira, Mr Orlando Bridgeman and the king of dandies himself, George Bryan Brummel, his pretty face with the insolent turned up nose perched above the dizzy folds of an exquisite white neck-cloth and surmounted by a negligent array of silken blond curls.

Lord Cranmere, in his deep voice, thanked the prince for honouring the ceremony with his presence and expressed the hope that his Royal Highness would do still further honour to Selton Hall by presiding over dinner.

'No, 'pon my soul!' the prince answered. 'I've promised Lady Jersey to take her to Hatchett's to choose her new carriage. A new carriage is no light matter and it's a long way to London. I must be off — '

'You will leave me, tonight?'

Marianne saw with surprise the lines of displeasure form round her husband's mouth. Was he then so disappointed to lose his royal guest? For her own part, she was only too desperately anxious for all these people to be gone and leave her alone at last with the man she loved. All the young couples in the novels she had read had asked nothing better than to bid their guests goodbye.

The prince's pleasant, rather foolish laugh rang out again.

'Are you so afraid of being left alone, on your wedding night?' That's not like you, Francis – but take heart, not all of me is going. I am leaving you the better part of me. Moira will stay and so will our American. And then you've your pretty cousin?'

This time, it was Marianne's turn to suppress a look of disappointment. Foppish Lord Moira, with his exquisite clothes and a manner so lethargic that he seemed more than half asleep, meant nothing to her but she had not had to exchange more than one glance with the person the prince had referred to as the American to know that she disliked him. And then there was the 'pretty cousin', Ivy with her airs and graces. From the very first she had treated Marianne as a raw country miss and flaunted a provoking 'cousinly' intimacy with Francis.

Turning her head away to hide her annoyance while Francis, on the contrary, appeared much reassured, Marianne met the amused eyes of the American himself. He was standing a little way away from the group around the prince, by one of the windows. Hands clasped behind his back, legs a little apart, he looked as though he had only happened to alight there by chance and formed a strong contrast with the other men present. This contrast had been the first thing to strike Marianne when he was introduced to her and she had been ruffled by it, as though the stranger's air of careless unconcern, verging almost on indifference, had been a direct insult to the irreproachable elegance of the others. It was not just his complexion, tanned by wind and weather, that offended her in comparison with the Englishmen with their pink, well fed faces. They were aristocrats, great landowners most of them, he was only a sailor probably owning nothing more than his ship, a ranger of the seas, 'a pirate'. Marianne had dismissed him instantly. It passed her comprehension how the son of an English king, a man who would be king himself one day, could find any pleasure in the company of a man who dared to turn up at a wedding wearing boots. All the same, her dislike had not prevented her from remembering his name. He was called Jason Beaufort. Francis had remarked with his habitual carelessness that the fellow came of a good Carolina family, descended from the French Huguenots obliged to flee to the new world after the revocation of the Edict of Nantes, but Marianne suspected her new husband of an excessively complaisant attitude towards anyone accepted by the prince.

'In spite of his looks, he's a gentleman—'

Thus the final judgment pronounced by Francis's handsome lips. Even so, Marianne was none too ready to agree. Although his manners were perfectly correct, she sensed in Beaufort something purposeful and menacing which made her uneasy. Accustomed, early in life, to the fierce pleasures of the chase, she often found herself comparing human beings to the animals she loved but whereas Francis reminded her of a splendid thoroughbred, she saw Jason Beaufort as a hawk. He had the hawk's bold profile, bright eyes and the lean, rangy look that yet gave an impression of dangerous vitality. Even the slender brown hands emerging from cuffs of delicate white lawn recalled the talons of the bird of prey while the look in those bright blue eyes was unnervingly intent. All through the ceremony, Marianne had been uncomfortably conscious of it on her neck and shoulders. She had found herself avoiding those eyes because, for all her native courage, she found it hard to meet them.

He was smiling, just now, as he looked at her. A thin, crooked smile revealing a lightning glimpse of very white teeth. Marianne's hand tightened on her husband's. She hated that slow, appreciative smile which made her feel somehow ashamed, as though the American were able to pierce through the mystery of her clothes and lay bare her girlish body. She actually shivered as she saw him abandon his idle stance and come towards her with his rolling sailor's gait. She looked away, pretending she had not seen the movement.

'May I be allowed to offer my compliments and good wishes?' The American's lazy voice spoke from so close behind her that she seemed to feel his warm breath on her neck.

Good manners obliged her to turn round but she left it to Francis to reply. His white hand clasped Jason's brown one as he exclaimed with a heartiness surprising to Marianne: 'You may indeed, my dear fellow! The good wishes of a friend have a value of their own and yours I know are genuine. We can count on your company?'

'Delighted.'

The blue eyes rested on Marianne's tight face and she thought furiously that he was aware of her dislike and amused by it. However, he had the good manners to go no further and merely bowed as the young couple moved away and turned their steps towards the Duc d'Avaray and the Bishop de Talleyrand-Périgord, who had come on behalf of Louis XVIII to honour the marriage of a countrywoman both of whose parents had perished in the Terror.

These two were standing somewhat apart, in lofty isolation over by the fireplace, making up by an austere dignity of bearing for their reduced situation as exiles. The simplicity with which both men were dressed formed a strong contrast with the elegance of the Prince of Wales and his friends. Marianne, in her old-fashioned dress, made a charming foil to their stiff, outmoded dignity. As the bride made her curtsey to the royal envoys, Francis had the momentary illusion that he was back at Versailles twenty-five years earlier and something of this showed in the involuntary respect with which he bowed. The smooth voice of the Duc d'Avaray was already extending the royal felicitations to the young couple, then, turning to Marianne, the old nobleman went on:

'Her royal highness, Madame la duchesse d'Angouleme[2] has been graciously pleased to send to you, my lady, this special token of her esteem. Madame has asked me to give you this, as a remembrance of her—'

He held out a small locket of blue enamel set with brilliants enclosing a fine lock of white hair. When Marianne gazed uncomprehendingly at the strange gift, d'Avaray went on:

'This lock was cut from the head of Queen Marie-Antoinette before her execution. Madame wished you to have it in memory of your noble mother who gave her life for the Queen.'

Colour flooded the girl's face. Unable to say a word, she sank into a deep curtsey leaving it to Francis to express her grateful thanks. Her feelings were, in fact somewhat mixed. These continual reminders of the past at a time when she stood on the threshold of a new life which she passionately hoped would be filled with the love and worship of a single man were more painful than pleasant. To Marianne, her mother was no more than a friendly ghost, the image of a smiling face pictured in an ivory miniature, but on this day the image had grown to the point of obliterating her own personality. There were moments when she wondered if it were really Marianne d'Asselnat and not Anne Selton who had married the handsome Francis Cranmere...

As he led her out into the hall to say their farewells to the prince, Francis glanced at Marianne's hands clasped round the locket.

'An odd present for a young bride,' he murmured, 'I hope you are not superstitious?'

She smiled bravely, thrusting away the momentary cloud.

'What is given in good faith cannot bring bad luck. This gift is precious to me, Francis.'

'Truly? I am glad. But, for the love of heaven Marianne, put the precious locket away in a box and don't wear it. Why do these damned demented Frenchmen always have to be waving the shadow of their frightful guillotine? I suppose it helps them keep alive their grievances and their thirst for revenge. And, I daresay, to forget that Napoleon is in power and they are only reflections of a vanished age.'

'You are very hard on my poor countrymen, Francis. Do you forget how

---

[2] Madame Royale, the daughter of Louis XVI and Marie-Antoinette.

much Madame has suffered? And I find it strange, that you, an Englishman, have a good word to say for the Emperor.'

'I detest Napoleon as much as I pity Madame Royale,' Francis retorted coldly. 'But I cannot approve of those who find it so easy to ignore the facts. But after all, politics seems to me a dry subject for your pretty head. Forget all about the revolution, Marianne, and concentrate on pleasing me.'

Dinner that night seemed to Marianne incredibly long and tedious. There were few guests and little gaiety. Certainly, it bore little resemblance to a wedding breakfast. Besides the young couple there were only the Abbé de Chazay, Lord Moira, Jason Beaufort and Ivy St. Albans and the guests had too little in common for lively conversation. The talk, at first commonplace, gradually died away. The Abbé de Chazay whose thoughts were no doubt already on his coming journey and the carriage which waited, ready harnessed, at the door, spoke little, the American not at all, contenting himself with observing Marianne with embarrassing attention. Only Francis and Moira talked about horses and hunting. Lady St Albans, following the bride's example, took no part in the discussion.

Ivy's dainty fingers were engaged in the mechanical rolling of little pellets of bread on the damask tablecloth. Marianne wondered why it was she could not bring herself to like this exquisite cousin of Francis.

Apart from her never allowing anyone to forget her connection with Lord Cranmere and her way of treating Marianne like a slightly backward child, Ivy St. Albans was the perfect picture of gracious sweetness. Some years older than Marianne, she was of medium height but her fairylike slenderness and still more the knot of pale gold ringlets which she wore high on her head made her seem taller. She had very delicate features, illuminated by a pair of languishing China blue eyes but although her mouth was as small as all the current canons of beauty could demand, there was something about her which Marianne found faintly shocking. It may have been her smile which had too close a look of Francis, perhaps that irreproachable and utterly feminine elegance which made the young girl feel, beside her, both countryfied and overdressed.

This evening was worse than usual. In her spreading lace-trimmed panniers, Marianne felt like some massive Chinese vase placed next to a fragile Tanara figurine. Her outdated furbelows only served to set off to advantage Ivy's wisp of a clinging muslin gown, the same blue as her eyes, cut low in the bosom to reveal the soft curve of her shoulders and caught in below her breasts by a chain of fine antique cameos that matched the fillet binding her fair curls. A long matching scarf completed an ensemble which, while stunningly simple, owed much of its effect to the perfection of the figure it covered. Ivy St. Albans, like many other Englishwomen, had taken to wearing muslin winter and summer because Napoleon was known to dislike it so much that the ladies of his court were virtually forbidden to wear it.

Marianne could never picture Ivy in anything but muslin. She had been wearing a dress of white muslin when Marianne met her for the first time, that day last summer in Bath. Lady Ellis had dragged a cross and distinctly unwilling Marianne away from her beloved woods with the two-fold object of taking the cure herself and at the same time introducing her niece into society. But the girl had felt instantly out of place amid the elegant crowds thronging the famous spa. There was too much noise, too many people, too much gossip, too many shrill, overdressed women and too many dandies with their bored and insolent airs and their passion for wagers.

And then, one morning as the two women were driving along Milsom Street after making some purchases, Lady Ellis uttered a cry and ordered the driver to stop. A couple were passing by on foot and Marianne's heart beat unaccountably faster. The woman was beautiful, certainly, and the height of elegance in the simple white dress which served to set off a miraculous chip-straw bonnet covered with a froth of delicate lace but Marianne had no eyes for her except to envy her escort. He was surely quite the finest man that ever was. Moreover, it was to him that Lady Ellis's rapturous exclamation was addressed.

'Francis, Francis Cranmere! My dear child, how good to see you again. Don't tell me you don't recognize me?'

The gentleman's handsome, disdainful mouth had curved into a smile.

'Lady Selton!' He responded instantly, 'could you doubt my knowing you? England is full of women but I'll take my oath there is only one Ellis Selton. Your most obedient servant, my dear lady.'

Removing the beaver hat he wore so elegantly tilted to one side, he bowed over Lady Selton's fingertips and her niece was able to observe, to her considerable astonishment, that her spinster aunt was quite flushed with pleasure. However, the young man's grey eyes immediately travelled on inquiringly to Marianne and she felt herself instantly purple with embarrassment. In her plain cambric dress adorned, thanks to the clever fingers of her maid, only with a single embroidered panel she felt suddenly horribly dowdy. Any comparison between herself and the lovely stranger was so little to her advantage that she felt ready to die of shame and was incapable of saying anything intelligible when her aunt presented her to: 'My dear Francis, the son of one of my oldest and dearest friends', and then to 'his charming cousin, Lady St. Albans'.

A few words more, an exchange of addresses, and then they parted with promises to meet again. The carriage moved away with Marianne on the verge of tears. All at once, she wanted desperately to make this fine gentleman notice her, to dazzle him with her wit and brilliance, while he had probably seen her merely as some kind of silly schoolgirl. Her aunt had laughed and teased her about it.

'But there,' she added with a sigh, 'I can scarcely blame you, these

Cranmeres are irresistible charmers, and Francis is the living image of his father. No man could ever think seriously of competing with Richard Cranmere.'

'Was he so very much admired?' Marianne asked in a small voice.

'Oh, the women were wild about him, every single one - more's the pity –'

The conversation had gone no further. Lady Ellis had lapsed into a reminiscent silence which the girl did not like to interrupt. She had learned later, by means of interrogating Jenkins, the old housekeeper, that her Aunt Ellis had once been madly in love with Richard Cranmere and had hoped to marry him but he had fallen instead for Marianne's mother, Anne, and Anne was already in love with a French diplomat. On her engagement to Pierre d'Asselnat, Lord Cranmere had gone away. His travels had taken him to India and it was there that he had married and that Francis had been born. The young man had returned home some ten years previously to take possession of a small inheritance not far from Selton Hall. At that time, he had called frequently on Lady Ellis, drawn to her by their mutual passion for horses. Then, succumbing to the attractions of London, he had sold the little estate which must have formed the bulk of his fortune and they had not seen him since.

'And probably will not see him again until the next chance encounter – in ten years' time!' Marianne had sighed.

But she was mistaken. Francis not only called on his old friend in the house she had taken for the season in Bath but, in September, he actually came to Selton Hall.

These visits plunged the young girl into an ecstasy of excitement. To her romantic imagination, Francis became Tristan, Lancelot, the Swan Knight come from distant shores to break the spell which held her captive. No legendary hero could live up to him. Francis was a hundred times more wonderful than all the knights of the Round Table put together, Merlin and King Arthur included. She began to day dream about him, basing an infinity of delight on a look or a smile, and building up reserves of happiness on which to live until his next visit. Francis behaved, in fact, charmingly to her. To her great surprise he would even sit by her now and then and talk to her. He asked her about her life and her amusements and, thinking of his life in London where he kept company with the noblest and most brilliant of the realm, she was ashamed that her conversation was all about dogs and horses and the countryside. She was so greatly in awe of him that one day, when Lady Ellis begged her to sing for Francis, she was unable to produce a single note. Her mouth was so dry that no sound came. By nature, lively and unselfconscious, in his presence she became shy and gauche. It was true that on that particular evening, Ivy had accompanied her cousin and her fragrant presence was not calculated to boost Marianne's confidence. The lovely cousin with her sophisticated elegance and unfailing sweetness was a sore trial to her nerves. She was like the fairy Vivien – but Marianne had never been fond of Vivien.

Her day of triumph had come out hunting when, for a whole day, she had galloped at Francis's side across muddy fields and through autumnal woods. Ivy, who disliked horses, had followed with Lady Ellis in the carriage. Marianne had Francis all to herself and she thought she would die of happiness when he complimented her on her faultless horsemanship.

'I know few men who ride as well as you,' he told her, 'and no women.'

There was a genuine warmth in his voice and in his eyes that flooded the girl's heart with joy. At that moment he really sounded like a lover. She smiled at him with all her heart.

'I love to ride with you, Francis. I feel as if I could go on like this to the end of the world.'

'Do you really mean that?'

'But – of course! Why should I say it if I did not?'

He made no answer. He merely leaned from his saddle and looked into her face and, for the first time, she was able to meet his gaze without embarrassment. Still, he had said nothing but as he moved away, he smiled briefly.

'Good,' was all he said. Then, apparently forgetting all about her, he gave his horse its head, leaving Marianne to wonder whether or not she had said something stupid.

After that day's hunting he had vanished for some time, and in any case her aunt's sudden illness had to some extent driven him from Marianne's mind. Then, one evening, two days before her death, Lady Ellis had sent for her niece.

'I know I am dying, child,' she told her, 'but I shall go in peace knowing that I shall not leave you alone.'

'What do you mean?'

'That Francis has asked for your hand and you shall marry him.'

'Mine? But – he has never spoken to me –'

'Stop babbling. I have not much time – he is a man who cannot fail to make you happy. He is twenty-eight now and will be able to give you the guidance and support you need. Besides, in bestowing you on him, I am remedying an injustice on the part of fate. Francis has no fortune of his own, now he will have ours – he will join you as the master of Selton – and when I am laying there, across the park, I shall be glad to think of my beloved home in your hands, both of you. That way, I shall never really leave you –'

Exhausted from the effort of speaking, Lady Ellis closed her eyes and said no more. Marianne left the room torn between a curious mixture of terror and delight. It seemed fantastic that Francis should want to marry her, a simple country girl, when there were so many women all anxious to please him. It gave her an odd sense of triumph. She felt at the same time very proud and very apprehensive.

'I shall never be worthy of him,' she thought. 'I shall always be doing something improper, and he will think how silly I am –'

It was this fear which returned, intact, to plague Marianne during her wedding dinner. She gazed with mingled joy and pride at Francis, sitting opposite her in the high-backed chair, long empty, that belonged to the master of the house. He sat in it so carelessly and naturally that the young bride was filled with admiration. For her own part, Marianne was all too conscious that she was now occupying the mistress's chair where, all her life, she had been used to seeing her aunt.

Ivy's soft voice broke in on her thoughts.

'I think it is time for us to withdraw, Marianne, and leave these gentlemen to smoke and drink in peace.'

Marianne jumped, realizing suddenly that everyone was looking at her and that the servants had already placed decanters of port and brandy on the table. She got to her feet, blushing in confusion for forgetting the time.

'Of course,' she said. 'We will leave you – I – I think I shall retire – a little tired –'

Already she was beginning to panic. Visibly unsure of herself, she went to bid farewell to the Abbé de Chazay who kissed her tenderly, unable to conceal his emotion. Inclining her head to the rest of the company, she let her eyes dwell a little alluringly on Francis as though begging him not to stay too long with his guests. Tonight was her wedding night and it belonged to her alone and no one had the right to rob her of even the smallest moment of it. But Francis merely smiled.

The two women left the room, Marianne feeling that her billowing silk dress sounded like a small typhoon. She could not wait to get it off, to be herself again. When they reached the foot of the stairs she turned to Ivy and found the other woman's blue eyes observing her while a thin smile twisted one corner of her lovely lips.

'Goodnight,' she said with nervous abruptness. 'Forgive me for leaving you so early but I am very tired and –'

'And you want to go and prepare yourself for the most important night of your life!' Ivy finished for her with a little crow of laughter which the bride found extremely irritating. 'You are right; Francis is not an easy man –'

The directness of this remark brought the colour flooding into Marianne's face but she said nothing. Picking up her wide skirts, she ran upstairs, her lace veil floating comet-like behind her. But Ivy's light, mocking laughter pursued her all the way to the door of her room.

CHAPTER TWO
Duel

The room was like a miniature archipelago with lace panniers, the great satin gown, wicker hoops and innumerable petticoats strewn about like a succession of pale islands. Marianne, now wearing only a simple bedgown made of fine lawn edged with lace and trimmed with narrow green satin ribbon, found herself gazing once more at her own familiar image mirrored in her glass. She saw a tall girl regrettably dark for an age which liked its women fair, and with a figure not yet fully rounded out. She had long, shapely legs, small hips and the neatest waist in all England. Her neck was long and slender, supporting an unusual heart-shaped face with high cheek bones and strong, proud features. The eyes, curving a little upwards at the corners to meet the sweep of delicately arched brows, were an elusive sea-green flecked with gold, and, almost as striking as their strange colour was their wilful, challenging expression. Even so, odd as it was, Marianne would have liked her face if it had not been for the big, soft mouth and the pale amber colouring of her smooth skin which gave her a faintly gypsy-like appearance and, in her own opinion, ruined everything. The canons of beauty of the day demanded cheeks all lilies and roses and Marianne was made miserable by her gipsy complexion for which not even her faultless hands or the heavy mass of silky black hair that fell below her hips could make up. Marianne's looks came from her father. Her mother had been all fairness but there was too much of the old stock of Auvergne in the girl's blood, with its occasional reminders of the Moorish knights of Abd-ar-Rhaman, joined to that of a Florentine ancestor. Gentle Anne Selton's British looks had been submerged.

Marianne sighed regretfully, thinking of the languishing eyes of Ivy St. Albans. She tried to restore her confidence a little with the thought that Francis had chosen her, had asked for her hand and surely that must mean beyond doubt that he liked her. Only, he had never told her that he loved her, had never even shown any disposition to make love to her although it was true there had been scarcely time. It had all happened so quickly. All the same, Marianne faced the night with trepidation, as though she stood on the borders of an unknown land, filled with half-suspected pitfalls. The books she was so fond of were generally rather reticent about wedding nights. The young bride would appear afterwards, blushing with her eyes modestly downcast, but with an invariable inward glow which, for the moment at least, Marianne was at a loss to explain.

She turned from the mirror to smile at Mrs Jenkins who having roundly refused to allow anyone else to attend her 'baby' on this great occasion, was now picking up the scattered garments. She smiled back.

'You look lovely, Miss Marianne,' she said, 'and everything will be all right. So don't look so dismal!'

'I am not dismal, Jenkins – only nervous. Do you know if the gentlemen have left the table yet?'

'I'll go and see.'

Mrs Jenkins went out, her arms filled with lace and petticoats, while Marianne drifted aimlessly over to the window. The night was still and black with not a star in sight. Long trails of mist rolled wraith-like across the park. There was practically nothing to be seen but Marianne did not need sight to see in her mind's eye the vast, sweeping dark green lawns of Selton Hall, barely touched as yet by autumn. She knew though that they lost themselves in the distance beneath the heavy shade of centuries-old oaks. Beyond lay the quiet hills and deep woods of Devonshire where she could gallop for days at a time on the track of fox or deer. This was the time, before the onset of winter, that Marianne loved: the misty mornings and long evenings spent around the wood fire roasting chestnuts and, later on, skating on the frozen ponds, silver blades flashing with the exhilarating rush of speed past reed beds white with frost. All these had been the simple joys of her girlhood. Marianne had never known, until tonight, how much she loved the old house and grounds and the English countryside, the red earth and soft hills which had closed like strong arms round an orphan child. Standing on the brink of the night which would give her to Francis, she wished that she could run out once more into the wood, because the trees seemed to communicate to her some deep power against which fear and worry broke in vain. And, just at this moment, she knew that she was dreadfully afraid, afraid of disappointing him, of being thought plain or stupid. If only Francis had taken her in his arms once, just once. If he had only murmured some words of love to give her confidence and overcome her modesty – but no, he had always been polite, even affectionate, but Marianne had never yet glimpsed in the grey eyes of her betrothed that flame of passion she so longed to arouse. No doubt tonight would bring her all these things. The words to sweep her off her feet and the overmastering caresses. Meanwhile, she waited in a state of feverish anticipation which left her mouth dry and her hands icy cold. Surely, no girl was ever half so ready to become her husband's adoring and submissive slave, for Marianne admitted secretly that there was nothing she would not do for love of Francis.

She was, of course, largely ignorant of what was meant by the phrase, 'belonging to someone'. Aunt Ellis was no longer there to tell her, even supposing she herself had ever known, and old Mrs Jenkins certainly could not but she had a vague idea that its effect would be a transformation so complete that her whole being would be altered by it. Would she love the trees and the countryside tomorrow if Francis did not love them too?

A slight creak as the door opened broke into her thoughts. It was Jenkins coming back and Marianne turned quickly from the window to meet her.

'Well' she asked. 'What is happening? Have our guests retired yet?'

Mrs Jenkins did not answer at once. She took off her spectacles and began wiping them carefully. Marianne knew instantly that something was wrong. Jenkins always did that when she wanted time to think before she spoke.

'Well?' Marianne asked again.

'Most of them have gone up, my lady,' the housekeeper said at last, restoring the spectacles to her nose.

'Most? Who is still down there?'

'Your husband – and that foreigner, the man from America.'

Marianne's lips tightened ominously. What business had this American to keep Francis downstairs at an hour when all his thoughts should have been for his young bride? Certainly, Jason Beaufort was the last person she wished to hear of just at that moment.

'Are they still at their port?'

'No. They are at cards.'

'At cards! At this hour?'

Mrs Jenkins spread her arms in a gesture of helplessness at Marianne's incredulous expression. The girl opened her mouth to say something but changed her mind. Slowly, she turned on her heel and went back to the window. Not even to old Jenkins who had brought her up would she show her disappointment. How could Francis dawdle over a stupid game of cards while she waited for him, trembling with an excitement that tied her stomach in knots and made her feel sick.

'Cards!' she said between her teeth. 'He plays cards while I wait for him!'

A spark of anger had begun to mix with her disappointment. Aunt Ellis had set great store by good manners and she would never have tolerated Francis's playing cards with a friend on his wedding night. It was not done in novels either. It was a small thing, perhaps, but the incident brought home to her just how much she missed her aunt.

'Now he is all I have,' she thought bitterly. 'Surely he must understand that? I – I need him so.'

She shut her eyes tightly to force back the tears. Her anger rose. Patience was never her most shining virtue and now it made her so cross to think of her husband wasting his time with Beaufort that she had to fight back a sudden impulse to rush downstairs and drag him away. It was bad enough that the man had been invited to spend the night in the house at all. It seemed to Marianne that his presence hung over it, if not exactly as a threat, certainly as an incubus. This may have been due simply to her dislike of him but, however much she tried to talk herself out of it, the sense of a shadow looming over Selton Hall remained.

'Won't you let me put you to bed?' Mrs Jenkins spoke hesitantly from behind her. 'It would be best – well more fit for you to be in bed when your Francis comes.'

'When will he come?' Marianne blurted out angrily. 'Will he come at all?'

Her pride and her love were both suffering. She must count for very little in Francis's eyes. But perhaps, after all, his concept of love was very different from a seventeen-year-old girl's. But she saw Jenkins looking at her unhappily and relented.

'I'm not feeling sleepy,' she said with an assurance she was far from feeling. 'I would rather stay up. But you, my good Jenkins, you go to bed. I – I shall read for a while.'

To support her words, she took a book at random from a small bookcase and, settling herself in an armchair, bestowed on Mrs Jenkins a smile which did not deceive that good woman in the least. She knew Marianne too well not to see through any such attempt to pull the wool over her own or anyone else's eyes. However, thinking it quite right and proper for her young lady to behave with a dignity in which, to Mrs Jenkins way of thinking, her husband was at that moment singularly lacking, the housekeeper did not insist. With a prim 'goodnight, my lady,' she dropped a curtsey, smiled warmly and withdrew.

She was hardly gone before Marianne flung the book into a corner and gave way to scalding tears.

Was it possible a game of cards could take so long? Two hours later Marianne had exhausted every possible outlet for her disappointment and exacerbated nerves. She had walked up and down the room until her feet trembled, gnawed her handkerchief to shreds and wept her heart out until she was forced to wash her face in cold water to remove the traces of tears. Now, dry eyed but with burning cheeks she admitted at last that she was frightened, simply frightened.

What could be keeping him so long? No game of cards could warrant such behaviour on one's wedding night. Perhaps something had happened to Francis. At once, the girl's imagination began building up a succession of improbable catastrophes. He might be ill. She was seized by a mad, childish longing to run downstairs and see what was the matter but some remnants of pride made her pause in the doorway. Suppose Francis were really sitting calmly in the drawing room playing whist? What a fool she would look—

Forcing herself to think calmly, she decided to do the only thing which seemed to her properly dignified and at the same time to offer a little balm to her wounded feelings, lock her door, go to bed, put out the light and sleep or at least pretend to since she knew that underlying her anger was a wretchedness that made the chance of sleep remote.

All around was the silent house. The noises of the sleeping countryside came to her through the open window. The belated shriek of a nightjar sounded somewhere deep in the woods. Marianne went to the door, shot the bolt and, tugging off her dressing gown as she went, hurried into bed. But she had hardly laid her dark head on the lace pillow, after first hurling the one intended for Francis viciously to the ground, when there was a soft tap at the door.

Her heart lurched in her breast and she lay frozen, not knowing what to do. She was torn between resentment, whispering to her to leave the door shut and pretend to be asleep, and love telling her to run to meet him with open arms now that he had come at last. The tapping came again, a little louder. Marianne could bear it no longer. She slipped out of bed, ran barefoot to the door and opened it. Then she stepped back with a gasp of surprise. There, standing in the doorway, was not Francis but Jason Beaufort.

'May I come in for a moment?' the American said. He smiled, revealing a flash of strong white teeth. 'I have to speak to you—'

Suddenly conscious of the extreme thinness of her nightgown, which offered nothing in the way of concealment, Marianne fell upon her robe with a cry of horror and wrapped it hastily around her. Once safely enveloped in its many flounces of lawn and lace, she felt sufficiently confident to face her unexpected visitor. Anger at being so surprised made her voice tremble as she said coldly:

'You cannot be aware of the impropriety of such a visit at this hour, sir, or you would scarcely have ventured to knock on my door. What you have to say must be very grave to justify such behaviour. I am awaiting my husband and—'

'Precisely, and I am here to tell you he will not come – not tonight at least!'

Instantly all Marianne's anxieties returned and she blamed herself bitterly for disregarding them. Something had happened to her Francis! But the American had read her fears in her eyes before she had time to utter them.

'No,' he said, 'nothing terrible has happened to him.'

'Then you have been making him drunk?'

Without waiting for a permission which was not forthcoming, Jason came inside and shut the door carefully behind him regardless of Marianne's frown. He was inside the room almost before she was aware of it. He looked at her and began to laugh.

'Well, what kind of education have you had, my lady, to make you think that only the fact that he was dead drunk would keep a husband from his marriage bed? Where the devil were you brought up?'

'My education is no concern of yours,' she snapped, stung by the American's laughter. 'Only tell me what has happened to Francis and then go!'

Jason made a face and bit his lip.

'Hospitality would not seem to be your strong point either. However, what I have to tell you will take a little time – besides being somewhat delicate. May I?'

With a slight, mocking bow he went and sat down in a large tapestry-covered armchair that stood beside the fire, stretched out his long-booted legs comfortably and looked up at the girl.

Marianne stood quivering beside the bed, her arms crossed over her breast, visibly struggling against a growing anger which made her eyes gleam like two hard green stones. The intruder looked at her thoughtfully for a moment, touched despite himself by her obvious youth and perhaps also by some private scruples. She had the animal grace of a young thoroughbred yet at the same time a warm femininity which touched some deep cord in the American. He found himself dwelling with a good deal of pleasure on the tantalizing and delightful vision he had beheld a moment before when she opened the door. But as he looked at her, a kind of rage welled up in him against Francis Cranmere and also against himself for being, through his own fault as much as the Englishman's, in this impossible situation.

At length, his silent scrutiny became too much for Marianne.

'Sir,' she broke out furiously, 'I warn you if you do not leave my room at once, I will have you thrown out, perhaps not by my husband, since you tell me he will not come, but by my servants!'

'If I were you, I would do no such thing. We, that is your husband, yourself and your humble servant are already in a somewhat delicate situation without your making it any worse by causing a scandal in the middle of the night. Leave your servants in their beds and listen to me.

Come over here now and sit down. I have told you, I must speak to you seriously and I ask you to hear me with patience.'

All trace of mockery had vanished. The sailor's blue eyes were hard as granite. The words were an order and, automatically, Marianne obeyed. She came slowly and sat down facing him as he had said, forcing herself to be calm. Her instinct told her that something was coming for which she would need all her self-control. She took a deep breath.

'I am listening,' she said coldly. 'But be quick. I am very tired –'

'It doesn't show. Listen, Lady Cranmere (he stressed the name deliberately), what I have to tell you may seem strange but I reckon you can stand a shock without flinching.'

'You are too kind. To what do I owe this good opinion?'

Marianne said lightly making an effort to conceal her growing alarm. What could the man be getting at?

'Mine is a hard life and I can judge a person's worth,' Beaufort answered curtly.

'Then be good enough to cut these preliminaries and come to the point. What are you trying to tell me?'

'This. I played cards with your husband this evening –'

'At whist? I know – for several hours, I believe.'

'That is so. We played and Francis lost.'

The girl's lovely mouth curved in faint scorn. Was that all? She thought she knew what the American had in mind. A mere matter of money.

'I do not see how that concerns me. If my husband has lost, then he will pay, of course.'

'He has paid, but that is not all. Will you pay, also?'

'What do you mean?'

'That Lord Cranmere has lost not only everything that he possessed, which was little enough, but also all the dowry you have brought him –'

'What!' Marianne had gone very pale.

'He has lost your fortune, your lands placed in his keeping, and the house itself with all that it contains – and more besides!' Beaufort spoke with a contained fury that frightened Marianne. She stood up but her legs refused to bear her and she had to lean on the arms of her chair. Everything seemed plunged into confusion, she felt as though she was going mad. Even the solid walls of her room seemed to be swaying and lurching wildly.

She had often heard her aunt and the Abbé de Chazay discussing, in shocked whispers, the extraordinary passion for gambling which possessed the youth of England, the endless, hectic gaming parties at which fortunes changed hands, the absurd bets on the most improbable things for the sake of which men were willing to stake even their lives. But it had never occurred to her that Francis, so calm and aristocratic, with his extraordinary self-possession, might indulge in such follies. It was not true! It could not be true! It was not possible.

She favoured Beaufort with a glance of biting contempt.

'You are lying,' she said as calmly as she could. 'My husband is incapable of such a thing!'

'How do you know? For how long have you known the man you married today?'

'My aunt knew him from a child. That is enough for me.'

'Who can claim to know what moves a woman's heart? I imagine Lady Selton was ignorant of Francis Cranmere's passion for gaming. At all events,' the American went on in a harder voice, 'I have not lied to you. Your husband has just lost all that you possess – and more besides.'

Marianne heard him with growing annoyance. She disliked his easy manner and the steady gaze of his blue eyes but his last words awoke an echo in her mind.

'That is the second time you have said that. I do not understand. What do you mean with your "and more besides"?'

Jason Beaufort did not reply at once. He could feel the young girl's nerve stretched taught as a bow string, perhaps at that limit of tension that comes before the breaking point. But she had weathered one storm and he liked that. It pleased him to have a worthy opponent.

'Well, why don't you answer me?' Marianne said cuttingly. 'Are you afraid, suddenly, or are you searching for some suitable lie?'

'I was merely wondering,' the American said gently, 'how you were going to take the remainder of what I have to – shall I say, confide.'

'Say what you like, but say it quickly!'

'After Lord Cranmere had lost everything, when he had nothing left to stake, he lost his temper and volunteered to win back all he had lost at one go. He proposed to stake, against all his former property, something infinitely more precious than all ...'

He paused again, hesitating to say the words which, in the presence of those clear eyes, seemed monstrous and out of all proportion. And Marianne's throat was so dry with fear that she could find no voice to bid him go on. Her 'what?' was scarcely more than a whisper.

'You,' Beaufort answered quietly.

One single little syllable but it seared into Marianne like a shot from a pistol fired at point blank range. For a moment, she thought that she was going to faint. She stepped back, and back again in an instinctive search for support, groping behind her until her icy hand met the warm, comforting stone fireplace. Now, she knew she was going mad – unless it were he, this insolent creature, he was the madman. But he seemed so cool, so self-assured, while she seemed to be falling headlong ... A wave of sick disgust swept over her. At least the walls of the house were there, certain and solid under her hands, to lean on otherwise she would have been sure that this was some nightmare. She flung her thoughts in Beaufort's face:

'Either I am mad, sir, or you are. Am I a slave to be sold or bartered at will? Even supposing Lord Cranmere to have been so vile or so rash as to stake the property placed in his keeping today, even then, he can only lose what belongs to him – and I do not belong to him!' The savagery in her tone startled the American.

'In the eyes of the law,' he said, and his voice was gentler than ever, 'you do belong to him. And let me make it clear, it was not you yourself, or your life he staked, but only this one night. It is this night which now belongs to me. The loss of that vast stake made it my privilege to come to you here, in place of your husband – to exercise his rights.'

No, this was too much! Who had ever heard of such a thing? Not even the abominable Lovelace, the persecutor of the unhappy Clarissa Harlowe whose adventures Marianne had read not long before, would ever have dared to suggest anything so improper! With what sort of creature did this impudent foreigner think he had to do? Marianne drew herself up to her full height and racked her memory with childish fury for some of the more vulgar and incomprehensible insults overheard in the stable yard. She felt as though they would relieve her feelings mightily. When, inevitably, nothing came to mind she was obliged to be content with pointing imperiously at the door.

'Go,' was all she said.

Instead of obeying, Jason Beaufort swung round and gripped the back of a chair, resting one knee on the seat. Marianne saw the knuckles of the brown hand whiten.

'No,' he answered coolly. Then, his eyes held by the pale graceful figure and by the disturbing recollection of the form half-seen not long before, he went on: 'Listen, and try to hear me out without losing your temper. You don't love that pompous selfish fop; you cannot love him?'

'I am not obliged to discuss my feelings with you – and I ask you once again to go.'

The American's jaw tightened. So, this chit thought she could impose on him with her queenly airs. Furious with himself, more than with her, he took refuge in anger.

'So much the worse for you!' he said grimly. 'At all events, he's lost you. No woman can go on loving a man who could gamble away her first night of love – not unless she had sunk as low as he. By his consent, you are mine for this full night. Come with me – come away with me – use this night he has relinquished to gain your own freedom! I'll not touch you but I'll take you with me, to my own country, out of his reach – I will make you happy – There before us is the sea to divide you forever from a man unworthy of you—'

'And unite me with another, at least equally unworthy!' Marianne retorted. Gradually, as he became more feverishly urgent, she had been recovering her self-possession. For the first time in her life, she was discovering power over a man, sufficient at least to disturb this disagreeable American. She gave way to the perfectly natural temptation to abuse it.

'If the chivalrous feelings you possess towards me are genuine sir, then you may prove it very simply ...'

Halted abruptly in the midst of his wholly unpremeditated outburst of feeling, Jason Beaufort asked curtly:

'How?'

'By returning the house, land and property which you have acquired by such dubious means. They have been in Lord Cranmere's possession for too short a time for him to have any right to dispose of them. Then, yes, I might think of you not merely without anger but even with friendship. As for my being yours, even for an hour, I think you can scarcely have imagined it?'

A gleam of anger showed in the American's eyes. His hawk-like features seemed to become even harder. He turned his back abruptly, perhaps to shut out the seductive vision of the child woman who had seemed so innocent but was now exhibiting an alarming self-possession.

'Impossible,' he said flatly. 'For me, that game of cards was a chance in a lifetime. My ship, the *Savannah Belle*, was wrecked on your Cornish rocks. Only three of us escaped and everything I had went down with my ship. With the money from your estates, I can get another vessel, crew, provisions and cargo. Even so—'

He turned suddenly, a prey to a desire stronger than reason, and fixed her with burning eyes.

'Even so,' he went on hoarsely, 'I'll give you back the house and lands, I'll even be fool enough for that if you will pay the final debt. Give me this night – and the morning I will be gone. You shall keep it all.'

He was moving slowly towards her as he spoke, drawn irresistibly by the graceful elusive white figure. Marianne had a lightening vision of what might follow. An hour in this man's arms and then he would go away and leave her once again mistress of Selton Hall. But these last minutes had taught her to be suspicious and she knew that it would be a long time before she could trust a man again. How could she be sure that when dawn came and once this spasm of desire, which even she, young as she was, could read naked and demanding in the man's taut face, was satisfied, how could she know that then he would keep his promise and give up the wealth he claimed *to* need so badly? A moment ago, he had promised not to touch her if she went with him and now, he dared to claim payment of the shameful debt!

All this rushed through her mind as Jason came towards her. He was reaching out to touch her when Marianne recoiled instinctively.

'No!' she cried. 'Take everything there is since you claim that it is yours but you shall not touch me. Not you or anyone! At dawn tomorrow you may drive us out of here, Lord Cranmere and myself, but until then my bed shall be my own.'

The reaching hands fell back. Jason drew himself up with a supreme effort to recover his control. Marianne saw the lean face which, a moment before, had been heavy with passion stiffen into a scornful mask of stone. He shrugged.

'You are a fool, Lady Cranmere. All things considered, you and your husband make a noble pair. I wish you every happiness. It will not be long, I think, before you discover the joys of living from hand to mouth with a man for whom you no longer possess any commercial value. But that's your affair. Keep your Francis since you care for him so much. You may remain here for a few more days until my man of business can take possession of the estate. For myself, I am leaving at once. Goodbye.'

He bent his tall figure in a curt bow, turned on his heel and strode to the door. In spite of herself, Marianne made a move to follow the man who was taking with him, as though it were of no account, all her childhood memories and everything she held dear. She had the heart-breaking thought that Aunt Ellis who had so loved her home would rest now, along with all the other Seltons, on land belonging to a stranger. Yet even then it did not occur to her to beg. Her pride forbade it. Her throat constricted and suddenly she wanted to cry.

'I hate you!' She wailed through clenched teeth. 'You can have no idea how much I hate you! I'd like to see you dead and while I live, I shall go on hating you!'

He turned again and looked at her. One corner of his mouth lifted in his mocking smile.

'Hate me as much as you like, Lady Cranmere. I'd a hundred times rather hate than indifference. After all, don't they say that on a woman's lips hatred and love taste much the same? A happy thought – I may as well find out?'

Before Marianne could guess what he meant to do, he had taken three steps across the space that divided them and caught her in his arms. Half-stifled, her head reeling, she found herself imprisoned in a grip of steel, her lips sealed by a hard demanding mouth that bore down relentlessly on hers. She struggled furiously but Jason held her fast, and for all her frenzy to escape there was little she could do. Alternate hot and cold waves seemed to run through her body, mingled with another strange and still more disturbing sensation. Unconsciously, Marianne's struggles grew feebler and ceased. That other mouth was so warm after the chill she had endured and by some miracle it had become suddenly soft and caressing – dazedly, Marianne was aware of a hand stealing up the back of her neck beneath the silken masses of her hair, imprisoning her head. It was like a dream – a not altogether unpleasant dream. And then, abruptly, she found herself released, standing alone while the world swayed about her, weak-kneed with a ringing in her ears. The American's horrible, mocking laughter sounded close by.

'My thanks for your co-operation, but do not forget you still owe me a night. One day, I shall come to claim it. What a pity it would be to miss the chance of making love to such a woman. You are made for it.'

At the sound of the closing door, Marianne, scarlet with shame, opened the eyes which she had closed to shut out the sardonic face of her tormentor. He had gone. She was alone at last but alone as she might have been in the midst of the ruins. Of her world, the world of her childhood, nothing remained. House, fortune, love and all her most cherished illusions destroyed in an instant. All that remained was a few, still-warm ashes soon to be scattered by the wind. The estate would be sold so that one more ship might sail the seas!

A horse's hoofs clattered beneath the window, diminished and died away. Marianne had no need to look to know that Jason Beaufort was gone, fleeing the wreck that he had brought about. Now she, Marianne, must think what to do about the disaster he had left behind.

She sat down calmly in the armchair so recently occupied by the American. Around her, the house was silent once again.

When, half an hour later, she emerged from her melancholy thoughts she felt as though she had been born anew as a result of some painful and unaccustomed new process of gestation. Very little remained of the innocent young Marianne who had plunged headlong with such blind infatuation into the mirages of calf-love.

Now, her only feeling was anger, an anger nothing but vengeance could assuage. This vengeance, Marianne was determined to exact at once. Francis had betrayed her, sold her, degraded her and for that he would pay.

Calmly she slipped out of the frilly gown and gauzy nightrobe for which she no longer had any use and put on instead a dark green riding habit. She twisted her hair into a hasty knot on the nape of her neck and left the room. Out on the landing, she was struck by the heavy, almost brooding silence of the house, an ominous, waiting silence like that of a wood before a storm when all living creatures, beast and tree seemed to hold their breath.

Throwing the skirt of her habit over her arm, Marianne glided soundlessly down the great oak staircase, a slight shadow in a world of shadows. On the last step, she paused. Everywhere was so dark. Where could Francis be? He had arrived at Selton Hall only an hour before the wedding ceremony and no room had been set aside for his personal use.

The girl's quick ear caught the clink of a glass and at once, sure of her direction, she made her way to her aunt's boudoir and opened the door. Francis was there. He was lying back in a big armchair, elegantly shod feet resting on a table covered with green baize which also held a big bronze candlestick, decanters and some glasses. His back was to the door and he did not hear Marianne come in. She paused for a moment in the doorway, looking with fresh eyes at the man whose name she bore. A pang in the region of her heart told her that anger and disappointment had not been enough to kill her love. He fascinated and repelled her, like the curious plant she had seen writhing its lipid tentacles in Lord Monmouth's glasshouses at Bath which devoured insects and small mammals. Her love for him was an unwholesome plant which she was determined to tear out by the roots, even if her heart were torn apart for ever in the process. But oh, how it hurt!

With a mixture of pain and fury, she allowed her eyes to dwell once more upon her husband's handsome face, the mouth for whose kisses she had longed, and the slender hand with which just then Francis was idly turning his full glass to catch the firelight. Those hands would never caress her now because she was here with the single intention of killing Francis Cranmere.

Leaving her husband's recumbent figure, Marianne's eyes flicked rapidly round the room and came to rest on a pair of fine Milanese swords which formed part of the decoration of this strange boudoir full of riding whips, weapons and spurs. She had used those swords more than once in practice bouts with old Dobbs who had taught her to fence. Noiselessly, she reached down one of the weapons, a strong, slender blade she knew well. Her fingers closed on the hilt and, settling it firmly in her grasp she moved forward without a sound. The blade would pass easily through the padded chair and the thickness of the man's body and Marianne was ready to strike so, from behind, without remorse as the executioner lets fall his axe on the condemned man kneeling at his feet. Hers was the hand of justice. This man had betrayed her, broken her heart. It was right that he should die. She drew back her arm. The sword's point touched the leather upholstery of the chair.

But slowly, she let her arm fall. The blade dropped. No, she had doomed him but she could not strike like this, from behind. She hated him with all the strength of disappointed love but she hated even more the thought of killing like a coward without giving her victim the least chance to defend himself. Her natural honesty recoiled from such a summary execution, even if Francis had deserved it a hundred times over.

The thought came to her: since her conscience demanded that the villain must have his chance, why not force him to fight a duel? Marianne was an expert swordswoman and knew her own strength. She stood a fair chance of beating, and killing even a skilled opponent. And then, supposing Francis proved himself the stronger and overcame her, she would die without regret, taking her shattered love and unsullied chastity to a place where such things no longer mattered.

She stepped out from the shadow of the chair and slashed the air with her sword. At the hiss of the blade, Francis turned his head and stared at her with a real surprise that gave way almost at once to a mocking smile.

'Here's a strange turn-out for a wedding night! What are you playing at?'

Was that all he had to say after his outrageous conduct? He might at least have shown some shame! But no, he was as carelessly at ease as ever! And dared to mock at her!

Ignoring the irony in the question, Marianne mastered her anger sufficiently to say coldly:

'You played for me like a paltry handful of guineas, sold me like a slave! Don't you think you owe me some explanation?'

'Oh, is that all?'

With a weary smile, Francis Cranmere settled himself more deeply in his armchair, set down his glass and clasped his hands across his stomach as though composing himself more comfortably for sleep.

'Beaufort is a romantic. He was ready to stake all the treasures of Golconda against you –'

'Which he did not possess.'

'As you say. But I do believe, if he had lost, he would have been prepared to steal to match your worth. Damme m'dear, you've an admirer there – unfortunately, it was I who lost. But there, there are some days when one is quite out of luck.'

His airy tone whipped up Marianne's anger. Suddenly his handsome, insolently smiling face maddened her beyond bearing.

'And you supposed that I would pay for you?' She said angrily.

'Lord, no! You've plenty of breeding, even if you are half French. I was pretty sure you'd send our American friend to the right-about. And so you did because I heard him riding off and here you are! But what the devil are you doing with that sword, put it down, do, before you have an accident.'

He put out an arm, more sleepily than ever, refilled his glass and carried it to his lips. Marianne noticed with disgust the dark red flush that was beginning to spread over his aristocratic countenance. Already, he was very nearly drunk. She saw him slip his fingers nervously inside his high muslin neckcloth to loosen it. She watched with contempt as he tossed back the last amber drops in his glass before saying curtly:

'Get up!'

He merely raised one eyebrow questioningly.

'Get up? Why should I?'

'I think you can scarcely mean to fight from an armchair.'

As she spoke, she reached down another weapon and tossed it to him. He caught it automatically, incensing Marianne further. Drunk he might be, but not enough to make him clumsy. He lacked even the degrading excuse of sottishness.

Francis was contemplating the bright blade with amused astonishment.

'Fight? Who shall I fight?'

'Me! Come, sir, get up! By making me the object of your sport you have offered me a deadly insult. You shall give me satisfaction. The name I bear does not permit an offence to go unpunished.'

'In future you bear my name, and I have the right to do what I will to my own wife,' Francis cut her roughly short. 'You are mine, body and soul, you and your possessions. You are nothing – except my wife! So now, stop behaving like an idiot and put away that sword. You don't know what you are doing with it.'

Marianne flexed the supple blade between her hands and smiled scornfully.

'As to that, I invite you to be the judge, Lord Cranmere. Besides, the name that I alluded to was not yours. That, I have done with! I reject it utterly! It is the name of d'Asselnat I mean. That name, you have sullied and betrayed in my person. And I swear to you shall not live long enough to boast of it.'

Francis's mocking chuckle cut short her words. Marianne listened without flinching while he lay back in his chair, his eyes on the ceiling, opened his mouth wide and roared with laughter. The man she had seen in this last hour was so different from the one she had imagined that his behaviour no longer had the power to hurt her. For the present, she felt nothing at all. Suffering would come later. Just now, Marianne was still under the effect of the revelation and the anger it had brought. But Francis was chuckling:

'You know, you're unbeatable? It must be your French blood gives you your taste for the dramatic. Anyone who saw you now, like Nemesis got up in green worsted, would die with laughter and refuse to believe their eyes. Come now, m'dear,' he went on carelessly, 'drop all these tragedy airs. They suit neither your age nor your sex. Go back to bed. Tomorrow, we have arrangements to make. Disagreeable ones, I admit, but unavoidable.'

With a sigh of irritation, Lord Cranmere at last hoisted himself from his chair, stretched his long limbs lazily and gave vent to a prodigious yawn.

'A damnable evening! That American had the devil in his fingers. Rolled me up like a bundle of dead leaves –'

Marianne's voice cut through his words.

'Lord Cranmere, I think you have not understood me. I will no longer be your wife.'

'Do you see any help for it? We are properly married, you know.'

'At first, I thought of applying to Rome for an annulment, it would not be difficult for the Abbé de Chazay to obtain one. But that would not cleanse the honour of my name. And so, I have decided to kill you and become a widow – unless, of course, you should happen to kill me first.'

An expression of profound boredom descended on Francis's perfect features.

'Are you still harping on that? Surely, the woman's mad. Where have you ever seen a man fight a duel with a woman? A woman? With a child! I have already told you, go to bed. A good rest will put such nonsense out of your head.'

'I am past the age of being sent to bed! Will you give me satisfaction, yes or no?'

'No! You may go to the devil, you and your ridiculous French notions of honour! Whatever possessed your mother to marry one of the damned frog-eaters! Truth is, must have been a bit mad herself, I heard the Duke of Norfolk offered for her and –'

He broke off with a cry of rage and pain. Marianne's sword hissed with murderous fury and carved a long weal on Francis's left cheek. He sprang back, clapping his hand to his hurt face and drew it away wet with blood.

'Coward!' She spat at him between her teeth. 'I'll make you fight me! Defend yourself or by the memory of my mother whom you have insulted, I swear I'll pin you to the wall!'

A dark flush of anger swept over Francis's face. His grey eyes flamed. In that instant, Marianne read in them, naked and violent, the lust to kill. Seizing the sword which still lay on the table, he bore down on her, an evil glitter in his eye.

'Have it your own way, damn you!' he muttered.

With one swift movement, Marianne whipped off the long skirt of her riding habit which threatened to impede her movements and stood up in boots and breeches. In an instant, she was on guard. At the sight of those long, slim legs and hips, outlined with anatomical precision by the close-fitting silk, a twisted smile crossed Francis's face.

'Gad, what a shape. And there was I thinking this marriage had nothing more to offer! Why, a moment ago I'd quite made up my mind to kill you. Now, damme if I won't be satisfied with disarming you – or perhaps pinking you – very lightly – just enough to make you properly submissive to the exercise of my conjugal rights. There's nothing like a taste of the whip to tame a filly without breaking her spirit. I like my mounts to have some fire in their veins!'

Even as he spoke, he had engaged. A feverish flush was on his cheeks and a wild light in his eyes. For the first time, Marianne saw revealed the cruelty of that mouth from which she had looked only for kisses. As he fenced, Francis favoured her with a detailed description of what lay in store for her when he had her at his mercy. Confronted with the blazing contempt of this seventeen-year-old girl, all vestiges of shame or self-restraint were stripped from him and sheer hatred made him determined, at all costs, to bend her to his will.

Sunk in her own misery and loathing, Marianne heard without properly understanding, without even really listening to his words. The wonderful picture she had built up of Francis was slowly and finally crumbling away, leaving in its place only a half-drunk man, whose handsome mouth spat out a stream of obscenity. And, insensibly, implacably, overcoming disgust, there came the renewed desire to kill.

But gradually, the odious voice fell silent and at the same time an expression of surprise replaced the anger on Francis's taut features, a surprise that was soon tinged with uneasiness. This slender, dark girl, with the defiant green eyes was fighting with the skill and address of an experienced duellist. There was no opening in that unwavering guard. The slender, bright blade seemed everywhere at once, multiplied a hundred, a thousand times by Marianne's supple wrists. The girl fought like a tigress, continually circling her opponent, changing her guard a dozen times. The foils rang together ominously, meeting faster and faster as Marianne forced Francis Cranmere to a killing pace.

Like all the prince's circle, young Lord Cranmere was a keen sportsman and accounted an excellent blade. All the same, he had his work cut out to defend himself against the lithe green-clad figure darting into the attack from all quarters at once, yet never, for all that, failing to parry adroitly in defence of her own skin. Not a muscle stirred in the lovely face but Francis could tell from the fierce light in her eye how deeply she relished this moment. He had a disagreeable sensation that she was playing with him. At the same time, his throat constricted with sudden desire. She had never seemed to him so lovely, so desirable. The excitement of the fight had put colour in her smooth cheeks, a rosiness on her lips. Her fine linen shirt, soaked now with sweat so that it clung alluringly to her body, was open at the throat, giving promise of the rich swell of her breasts.

Enraged to find himself thus held at bay by one he had regarded as no more than a pretty, love-sick goose and eager to make an end, the sooner to enjoy her, Francis lost his head and began to make mistakes. There was, in addition, the fatigue of a heavy night at cards and the fumes of alcohol misting his brain. Marianne saw this and redoubled her agility. Francis lunged, aiming for a decisive thrust. She parried by a hair's-breadth and then, slipping with a quick, snake-like movement under her adversary's blade, thrust home. Her point buried itself in Francis's breast.

The young man's grey eyes widened with a look of enormous surprise.

The sword slipped from his suddenly loosened grasp and clattered to the floor. He opened his mouth to say something but nothing came, only a gout of blood which dribbled down his chin. He crumpled where he stood and, slowly, Marianne drew out her sword. She let it fall, without even thinking to wipe it, and went on her knees beside the wounded man. His eyes were already clouding. Her throat tightened and suddenly she wanted to cry. Her hatred had left her now that he was dying.

'You did me a great wrong, Francis – I am avenged. Now, die in peace. I have forgiven you.'

From beneath half-closed lips his eyes sought for her and his hand groped to touch her. A ghost of a smile touched his lips.

'A pity,' he murmured. 'I could – have loved you –'

He closed his eyes with a groan. It was then, as she still knelt by him, Marianne heard a fearful shriek behind her.

'My God! Francis –'

Marianne turned quickly and was just in time to jerk herself backwards to avoid being knocked down by Ivy as she cast herself sobbing onto the lifeless body. She had not heard the door open or seen the other girl enter. How long had Francis's cousin been there? How much had she heard? Marianne looked down at the graceful form, prostrate amid the swirling folds of her white gown, and frowned, wondering at the violence of her grief. Ivy was clasping Francis's body and uttering whimpering cries, like a wounded animal, out of all proportion in Marianne's estimation with the natural grief to be felt for a mere cousin. But she had little time to wonder before Ivy rounded on her, her face streaked with tears and rendered unrecognizable by grief and malice.

'This is your doing, I suppose,' she said fiercely. 'You found out at last that he did not love you, that he could not love you – and so you killed him! It wasn't enough for you to bear his name, to be his wife before the world, to have the right to serve him –'

'Serve him? You are out of your mind!' Marianne's lip curled scornfully. 'The women of my house do not serve! As for this man, I killed him in fair fight! There are two swords –'

'But only one has blood on it! You jealous little French slut, you knew it was me he loved and you could not endure it!'

'He loved you?' Marianne was genuinely astonished.

Ivy St. Albans's lovely face was transfigured with the fearful joy of flinging the searing truth in the teeth of her hated rival.

'He was my lover! For months now we have been united, body and soul. He would have married me, but neither he nor I had money. Then you turned up, you and your old fool of an aunt. It was just what we needed; a pair of silly women who asked nothing better than to drop a fortune at his feet. It was child's play for Francis to win you. Everything went off as he had

47

hoped, better even since the old woman had the sense to die and leave you everything! But then you guessed, didn't you, that he meant to keep you tucked away down here in the country while he lived with me in London, with me and your money! It was that you could not stand —'

Marianne listened in amazement to this eruption of fury and hatred. Horrified, she saw at last the cynical calculation, of which she had been the object, and cold-blooded way in which these two had coolly set about playing on her own innocence and her aunt's goodness. Even more than the insult, which had already been wiped out, it was the contemptuous way this creature dared to speak of her aunt's memory that roused her anger.

'You would not have enjoyed my fortune for long,' she said coldly. 'Your precious Francis lost it all tonight; the little of his own he had left and everything I brought him. The master of Selton Hall at this moment is Jason Beaufort!'

The news struck Ivy like a thunderbolt. Her fine blue eyes dilated, her jaw dropped and a deathly pallor spread over her face.

'All – the whole fortune?'

'All! I have nothing left but my honour, and even that he dared dispose of. He deserved to die, you see! I could have shot him down, from behind, like a mad dog or stabbed him in the back. I gave him a chance. He lost. The worst for him.'

'And for you, also. You killed him, you shall hang!' Ivy screamed, no longer able to contain her fury. 'I shall testify against you! You dared to strike him, you, who should have been too happy just to be his humble slave! But you are forgetting the Prince of Wales. The prince is his friend and he will not let your crime go unpunished. I am here and I will not rest until I have brought you to trial and then I will tell all the lies I need. And the day they put the rope round your neck I shall be there in the front row – to cheer!'

Beside herself with rage, Ivy began calling loudly for help and ran to the hearth to pull the bell that hung there. But, quicker than she, Marianne was before her and as Ivy ran into her she clapped a hand across her mouth.

'Be quiet you little fool! You will wake the whole house —'

Biting savagely at the fingers clamped across her lips, Ivy wriggled herself free and said venomously:

'I mean to wake everyone! Lord Moira will come and he will listen to me! You will be locked up until you can be brought to trial.'

'My servants will defend me.'

'Not against the prince. They are all loyal Englishmen and to them you are only a foreigner, a nasty little Frenchwoman, a papist who has killed her husband! They will believe me —'

Marianne's brain worked quickly. But, though she tried to reassure herself, fear began to gain on her, whispering that Ivy was right. It was true.

Respect for the tradition was strong at Selton Hall and for all her servants, except perhaps for Dobbs and old Jenkins, she would be only her husband's murderer. They would forget everything but her French blood and her Catholic faith. If Ivy screamed for help, then she was lost – and Ivy was going to scream, was screaming already –

In her terror Marianne seized hold of the first object that came to hand which happened to be a long duelling pistol that lay on a chest. She grabbed it by the barrel and struck with the butt. The blow caught Ivy St. Albans on the temple and she dropped without even a sigh. But this time her rival wasted no precious seconds contemplating the prostrate figure stretched in its virginal drapery beside the lifeless form of Francis. She did not even pause to find out whether Ivy still lived. She had to escape, and escape with all speed. Already, it seemed to her that she could hear people stirring somewhere in the house. They would come and find her with the two motionless bodies, they might be coming even now – with a shock of horror, she seemed to see the shadow of the gibbet already looming over her.

Without knowing how she did it, she almost staggered from the room, blundering heavily against the furniture, and dashed up the stairs to her room. There, she snatched up the pearl necklace that had been her mother's, the duchesse d'Angoulême's locket and a purse containing a little money and then, shrouded in a big, black hooded cloak, she hurried out again without a backward glance, slipped noiselessly along the darkened gallery to a small stairway built into one of the turrets. From there, she made her way to the stables without encountering a living soul.

CHAPTER THREE
The Old Roots

The wind had risen, bringing with it a cold, dense rain that whipped against Marianne's face where she stood, her eyes heavy with tears, gazing at the silent mausoleum where her ancestors lay at rest, but she did not feel it. The night was so dark that the dome and the white columns loomed up, blurred and ghostly, like a mist before her eyes. It was as though the tomb of the Seltons was already receding into the past, falling back into darkness and distance in spite of the girl's desperate efforts to impress each line of it upon her memory. She thought with pain and bitterness that this was all she had left in the world, this acre of land and the marble beneath which her ancestors lay.

Driven by a compelling need to feel less wretched and alone, she pushed open the creaking gate and laid her cheek against the cold, damp stone as, when a little girl in need of love, she had run to hide her face against a grey silk skirt.

'Aunt Ellis,' she moaned, 'Oh, Aunt Ellis – why?'

It was the cry of a lost child, but there was no one to answer. Why had her quiet, sheltered life been suddenly transformed into this irretrievable disaster? Marianne felt all the incredulous terror of a passenger on board ship who suddenly exchanges the safety and comfort of his cabin for the icy tumult of the storm, finding himself snatched from his warm bed and plunged into the sea, clinging to a spar.

But she might as well have tried to warm the cold marble tombs in her arms. All was still, cold and silent. And yet, there was an agonizing pain in trying to tear herself away. Going, she would leave behind her all her childhood and all the happiness she believed that she had known.

But time was short. Back in the direction of the house, voices were already shouting. They must be looking for her even now. Then, suddenly a thick column of smoke rose above the trees and a long flame shot skywards. Marianne moved a few steps away from the mausoleum.

'Fire!' she muttered. 'Selton is on fire—'

What could have started it? Her first impulse, seeing the old house in danger, was to rush back but a sudden grim satisfaction made her pause. Let the noble old house burn rather than see it in the hands of the American! It was better so! Then there would indeed be nothing left of all her memories, nothing but the indelible scar she bore in her heart, and this white marble monument.

Brushing away the tears that ran down her cheeks with an angry gesture, Marianne went to the place where she had left her horse and climbed wearily into the saddle. Her thoughts went back suddenly to her flight from the boudoir. She had no clear recollection of how she had got out of the room but she did recall hearing some kind of dull thud as of a piece of furniture overturned. The candles on the table! Had she knocked them over? Had she been the unwitting cause of the fire? A picture crossed her mind of the two still forms left lying in the room but she thrust them back angrily. Francis was dead. What difference if his body were reduced to ashes. As for Ivy, Marianne felt nothing but hatred for her.

Standing up in the stirrups, she looked back for an instant to where, above the treetops, the roofs of Selton stood etched against the ruddy glow of the fire as though against a bloody dawn. An indistinguishable murmur of voices reached her but, for Marianne, the insubstantial barrier of trees had become a symbol, cutting her off forever from a world already falling into ruins. It was right that it should be so, and, thinking she had wasted enough time, she raised her hand in one last gesture of farewell to the monument and then, digging in her heels, made off at a canter into the woods. The wind of her going filled her ears, drowning out the roar of the fire.

In her present terrible plight, there was only one person who could help her. Her godfather. Marianne knew that if she was to save her neck, she must leave England. The Abbé de Chazay was the one man capable of assisting her in this. As ill luck would have it, he was probably off on one of his long journeys. He had told her, the previous evening, that he meant to travel to Rome in answer to a summons from the Pope and, as he kissed his goddaughter goodbye, he had mentioned taking ship at Plymouth the following morning. Marianne, too, must be on that boat.

Fortunately for her, she knew the country well and there was no lane or by-way with which she was not familiar. She travelled by a short cut across country which brought her to the outskirts of Totnes, from where she had nearly twenty miles to cover to reach the great port before the tide but her mount, one of the best hunters in the stables, had strong legs.

There seemed to be a faint lightening of the darkness. The rain had come on more heavily, driving away the mist, and the moon, shining out between thick blankets of cloud, nonetheless gave sufficient light to enable Marianne to see her way without difficulty. Bent over her horse's neck, her hood pulled well down over her eyes, she hunched her back against the downpour, disregarding the water trapped in the sodden folds of her frieze cloak and concentrating wholly upon the route she had to follow.

When at last she caught sight of the ruined towers of an old Norman castle looming in the darkness above a village of straggling white houses, Marianne turned off into the hills that lay on her left and rode full tilt for the sea.

The boy lifted his arm and pointed out into the roadstead.

'Look! That's the *Fowey*. Just turning into the Sound.'

A wave of despair swept over Marianne. Too late! When, breathless and exhausted, she had fallen rather than dismounted from her horse on the old quay at Plymouth known as the Barbican, the Abbé de Chazay had already left. Out there, on the sparkling water plucked by the wind into choppy wavelets, the lugger was plunging gaily out to sea under full sail, carrying with it her last hope.

'You are sure,' she asked the boy without conviction, 'that the French priest was on board?'

He raised his hand and spat with dignity, 'Sure as my name's Tom Mawes! Carried his traps from the Crown and Anchor meself, I did! Take you there, if you like? Best inn in town, right by St. Andrew's Church.'

With a shake of her head, Marianne declined this offer and the boy shrugged and strolled away, muttering under his breath something about 'blasted females' with no proper notions of the reward due to goodwill. Marianne walked on a little way, leading her horse, and sat down on one of the large stone capstans used for tying up vessels. All her strength and courage had drained away. Out there, on the green water, the little ship was slowly disappearing into the pale sunlight of a wintry morning that had clothed the hills around the bay in bluish mist. This was the end. Now, she had not one friend left on English soil, no one to whom she could turn for help. Now, she had only herself to rely on. It was necessary to escape, and to escape quickly, but where could she go?

The deserted Barbican was slowly coming to life. Fishing boats came in and the heaped baskets were swung up onto the stone quay, filled with plaice and sole, still wet and shiny. Granite-coloured crabs waved their black pincers from inside lobster pots and there were great clumps of greenish seaweed studded with deep purple mussels. Housewives hurried by, their starched caps bobbing, bearing great baskets on their arms and casting curious glances at the pretty, tired-looking girl dressed in boy's clothes and holding a blood-horse by the bridle.

At last, their silent scrutiny brought Marianne back to an awareness of herself and she got up, unable to endure the continued bombardment of so many curious glances. At the same time, she realized one simple fact. She was starving hungry. It may have been the sight of all that fish, the intoxicating smell of the sea, the fresh breeze, but whatever the cause, her stomach was crying out for food as only a seventeen-year-old stomach can. Yesterday, at that dreadful wedding dinner, she had been too agitated to eat much and she had taken nothing since.

Was it really only yesterday that she had married Francis! It seemed an eternity since that wedding ceremony. So, it had needed only a few hours to make her first an outraged wife, then a widow and now a criminal and a fugitive from justice who would soon be hunted down, if they were not already on her track. But when she thought of those who had so cruelly wounded her, no remorse troubled her mind. They had deserved their punishment and in striking them down she had done no more than avenge an insult to her honour, as any man of her family would have done. Only, when she thought of Francis, she was conscious in her inmost heart of a kind of vertigo, as though she stood on the brink of a precipice, and a bitter taste of ashes in her mouth.

With an effort of will, she drove out these gloomy thoughts. Marianne was young and strong and determined with all the force that was within her to overcome the malign fate which dogged her and to do that, it was necessary to remain alive. And, first and foremost, to eat, rest and think. She looked around her, searching for the boy she had spoken to earlier but he had vanished. However, she remembered what he had told her. The Crown and Anchor was the best hostelry in Plymouth and situated not far from St Andrew's Church. And there, rising above the steep pitched roofs, was indeed a Gothic tower which undoubtedly belonged to the former Catholic cathedral. A narrow, twisting street led her towards it and before long, she discerned the ancient timbered facade, gleaming leaded casements and impressive sign of a substantial old inn. Giving her horse into the care of a groom who appeared as though by magic, Marianne entered the inn and descending a few steps found herself in a large and welcoming common room adorned with much gleaming copper and brass with a large table in the centre and a number of smaller tables disposed around it, all covered with clean white cloths. A good peat fire burned in the hearth and a number of lusty serving wenches, their cheeks red and polished in the glow from the fire, tripped about the room bearing loaded trays.

There were few people about as yet and Marianne was able to slip unnoticed into a seat at a small table somewhat in the shadow of the wide chimney piece. From the maid-servant who appeared almost at once, she ordered oysters, a crab, a dish of the clotted yellow Devonshire cream she adored, as well as tea and toast. Then, as the girl sped away in a whirl of crisp petticoats to carry out her order, she tried to take stock of her position. Everything that had happened to her seemed so very improbable. Not even her beloved novels brought any guidance! None contained any situation remotely comparable to her own. She had, to be sure, a little money, but so very little. It would not enable her to subsist for more than a week. Then, she had to find a passport without having recourse to the authorities in the county, and find a boat prepared to face the considerable risks involved in running the blockade which had existed on all traffic between England and France for the past three years. All that would take money, probably a great deal of money. Marianne still had the pearl necklace she had brought with her but if she were to sell that here, quite apart from the dangers involved in such a sale and the questions to which it would give rise, she would have very little left to live on wherever she eventually took refuge, or where fate might decide to place her. And, to tell the truth, it mattered little to the fugitive where the winds might carry her, provided they put a sufficient distance between herself and the hangman's noose. So, she must keep the necklace.

Suddenly she thought of her horse. He was a valuable animal and by selling him she might perhaps obtain enough money to pay her passage on some vessel whose master would not be over scrupulous in the matter of payment. At all events, it would be less dangerous than the necklace.

Somewhat heartened by her plans, Marianne did full justice to her breakfast and, by the time she had swallowed the last mouthful of cream, she was feeling very much better. Her clothes had dried. Warmth and nourishment had restored some measure of elasticity to muscles chilled and stiffened by hours on horseback. A gentle drowsiness crept over her and, bit by bit, her eyelids began to droop.

All at once she sat up with a start, wide awake on the instant. A man had come into the room, from the staircase leading to the upper floor where the guest bedchambers lay.

The newcomer was tall, thin and very ugly, grey-faced and hollow chested; he was aged about fifty but looked at least twice that on account of his evidently decrepit state of health. He was followed closely by two servants who hovered anxiously in the way of those members of a superior household whose duty was to be constantly alert to attend to their master. His out-moded garments, red heeled shoes, bob-wig and three-cornered hat suggested the émigré, and so indeed he was. Marianne knew him. Only the day before, he had been present, along with Monseigneur de Talleyrand-Périgord, at her marriage. It was the Duc d'Avaray the confidential friend and favourite of Louis XVIII, the Castor to his Pollux, out-of-office Sully to his would-be Henri IV.

Yesterday's ceremony had been interrupted more than once by the duke's cavernous coughing, and he was coughing again now on his slow progress through the coffee room at the inn. It was no secret that the Duc d'Avaray was dying of consumption.

He sat down heavily without seeing Marianne at a table close to hers occupied hitherto by a middle-aged man, a steward to all appearances, who rose at his approach. But the first words they exchanged made the girl prick up her ears.

Pushing aside the dish of steaming mutton set on the table with an expression of disgust, the duke sipped his tea slowly and sighed.

'Well, my good Bishop, have you found a vessel?'

'I have found one, Your Grace, though I had a job,' the man answered speaking with a strong Welsh accent. 'The man is a common smuggler, a Portuguese but his ship is seaworthy and sufficiently commodious. He has agreed to carry you as far as Madeira. We sail on tonight's tide.'

D'Avaray's sigh betrayed more resignation than delight.

'Excellent. Now I can only put my trust in the gentle climate of the island. I may perhaps recover.'[3]

Marianne listened to no more. Hope surged up in her. This man was leaving England, he had a vessel and since that vessel was a smuggler her master could not be too particular in the matter of formalities. For her, this meant safety, luck beyond hope which she could not afford to lose. She shrank back in her corner, hardly daring to breath, observing the two men and watching for the right moment to introduce herself. The duke was a sick man himself and could not but feel compassion for her distress. If he were willing, she would care for him, make herself his nurse, his servant – she was prepared to offer any devotion in exchange for a helping hand.

The two men finished their meal in silence then, as the duke ordered a fresh pot of tea, Bishop took his leave, saying he would carry the news to Monseigneur de Talleyrand-Périgord, who had accompanied his friend d'Avaray to the port but was at that moment visiting some émigrés settled in the town. The room had gradually emptied of company and now the duke was alone. Marianne judged that the moment had come. She rose to her feet.

As she stood before him, the old gentleman was seized by another fit of coughing.

'Your Grace – with your permission. It is imperative I speak with you –'

Watery eyes gazed up from a congested face.

'What – d'ye want?' he gasped. 'Go away!'

For answer, she slipped into the seat vacated by Bishop and, pouring some water into a glass, offered it to the duke.

'Drink slowly, it will soothe you. Afterwards, we will talk –'

Mechanically he obeyed. He emptied the glass and, by degrees, recovered his normal complexion. Taking out a large handkerchief, he

---

[3] The duc d'Avaray died the following year in Madeira.

mopped the sweat from his yellowed brow.

'I thank you,' he said unsteadily. 'What may I do for you?'

Marianne leaned forward so that the firelight fell directly onto her face.

'Look at me, my Lord Duke. Yesterday at Selton Hall, you were present at my wedding. Today, I am lost without your aid.'

Marianne's voice was hoarse with emotion and she almost choked over the last words while the duke's lack-lustre eyes grew round with astonishment.

'Mademoiselle d'Asselnat! Lady Cranmere, I mean. What are you doing here? What has happened?'

'Something very terrible. Yesterday I had a house, wealth, a husband and a name. It is all gone, nothing remains.'

'Nothing? How is this possible?'

'The house is burned down, the fortune lost, the husband dead and the name such as I shrink from—'

Swiftly, righting down her grief, Marianne described for the duke the events of that terrible night. As she spoke, she felt the horror and misery sweep over her again. She was still little more than a child and a child oppressed by burdens too heavy for her to bear. It was a relief to confide in someone even this stranger who did not, however, appear to be greatly struck with compassion. On the contrary, as the tale advanced, Marianne saw to her dismay the gentleman's weary face assume a closed expression while his eyes hardened with suspicion. Clearly, he did not believe her. She tried to add more urgency to her appeal for help but, when she had finished, the duke merely observed shortly:

'A strange tale, to be sure! So you killed your husband in a duel? Who do you think will believe that?'

'Why, you, since it is the truth! He did me a great wrong. I called him out and killed him.'

D'Avaray gave a weary shrug.

'My child, you will have to think of something else. No man worthy of the name would ever cross swords with a woman. Besides, who ever heard of a woman whose sword play was good enough to kill a man in the prime of life? Not since Joan of Arc and you are no Joan of Arc, I presume?'

Stung by the sarcasm, Marianne said bitterly:

'Your mockery is misplaced, my Lord Duke. As God hears me, I swear I have spoken only the truth—'

'Do not swear! I am no believer in oaths. You women use them as you like—'

'Very well, if I am lying, what do you think happened?'

'I will tell you. Your husband staked your fortune and lost it. I have heard sufficient of Lord Cranmere's reputation to accept that may well be true. But, rather than confessing it to you, he went instead to his cousin. All the world knows he was her lover. You surprised them and, in a frenzy of rage and jealousy you stabbed your husband, struck down his companion and to make doubly sure they would not escape, set fire to the house. After all, it no longer belonged to you –'

'You forget Jason Beaufort – and Lord Cranmere's shameful bargain with him –'

'A bargain which exists only in your imagination. You needed some justification for your murderous act.'

'He can bear me out. He knows I have spoken the truth.'

'If that is so, you may confidently place yourself in the hands of the law. You have only to send for him. With him as your witness, you may well prove your case –'

'But where is he to be found?' Marianne cried desperately. 'He is a sea captain – a pirate, I daresay – and the sea is very large.'

'If I have understood your story correctly, he is a sea captain without a ship. He must either get another or have one built. Search the English ports and you will find him soon enough.'

'Do you expect me to run after a man I hate, who has taken everything from me and would have taken even my honour? Do you expect me to beg his help, his evidence to clear me of a crime I have not committed?'

The duke rose with an effort and nicked a speck of dust from his old fashioned lace cravat.

'I have no expectations at all in the matter, my child. It is, quite simply your only chance –'

A heavy silence followed. Marianne saw her best hopes disappearing.

'You mean, you will not take me?'

D'Avaray spread his wasted arms helplessly before replying.

'You cannot think it! It is true, I am going for the sake of my health but I am still high in the confidence of his majesty King Louis XVIII. The King's position is such that no breath of a scandal must come near him. And yet you ask me, his friend, me, Antoine de Bésiade Duc d'Avaray to give protection to a murderess fleeing from the English justice? It is madness!'

'My parents gave their lives for their sovereign and yet when I, their daughter, ask for help it is denied me. The King is my King as well as yours. I, Marianne d'Asselnat, have a right to claim aid and comfort from him.' There was pride in the girl's voice.

'By your marriage, you are English. The King of France can do nothing for you. What little power he has, he owes to those who are worthy of it!'

Stunned by the old duke's harshness, Marianne felt suddenly very tired, tired to death of this exhausting battle with a man who refused to understand. Determined to make one last, desperate effort, she said hopelessly:

'But if you help me, would he ever know? I do not ask you to take me to

Madeira. Only, set me ashore anywhere, even France. What does it matter?'

'It may not matter to you but you forget the hounds of Bonaparte. In France, Madame, I am a proscribed émigré. Merely to approach my country is to risk my head. But if it is your desire to go there, you may easily find some fisherman who deals in contraband, here in this very town, who for a consideration will certainly put you ashore somewhere on the coast of Normandy or Brittany.'

Marianne gave a little shrug.

'What could I do in France? I have no family there anymore. But then, nor have I anywhere.'

A sardonic gleam came into the gentleman's red-rimmed eyes. He gave a dry cackle of laughter.

'No family? Oh but you have. I know of two persons at least connected to you by blood.'

'Two? How can this be? No one has ever spoken of them to me.'

'They are little enough to boast of. I should think Lady Selton preferred to forget that part of the family but the fact remains that you have two cousins, one closer than the other, to be sure, but the second a person of some standing!'

'Who are they? Tell me quickly,' Marianne said eagerly, her dislike of the old duke momentarily forgotten.

'Ah, you would like to know. It does not surprise me and, from what I have just learned of you, you should deal very well with both these ladies. One is a poor demented creature, your poor father's cousin. Her name is Adélaïde d'Asselnat. She never married and long ago severed all connections with her family on account of her disgraceful opinions. La Fayette, Bailly and Mirabeau were among her friends and there was always a welcome at her house in the Marais for all those wretches responsible for overthrowing the throne of France. She must, I believe, have gone into hiding during the Terror to have escaped the guillotine which devoured the first masters of the revolution as well as its nobler victims. But I presume she must have reappeared and should not be surprised to learn that she had become transformed into one of Bonaparte's most loyal subjects. As for the other – she stands even closer to the Corsican ogre.'

'Who is she?'

'Why, his own wife. Citizeness Bonaparte, whom they call the Empress Joséphine nowadays, has for her maternal grandmother a Mary Katherine Brown of the Irish family. She was the daughter of a Selton and married Joseph-François des Vergers de Sanois. Her daughter, Rose-Claire, married Tascher de la Pagerie, whence Joséphine.' The duke gave a twisted smile. 'Family history holds no secrets from us,' he added sardonically. 'We have time enough in our exile.'

Marianne was a prey to a host of contradictory feelings. The knowledge of her close connection with the wife of Napoleon gave her no pleasure, quite the contrary, for throughout her childhood she had been used to hearing her Aunt Ellis alternately abusing and deriding the man she never referred to as anything but 'Boney'. Lady Selton had taught her to hate and fear the Corsican oppressor who had dared set himself up on the throne of the martyred king, to blockade England and crush all Europe under his heel. To Marianne, Napoleon was a monster, a tyrant spawned by the hideous revolution which, like a vampire, had sucked the finest blood of France including that of her own parents. She left d'Avaray in no doubt as to her sentiments.

'I have no call to seek help from Madame Bonaparte – but I should be glad to see my cousin d'Asselnat.'

'I am not sure I approve your choice. The Creole is well connected. She has even a few drops of Capet blood in her veins, a little secret unknown to her husband and which may yet cost him dear. While the demoiselle d'Asselnat is only a foolish old woman whose sympathies are scarcely more creditable. Now, permit me to take leave of you. I have matters to attend to.'

Marianne too had risen. Standing, she was a head taller than the duke. She looked down at the sick man whose shoulders were once more in a terrible spasm of coughing.

'For the last time, my lord Duke, will you not take me?'

'No. I have told you my reasons. Permit me to die with nothing with which to reproach myself. Your servant, madame.'

He bowed, so slightly as to make the courtesy an insult. Marianne coloured angrily.

'Wait one moment, if you please!'

Taking from her bosom the locket presented to her the day before, she flung it furiously onto the table.

'Take this back, my lord! Since I am no longer one of you, I have no claim to it! Remember, I am English now and a criminal to boot.'

For a moment, the duke looked at the jewel gleaming on the soiled cloth. He put out his hand to take it, then changed his mind. He looked up and regarded Marianne with mingled pride and anger.

'It pleased her Highness to make this gift in recognition of your mother's sacrifice. To return it would be to offend her. You had better keep it. After all,' he went on with a chilly smile, 'you are at liberty to throw it in the sea if you do not want it. It might even be better so. As for you, may God help you for you will escape neither His anger nor your punishment, not if you flee to the ends of the earth!'

He moved away leaving Marianne angry and mortified as well as bitterly disappointed. Everything she trusted, everything she believed in seemed fated to crumble to dust in her hands. Never she swore, would she forget this humiliation. But, for the present, some other means must be found.

By evening Marianne was once again on the old Barbican. She had sold her horse for a good price and further exchanged her riding clothes for a good plain dress of brown wool and a thick cloak with a deep hood worn over a white linen mob cap, and a pair of stout shoes and coarse woollen stockings. She had never worn such garments before but she felt comfortable in them and very much safer. Her money and the pearls were stowed away in a strong canvas pocket sewn into her petticoat. Dressed like this, she was no longer an object of curiosity and would be able to roam the Plymouth waterfront very much as she liked. Her next task was to find a vessel that would carry her to France. In this, time was against her and every hour that passed increased the danger of discovery and arrest.

Unfortunately, knowing no one in the town made it hard to know whom to approach especially in so delicate a matter as a clandestine passage. For a long time, Marianne walked up and down the quay, watching the comings and goings of sailors and fishermen all around her, often tempted but never quite daring to approach them. She wandered on in no particular direction, oblivious of the cheerful bustle of the harbour. As evening drew on, the wind sharpened. Soon she would have to find an inn to spend the night, somewhere more modest than the Crown and Anchor, but she could not yet bring herself to do so. Tired as she was, she could not help feeling somewhat nervous at the prospect of being shut up for the night between four walls and was besides quite sure she would not be able to sleep.

As she passed Charles II's fort, one of the sentries called after her. With a nervous shiver, she hurried on, hugging her cloak more closely about her. The man laughed and uttered some coarse pleasantry but made no attempt to come after her. She saw the old Smeaton fire tower a little way ahead, its bright light a nightly warning of the dangerous approaches to the great port. Bleak and lonely on its rock, rising above the sand, the beacon with the great iron cage that held the light and its supporting masts looked like nothing so much as a great ball of wool stuck on to knitting needles. The flag hung like a wet sheet from the upper platform, so sodden with rain that the wind barely stirred it. There seemed to be no one about and this loneliness, with the moaning of the wind, gave the place a somewhat sinister aspect. Marianne almost turned back but then she saw an old man sitting on a rock right beneath the grey tower and smoking his pipe. Timidly, she went up to him.

'If you please—' she began.

The old man cocked a bushy eyebrow under the faded red stocking cap, revealing a wickedly bright eye.

'What are you doing out here, at this time of night, my pretty, eh? The sailors from the fort have an eye for a pretty girl and the wind's getting up. Likely it'll blow your bonnet over the windmill!'

There is often a secret, unspoken sympathy between the very old and the very young. The old man's friendly tone gave Marianne confidence.

'I know no one in this town, and I must find someone to ask. I thought that, perhaps you might —'

She did not finish. The old man's eyes had quickened and he was studying her with the keen glance of a seaman, accustomed to noting the minutest variation of sea or sky.

'You are no country maid, though you may dress like one. Your voice gives you away. No matter, my girl. What do you want to know?'

In a low voice, as though ashamed of what she had to say, Marianne told him:

'I must find a vessel to take me across the sea – and I cannot tell who to approach.'

'Why, the Harbour Master, of course! It all depends on where you want to go —'

'To France.'

The old man gave a low whistle which vanished on the wind.

'That's another matter entirely, but even there, the port office may be able to do something for you. You must not think our brave English lads are frightened of Boney and his war dogs. There are still some who run the blockade.'

'But I cannot go to the port office,' Marianne broke in impatiently. 'I have no papers. I – I have run away from my parent's house and I have to get to France.'

The old man thought he understood. He chuckled loudly, winking and nudging her with his elbow.

'Oho, you cunning little rascal! Off to join your sweetheart, eh my pretty? That's why we don't want to be noticed, is it? Frightened the Runners'll be after you to take you home again, eh?'

'Yes, you have guessed. But who will take me?'

'No one without money!'

Modestly turning her back on him, the girl quickly raised the hem of her skirt, fumbled in her canvas pocket and withdrew a shilling which she placed in the old man's hand.

'Here, I have a little money. But for pity's sake, if you know of any sailor or fisherman, even a smuggler who might take me, tell me his name —'

The old man held up the coin to study it then tossed it in his hand with evident satisfaction before thrusting it into his pocket. This done, he returned his attention to the girl and looked at her doubtfully.

'There is one I know,' he said with some seriousness, 'but I'm not sure if

I ought to send you to 'un. 'E'd sell 'is own mother for a shilling and for a guinea'd kill her with 'is own hands.'

'I will take the risk. Tell me where I may find him.' A sudden, instinctive caution made her add: 'At all events, I could not give him more than a guinea. That is all I have—'

The old man sighed. He rose and stretched himself with a groan.

'Dang me, old I may be but I'll not let you go alone to find Black Fish. If so be as you've another shilling to quench an old man's thirst, I'll take you and put in a good word for ye.'

'Black Fish?'

'That's what they call 'un. Never heard's right name. But you can trust Nathaniel Naas, I've never met a better sailor – or an uglier!'

Once again, Marianne felt in her pocket and drew out a shilling which she gave to old Nat and a golden guinea which she kept in her hand, being determined not to reveal the whereabouts of the remainder of her treasures to one whom she strongly suspected of being a pirate. The old man pocketed the second shilling and limped away. It was now quite dark and the wind had dropped though a biting cold air still came in from the sea.

'It'll not be warm out there tonight,' the old man said, digging his hands deep in his pockets. 'I'd rather face a bowl of punch than the breakers in the Sound.'

In single file, they made their way back to the Barbican. Nathaniel Naas stopped beneath a battered sign at the end of the old quay and pushed open the low door of a small tavern. A dim, orange light filtered through the grimy windows. Marianne was met by a nauseating reek of alcohol, fried fish and human sweat, together with a confused babble of drunken voices. Above it all, floated the crude air of a sea shanty. The girl drew back in terror. She had never imagined herself entering such a place. The old man glanced at her dubiously.

'You're quite sure? Shall I go in?'

Marianne clenched her teeth to still their chattering. She was cold and frightened and she wanted to go to sleep. She had reached very nearly the end of her strength. She had to get it over with.

'I am sure,' she whispered.

'Then you just wait there.'

He went inside, leaving her alone in the darkness. The quay was empty now. Lamps had been lit in the houses, conjuring up a picture of families within gathered warmly round the tea table. The girl's heart contracted. She felt suddenly very weak and very much alone. The muscles in her throat tightened and all at once she felt as if she wanted to cry while, at the same time, a tempting voice within her was urging her to give up, to go back and abandon herself to her fate. She felt chilled to her very soul. There were some people, she believed, whose lives collapsed without warning and ceased to have any meaning. Perhaps her life was like that, and no longer worth living. Perhaps it would be better to give herself up. Certainly, she had lost any inclination for the part of a heroine in a romance.

The forest of gently dipping masts in the harbour swam before her eyes. Some had their riding lights lit, like intermittent red stars in the darkness. For a second, Marianne was on the point of taking to her heels and running away but the sound of footsteps prevented her. Someone was coming along the quay and her instinct for self-preservation reasserted itself. She made out the dark figures of two men and drew back, shrinking out of sight into a dark, narrow passage running alongside the tavern.

The iron lantern swinging above the tavern door threw a bright patch of light, barred with a shadow like a cross, on to the cobblestones below and this enabled the girl to obtain a clearer view of the two men strolling towards her at a leisurely pace. One was much taller than the other. He wore long seaboots and was muffled in a black cloak. The other barely reached to his shoulder but made up in plumpness for what he lacked in height, for he was almost as broad as he was long. As far as Marianne could tell, he seemed to be dressed like a country lawyer in a frock coat and beaver hat. He must be the owner of the high, fluting voice which Marianne had heard first. Abruptly, another voice, hard and authoritative, broke in but this time Marianne was able to hear the words. What she heard caused her to listen intently.

'You are certain she is here?'

'She was seen at the Crown and Anchor,' the other, lighter voice answered. 'It was certainly she – '

Icy sweat trickled down Marianne's spine. The words brought back the consciousness of her position and she felt her heart lurch in her breast. Who were these men? Was it imagination or had she heard that deep voice before? In her sudden desire to get a sight of its owner, she almost left her hiding place but, as if he had been aware of her secret wish, the taller of the two men paused beneath the lantern, took something from his pocket and jumping on to a stone mounting block, inclined himself towards the flame, flickering in its metal cage, in order to light a cigar. The light fell full upon his face and Marianne bit back a cry as she recognized the hawk-like profile and restless expression of Jason Beaufort.

Her heart beating wildly, she pressed herself back against the streaming wall of the building and closed her eyes in a childish effort to shut out that terrifying face. She was sure now; it was of herself that he had been speaking a moment before. So, not content with ruining and insulting her, the American had now descended to hunting her down like a common constable.

Anger took hold of her, all the fiercer because she was powerless. She wished now that she had not let him escape! He had deserved death as much as Francis, and yet he lived. From behind the fragile lids of her closed eyelids, she heard the scrape of Beaufort's boots as he jumped down and then, once again, the voice with the faint southern accent which was all too familiar now.

'Well, she'll not go far. She's too easily recognized and clever as she is, she'll not escape for long. The noose is already waiting for her.'

Marianne thought she would faint at this grisly prophesy. There was a sick taste of fear in her mouth. She could almost feel the roughness of the rope around her neck and instinctively she put up her hand to her throat as she tried to squeeze herself back even further into her refuge. If only the wall could have opened and swallowed her up.

Meanwhile, the two men were walking on, moving away from the passage and out of earshot. Had they said anything else? The drumming in her ears had prevented her from registering anything but the diminishing sound of their footsteps. Even when these had died away completely, she still dared not open her eyes so great was her terror of seeing Beaufort's face once again before her. But someone, close by, was calling her.

'Hoy! Little maid, where are you?'

That must be old Nathaniel. Taking a deep breath to calm the frantic beating of her heart, she emerged from her hiding place.

'Here I am.'

The old man smiled, revealing the remnants of some teeth which had long forgotten what it was to be white. He was rubbing his hands, apparently well pleased with himself.

'Come with me,' he whispered. 'I think it'll fadge. Black Fish sails tonight with the tide – wants a look at ye –'

Taking her firmly by the hand, he drew her to the tavern. Marianne suffered him to lead her without resistance and immediately found herself in a lighted room where the atmosphere was like a dense fog, reeking in equal parts of rum and tobacco smoke from the long clay pipes of the drinkers huddled beneath the low ceiling. There were fishermen, sailors in stocking caps and a sprinkling of marines in blue uniforms and hard black hats, all of them, with their girls, drinking shouting and singing at the tops of their voices. In a corner by the soot-blackened hearth, a boy knelt at a big, wooden tub washing the tankards as they were brought to him by a moustachioed serving wench. Marianne's entry in the wake of old Nat provoked an outburst of shouts and coarse jokes. Voices called out from all parts of the room.

'Cor, she's a ripe 'un! Hey, sweetheart, come and have a drink with me?'

'By the guts of old Noll, she's the girl for me! D'ye see those eyes, Sam? Clear as the sea the day after a storm!'

'Stow it, Harry! She's not for your picking. Look at her! I'll wager she's a virgin.'

'No harm in finding out! Here, darling! Over here!'

Hands reached out, striving to encircle her waist, or pinch her bottom. Scarlet with shame and terrified in case there should be someone there who knew her face, Marianne eluded them as best she could. Cursing and shoving lustily, old Nat managed to keep off the boldest but he had no easy job. Marianne clutched her cloak around her and tried to dodge the grasping hands, keeping her eyes on the ground so as not to look at the flushed faces of the men and darkling eyes of the girls. Suddenly, a loud voice thundered above the din.

'Stow that racket! And hands off! Leave the girl alone. It's me she's come to see.'

An enormous man had risen from his seat by the bar at the far end of the room. From the colour of his hair and the thick growth of beard that sprouted from his chin, Marianne guessed that this was Black Fish and forced back a gasp. Old Nat was right, never had she seen anyone so ugly. He was a giant of a man, black haired and swarthy skinned. His broad face, with its shapeless features and wide, fleshy nose, might almost have been flattened by a blow from some gigantic fist. The eyes, so bloodshot as to obscure whatever colour they might have had, spoke of long familiarity with the bottle. His bear-like form was clad in a striped jersey with, over it, a faded red coat which still retained some remnants of gold braid. An ancient cocked hat adorned with an enormous green cockade sat jauntily sideways on his pigtailed head. Loud-voiced and powerful, brandishing the inevitable pipe, Black Fish loomed up through the thick fug that filled the room like some weird and menacing Father Neptune. It was all Marianne could do to keep from crossing herself. But already a vast hairy hand had grasped her arm and was drawing her irresistibly forward. She found herself seated on the form facing old Nat who was chuckling and rubbing his hands.

'Its just as I told ye, lass! He's a right one is Black Fish —'

More frightened than she was prepared to show, Marianne privately considered that this Black Fish bore a striking resemblance to the pirates whose exploits she had devoured with such relish when safely between the covers of a book. The reality was quite a different matter. The man before her had no black patch over one eye or wooden leg but, these details apart, he seemed the living image of a gentleman of fortune. And so ugly! The prospect of finding herself alone at sea with this dreadful man made her shudder. But for the alarming words she had overheard pass between Jason Beaufort and the short stranger, she would probably have abandoned all thought of any closer acquaintance with this terrifying individual. But the American's presence in the city brought the shadow of the scaffold more menacingly close and she had no choice but to escape by any means and in whatever company, even that of the devil himself if need be.

Black Fish was watching her knowingly from beneath his bushy black brow. He leaned heavily across the table and thrust his face into hers.

'Not so keen now to sail the seas with old Black Fish, eh lass?'

Marianne gritted her teeth and forced herself to look her fearful acquaintance in the face.

'I am obliged to go to France. It is a matter of – of life and death!'

The mariner opened his mouth in a roar of laughter, letting out a gust of pungent, rum-laden breath.

'You love your young coxcomb as much as that do you? You can't be afraid if you mean to cross the Channel at the end of November!'

'I am not afraid of the sea and I wish to go to France. Will you take me?'

'That depends. What'll you pay?'

'A guinea.'

'Not much for the risk of a brave man's life. Well, let's see your guinea then at least we'll know you speak the truth.'

For answer, she opened her hand. The lamplight gleamed for an instant on the heavy gold coin with the plump profile of King George III as it lay in her palm. Black Fish reached across and took it. He bit it and gave her a wink.

'Good enough. It's a bargain, my girl. I'll take you. You're lucky, I've business of my own with the French dogs. Your guinea will serve.'

At once, Marianne felt her spirits revive. Now that he had agreed to take her, hope and courage returned and she was able to fight with all her strength against the insidious counsels of despair. She refused to think that this man might betray her or, having taken her money, that he might leave without her. In any case, she was determined not to let him out of her sight.

'Thank you,' was all she said. 'When do we sail?'

'You seem in a mighty hurry – where do you lodge?'

'Nowhere. If we leave tonight, I have no need of a lodging.'

'Very well, we stay here until ten and then go aboard.'

'The tide is not full until midnight –'

'Bright as a button, ain't we! But over inquisitive. I've things to do before we put to sea, my pretty! Here, drink some of this! Proper turnip head you've got on you.'

"This" proved to be a glass of steaming grog which Black Fish shoved towards his passenger. Marianne eyed the pungent beverage suspiciously. She had never tasted spirits and was on the point of saying so.

'But – I do not know –'

'You don't know but what it mightn't make you ill, eh? Never tried it before?' Bending forward suddenly so that his beard almost touched Marianne's ear, he muttered rapidly: 'Try and drop the flash talk if y' can. Ye'll get yourself noticed –'

Taken by surprise, she gave him a startled glance then seized the glass and bravely swallowed down a draught of the burning liquid. She gasped, choked and began to cough wildly while Black Fish thumped her mightily between the shoulder blades and roared with laughter.

'Takes you back a bit, at first,' he agreed encouragingly. 'But you'll get used to it –'

The worst of it was that this curious assertion proved correct. Once she had got her breath back, Marianne discovered that the grog had power to spread an agreeable warmth through her exhausted body. It flowed down like a fragrant, fiery river. All in all, she found it very good. She took another sip, rather more cautiously this time, to Black Fish's huge delight.

'We'll make a sailor of her yet!' he boomed, smashing his fist down on the table with such force that old Nat, who for some moments past, had been fast asleep and snoring with his head on his arms, sat up with a start. He sat there, blinking helplessly, still half asleep.

'Go home to bed, Nat,' Black Fish told him. 'Time old grandads were asleep. We'll have another jar, me and the lass, then we'll be off.'

Hiking Nat unceremoniously to his feet, he picked up the red hat which had fallen off the old man's head and stuck it on again at random. Then he gave him a push towards the door.

'G'bye, little lass,' old Nat mumbled. 'God speed –'

'That's enough! Off with you, now!' Black Fish cut him abruptly short.

Marianne, too, felt very much inclined for sleep. She was warm now and the rum, as well as filling her with a comfortable sense of well-being, was making her very sleepy. Viewed through the soothing veil of alcohol, her terrors faded, leaving only an insuperable weariness. However, she was obliged to sit a whole hour more with drooping eyelids, watching Black Fish consume quantities of rum and smoke pipe after pipe. In all this time, he paid her no attention at all. He sat with his eyes fixed vacantly on some point in the smoke-filled room and seemed to have forgotten his companion altogether. She sat bravely on, waiting patiently for him to give the signal to leave. The crowd about them had thinned. Two or three men were throwing dice while others were gathered round a table listening to the battle yarns of a quartermaster of marines. A drunken sailor in a corner was singing a tuneless refrain and periodically thrusting away a girl who was trying to take him home. Black Fish and Marianne sat on unnoticed. She was beginning to wonder for how much longer this would go on when the black wooden clock struck ten.

On the last stroke, Black Fish hoisted himself to his feet and, still without looking at her, laid hold of his companion's hand.

'Come, it is time,' was all he said.

Their departure occasioned no remark. Once outside the low doorway with its leaded panes, they were caught up in a fierce gust of wind bringing with it a strong smell of the sea. Marianne breathed in deeply with a sudden exhilaration. The wind smacked of freedom. And suddenly, standing there in the inn doorway, she discovered a new meaning to her flight. Her first thought had been undoubtedly to save her life but as she smelt the sea breeze it came to her suddenly that there was a fierce joy in severing the last ties that bound her, leaving her moorings behind, tearing up the old roots and drifting off into the unknown guided only by her own will. Impulsively, she held out the folds of her cloak, letting the wind swell them, as though she would offer herself to be picked up and carried away by it.

Black Fish had been watching curiously. 'Sure you're not frightened?' he asked suddenly. 'It'll be a hard night!'

'I don't care! It's good, this wind! And besides,' she suddenly remembered her role, 'I am happy, I am going to meet –'

'No!' he interrupted her roughly. 'Don't talk to me about your lover! I don't know why you want to go to France, but it is not for a man.'

'How did you know?' she asked him, making no further attempt at denial.

'One's only to look at your eyes, my beauty! Not a spark of love in them! When I looked at them just now, when old Nat brought you to me, I saw just one thing. Fear! That's why I'm taking you, because you are afraid. I've no truck with love. It's a waste of time! But fear now, there's some sense in that. Now come, it's time we were off! There's things to do before we put to sea.'

Black Fish spat magnificently, stuffed his pipe in his pocket and ramming his improbable hat down on his head against the wind, set off with great strides along the quay. Marianne followed him, still wondering why this hideous pirate should fill her with such instinctive trust.

CHAPTER FOUR
The Stormy Seas

Black Fish's vessel, the *Seagull*, lay at the far end of the Barbican, not far from the stone set up to mark for all time the berth of the *Mayflower* before she had set sail across the Atlantic to New England with her cargo of Pilgrim Fathers. Beneath her grimy appearance and chipped green paintwork, she was a handy little sloop with well-caulked seams and a snug cabin into which, on Black Fish's orders, Marianne descended.

'You stay there, and not a sound! We don't want to tell the coastguards we're here.'

He turned his attention to the sails and the little vessel slipped slowly out of harbour. But, to the not inconsiderable surprise of his passenger, instead of making for the open sea, Black Fish turned up the estuary of the Tamar in the direction of the naval dockyard. Curious as to the reason for this behaviour, she crawled on hands and knees out of the cabin and whispered: 'Where are we?'

'I told you I've something to do. Another passenger to take on board. Now, that's enough. One more word and its down to Davy Jones with you!'

He was stowing the sail as he spoke and now produced a great oar with which he began sculling noiselessly but with an effectiveness that did honour to his strength. Now that they had left the beacon behind them, the darkness was complete, only pierced now and then by the distant riding light of some vessel. At night, the tower crowned with its glowing brazier was a fantastic sight, but Black Fish had made a considerable detour in order to avoid the stippled red light thrown on the dark water. Clinging to the rail of the tiny vessel, Marianne breathed in the night air greedily and stared at the ghostly shapes of the hills gliding past with the occasional bright point of light. The sloop worked slowly up the estuary, fighting the current. It was not long to high tide and the swell was already making itself felt in a short, choppy sea. Black Fish must be straining every muscle but he was a man of uncommon strength, well able to do the work of two. Marianne thought that he must also have cat's eyes to find his way in such conditions, although now that her own eyes were becoming accustomed to it, she was able to make out some small shapes.

Abruptly, as they passed the crumbling stonework of an old, disused mole, Black Fish stopped sculling, shipped his oar and tied up to what must have been an ancient ring in the wall. Seating himself in the stern, he cupped his hands about his mouth and mewed three times like a gull, with a realism which astonished Marianne. After that, he seemed to listen for something.

Marianne, full of curiosity, was about to speak, but he waved her curtly to be silent and she subsided meekly.

It was getting colder and there was something forbidding about the darkness and silence of their surroundings. Not far away, a number of dark shapes loomed up looking like a barricade of huge ships lying across the Tamar. Even the slap of the waves had stopped. The monsters lay huge and motionless, a lantern burning here and there, and the water in between them and the sloop looked curiously flat, smooth and thick, like cream. It gave off a faint smell of mud. Unable to contain her curiosity any longer, Marianne crept closer to Black Fish and in spite of his prohibition, whispered softly: 'What is it? Where are we?'

Black Fish pointed to the dark shapes.

'The hulks,' he said simply. 'You know what they are?'

Marianne knew, she had heard of the old ships, no longer seaworthy, with their barred ports, that were used as prisons to house those of Boney's sailors who fell into English hands.

'Admirable prisons,' Aunt Ellis had often said with satisfaction, 'only too good for them, I dare say! They say some manage to escape —'

But what were they doing here? Why this mystery? Black Fish was speaking again in a low voice.

'The *Europa*, the *St Isidore*, the *St Nicholas*, each one of them a hell! The French are crammed in there so tight that every night some die of suffocation —'

To her surprise, Marianne heard a note of anger in the big man's voice and she did not hide her astonishment.

'But they're enemies! You ought to be glad. But it seems to grieve you.' The beginnings of an oath escaped Black Fish but he controlled himself at once and only said gruffly: 'I am a seaman, not a jailor, and they too are seamen —'

Suddenly Marianne understood.

'Do you mean – you are going to help one of them to escape?'

'Why not? He is like you, willing to pay. I'm helping you to escape. So keep your questions to yourself. Now, keep your trap shut or you'll have us spotted.'

Marianne did not persist. She was made forcibly conscious that now she was only a girl, like any other, less than others even, because she was obliged to hide and flee. She had no choice but to accept, humbly and in silence, what fate might send her, even to being ordered about by someone who was practically a pirate.

But in a moment, her thoughts were distracted by something very odd that seemed to be happening. Something appeared to be crawling towards them over the water. Marianne could not make out what it was precisely. Again, Black Fish imitated the gull's cry softly beside her and she almost cried out. There was something frightful and terrifying about the blurred form spread-eagled on the water. She pointed with a trembling hand.

'There – do you see?'

'Quiet. It's him.'

Marianne's eyes were by now sufficiently accustomed to the darkness for her to be able to see that the figure was in fact that of a man. She was about to ask another question when Black Fish prudently forestalled her by whispering hastily: 'The hulks are anchored in a muddy creak. We're at the edge of a lake of liquid mud. It's a death trap – if he tries to stand up, the mud will suck him down –'

This time, it was fear that kept Marianne silent. Her heart was in her mouth and her eyes wide with terror as she followed the fugitive's agonizing progress. The first hulk was not very far away but to her the distance seemed immense, and then there was the additional danger that the prisoner's flight would be discovered or of his being overcome by cold in the water. The man must not be recaptured because if he were, she would be taken with him. He must succeed for her own life to be safe. Moreover, in her heart of hearts, she admired the courage of a man, who, to regain his freedom, would risk a hideous death in the slimy depths of that perilous sea of mud.

Black Fish, paying no more attention to her, was bent over the rails, leaning as far out as he could and holding the oar at arm's length.

He gave the gull's cry once more, then Marianne heard him whisper in French: 'Over here, lad. One more heave-there you are!'

There was something so timeless and improbable about the whole of this night that now she was no longer even astonished that a one-time English pirate should express himself with perfect familiarity in the language of Voltaire. It was no stranger than everything else. Nothing, in any of the books that she had read, not even Robinson Crusoe itself, had been anything like this.

She heard the sound of someone gasping for breath, followed by a muffled, wordless cry and then the boat lurched violently. Black Fish came upright hauling after him, as though dredged from the bottom of the sea, something heavy, wet and slimy which he deposited upon the deck where it lay motionless. But for the rattle of the man's breathing, Marianne would have thought him dead. Without wasting a moment, Black Fish took him by the feet and dragged him towards the cabin. Marianne, listening eagerly, overheard a scrap of dialogue, likewise in French.

'Not too bad, was it?'

'No. I've known worse, but we must be away from here – I think a spy saw me go! Oh God, it's cold!'

'Here, wrap this round you. When you're dry, I'll get you some clothes. And take this. There's rum in the flask – then try and sleep. We'll get off now. Tide's all but full.'

In fact, Marianne noticed a tremor of the ship's planking where she lay at the edge of the mud, as though something were working and writhing below. Black Fish reappeared, cast off and shoved the boat away from the old jetty with a strong push of the oar. Not before time. Lanterns were moving like will o' the wisps about the hulk and a light shone out through barred portholes, revealing gesticulating black figures. Soldiers could be seen, trailing their guns. But the sloop, freed from the mud by a lusty stroke of the oar, was already passing behind the crumbling stone jetty, back into the main stream of the Tamar. Black Fish stuck to his oar, rowing like a trojan, and now, with the current in her favour, the light vessel was making a good speed. Marianne watched, fascinated. The man was like some fantastic human machine and thanks to him the heavy ship seemed endowed with an extraordinary driving force. She was just passing the beacon, lying well out in the middle of the estuary, when the gun boomed out behind them. Black Fish cursed without troubling to keep his voice down.

'A thousand thunders! The escape's discovered! We're lucky though, wind's getting up –'

It was doing more than getting up, it was blowing with a force that Marianne found terrifying. Suddenly, the estuary had become huge. The shore line had receded on either hand, leaving a broad expanse of sea, the waves capped with curls of foam. Imperturbably, Black Fish set the sail and took the helm. The sail gave a crack as the wind caught it and swelled triumphantly. The sloop bounded forward, running for the open sea. Once past the final buoys and nothing but the wide waters lay before them. The echo of the gun was lost in the roaring of the wind.

'We've sailed right into a storm –' Marianne shrieked breathlessly.

'This? A storm?' Black Fish laughed. 'You wait till you see a real storm, lass. You won't forget it. This is just a nice little slice of wind to see us on our way, strong enough to make the coastguards think twice about sticking to our heels. And don't come telling me you're frightened. I warned you.'

'I am not frightened!' Marianne declared fiercely. 'And to prove it, I shall sleep here!'

'You'd be better in the cabin.'

'No!'

The real reason was that she could not bring herself to go down there. In the cabin was the unknown man, the escaped prisoner who must be some kind of desperado since he was one of Napoleon's fearful Frenchmen. Marianne was a hundred times readier to face the battering of the wind and even the occasional dollop of sea water than the company of a man whose very presence on board only made her the more conscious of the evils of her own situation. The only distance now between the escaped prisoner and the erstwhile mistress of Selton Hall was in Marianne's own will. And yet, now that she had nothing to do but wait for the approach of the French coast, her accumulated weariness overcame her. She was so tired she could have gone to sleep lying in a puddle. Besides, the unaccustomed heavy fumes of the rum were beginning to make themselves felt.

'As you like,' Black Fish said. 'You can wrap this round you.'

It was a length of sail cloth, coarse to the touch but dry and thick enough to be almost waterproof. Marianne folded it round her gratefully, making a kind of cocoon with herself inside. Then, curled into a ball like a cat in a basket with her head on a coil of rope, she closed her eyes and fell instantly asleep.

The face which Marianne beheld when she opened her eyes was a pleasant one. Clean manly features framed in a short golden beard and grey eyes, at present filled with admiration. For a moment, she thought it must be a continuation of her dream which had transported her temporarily back to Selton which still seemed so close. But the world to which the face belonged was a long way from the quiet English countryside. It was a turbulent, watery world of grey skies with heavy clouds racing as far as the eye could see, of salt spray and icy waves rising and falling in a froth of boiling foam. Towering above this world of water was the massive figure of Black Fish standing at the *Seagull's* wheel, great hands clamped to the spokes, as huge and outlandish as some sea god from a nightmare.

The man with the fair beard put out a hand and touched Marianne's damp cheek with one finger.

'A woman!' he murmured, as if unable to believe his eyes. 'A real woman! Do they still exist?'

Black Fish's thunderous laugh rose above the roar of the wind.

'They surely do, and a darned sight more of them than is any good for the peace of honest lads like you and me! Take no notice of her, lad.'

'She is pretty, though—'

'She's well enough, but what her lay is, I don't know. Told me some yarn about wanting to go to France to find some boy, but that's a lie, I know. If she's not scared to death, then I'll be hanged. She's scared and running from something, maybe the law – likely she's a thief. With her pretty face, she's prigged some swell cove's dibs, I shouldn't wonder, and now they're after her—'

Throughout this dialogue which took place in French, Marianne had managed to keep silent but to hear herself accused of theft was more than she could bear. Pushing aside the canvas, she burst out fiercely in the same language:

'I am not a thief and I forbid you to insult me! I did not pay you for that!'

Both men gaped at her in surprise and Black Fish almost let go of the helm.

'How's this, you speak French?'

'Why not?' she said haughtily, 'Is there a law against it?'

'No – but you might have said!'

'I do not see why! You did not tell me that you speak it – like a native!'

'That's enough sauce from you, my girl,' Black Fish growled. 'I'd talk a bit less flash, if I were you. There's nothing to stop me taking you by the scruff and pitching you overboard. You seem a funny kind o'mort to me. Whose to say you ain't a spy?'

Marianne was too angry to be frightened.

'No one,' she retorted. 'And if you wish to throw me in the sea, feel free to do so! You will be doing me a service. I regret only that I was mistaken in you. I took you for a smuggler. It seems, however, that you are a murderer!'

'Hell and damnation—'

Black Fish, red with anger, had dropped the helm and was about to throw himself at the girl. At the strong risk of being hurled overboard himself, the fugitive from the hulks cast himself bodily between them and thrust back the giant who stood uncertainly, his fist still raised.

'Nicolas, are you out of your mind? Behave yourself. Can't you see she's only a kid?' Turning to Marianne, he asked her kindly: 'How old are you, little one?'

'Seventeen,' she said reluctantly. Then added almost at once: 'Why do you call him Nicolas?'

The young man began to laugh, showing firm strong teeth.

'Because it's his name. You don't think he was christened Black Fish? And you, what are you called?'

'Marianne—'

'A pretty name,' he said with approval, 'but Marianne what?'

'Marianne nothing! Is it any of your concern? I have not asked you questions!'

He drew himself up and made a ceremonious bow, rendered absurd by the enormous garment Black Fish had found for him to wear.

'I am Jean Le Dru, native of Saint Malo—' he paused and added with a simple pride which did not escape Marianne, '– and I sail with Surcouf!'

Had he been a king's son, he could not have said it with more pride.

Marianne did not know who Surcouf was but, feeling suddenly drawn to him in spite of herself, she smiled and said: 'I had thought you to be one of the Corsican's men.'

He stiffened, frowned imperceptibly and looked at the young woman with narrowed eyes.

'Surcouf serves him and I serve Surcouf. And let me add that when we speak of him, we say the Emperor!'

He turned without further comment and went to seat himself beside Black Fish. Realizing that she must have wounded him in his convictions, Marianne inwardly cursed herself for a fool. There had been no need for her to show her dislike of the man he spoke of with such ceremony as the Emperor. He was a Frenchman and she in his power for, to her great surprise, Black Fish had not reacted as a loyal Englishman should have done. Throughout the brief contretemps, he had not stirred, content with staring vaguely out to sea. She wondered if Black Fish were really English. The way he spoke French gave some room for doubt.

Left to herself, Marianne tried to retreat once more into her shell of damp canvas and go to sleep but this proved impossible. The vessel was pitching badly in the choppy seas of the Channel and Marianne became suddenly very much aware of the movement. Beyond the rail, the grey waves fell into deep hollows as though the sea would open up beneath the ship, then swelled up again, driven by the wind. The horizon had disappeared. Now there was no land in sight, not even a rock, only the sea birds and the universal grey waters through which the sloop plunged blindly on, her sails strained to breaking point.

Marianne was suddenly overcome by an appalling feeling of nausea. She closed her eyes and let herself go. It seemed to her that she was dying. That everything was falling to pieces around her and her stomach responded to every lurch of the vessel. Never having been sea sick before, she did not know what was happening to her. She tried to stand up, clinging to the rails, but once again the sickness overpowered her and she sank back utterly exhausted on to the deck.

The next thing she felt was two hands holding her and someone lifting her up. Something cold was pressed against her mouth.

'Feeling bad, eh?' the voice of Jean Le Dru said in her ear. 'Drink this, it will do you good.'

She recognized the strong, pungent smell of rum and swallowed some mechanically. But her empty stomach rebelled against the spirit. Abruptly thrusting aside the arm which held her, she opened wide terrified eyes and made for the ship's side with a strangled yell.

For the next few dreadful minutes, Marianne forgot all dignity in the spasmodic heaving of her stomach. She did not even mind the sea which slapped her face wetly, although this helped to revive her. She clung to the rail while Jean, his arm clamped securely round her waist, did his best to stop her falling overboard. When the violent retching subsided a little at last, she sagged like an old pillowcase and would have fallen if the Breton had not caught her. Gently, with almost motherly care, he laid her back on the canvas and covered her as best he could. Black Fish's voice came to her, as though through cotton wool.

'Shouldn't have made her drink. Probably hungry.'

'That's the best bout of seasickness I ever saw,' the other answered.

'I'd be surprised if she could swallow a mouthful—'

But Marianne was past joining in the argument. She was conscious of nothing but the moment's respite granted her by this sudden frightful illness and, hardly daring to breathe, was watching for the smallest sign on the part of her body. The lull was in any case only a short one, for after a few minutes the retching began again and Marianne was once more a prey to seasickness.

With the fall of night, the gale became a tempest and curiously Marianne's sickness grew less. The pitching of the vessel became so violent that it put an end to the nauseating lurching of her stomach. She emerged at last from the depths of misery in which that hellish day had passed but only to meet another kind of horror, this time fear.

When she first crawled out of the small cabin where Jean Le Dru had placed her to be a little out of the wet, it seemed to her that the world was disintegrating around her. Murky clouds scurried across an inky sky beneath which the sea was erupting in all directions. The two men had lowered the sail but still the boat was dancing like a cork in the boiling waters. From time to time, it plunged into a wall of mist so thick that it was hard to tell whether it belonged to the sky or was cast up as spray by the raging sea. They would emerge for a moment, only to rush headlong into another bank of mist. It seemed as though some giant hand took hold of the little sloop and hurled it like a ball through the midst of the storm, now and then dropping it for a moment only to pick it up again and toss it further.

But what frightened Marianne most of all was the faces of the two men. Through the waves crashing over the side, she glimpsed Black Fish, still clinging to the wheel, his back bent against the raging wind. Jean was finishing sewing the sail, fighting against the blinding sea. Both were soaked to the skin but they seemed not to care, though their tense faces betrayed their anxiety.

Black Fish saw Marianne and yelled above the wind.

'Stay in the cabin! You've no business here. You'll get in the way and risk being swept overboard!'

'I can't breathe down there,' she shouted back. 'I'd rather be out here—'

Jean hurried over to her, put his arms round her and tried to force her back inside but she clung to him.

'Please, let me stay with you – I'm frightened, all alone —'

She broke off as a wave hit her. Another followed and she was soaked from head to foot but only clung more firmly to her companion. In the same instant, a cry of terror escaped them both. The mist had parted suddenly revealing a sheer black cliff rising directly ahead. Their cry was echoed by the helmsman.

Jean caught Marianne to him instinctively. Convinced that their last hour had come, she closed her eyes and pressed her face into his shoulder. The young man's arms were so strong and reassuring that she found to her surprise her fear lessened. In a moment or two she was going to die in the arms of a stranger and yet, deep down, it did not seem to matter very much. Perhaps it was even right that it should be so since her life had fallen into this meaningless idiocy. It felt good to be held close against a man's chest and, was she dreaming or was a pair of warm lips pressed to her forehead?

But the crash never came. Black Fish wrenched at the helm and the small boat went about so suddenly that Marianne and Jean lost their balance and tumbled on the deck. When Marianne opened her eyes again the glistening wall of rock was slipping past within an arm's length of the ship's quarter. Behind her, she heard the seaman cursing with a violence in keeping with the fright he had had.

'What was that —?' asked Jean Le Dru.

'The Dover rocks, I think,' Black Fish answered. 'I did not think we were so near. We had a lucky escape!'

To restore himself, he called for the flask of rum, swallowed a large draught and then devoted himself once more to steering the sloop, which, once past the rocks, was heading into a fresh bank of mist and spray. But Jean was worried and showed it.

'How came we near the Dover rocks? They are not on our course.'

'I'm doing my best,' Black Fish growled. 'My compass is all to pieces. I'm steering by guesswork.'

'Then the Virgin and St Anne d'Auray protect us.'

This pious wish was lost in the howling of the wind which just then redoubled its violence. A wave crashed over the side, and Jean led the gasping Marianne firmly back to the tiny cabin. Black Fish alone remained, standing amidst the tempest like Atlas bearing the world on his shoulders.

'Ship ahead! We're saved!'

There was both triumph and relief in Black Fish's voice. He was echoed by Marianne and Jean. For hours they had been running blindly before the storm. The *Seagull's* case had been desperate. Not many cables' lengths from the dread Dover rocks, an underwater reef had damaged the rudder. They had tried to hoist the sails but these were carried away when the mast collapsed before a gust of exceptional force. Since then, the vessel had drifted, blind and helpless, at the mercy of the untrammelled waves. The worst moment for Marianne had been when she saw Black Fish leave the helm to come and sit with Jean and herself. She had grown used to seeing the enormous sailor as a kind of ocean god, as much a part of his vessel as of the sea itself. The boat was soundly built and yet the storm had battered it savagely, the man seemed indestructible and yet he too was beaten. In her wretchedness, she could not help saying: 'Is there no hope?'

Black Fish shrugged. 'What else can I do?' he said gruffly. 'Row? You can try it if you like but I've done all I can. Now, it's in the lap of the gods.'

He pulled his sodden and ridiculous hat down over his eyes irritably, as though he meant to sleep, but his eyes, beneath the dripping brim, were watchful. He was the first to spot the stern lights of a vessel which in their present situation was a blessing from heaven.

'We are saved,' Marianne repeated, her nerves too much on edge to feel much relief. 'Saved!'

But Jean was less optimistic.

'Wait and see what vessel she is first,' he growled. 'They may be pirates and refuse to take us aboard. We're not much in the way of a prize. Or they may be English and send me back to the hulks.'

But Marianne could not believe that the captain of any vessel could be so heartless as to send three luckless passengers aboard a fishing boat coolly to their deaths on such a black and dreadful night. Eyes smarting from the salt and so wet through that she could no longer even imagine what it was to be dry, she gazed with passionate intensity at the twin stars dancing in the murk, reminding her of the big ships she had seen in Plymouth Harbour, as stout and comforting as a warm inn at the end of a wintry frozen forest. How she longed to escape from this hell of wind and water, the cold and fear! In this moment of great peril, she was once again a terrified child, grasping at the least protection, the smallest help, the slightest hope, only so she might be less cold and frightened.

'The wind's driving us towards her,' Black Fish said. He was clinging to the halyards and peering into the darkness. Almost at once, he gave another, louder shout.

'We must be near a harbour. I can see another light to starboard.'

He broke off with a gasp while Marianne flung herself into Jean's arms with a shriek of terror. The darkness had lightened suddenly and in that instant the shape of a huge reef slipped by to starboard at an alarming rate, followed by another. The rudderless sloop was driving forward like the wind and the lights of the vessel ahead were drawing nearer at a dizzying rate. Soon, its shape could be seen, dark against the sky. Then all at once, a sliver of moonlight slipped between the clouds and lighted on the boiling waters, revealing the tragic outline of a big merchantman yawing drunkenly amid the battering of the hissing, foaming waters beneath her. Her tall sails hung like wet rags uselessly from masts like black and naked trees. At the same time, huge glistening rocks, carved in fantastic shapes, appeared for an instant and were gone, rocks whereon danced the second light which Black Fish had taken for the entry to a harbour. Jean Le Dru's shriek nearly burst Marianne's eardrum.

'Wreckers!'

He shook his fist wildly at the coast with its deadly trap, his whole body trembling with anger. Marianne felt him shaking against her, vibrating like the vessel itself, and her instinctive liking for the boy increased. His indignation communicated itself to her own heart, just as Jean's nervous excitement was something she felt in every fibre of her own body. Curiously enough, at that moment, such is the bond of the common danger, the escaped prisoner from the hulks and the daughter of the Marquis d'Asselnat were as one.

Jean was speaking again, spitting out his words. 'They fasten a lantern to a cow's horns and lead it up and down the shore to make doomed ships believe they see another vessel. That is what happened to the big merchantman and his lights drew us. They are vultures, devils!'

In her unconscious need to soothe her brother in terror, Marianne tried to conceal her own fears because she sensed that Jean would need all his strength and quickness for what was to come and also because it was important to her that he should still be a solid rock to lean on. Staring at the vague outline of the coast, she asked: 'What coast is this, do you know?'

It was Black Fish who answered in a voice as calm as though the danger no longer concerned him.

'It is one of the most dangerous places on the coast of Brittany. They call it Paganie, "pagan land", and it is true that its inhabitants are fiercer than any pagan. It is a cruel, desolate spot, relying on the sea for everything. The people make sure it gives them what they need.' There was a sudden gentleness in his voice as he added: 'I think, lass, this time it is death.'

It was true, the little boat was caught up in a whirl of hissing spray. Around the three unfortunates as they clung to one another, the sea roared in the rocky cove but another, more terrible noise rose above the sound of the tempest. In the same instant, fires sprang up on the shore, throwing a tragic light over the sea. Screams and shouts rent the night, mingling with the crackle of burning wood. The huge bulk of the merchant ship seemed to rear up and fall back with a sound like thunder. A wave, higher than the rest, had cast her, belly-down on a jagged reef and what Marianne and her companions had heard was the sound of her hull splitting. Marianne could see small black figures clinging to the vessel's bridge and spars. She saw other figures armed with torches running back and forth on what must be a small beach. Then she saw no more because the sloop in her turn was rushing to her doom and terror overcame her. Marianne had been preserved until that movement by the tragic grandeur of the sight but now she fully realized her own mortal danger. She stared with eyes of horror at the black waters foaming so close, waters which in a few minutes more would close over her.

Still clinging to Jean, she crossed herself earnestly, muttered a prayer and had a brief thought for her Aunt Ellis whom she now went to join and even for Francis and Ivy. Were human quarrels carried over into the next world? It hardly seemed to matter. What mattered was that she should be forgiven for the twofold crime she had unwittingly committed. Next, she made up her mind to close her eyes to shut out the terrible scene of the shipwreck, and that she would never open them again. But first, she glanced up at the young man whose arms were round her. He was standing like a statue, head held high and his face might have been carved out of marble as he stared at the doomed vessel. Marianne felt his body trembling against hers. But then he became aware of her movement and looked at her like one awakening from a dream. It was only an instant. Then he was gripping her shoulders.

'And of course, you haven't the faintest idea how to swim? You've never learned! They don't teach girls that kind of thing where you come from –' There was a kind of desperate violence in his voice.

'But – yes, I learned to swim. In a river, certainly, not in this –' She jerked her head towards the raging sea and shuddered.

'If that is true, you may yet escape,' said Black Fish's loud voice beside her. But Marianne was beginning to understand all that was meant by that word, swim, and felt as much terror as though she had never learned. She clung to Jean with all her strength.

'I can swim – but I'm frightened! I'm so frightened! Don't leave me, I beg of you, don't let me go – without you, I am bound to die.'

A softness came into the boy's tense face. Faced with the terror of this child, he forgot his own fear and thought only of protecting her. There was such beauty in the supplicating eyes, such loveliness in the face raised to his that all at once, he felt in himself the strength of twenty knights. Impulsively, he clasped her to him.

'No, I will not let you go! I will hold you tight. I'll hold you so close that the sea shall not get you –'

'No rash promises!' Black Fish growled. 'Once in the water, its every man for himself but the Devil's in it if between us we can't get her out of this – always supposing we can get ourselves out of it.'

But Jean was not listening. Impelled by the unconscious desire which had sprung up in him at the moment when he first looked on Marianne, he had set his lips on hers and for a brief moment, Marianne forgot her fears in the sweet tenderness of that kiss. In the same instant, the sloop lifted as though about to take wing, keeled over to one side and fell back with a dreadful tearing sound. Marianne and Jean were flung into the sea with such violence that their arms were torn apart and to her horror, Marianne found herself alone amid the white topped waves.

Deafened and blinded, she sank at first like a stone but then her will to live and animal instinct of self-preservation came to her rescue. Without quite knowing how, she struggled to the surface at last, half drowned, her nose and ears filled with water, but alive. To her surprise, she saw that she was much closer to the shore. A big wave rolled her over, mercifully cutting short her view of the terrifying spectacle before her. Men were running in all directions, shouting wildly. Some, completely naked in spite of the cold, plunged into the water armed with long gaffs which they used to draw the debris from the wrecked ship within reach. It was like a vision of hell and somewhere at the back of a mind half dead with terror and fatigue, Marianne found herself thinking that what she saw might well be devils.

Once again, she found herself able to breathe, and looked round wildly for her companions. Once again, a mountain of foam bore down on her and swallowed her. The sea tossed her to and fro like a cockle shell, now bearing her in towards the shore, then carrying her out to sea again only to bring her back once more. It was as though the waves were trying to batter her to pieces, the better to absorb her into their watery depths. Perhaps after all, that was what death was?

Then, suddenly, came searing pain, tearing at Marianne's right thigh. She gave one agonized shriek and then lost consciousness.

When she opened her eyes, it was to find herself in the power of demons. She was being roughly pulled about by two men, one feeling her all over while the other tore off her clothes. She felt the cold sand under her bare back and the burning pain in her side where the gaff must have wounded her in drawing her ashore but scarcely had she opened her eyes than she closed them again in horror at what she had seen. Two men were bending over her. They had long hair and the eyes that glittered in their filthy, hairy faces were the eyes of wild beasts. The one engaged in stripping off her clothes was stark naked, his huge muscular body covered in black matted hair. They were growling like animals, ripping off everything they could find about her and a kind of blind instinct told her that her only chance was to counterfeit death. She was so cold that it was almost true. But the two robbers were not interested in her condition, only in her garments. She heard the gurgle of triumph as they found the canvas pocket where she kept her modest wealth. They began talking together in a rough speech which she did not understand but she guessed that they were arguing over the pearls, the gold and the locket. What these men were taking was all the little she had left in the world and yet Marianne found it did not even make her want to cry. She was too cold and bruised and frightened to be aware of anything but her immediate physical sensations and could only pray with all her might that the men would be satisfied with robbing her and go away and leave her on the beach.

One other thought she clung to, that of her companions in misfortune, Jean and Black Fish. Where could they be? They were seamen, familiar with the worst of storms and must have come to land at the same time as herself or sooner. But she sensed that she was alone. If they still lived, they would not have abandoned her at the mercy of these dreadful men! Jean had promised to look after her. He had kissed her, as though he truly loved her – yes he must be dead. And it seemed to Marianne that she had nothing left in all the world.

Timidly, she half opened her eyes. The two men were standing a few yards away from her, still arguing, but the scene beyond was like something out of a nightmare. The wreckers were busy dragging chests and bales of all descriptions up on to the sand. All about were bodies thrown up by the sea, those of the seamen from the merchant vessel, some already dead, others perhaps still living but only to be finished off without mercy by the wreckers with knives or bludgeons. Further out on the rocks, lay the dying ship, a great hole in her side.

Marianne caught herself thinking idiotically of accounts of shipwrecks she had read in days gone by. They had been nothing like this. She thought of the heroine of *Paulet Virginie*, preferring death to the idea of taking off her dress. How stupid! Wasn't she herself half naked at the mercy of these men?

As her wits returned, she saw that the sea had thrown her up at one end of the beach. There were rocks close by, rocks among which it might be possible to hide. Absorbed in their booty, the two robbers seemed to have lost interest in her and it was so cold, here in this icy wind.

Very slowly, she began to crawl but however slight the movement, it was noticed. The two men were on her in a second and Marianne found herself pinned helplessly to the ground. With eyes wide with horror, she saw one of the men, the one who still wore some clothing, take from his belt a long cutlass which flickered redly in the glow of a nearby fire. He was already bending down holding the cutlass to her throat when a figure leapt out from among the rocks. Caught off his balance from behind, the man rolled over on the sand. At once, his attacker was upon him and the two men began a savage struggle in which the robber's knife gave him the advantage of Jean Le Dru. The other ruffian was still holding Marianne down so that she could only watch the fight helplessly. But though helpless she was full of hope. If Jean had escaped from the sea and was here on the beach fighting for her, why should not the giant Black Fish also reappear. That would considerably increase their chances.

Jean was bigger than his adversary and must have made up for a good deal in sheer strength but even so, his spell on the hulk *Europa* and, more recently, his fight for life against the sea, had weakened him to such an extent that it was soon apparent both to the girl and to her guard, who showed his delight by a series of animal grunts, that the robber would soon have the upper hand. And still Black Fish had not appeared. With a rush of pity and terror, Marianne realized that all was lost. The other man was already on top, and kneeling on his chest while Jean tore vainly at the hands around his throat which were slowly choking him. In her terror, Marianne cried out in French.

'For pity's sake! Do not kill him!'

An evil laugh was the only answer but, like an echo of the girl's despairing cry, an icy voice commanded:

'Enough! Let the man go, Vinoc!'

Obedience was instant. Jean Le Dru found himself released while the two robbers retreated, cringing fearfully. The man who had appeared out of the shadows like some ominous night bird was evidently the chief of the wreckers. He was a tall man, dressed in a peasant's sheepskin coat and baggy canvas breeches caught in tightly at the knee, and black felt hat, and his hair hung in short plaits on either side of his face but above these rustic garments, a great black cloak hung from his shoulders, stout leather gauntlets protected his hands and his features were concealed by a black velvet mask. All that could be seen of his face was a strong mouth whose corners drooped in an expression of perpetual disdain and unusually brilliant eyes of some indefinable colour. Seeing those eyes rest thoughtfully upon her, Marianne flushed scarlet with shame and huddled with her arms across her breast in an attempt to hide her almost complete nakedness in the shadow of the rocks. With the frigid smile which never reached his eyes, the unknown shrugged off his black cloak with a quick movement and, tossing it to her, spoke to the two men.

'Take her!' he ordered. Then, pointing to Jean Le Dru who stood before him, still shaking from his fight, he added carelessly: 'Kill him.'

Marianne hastily wrapping herself in the cloak which, she noticed, had about it a smell of verbena totally unexpected in a wrecker, was about to protest but Jean was before her.

'If that is your verdict, why did you stay the fellow's murdering hand a moment ago?' he cried bitterly.

'A reflex. The woman's scream perhaps. And you fought well. I wished to see who you were —'

'Nothing – or no one, as you like! A Frenchman, a Breton like yourself. That is why I do not understand why you would kill me.'

Marianne followed this exchange with amazed disbelief. Beyond a doubt everything that happened to her was fated to have the incoherence of a bad dream. Was it really she, Marianne, sitting here on a rock on a storm ravaged Breton beach, dressed only in a cloak lent by a robber, guarded by wreckers, while a man in a black velvet mask argued about life and death with a prisoner escaped from an English hulk? When she was a little girl, old

Jenkins, who loved stories, had told her a host of fabulous tales about the adventures that had befallen poor wretched souls in olden times who were dogged by persistent ill luck. She had heard, too, of the fearful things which had taken place in this land of France ever since the people had run mad and drowned their aristocracy in a bath of blood, and an ambitious Corsican clambered on to the Imperial throne. All this she had been told, and much more she had read but she would never have believed that such things could happen to her. But one cannot be suddenly confronted with life in the raw and remain unchanged. Little by little, Marianne felt her scruples crumbling away, and all her former weakness and false modesty disappearing. Such things seemed stupid and meaningless.

But Jean and the masked stranger had not finished speaking.

'No witnesses and no survivors, that's the first rule in this business –'

'Some business! Wrecking –'

'Don't dismiss it so lightly. It's a good living and, in these times, that is something to think of. After all, I am offering you a chance. Swear to serve me faithfully as one of us and I will spare your life. Stout hearts are not so easy to come by.'

Jean shrugged with unconcealed contempt.

'Serve you? How? For work of this kind,' he indicated the ravages on the beach, 'all you need is thieves and murderers, not sailors. I am a sailor, one of Surcouf's men!'

Once again Marianne heard the note of pride in his voice and it made her curious. Who, she wondered was this Surcouf for Jean to be so proud of him? However, it seemed the masked man knew who he was well enough. His fists clenched and his voice came thinly through set jaws.

'The Sea Fox, eh? "Baron Surcouf"? Bonaparte's henchman? You have just signed your death warrant, my lad! Besides, I've wasted enough time with you. Do your work, men –'

'*No!*'

Unable to help herself, Marianne sprang forward impulsively, her aching head held only one idea, to save the life of the man who had fought for her when he might have stayed quietly in his hiding place among the rocks and watched her die, the man who had guarded and protected her in danger and who, when it seemed that death was on them, had kissed her – she clung with both hands to the masked man's arm and thought sprang to her mind that she might as well have clutched an iron bar.

'No, do not kill him! He's lying – he does not know what he is saying. He serves not Surcouf but me! He would not say so for fear of revealing who I am but I cannot see him die because of me.'

'You?' the stranger said with a lift of his eyebrows. 'Who then are you?'

'An aristocrat, like yourself – for you are noble, are you not? Your voice and your speech declare it –'

84

To save her life she could not have said what made her say it. But whether divinely or diabolically inspired, her words had certainly succeeded in gaining the stranger's attention and something told her she had not been mistaken. A spark of curiosity showed in the man's eyes.

'It may be so. Know, however that men call me simply Morvan. But you have still not told me who you are.'

'My name is Marianne d'Asselnat. My father and mother went to the guillotine for trying to save the queen.' Suddenly she remembered Madame Royal's curious gift and added urgently: 'Tell your men to give you what they took from me. You will find there, as well as a little English money and my mother's pearls, a blue enamel locket containing a lock of white hair. It was given to me by the Duchesse d'Angoulême and the hair belong to the martyred queen!'

Marianne was amazed, as she heard herself speaking, that it all came so naturally. She had slipped effortlessly into the voice and accent of a fanatical royalist even though, in the inn at Plymouth, she had turned her back upon the émigrés who, in the person of the Duc d'Avaray, had rejected her. But it seemed quite fair to use them in order to save the life of one who served Napoleon – and of course the unknown but undoubtedly celebrated Surcouf!

It seemed that she had almost won her point. Morvan beckoned imperiously to the two men who had been standing a little way off holding Jean and waiting passively for the order to kill him. A few brief words in the strange rough speech which must be the Breton dialect and Vinoc, scowling to himself, handed over to his chief the jewels stolen from Marianne. Morvan took the pearls and put them in his pocket without a word, then he strolled over to one of the fires, holding the locket in his hand. The glow of the flame fell on his grim face with its black mask behind which the eyes burned like hot coals. Marianne threw a quick, anxious glance at Jean. She was afraid he might have heard the rather unorthodox way in which she had defended him. But he had heard nothing. He was leaning back against a rock with his eyes closed in an attitude of utter weariness, still flanked by his guards, simply waiting for his fate to be decided.

Now Morvan was coming back. This time, as he approached Marianne he uncovered and bowed with unexpected grace, his black hat sweeping the sand.

'I crave your forgiveness, Mademoiselle d'Asselnat, for this discourteous welcome. Believe me, I could not know that you were in this wreck. If you will take my arm, I shall be honoured to conduct you to my house where you may rest yourself – and we shall have some speech together.'

Delighted to have won even a moment's respite, Marianne did not stop to ask herself what he meant to talk about.

'And my servant?' she asked, before accepting the proffered arm. 'I hope you mean to pardon him?'

A smile which Marianne judged far from pleasant appeared below the black mask.

'But naturally. He shall follow us but his rash words have made him suspect and he must be watched. Do not take offence at this.'

The two robbers, both of whom were now dressed, brought Jean Le Dru forward, almost dragging him for he was clearly at the end of his strength. Morvan glanced keenly at the young man then gave his orders in a low, distinct voice.

'Take him back to the manor. His life is spared. He is only a lackey, in the service of the young Marquise d'Asselnat, who comes from our exiled princes. But he had lied to me and must be punished. Lock him in the tower.'

Marianne was overcome with fresh terror at these contemptuous words, realizing that Morvan was trying to provoke Jean into a denial. In fact, the young man had flushed angrily and was struggling to free himself. He was going to deny it, he was going to repudiate her and then Morvan would have him killed without a moment's hesitation. Marianne ran to him and clasped his hands as hard as she could.

'Be quiet, Jean – it is no use lying. I have told this gentleman what I had to tell him because it would have been stupid to throw away your life for nothing.'

He opened his mouth to cry out but the pressure of the small hands became more insistent and Jean merely shrugged and cursed.

'Very well, mademoiselle. I daresay you are right and I'm only a fool!'

But the look he gave her was not only devoid of any gratitude but so heavy with contempt that Marianne shivered. Now that Morvan had seen fit to proclaim her as an envoy of the exiled princes, she realized that in Jean's eyes she had become an enemy. A royalist spy, and the comradeship born of danger was dead. She was bitterly hurt without quite knowing why but Morvan was watching her and she made herself turn away in order to avoid rousing further suspicions. An aristocrat should not be unduly concerned about a servant. As it was, he remarked when she slipped her hand into the proffered arm: 'You take good care of your servant, my dear. I wonder if I was right to let him live. You set such store by it —'

Realizing that her pleas would not help Jean and that on the contrary, she was bound to play the part she had assumed right to the end, Marianne merely shrugged in her turn and answered:

'Faithful servants are rare, especially for an exile. Now, Monsieur Morvan. I should be glad if you would conduct me to your house. I am tired and perished with cold.'

She said no more and allowed the wrecker to lead her to his unknown dwelling but inwardly she was full of trepidation. She placed little trust in this man who, while admitting his rank, had not unmasked for her, a man who killed in cold blood, a wrecker who could plunder and steal and who had slipped her pearl necklace into his pocket quite unconcernedly. All she hoped to gain was a little time to rest and food for her exhausted body. But she had no illusions about what must follow. As soon as she was better, she would make her escape, taking Jean with her, he no doubt to rejoin his famous Surcouf, she to try and find what little family she had left.

The wreckers had been keeping the plunder from the wreck about the fires on the beach but there was still a good deal of debris floating between the ship, now three quarters submerged, and the shore. Men were still plunging into the water, in the grip of a frenzied and unremitting lust for gain. But the storm was abating and already the tide was on the turn. The thunder of the waves which, only a moment before, had been breaking on the rocks in great fountains of spray, gave way to a degree of calm in which the men's frenzy also abated. The waters began to go down and, at the same time, a greyish light touched their surface and spread over the sky. Dawn was not far off and Morvan, moving slowly up the beach with Marianne, paused to sniff the air and, taking a silver whistle from his pocket, blew three short, piercing blasts which had the effect of stopping his men in their tracks. He raised his arm and pointed to the sky. Regretfully, the wreckers left the water and made their way to the fires where they set about loading the chests and bales on to their shoulders. The corpses were left where they lay. Marianne passed quite close to one of them and closed her eyes to shut out the poor, sightless face. If she valued her life, she dare not let the man beside her see how deeply he appalled her. Little by little, she was learning the hard way that most cruel of all lessons, that if she were to survive, she would have to lie, cheat and use all her wits to do so. It was a lesson she would never forget. With the exception of the poor young man now being dragged along behind her and possibly of Black Fish whose giant corpse must still be floating somewhere in the receding waters of this hateful bay, her first contacts with men in this wide world had brought her nothing but disgust and a profound contempt. In future, she meant to emerge victorious from any further brush with them, at least so far as the still untried limits of her strength allowed.

A mizzling rain began to fall from skies of unrelieved dark grey. The fires were out and the growing daylight glimmered on wet, seaweed covered rocks. Somewhere inland, a cock crowed hoarsely. Marianne's feet stopped sinking into sand and trod on hard ground covered with dry grass. This, then, was Brittany.

CHAPTER FIVE
Morvan the Wrecker

The manor house belonging to the man who called himself Morvan lay at the end of a hollow road, at this season deep in mud, between high banks crowned with gorse and stunted ash trees which turned it into a long, greenish tunnel; a crumbling sixteenth century façade flanked by turrets. Some way off, in a dip in the ground, was a small village made up of a few low cottages with walls of grey granite and roofs of heavy thatch. The sea was close by, overhung by ragged cliffs that, to the south, curved back sharply inland to form a narrow estuary. Out on the heath, a pair of standing stones like lonely sentinels kept their gloomy vigil among the gorse and whin bushes while on the summit of a nearby hill the remains of a stone circle lay in the short grass, waiting endlessly for the return of a sun worship now gone for ever. But of all this, in the livid light of a rain-sodden dawn, Marianne saw little. She was too frozen and exhausted to notice anything but the bed which Morvan conjured out of the wall by opening a wooden panel carved in intricate, lacy patterns. The mattress was stuffed with seaweed, the blankets rough wool and the sheets raw, unbleached linen but she threw herself down on them as gratefully as a hunted animal and fell instantly asleep.

When she awoke at last from the deep, dreamless sleep which had possessed her, Marianne saw that it was dark again. Candles were burning in silver sconces, a fire roared up the soot-blackened chimney and before the ancient stone hearth an old woman in a black gown and white cap was busy laying out some clothes on a bench while she watched the great cauldron of water set on to boil. Her face had the sunken look of those whose teeth have gone and there was something uncomfortably witch-like about the dark shadow thrown by the flames on to the old-fashioned coffered ceiling. Her jaw moved continuously above the froth of ribbons fastening her bonnet.

The wooden bed creaked as Marianne sat up. The crone turned colourless eyes on her beneath wrinkled, tortoise lids.

'You can be stirring now. Here's clothes for you and hot water to wash.'

The old woman's peremptory tone nettled Marianne, accustomed to the quiet deference of her own servants.

'I'm hungry,' she said sharply. 'Get me something to eat.'

'Time enough,' the old woman told her calmly. 'Dress yourself and join the master. If he means you to eat, you will eat.'

She hobbled out of the room, leaning on a knotted stick, taking no further notice of the girl. Marianne scrambled over the fretwork side of her strange bed and found herself standing on a bench from which she could step down on to the floor of beaten earth which still showed, here and there, some remnants of coloured tiles. The room itself was of noble proportions and some traces of gilding glinted here and there among the plentiful cobwebs on the ceiling. But it contained no furniture beyond three of the curious cupboard-beds, their walls carved in primitive but oddly attractive designs, the benches by which they were reached and those by the hearth on which, in addition to the clothes, stood a basin, some soap and towels. The old woman had built up a roaring fire in the hearth and Marianne was able to wash in great comfort. She did so with a good deal of pleasure and finished by washing the sand and salt out of her hair, throwing bowlful after bowlful of dirty water out of the tiny window without a thought of where they might be landing.

At last, she felt clean again. She twisted her hair into thick braids and wound it round her head, then turned her attention to the clothes provided for her. She was surprised to find them remarkably grand for any peasant woman. The gown was leaf green damask trimmed at the hem with gold embroidery and there was a small satin apron of the same green edged with lace. A big lace shawl and a muslin cap shaped like a small hennin, with a pair of dainty, buckled shoes, completed the outfit. Marianne's pleasure as she put it on was truly feminine. Taking down the old mirror which hung in a corner, she contemplated herself in it with some satisfaction. The dress might have been made for her. The velvet bodice sat well on her slender waist and the green silk matched her eyes. Draping the Irish lace shawl gracefully round her shoulders, she pirouetted lightly and made for the door.

The two rooms leading out of the large bedchamber showed the same state of dilapidation and neglect, with bare walls showing here and there a glimpse of frescoes in which pallid figures wandered among peeling fields, great overmantels with broken carvings, a complete absence of furniture and abundance of cobwebs so thick they hung like cloudy drapery from the ceiling. For a moment, Marianne wondered if Morvan had brought her to a wholly deserted house but then the sound of voices reached her through a half open door. She went towards them and pushed the door open wider.

The room which met her eyes might just as easily have been the dining room of the great house, by reason of its immense table, the chapter house of a monastery, on account of its vaulted ceiling and the massive, black wooden crucifix on the end wall, or simply a warehouse, from the quantities of chests, bales and packages of all descriptions that lay about on the ancient studded leather armchairs and innumerable stools. A great many of these parcels had been ripped open, revealing lengths of silk or woollen cloth, bales of cotton, bags of tea and coffee, tanned hides and a host of other things, all the more or less recent spoils of wrecks washed up by the sea. But Marianne had scarcely a glance for all this because, right in the midst of all the confusion, a blistering argument was in progress between the chief of the wreckers and a very pretty girl dressed in much the same costume as herself except that her dress was rose pink satin and her shawl of Chinese silk embroidered with apple blossoms.

That they were quarrelling was clear only from their angry voices because the words were in the Breton language of which Marianne could not understand a word. She saw, however, that the girl was nearly as dark as herself with a fine pink and white complexion and an expression in her hazel eyes of quite unbelievable hardness. She also noted, with some surprise, that while Morvan had removed his hat, he still wore his black velvet mask. But by this time, the girl had heard someone come in. She swung round and, seeing Marianne, turned her anger against her.

'My dress!' she exclaimed furiously, this time in excellent French. 'You dared to give her my dress – and my shoes, and my beautiful Irish shawl!'

'I did indeed,' Morvan answered her coldly without giving himself the trouble of raising his voice, 'and I shall dare a great deal more Gwen, if you continue to scream in that way. I cannot bear people to scream –'

He was sprawled negligently in a chair, one leg hooked over the arm, playing with what seemed to be a brand-new gold-mounted riding whip.

'I shall scream if I like!' the girl retorted. 'That is my dress and I forbid you to give it to her.'

'It was mine before it was yours, since every stitch I gave you. You were half naked when I found you outside the prison in Brest, waiting to see your lover hanged, a thief like yourself – everything you've got on your back you owe to me, my girl. This, and this – and this too!'

With the end of his whip, Morvan lifted the gold chain round the girl's neck and flicked the lace at her sleeves with a contempt that made Gwen shake with fury. When he began to lift her skirts, she slapped them down and screamed at him:

'You gave me nothing, Morvan! What I have, I've earned. It's my share of the loot – and the price of the nights I've given you. As for that one –'

She turned to Marianne as though she meant to take her clothes back then and there but was stopped in her tracks when the other girl said coolly:

'I am sorry, believe me, mademoiselle, if I have unwittingly borrowed your garments, only consider how unfortunate had I been obliged to appear before this gentleman –' a brief toss of her head indicated the wrecker, '– dressed only in a blanket. I can only add that if you will be good enough to find me some others, I will gladly restore these to you.'

These mild observations acted on Gwen like a shower of cold water. The anger left her face and was replaced by astonishment. She stared at Marianne with new eyes then, after a moment's silence, muttered ungraciously: 'Oh very well! Keep them for now since you've no others. But,' her voice became sharply practical, 'try not to spoil them.'

Marianne smiled. 'I'll do my best,' she said. Gwen's words had told her a good deal and this, with the fact that her lover had been a thief, suggested that she was a peasant girl fallen on hard times. Marianne felt an odd kind of sympathy for her. In the past few days, she too had learned the meaning of fear, suffering and physical wretchedness. In Plymouth harbour she would have done almost anything to save her life and to escape from Jason Beaufort. Besides, this Morvan seemed decidedly unpleasant. There was something in Gwen's voice when she spoke to him that put Marianne instantly on her side out of feminine solidarity. The wrecker may have been aware of this because he sat up suddenly and waved Gwen away.

'Go now. I must talk seriously with this young woman. I will see you later.'

Gwen obeyed, without hurrying. She made her way over to the door, hips swaying under the Chinese shawl, but as she passed Marianne, she dropped him a wink, heavy with meaning.

'Seriously? She's too well stacked for that! I know you, Morvan. Get a pretty girl within reach, and you can't keep your hands off her. Take care, that's all. If you give her my place as well as lending her my clothes, you'd better watch out for her health – and your own. Have fun!'

Pulling a face at Marianne who felt her earlier sympathy evaporating fast, she swept out with the airs of an outraged queen. But the interlude had at least given Marianne a chance to recover her self-composure and now she was able to contemplate the chief of the wreckers without a qualm. He was, after all, only a man and Marianne had determined that no man would ever get the better of her again. Jason Beaufort's kiss, as well as his improper proposal to her, followed by Francis Cranmere's dying words and then by the looks and actions of Jean Le Dru had made her suddenly aware of her own female charm and of the power they gave her. Even the girl who had just gone out, even Gwen had in her vulgar way paid tribute to her beauty. She had said that she was "well stacked". Marianne was none too sure of the precise meaning of that curious phrase, but it seemed to be complimentary.

Seeing that Morvan remained slumped in his seat, playing with his curiously braided hair, and did not offer her a chair, she drew one forward for herself and sat down.

'If we are to talk seriously,' she said calmly holding her hands on her silk apron, 'then let us talk. But what are we to talk about?'

'You, myself, our business – I imagine you have a message for me?'

'A message for you? From whom? You forget that I was cast up here by the sea, I was not coming here of my own will. Since I did not anticipate the honour of your acquaintance, I cannot see how anyone should have given me any word for you.'

For answer, Morvan took from his pocket the blue enamel locket and swung it gently from his fingers.

'The person who gave you this cannot have sent you merely for the pleasure of visiting Brittany in winter.'

'Why should you think anyone sent me, or that I was coming to Brittany? One lands where one can in such a storm! That memento, I owe to my parent's sacrifice. You would do me a kindness by returning that and my mother's pearls. They have no business in your pocket.'

'We'll talk of that later,' Morvan broke in with a smile which made his mask look still more sinister. 'For the moment, I want an answer. Why have you undertaken this perilous crossing at the very worst time of year? No young woman of your name and breeding would undertake such a journey unless she were one of the king's amazons at least – or had a mission!'

Marianne had been thinking fast while Morvan was speaking. She was well aware that her best chance of safety lay in the air of mystery which surrounded her. To tell Morvan the story of the events which had destroyed her world and her illusions would be the greatest folly. While he believed her on the same side as himself, Morvan would treat her well. The idea of a mission was a good one to hold on to. Unfortunately, Marianne had never met the exiled royalty and had few contacts among the émigré population apart from Monseigneur Talleyrand-Périgord and, to her regret, the Duc d'Avaray. Of course, there was her godfather but she had no proof of the Abbé de Chazay's travels being in the service of the right king. God's service would be reason enough.

Through the holes in his mask Morvan's cold eyes were studying the girl. She had not noticed that silence had fallen between them while she was thinking. The wrecker repeated his question.

'Well, this mission?'

'Supposing I have one – and it is possible – it is no concern of yours. I see no reason to confide in you. And furthermore,' here she allowed a note of insolence to creep into her voice, 'even if I had a message for you I could scarcely give it to you since I do not know who you are.'

'I have told you. I am called Morvan,' he said arrogantly.

'That is not a name. And I would remind you that you have not yet been civil enough to show your face. To me, therefore,' Marianne concluded, 'you are simply a stranger.'

A gust of wind flung open one of the windows, sending it banging back against the wall and whirled through the room lifting the papers which lay on the tables. Morvan rose with a sigh of irritation and went to close it. On his way back, he paused to snuff a candle which was smoking, then came and stood squarely in front of Marianne.

'I will show you my face if I think fit. As for my name, it is long now since I had any but Morvan. I am known by that name, over there,' he added with a nod in the direction from which came the murmuring sound of the sea.

'I have nothing to say to you,' Marianne answered him coldly, 'except to ask you to return what is mine, in other words my possessions and my servant, and let me go on my way – when you have given me something to eat, that is, for to tell you the truth I'm starving.'

'And we shall sup very shortly. I did but wait for you. Let us settle our business first, however. I cannot eat with something nagging at me.'

'I can at any time. So let us get this over if you please, and ask whatever questions you wish.'

'Where are you going?'

'To Paris,' Marianne said with all the satisfaction of one telling the simple truth.

'Who are you going to see? The Red Herring? Or the chevalier de Bruslart? Although I doubt the latter's being in Paris.'

'I don't know. They would find me. I don't know who I have to deal with.'

Now it was Morvan's turn to look thoughtful. But Marianne could guess what he was thinking. He must be reasoning that a girl so young and inexperienced could not be the bearer of any perilous message and, in any case, would be unlikely to know its real worth.

Having reached this conclusion, he smiled at her, that wolfish smile which Marianne hated instinctively.

'Very well. I am willing to accept that and shall not force you to betray your secret – which might have unpleasant consequences for us both. But your coming is a blessing of which I should be foolish not to take advantage.'

'Take advantage? But how?'

'It is like this: I have already sent two messengers, one to the King at Hartwell House, the other to London, to the Le Comte. Neither has returned and for months now I have had no orders or instructions. I was getting desperate when the sea deposited you here like a miracle. You are a god-send! You could scarcely expect me to let you run away again without first giving me a little help?'

The tone was soft, almost caressing but Marianne forced back a shudder. There was something cat-like in this man and she liked him better when a spitting fury than with velvet paws. However, she managed to conceal her thoughts.

'How may I help you?'

'Easily. By remaining here, as my – guest,' an infinitesimal pause before the word, 'and queen of this sad house. Meanwhile, I shall see to it that your servant, the man by whom you set such store and who seems to me to have the air of something more than a mere servant, is sent back to England. He will go, with a proper escort, to the King – or to Madame Royale. Her Highness must have a great regard for you to have given you this precious locket. She will not be indifferent to the fact that you are detained here, unable to assume your mission, until I obtain satisfaction from the princes, or at least an answer to the question I have asked.'

Morvan was watching her reactions closely and Marianne needed all her self-command not to show her dismay. Yet the wrecker's plan contained nothing to delight her. Jean Le Dru would never consent to carry through the part she had forced on him if it meant a return to England and the hulk that awaited him in Plymouth or Portsmouth. He would tell the truth and would then be in imminent danger of having his throat cut by Morvan's men. And if Morvan were ever to suspect what she really was, a murderess fleeing from the rope, her own life would not be worth much more. Morvan was just the man to hand her over, bound hand and foot, to the English law if he thought it would serve his turn. She had to part company with this dangerous individual and the sooner the better. But meanwhile, it was vital to gain time and, when Morvan asked: 'Well? What do you think of my offer?' she was able to reply quite calmly and even summon up a smile.

'I think it is an interesting idea and one we might examine further at more leisure – when we have eaten for instance –'

Surprised, perhaps at her ready acceptance, Morvan gave a crack of laughter and offered his arm with a bow.

'You must indeed be very hungry. And you are quite right. My arm, my dear, and let us recoup our strength somewhat.'

The room in which meals were taken in Morvan's house bore no resemblance to a banqueting hall. It was simply a large kitchen with a floor of beaten earth. A granite fireplace of monumental proportions took up the whole of one side and inside it, in a niche in the soot-blackened wall, was a stone bench on which an old man, with grey hair straggling from under a battered hat, sat meditating with his chin on a knotted stick. At the far end, beneath the narrow window, a long box table, flanked by two settles, was set at right angles to the wall. On it were bowls and dishes made of a red earthenware and, next to them, a big wicker dish cover was attached by a long cord to a pulley fastened to the ceiling. The only light in the long, low room came from the flames in the hearth and from a pine torch stuck medieval-fashion into an iron ring in the wall. There was a strong smell of wood smoke. Apart from the old peasant dozing in the chimney corner there were only four people in the kitchen when Morvan entered with Marianne on his arm: the old woman she had seen when she woke up and was now busy with a large pan on the fire, Gwen and the two men whose acquaintance Marianne had made under such unpleasant circumstances on the beach. No one spoke. Gwen merely stuck her nose in the air and took her place at table with the rest.

Sitting beside her and facing the three men, Marianne could not help asking why Jean Le Dru was not present and where he was.

'Because in my house, as in other noble households, the servants do not eat with the masters. These – er, gentlemen,' he added in a mocking voice, indicating Vinoc and his companion, 'are my lieutenants. Your servant is lucky enough to be served in his own quarters – he is locked in the barn.'

With this explanation, Marianne was obliged to be content as Morvan began immediately to say grace. No respectable household would have bowed their heads more piously over their plates than the three wreckers and the girl Gwen. Deciding that in future nothing should surprise her, Marianne did the same, after which they addressed themselves to the meal in a silence befitting so noble a subject as food.

This too was of a kind quite unfamiliar to Marianne. A thick soup made of parched oats and a few pieces of bacon so fat that Marianne could not think of eating it, was followed by potatoes baked in the ashes. Seeing the others break them open on the edge of their bowls and then dip each spoonful in the cold milk of which there was a plentiful supply, she copied them and found it delicious. The buckwheat pancakes sprinkled with plenty of sugar which came next were good as well and she drank several bowls of milk. Only Morvan drank wine.

From where she sat, Marianne could see into a small room, like a store room, opening out of the wall next to the fireplace. Inside, under the now darkened window, stood an outsize table covered with a white cloth. Sitting cross-legged on this table was a small, wizened man. His skin was almost yellow, his hair dark and lank, his hands white and agile. A huge heap of materials of all colours had been pushed to one side, while this curious creature was busily engaged in putting away vast quantities of pancakes smothered in thick cream with which the old woman was plying him with unexpected goodwill. Marianne could see that they were talking a good deal but could not hear what was being said. However, since she was too young to contain her curiosity, she asked:

'Who is that man in there, eating among all the materials?'

'The tailor, saving your presence,' Morvan answered without looking round. 'It is the custom here to have such people to the house to cut and sew garments. They are clever with their hands and perform wonders. If you wish him to make you a gown, I shall be happy to present him to you.'

'Why does he eat alone in that little room?'

'Because he is the tailor, saving your presence!'

This time, Marianne looked at him wide eyed. Could he, by any chance, be laughing at her?

'Why do you keep saying "saving your presence"?' she said with a touch of insolence. 'How peculiar!'

'Because a tailor, saving your presence, is not a man and therefore one should ask pardon when mentioning him. That does not, however, detract from his skill. This one, his name is Perinnaïc, an artist in his way —'

No, Morvan was decidedly not laughing at her. He made the explanation calmly, as though it were the most natural thing in the world. Moreover, Marianne did not miss the venomous glance cast at him by the occupant of the small room. Perinnaïc must have heard what was said about him. Morvan had not troubled to lower his voice. Gwen raised hers sharply.

'He is a real artist,' she announced. 'He is sought all over Brittany and you should be proud that he consents to work in your muddy great barn when all the grand houses are after him.'

Morvan gave a short laugh.

'I was forgetting! Men may cordially despise the tailor, saving your presence, but the women adore him. I suppose you will be the same.'

Marianne said nothing but her eyes dwelled thoughtfully on the little man who had finished his meal and was once again working away earnestly with fine gold thread at some embroidery he was doing on a black velvet garment. What interested her was not so much the man's skill as the hatred she had glimpsed briefly in his eyes. Feelings of that kind directed towards Morvan were bound to strike a sympathetic chord in her. She made up her mind to ask for a dress, simply as a way of approaching Perinnaïc. And with her mother's pearls in his pocket, Morvan could well afford to buy her one!

The meal ended with a further blessing. Marianne rose and, without waiting for permission, made her way over to the tailor's little retreat. He did not look up at her approach but Marianne found herself instantly spellbound. Perinnaïc's thin fingers worked with extraordinary dexterity, creating on the black velvet a delicate tracery of strange, spiralling patterns that seemed to spring direct from his own whimsical imagination. Marianne was too much a woman not to admire the work wholeheartedly and still too much a child not to put her admiration into words.

'You are a very great artist!' she said softly and with real feeling, quite forgetting that the man would probably not understand her words. He looked up, however, possibly in response to something in her voice. Something approaching a smile warmed his shrivelled face but only for an instant. Perinnaïc's lashless eyelids dropped again at once and Marianne heard Morvan's insolent voice behind her.

'Decidedly, no woman can resist anything to do with clothes. Tomorrow, you shall choose a length of stuff and be measured. Oh, don't worry, it will be enough for him to take a length of your arm.'

Without troubling to thank him, Marianne went on immediately to tell him of her wish to see Jean Le Dru. She wanted to assure herself, that he was being properly treated. Unfortunately, Morvan was unimpressed by such concern. He merely told her in a bored voice that she need feel no anxiety for her servant, he was being well treated as she could see for herself from the size of the meal old Soizic was at that moment loading on to a large tray. But he had no intention of allowing his guest to converse freely with her "highly suspicious" servant.

'We shall see him together, tomorrow morning,' he concluded, 'when we inform him of what we would have him do. What can you have to tell him now that will not wait? It is dark, the day is done now and it is time to rest.'

'I am not sleepy,' Marianne snapped. She had slept all day and was now suffering at least as much from impatience as from real anxiety. She had to see Jean alone and explain to him what she wanted him to do to ensure the safety of them both. Pulling the precious Irish shawl more tightly round her shoulders, she went on, a little defiantly: 'What am I supposed to do? Crawl back into that cupboard thing I sleep in I suppose?'

Morvan laughed.

'You have no fancy for our box-beds, I see, but they can be very cosy when the air bites cold. However, since you are not sleepy, what would you like to do? You might take a walk but the night is dark and cold –'

'Thank you! But I have no desire for a second view of those poor murdered wretches on the beach.'

'You take me for a child, my dear. It's little enough we see of the coastguard and customs men in these parts, I agree they stand somewhat in awe of our rude manners, I believe, but one never knows. The drowned have been thrown back into the sea, the others properly buried. We did not kill so very many, you know.'

The last words were spoken in an ironic tone which made Marianne want to slap him.

Rather than arouse his suspicions, she agreed when he proposed a game of chess. At his command, an exquisite marquetry table was brought into the homely kitchen. Arranged upon it was a set of sparkling chess men made of silver and crystal and certainly very old. These were followed by two fragile armchairs upholstered in pale silk which were placed before the fire.

'This is the warmest place in the house,' Morvan explained taking one of the chairs and offering the other to Marianne. 'There is my own room, but the chimney smokes and one freezes there. Besides –' He gave a slow smile and his teeth gleamed wolfishly below the mask, 'we are as yet insufficiently acquainted for another, more enthralling game I might propose. Until proved otherwise, you are the guest sent by God – and, of course, by their Highnesses.'

'I seem to think,' Marianne retorted blandly, 'that it takes two to play that game – and you would find me less willing to engage in it than in this. I should, on the other hand, be very willing to see you at last remove your mask. I dislike that velvet face.'

'You would dislike what it conceals still more,' he answered harshly. 'If you must know, my pretty babe, I am disfigured. An unlucky sabre-cut at Quiberon yet, even then, I came out of that carnage alive and think myself lucky I escaped so lightly. So, let us leave my mask where it is and have our game.'

Chess had been the Abbé de Chazay's passion and Marianne had played the game as long as she could remember. Patiently, in the course of endless games she had developed her sense of strategy. She played well, with a speed and boldness that could disconcert even a skilful player. But tonight, her mind was not on the game. Her eyes scarcely saw the glittering pieces touched to gold by the dancing light of the fire, her ears were so busy straining to catch all the sounds of this unfamiliar house. Gwen had disappeared as though by magic. The old woman, Soizic, had gone off with her tray. Almost at once, the sound of her wooden shoes was heard outside the kitchen window. There must be an outer door somewhere not far away leading to the barn where Jean was imprisoned. The two "lieutenants" had shuffled out with an awkward "goodnight all", and shortly afterwards the little tailor had also made his way across the kitchen, carrying his candle, on his way to whatever hole had been allotted him to sleep in.

Now that he was no longer sitting down, Marianne saw with pity that he was a gnome-like creature with stunted legs much too short for a body whose development, apart from a tendency to be hunchbacked, was normal. He gave the players as wide a berth as possible and muttered his goodnight humbly enough but once again Marianne caught that glance of pure hatred directed towards Morvan.

Last of all, the old man in the chimney corner hobbled away, half asleep, and then the only sounds were the crackle of logs in the hearth and Morvan's rather heavy breathing. Little by little, the silence became oppressive. The mask and the angle at which his chair was placed left the wrecker's face in shadow, and Marianne had the unpleasant feeling that she was playing against a phantom; only the hands moving the pieces on the squares and violet-wood, seemed alive. It was a good hand, of almost feminine whiteness, the fingers long, perfectly formed and sensitive. Their colour apart, Marianne had seen another pair of hands like those, quite recently. They reminded her of Jason Beaufort's hands and the memory was not a pleasant one. On Morvan's however, Marianne's keen eyes were able to make out the faint mark of a star-shaped scar at the base of the third finger. She had always been fascinated by hands and by the strange, evocative power they had to conjure up a host of images. She had been fond of studying people's hands. These hands suggested something quite different from nights spent lurking in ambush on storm-lashed rocks, waiting for luckless vessels to fall into the trap – they suggested –

The hand was abruptly withdrawn and Morvan's coldly courteous tone dispelled his adversary's musings.

'Your mind is not on the game, my dear. That is my bishop you were about to move. Perhaps you are more tired than you thought? Would you rather we stopped for tonight?'

Marianne grasped at the chance he offered. She had better things to do tonight than to play chess. And so, with a rueful smile, she agreed that she did feel a little sleepy. Morvan rose, bowed and offered his arm.

'After such a night as you have passed, it is not surprising. I will take you to your room.'

The fire had burned down to a red glow and the cold had crept into the long, bare room but there were new candles in the silver sconces and the bed in the carved wooden alcove had been freshly made. A long cambric shift was laid out on the coverlet. But Marianne had no thought of going to bed. She began by throwing some logs on the fire and the flames burned up, bright and clear, driving away the gloomy shadows. That done, she went straight to the window and dragged aside the ragged curtain that covered it. She found to her fury that it was firmly barred and fastened with the aid of a padlock. It seemed that Morvan left nothing to chance. A wave of depression swept over her. She would never manage to get to Jean and tomorrow would bring disaster to them both. But how was she to get out? Morvan was almost certain to have locked the door and in fact that infallible recording device of memory was already telling her that she had heard the dry click of the key in the lock.

She went over to the door just the same, though without conviction, and lifted the latch but let it go again immediately. Someone on the other side was stealthily turning the key in the lock. Marianne drew back instinctively as, without a sound, the door swung open. The tailor's pale face loomed out of the shadows.

He put his finger quickly to his lips to still Marianne's exclamation of surprise.

'Ssh! May I come in for a moment?'

She beckoned silently, noticing that the odd little man spoke perfect French. He limped across to the panelled wall that concealed the cupboard bed and opened the doors. Then, having assured himself that they were empty, he turned back to Marianne who was watching him with astonishment.

'On the right of the barn door,' he whispered, 'you will find a hole in the wall. That is where they keep the key –'

'Thank you,' said Marianne, 'but how am I to get out of the house? Even my window is barred.'

'Yours, yes, but not the others and, in particular, not that of the room where I work. It will be a tight fit, but you are not large, and the barn is just opposite.'

There was a moment's silence. Marianne stared at the little hunchback in amazement. His small eyes were twinkling like stars and he seemed suddenly highly delighted.

'Why are you doing this?' she asked. 'You know I mean to escape – and you are putting yourself in danger.'

'Not at all. He will think that Madam Jealousy let you out. After all, who should notice a tailor – saving your presence? And for my reasons – say I like playing tricks on folk that are too cocksure – or that I have my own reasons for hating the Lord Morvan! Go, quickly –'

'Thank you again – but I owe you my freedom –'

'Not yet. I am not certain you will get away – or not unless you go alone.'

'What do you mean?'

'Nothing. You will see. But whatever happens, I will come back before daylight and lock this door, whether you have returned or not. Then, all will be safe. And, take my advice and leave that light shawl behind. Even in the dark, you could be seen.'

Letting fall the heavy lace, Marianne went quickly to one of the beds, stripped off a brown blanket and wrapped it closely round her. She was trembling with cold and excitement. She turned to Perinnaïc again.

'How can I thank you for what you are doing for me?'

'Easily!' The smile on his face was replaced by a look of sudden ferocity. 'See to it that Morvan's head rolls and I shall be repaid a hundredfold!'

Marianne repressed a shudder at the twisted hatred that showed in the hunchback's face.

'I don't see how I can do that. I don't even know his face –'

'Nor I. But he is absent very often and I know he goes to Paris. There, he must surely discard his mask. Try and find out who he is – and, if you succeed in sending him to the scaffold he has eluded for so long, then know you will have avenged countless unhappy souls! Go quickly now, I have talked too much and words are perilous.'

Marianne glided swiftly out of the room. Periannaic had given her a taper in a crude holder to light her but she remembered the way to the kitchen perfectly and soon found herself in the big, still warm room. The fire was still alight and judging that this would give her light enough, Marianne put out her candle and left it on the overmantel. She made her way into the little room, climbed on the table and set about opening the window, praying to heaven that it would not creak too much. To her great relief, it opened easily. Marianne leaned out.

It was a black night and the wind was blowing strongly but her eyes soon grew accustomed to it. Immediately facing her, she was able to make out a large squat building that could only be the barn. Quickly pushing out the encumbering blanket, she wriggled her slender body through the tiny opening. It was only just big enough and she scraped herself painfully in the process but the will that drove her was stronger than the pain. Then she was standing outside. The ground was hard with frost and the grass quite dry so that her feet did not get wet, but even so it was not very warm and Marianne was glad to wrap the blanket round her again. She hurried over to the barn, her light shoes making no sound. There was no one in sight and she had little fear of meeting anyone. She knew already from the way old Soizic had grumbled at having to take the prisoner's supper out to him that the Bretons were not fond of going out after dark for fear of encountering the ghosts of the dead.

She reached the barn and felt for the key but she had to stand on tiptoe to reach the narrow crack between two stones. At last, her fingers closed on the cold metal. Even then, however, it was not easy to discover the lock. Her hand shook with excitement and her heart beat as though it would leap out of her breast but when the key finally slipped into place, she found that someone must have oiled the lock recently because it turned easily and without making a sound. Somehow, Marianne found herself inside, blown in with a gust of wind. She had to lean on the door with all her strength to close it. Overcome by excitement, she closed her eyes and once again had the feeling that all this was somehow unreal and absurd, as though she were playing a part.

From somewhere inside the barn a voice spoke. 'So you've come? It's about time, I was just going to blow out my candle.'

Comfortably ensconced in a heap of straw, Jean Le Dru sat with folded arms looking at Marianne. The candle she saw was still alight although almost burned down. It was stuck to the tray beside the remains of the meal. She understood however why Perinnaïc had told her that if she meant to escape she would have to do so alone. Jean seemed to have suffered no ill treatment. Far from it. He had obviously been allowed to wash because his fair hair shone like gold and the beard had gone from his chin. He had been given dry clothes as well but there was a broad iron band around his ankles linked by a heavy chain to a massive ring embedded in the masonry of the wall. There must be a key to unfasten that chain, but Marianne had not got it.

Her face was such a picture of disappointment that Le Dru began to laugh.

'Yes, your friends have anchored me good and fast. But maybe, if they've given you the key I can see in your hand they've been good enough to give you the one that opens this little trinket as well?'

She shook her head. 'They're are not my friends,' she said unhappily. 'I found out where they hid this key – I was hoping that we could escape together, tonight.'

'Escape? Why do you want to escape? Aren't you happy here? I saw you trotting off like an honoured guest on the arm of that masked devil and, I will say, they've got you up like a princess. A Bretonne princess, of course, but then, in my view they're the best of all! And there's no denying it suits you. You look quite lovely in it.'

'Stop teasing me! We are not in a drawing room. We must find some way to escape, I tell you, or both of us are lost!'

'I am, at any rate. As for you, although I don't quite see how you are in danger my dear – marquise, is it? I am not stopping you running about the countryside on this charming night. For my own part, with your permission, I am going to sleep. It's not so bad here in this straw, all things considered. So I'll just wish you a good journey. Don't forget to shut the door when you go. There's a devil of a wind!'

'But you don't understand!' Marianne wailed almost in tears. She went down on her knees beside him. 'I am not what these people think.'

'Not an aristocrat? Who do you think will believe that? One's only to look at you.'

'It is true, I am an aristocrat, but I am not an agent of the king. Ever since I came, they have talked about nothing but conspiracy, the princes' agents and the Emperor's spies, but I don't understand a word of it. I know nothing about it – nothing, I swear to you!'

In her desperate longing to convince him, she had clasped her hands in a childish gesture of supplication. He must believe her. He must be her friend again, as he had been last night in the storm. She needed his man's strength so badly! And now, his beardless face made him look so unbelievably young, much closer to her than he had been before. There was something open and clean about him which was both attractive and reassuring. Running out of argument, she said in a small, frightened voice which all unknown to herself, touched a chord in the boy's locked heart.

'You see – I'm only seventeen.'

The grey eyes which had been so cold a moment before, softened suddenly. Stretching out his arm, Jean folded the girl's clasped hands in his one big one and drew her forward until she was sitting on the straw.

'Now,' he said quietly, 'tell me what made you run away from England. You were running away, weren't you?'

She did not answer immediately, uncertain whether or not to tell him the truth. Her experience with the Duc d'Avaray had shown her how fantastic and unconvincing her story sounded. On the other hand, she needed Jean too much to wish to deceive him. If she made up a story, he would know somehow that she was not telling the truth. And besides, she had had enough of lying. Abruptly her mind was made up.

'I killed my husband in a duel on our wedding night!'

'What?'

Marianne realized that she had succeeded in breaking through the shell of mocking indifference with which Jean surrounded himself. She saw, with a degree of innocent pride, his eyes widen and appear to change colour. She was vaguely conscious that he was altering his estimation of her. His lips barely moved as he said softly:

'Do you know what you are saying?'

'I know,' she said sadly, 'it does sound incredible but it is true.'

Encouraged by the instinctive trust which he inspired in her and by a deep longing to confide in someone at last, she told him all about the terrible events of her wedding night. She kept nothing back, and told her story with an honesty to which the Breton's own uncompromising nature responded. She knew he would not turn away from her and when, at the end, he nodded and put out one finger timidly to stroke her cheek, she was sure of his sympathy.

'Pity you're a girl. You'd have made a splendid boy! Held your own anywhere! But now, tell me why you are in danger and why you have to escape from here? What has that masked man done to you?'

'Nothing yet,' she assured him, touched by his concern, 'but we must find some way of leaving here, both of us, because we can do nothing alone. Meanwhile, I have come to ask you to stick to the same story. The chief of the wreckers thinks that —'

She embarked on the tale of her dealings with Morvan. Jean listened, as before, but this time when she stopped talking the warm glow had gone out of his eyes. He sat thoughtfully hugging his knee.

'If I take ship again for England, its back to the hulks! And this time, God knows when I will get out. Supposing I ever do get out!'

'But of course you can't go back! It is just a matter of gaining time. If you agree, I'll manage to delay things for a few days, perhaps even a few hours will be enough to give us time to escape. Yes, tomorrow night should do it. I have a friend in the house and before then I should have found out where they keep the key to this chain and then we can both escape! But if you tell him the truth when he asks, nothing can save us!'

Jean turned his head slowly and at the sight of his set face an icy trickle seemed to run down Marianne's back. Did he still not trust her? He was looking at her as though he would see through to her very soul. She was about to speak, put forward further arguments, but he silenced her.

'How far can I trust you? You stand for everything I hate, everything I am fighting against. If this is a trap, I shall be lost without Black Fish. And I am needed. No – you can escape, go now, tonight, and leave me. I'll manage somehow!'

'Indeed I will not! I will not go without you. Especially since you do not trust me. If I did, then you would certainly be lost! Morvan would slit your throat first thing in the morning without more ado.'

'And you are really determined to save me? Why?'

Why, indeed? Marianne could not have said clearly yet it seemed quite natural in her own mind. Their flight together from Plymouth, the dangers they had passed through had in some way bound them together. Jean's behaviour, his protectiveness and affectionate comradeship had found a way to her heart. She would have scorned to escape alone, leaving him helpless in Morvan's power. But if he did not understand this himself, she could not explain it.

Jean was evidently waiting for her answer. He had moved closer and she could feel his breath on her neck. Very gently, he cupped her face in his hand and turned it towards him, as though to read her thoughts in her expression. Marianne looked into the questioning blue eyes. His lips quivered a little as he persisted.

'Answer me, little girl. Why do you want to save me? Is it out of pity?'

'Oh, no! Not pity! But – friendship perhaps –'

'Oh, only friendship –'

He seemed disappointed. His hand moved lingering over Marianne's neck, caressed the curve of her shoulder and came to rest on her arm, as though loath to let her go altogether. Afraid that she had hurt him she asked:

'Aren't you glad I am your friend? We have been through so much together – and you saved my life on the beach when those men would have killed me.'

'That was nothing. I could not stand by and see you slaughtered like a sheep before my eyes. Any decent man would have done the same.'

'Yes, but I think that decent men are rare. But anyway, it is settled. I stay with you.'

Jean made no answer. Silence fell between them, a silence so deep that Marianne seemed to hear her own heart beating. It was warm in the barn and the hand lying on her arm was warm, too. She could feel the warmth through her sleeve and without quite knowing why, found it oddly comforting.

The candle flame was guttering. It would not burn much longer but Marianne found she did not want to go. She sensed that there was nothing more to say that, although he had not said it in so many words, Jean had agreed, but still she was content to linger.

Outside, the wind was howling round the barn but there, in the hollow of the straw, all was warm and cosy, a haven of peace in the midst of a tormented world, but Marianne had to force herself not to look at the chain which bound Jean. She had read a story once about a girl very much in love visiting the man she was to have married, in prison on the night before his execution. She had forgotten the name of the story but tonight reminded her of it a little. To be sure, there was no gallows waiting outside but at any moment, a word from Morvan could turn one of his men into an executioner.

Jean's hand crept up again to her shoulder. She turned her head and saw him looking at her with eyes that were strangely bright. His voice, when he spoke was husky.

'I am glad you are my friend but – I had hoped for something more – I had hoped you liked me a little. When I kissed you on the boat, you didn't mind.'

She opened wide astonished eyes.

'But of course I like you! Especially now that I can see your face. And I liked it when you kissed me. It – it made me feel brave again.'

'And supposing – I were to do it again?'

She felt his arm go round her waist to draw her to him but instead of answering, she only smiled and closed her eyes, waiting for his kiss. It was true, she did like him. He smelled of the sea, from which they had both come. His eyes were as blue as the sky and very soft. They were gazing at her tenderly, a hint of anxious pleading in their blue depths. Perhaps he loved her? He was the first young man who had ever dared come near her, with her own consent, for she discounted Jason Beaufort's stolen kiss. But this man in chains whose trembling lips were now close to her face stirred and troubled her all at once. She wanted him to be happy. Tomorrow he would risk his life again for her sake and she wanted to give him a little happiness in return. She let him kiss her, let him draw her down into the straw and even slid her own arms round his neck to make him keep on kissing her.

At one moment he left her lips and began to cover her face and neck with little, quick kisses, light as butterfly wings yet which drew from her a long, shuddering sigh which Jean did not miss. When he fastened on her lips again, he grew more daring and began gently to unfasten her bodice. Panting a little, her head on fire, Marianne did not resist. She felt on the threshold of some great and already overwhelming discovery. Her feminine instinct whispered to her that her body held some incredible surprises in store for her.

Her thoughts went back briefly to Francis Cranmere. His should have been the hands to awaken her to these new and strange sensations. Even through the turmoil of her senses, she realized that she was on the point of giving to this stranger something which by rights belonged only to a husband and yet oddly, she felt neither shame nor scruples. She was living now outside her past life, outside any normal existence. Why not give to Jean what the American, Beaufort, had so boldly demanded, what no woman could be sure of keeping once a man had made up his mind to take it from her by force or cunning? The wretched Clarissa Harlowe whose sad history Marianne had devoured in secret, had been given a sleeping draught by the unworthy Lovelace in order that he might wreak his will on her. Marianne was not entirely sure what wreaking one's will involved, but she was sure that Jean would need no potions to achieve his ends. Dimly conscious of the ties of flesh binding men and women, she felt no will to resist. His caresses were so gentle and roused such delicious sensations in her! Then, he seemed to grow delirious, muttering broken words she only half understood, and interspersing them with more and more burning kisses. It was quite the most thrilling experience that could happen to any girl and whatever happened next must be marvellous indeed –

Then, abruptly, the magic spell was broken and there was only crude, painful reality. Marianne screamed but Jean did not even hear. He had been starved for too long and now he fell on her, carried away by a hunger and a passion he could no longer control. Gone was the tender lover, gone the soft caresses and, in their place, an agonizing pain and a man who seemed like one possessed. Frantic with horror, she tried to struggle free, but he held her fast. She tried to scream and he stopped her mouth with another kiss, but the magic had departed. Now, Marianne endured it with muscles tensed and straining nerves. Then, quite suddenly, it was all over and, as if by magic, she was free.

Too stunned to move, she lay looking up at the dusty roof beams struggling with disappointment and a longing to burst into tears. So this was love? This, nothing more nor less? In that case, she could not understand why they made so much fuss about it in novels and why so many women and girls ruined themselves for its sake. It was nice to begin with, but, all things considered, not really very rewarding. All she had now was this vague feeling of disgust coupled with a strong sense of frustration. No, never in her whole life had she been so disappointed.

A gentle finger stroked her cheek and at the same time she heard Jean laugh softly.

'Why don't you say something? You made me very happy, you know. I'll not forget. And besides that, I'm glad I was the first.'

'How did you know?' Marianne said sulkily.

This made him laugh outright.

'What a little girl you are! It is something a man knows at once. Now, you must get back inside. The candle is nearly out and it is better your absence should not be noticed. Besides – I'm abominably sleepy!'

She propped herself on one elbow but the sight of his cavernous yawns only added to her disappointment. In her view, only a great deal of tenderness could have removed the disagreeable impression she had received. He was nice, but that was all and now she sensed he wanted to be left in peace.

'Tomorrow, then –' she said dully, 'what will you do?'

He smiled teasingly and winked.

'You're a cool customer! Don't worry I'll do what you want. I owe you that –'

He sighed luxuriously and curled himself into a ball then, having arranged his chain so as to cause the minimum of inconvenience, he folded his arms and shut his eyes.

'Sleep well—' he added sleepily.

Marianne sat back on her haunches and stared at his sleeping figure in bewilderment. Really, she thought resentfully, men were the oddest creatures. A moment ago, this one had been all fire and flames, half mad with love – and now, barely minutes afterwards, there he was sleeping peacefully having forgotten her very existence. Was there anything in this to justify the secretive smile and air of inward triumph common to brides in books after their wedding nights? Always, excepting the unfortunate Clarissa Harlowe who, having slept deeply throughout, was not even aware of what had happened to her. There did not seem to Marianne to be much reason to give themselves such airs! For her own part, she had quite made up her mind not to repeat the experience in a hurry, not even to please Jean! Oh no!

The candle put an end to Marianne's musings by going out altogether. All she could do now was go back to the house and climb into her bed in the cupboard. She sat still for a moment until her eyes grew accustomed to the dark and then got up, hunted for the key which she had put down somewhere near the candle and then left the barn, closing the door carefully behind her and putting the key back in its hole.

Outside, the night was darker than it had been. A high wind was blowing that tugged at her blanket and almost threw her to the ground. For a moment, she was tempted to make her escape then and there, alone, but she suppressed the thought bravely. It was not Jean's fault after all, if she did not find lovemaking very enjoyable and besides, if she were honest, she had to admit that she had to some extent asked for what had happened. In any case, she was bound to Jean by their mutual plot against the wreckers. A pact was a pact.

Turning her back on the tempting heath, Marianne regained her room by the same way that she had left it and got into bed.

She had hardly pulled the covers over her head when she heard the almost imperceptible sound of the key turning in the lock. The hunchback tailor had kept his word.

CHAPTER SIX
The Man of Goulven

When, the next morning, Jean Le Dru was discovered to have fled, Marianne felt as though the skies had fallen on her head. She had taken advantage of a brief spell of sunshine to walk out on to the stretch of bare heath land lying between the manor and the sea. The greasy peasant soup, which was all that was provided by way of breakfast, proved highly indigestible and Marianne felt a strong desire for fresh air. The fragrant tea and crisp toast of Selton Hall seemed a long way away. All thought of them was driven out of her head, when Morvan's cry of wrath rent the quiet morning air.

She did not understand at first what had happened. She was sitting at the foot of one of the strange sandy stones that were dotted about the countryside, watching the calm sea as it lapped lazily against the rocks where seaweed lay in bright green patches. A few patches of timid blue showed between great banks of white cloud against which the flying gulls were half invisible, and down in the hollow of the little bay, a few chimneys were smoking peaceably alongside the boats drawn up on the pebbles.

Some women and children were making their way down to the beach, armed with long boathooks and rakes with which, at low tide, they scraped the seaweed off the rocks and brought home the long, shiny ribbons that were the only wealth of this god-forsaken land.

After the passion of the night before, Marianne was glad to sit dreaming over this scene of beauty and tranquillity. As a result, when she saw Morvan coming towards her, her first feeling was one of irritation. Could the man not let her alone for a moment? The next moment he was on her, grabbed her arm and hauled her to her feet.

'Come back inside – you have deceived me, lied to me – well, you'll not do it again.'

'Do what again? Are you mad? What have I done now?' Marianne cried, stung to quick anger. 'And first of all, let me go!'

She wrenched her arm away. Morvan, forced to let go suddenly, staggered and almost fell. But Marianne could see, that under his ridiculous mask, his face was unusually red. His hands were clenched as he rounded on her again.

'Your precious servant! Whose loyalty you swore by! Well, he's run away and left you!'

Now it was Marianne's turn to stagger. She had expected anything, but not this and did not attempt to hide her shock.

'Run away?' she echoed. 'But – it's not possible! He couldn't.'

She was on the point of saying: 'He couldn't do that to me,' but she bit back the words. But Morvan was already going on.

'I thought so too and I took every care. I had him chained up in the barn. But this morning, when Soizic took him his food, she found the bird flown, the door wide open and the chain sawn through!'

Marianne was hardly listening.

'It's impossible,' she said again blankly. 'Impossible!'

Boiling with anger at such black treachery, she was struggling desperately to remember everything she could. The previous night's events passed through her mind with merciless clarity. Le Dru had been asleep when she had left him, and so deeply asleep that she could have sworn not even a thunderclap would wake him. The chain was unbroken and when she left, she had locked the door carefully and put the key back in its place. At that moment, she was quite certain Jean had no means of escape; if he had, he would have told her, and agreed to escape with her at once as she had asked. Her next thought was for the tailor. But Perrinaic had told her that if she meant to escape, she would have to do so alone. It was surely not he who had given the Breton the file to saw through the chain and opened the door. Then who? She had no time for further wondering. With an effort, Morvan had regained control of himself and was saying coldly: 'I am waiting for your explanation.'

Marianne shrugged and sensing that the only thing to do was to appear very cool, she plucked a long stalk of dry grass and began to chew it thoughtfully.

'What explanation do you expect me to give? I am like you; I do not understand. Perhaps he was afraid? If you had chained him –'

'I invariably chain all those who dare to utter certain names in my presence and I am beginning to think that I was mistaken in not doing the same to you. After all, I have no idea where you come from or who you are! All I know is what you have deigned to tell me –'

'Are you forgetting the queen's locket?'

'You might have stolen that. Come back with me now unless you would have me take you back by force. I –'

He broke off. For a moment or two, as he talked, he had been instinctively following with his eyes the movements of a small boat which had just rounded the headland on which he and Marianne were standing. She was running before the wind and her red sails struck a brilliant note against the grey sea. They could make out the shape of the man at the tiller and suddenly, born on a gust of wind, they heard his voice. He was singing gaily.

> '… We saw an English frigate
> Hard on our starboard bow,
> A-sailing o'er the briny deep,
> For to attack Bordeaux…'

The words of the song came to them with impudent clarity through the crystalline air. Behind her, Marianne heard an odd noise which she realized with a shock was Morvan grinding his teeth. The eyes that watched the small boat through the hole in his mask were those of a madman and Marianne felt a thrill of terror as they were turned on her.

'You hear? Will you still deny it? Where do you find your servants, Mademoiselle d'Asselnat? On the English hulks?'

'I still do not understand you!' she said with dignity.

'That song is known throughout the seven seas! It is the song of Robert Surcouf's men! And your so-called servant is one of them!'

'What nonsense! He has always served me faithfully!' Marianne spoke with such conviction that for a moment the other was shaken.

'It may be that you too have been deceived, but we shall know soon enough.'

'What do you mean?'

'Last night I had word at last. A messenger from the Comte d'Antraigues will be here before long. Then we shall get your position clear, my beauty. Until then, you will remain under lock and key!'

'What right have you?' Marianne protested. Remembering her ally the tailor, she felt safe in allowing herself to carry the matter with a high hand since she had every expectation of making her own escape that night.

'If someone is coming from London, he can only confirm what I have told you. Then, my friend, it will be up to you to explain why you have kept me here. You are delaying me.'

The assurance in her heart clearly disconcerted the wrecker but he pulled himself together, unwilling to go back on his decision.

'At all events, I shall personally keep a close watch on you. Come. We must go to the house and pay our last respects.'

'To whom?'

'To my lieutenant Vinoc. Your – er, servant killed him as he made his escape.'

The body of the dead man had been laid out on the table in the great hall covered with a white sheet. All the chests, bales and packages of all descriptions that generally cluttered the room had been removed for the occasion and large sheets had been hung from the ceiling on either side of the table, making a kind of white chapel around the body. Death had brought little nobility to the wrecker. Even when shaved, brushed and dressed in his best embroidered clothes, he retained, in his everlasting stillness, an immense ugliness and an expression of deep cunning. Marianne thought she had rarely seen such a dislikeable corpse. All those she had previously beheld had about them something quiet, gentle and noble which took away anything frightening about them. But this man had gone into the next world wearing the same ferocious expression that had been his in life. Old Soizic must have some similar thoughts to Marianne's because she wagged her head sorrowfully as she looked at the dead man.

'Died with all his sins upon him! You can see it in his face —'

None the less, she had placed the dead man's hands together and wound a boxwood rosary, but with an evident lack of enthusiasm.

At Morvan's command, Marianne stayed with the other women of the household, who were praying round the corpse in accordance with the strict funeral rites of the region. She had to exchange her bright clothes for a dress of black wool, probably also borrowed from Gwen, a black shawl and a headdress of the same colour. She had raised no objections to all this. Kneeling on a prie-dieu by Vinoc's feet with Gwen opposite her, pretending to tell her beads, she had at least a chance to think. On a stool between the two women stood a bowl of holy water with a sprig of dried boxwood in it. Marianne kept her eyes firmly fixed on it rather than on the dead man's unattractive feet. Whenever she looked up, she found Gwen watching her with a mocking, triumphant expression equally unpleasant to behold, although it undoubtedly gave food for thought. Why should the Bretonne girl look so pleased with herself? Because Morvan was treating Marianne as a prisoner at last or – she wondered suddenly whether there was very far to seek for the mysterious hand which had opened the barn door, sawn through Jean le Dru's chains and been responsible for his otherwise inexplicable flight. Short of being an utterly contemptible hypocrite, he had no reason to escape alone especially after Marianne had refused to go without him. No, there was something else – whoever had opened the door for him must have had to shake him awake and persuade him to go. Something told Marianne that she had won him over last night, and that at the cost of her own disillusionment she had gained his complete allegiance. To his simple, unsophisticated way of thinking, the fact that she had given herself to him made everything straightforward. Then what had been said to him to make him abandon her so callously, even putting her life in danger? It smacked of a woman's revenge.

Footsteps came and went behind her bent back, the clatter of sabots on the worn flagstones, the scrape of hobnailed boots; from time to time, a hand appeared, picked up the box twig and piously sprinkled the corpse. The villagers and local peasants were coming, as custom demanded, to pay their respects to their brother's earthly remains. That, in his lifetime, he had been an out and out villain made no difference. He was a Breton and he was dead and that, for all other Bretons, made him sacred.

In fact, it was really rather moving except that, hearing Morvan solemnly inviting everyone who came to the wake, Marianne began to feel anxious again. With all these people about, how would she ever manage to escape? Would she even be allowed to keep her room to herself? Morvan had promised that he would keep her under close watch in future, which was distinctly unpromising. Moreover, if it were Gwen who had been responsible for Le Dru's flight, she would be unlikely to stop there. Marianne could read in her spiteful expression that she would not rest until she had got rid of the intruder. To be sure, there was still – saving your presence – her friend the tailor, but would he be able to help her this time? With all this in mind, Marianne began to pray in good earnest, but for herself rather than for a dead man who was no concern of hers. She stood in dire need of heavenly aid.

A huge, hairy black hand took hold of the box twig and a deep base voice began intoning:

'De profundis clamavi ad te domine
Domine exaudi vocem meam…'

Marianne felt as though the great bell of the cathedral had sounded in her ear and clapped her hand to her mouth to hold back a cry. The man was a peasant of gigantic size. He wore the traditional Breton costume of wide, pleated breeches, caught in at the knee, embroidered waistcoat under a short cloth jacket with a goatskin coat over all. His long, black hair fell to his shoulders but beneath the blue bonnet of the men of Goulven, she recognized the face of Black Fish.

He was leaning on a massive cudgel, his eyes cast upwards, intoning as fervently as though he had done nothing else all his life. The peasants looked at him with some respect and even Gwen gazed up at him in fascination, enabling Marianne to overcome the inevitable shock at this sudden reappearance of one she had presumed drowned. How had he come there? By what miracle had he escaped the storm, the rocks and the wreckers? These questions were unanswerable but since she and Jean Le Dru had escaped unhurt it seemed quite natural, after all, that a force of nature like

Black Fish should have done so as well.

The peasants were now responding in chorus to the prayer for the dead and Marianne made an effort to remember the ritual words but she was far too agitated. Her mind remained a blank. Not that it mattered much. She was certain that Black Fish's coming was an answer to her prayer.

The prayer ended, Morvan left his place of honour in the room and came forward to greet the newcomer.

'I have not seen you before, my man. Who are you?'

'His cousin,' Black Fish answered pointing with one hairy finger to the dead man. 'Like him, I am from Goulven. I was coming to see him when I heard the news. Poor Vinoc! Such a good fellow!'

Before Marianne's astonished eyes, he wiped away what must have been quite imaginary tears. But he was convincing enough, for Morvan had no suspicions. He even made him welcome, bowing instinctively to the strict laws of baronial hospitality.

'In that case, remain. Watch with us and share in this night's meal.'

Black Fish bowed without speaking and moved back to join the group of peasants. With shoulders hunched, and both hands leaning heavily on his *pen bas*, [4] he was hardly distinguishable from the other men and Marianne returned to her prayers without being able to meet his eye. From that moment on, she could think of nothing but the silent figure upon whom so much might depend. She had no idea how he came there, or why, but she was convinced it was for her. She was a prey to a fever of excitement that soon made it quite impossible for her to remain on her knees any longer. She rose, putting on an agonized expression as if she were suffering from a pain in her knees. At once a peasant woman came to take her place. Morvan frowned but told her in a low voice to go and join Soizic in the kitchen. Marianne asked nothing better, but, much as she longed to make contact with Black Fish, she dared not pass too close to him on her way out. They had no chance to communicate until after nightfall, when the whole household gathered round the old woman whose part it was to intone a kind of funeral chant in honour of the dead man. There was, inevitably, a certain amount of confusion as everyone gathered around the bier and Marianne felt a touch on her elbow. A voice whispered in English:

'Tomorrow – during the burial – try and faint at the church –'

She looked round in surprise but all she saw was the pious face of a little old woman whose nose all but touched her chin, mumbling prayers through toothless gums. Only, a little way away, she saw the sailor's broad back moving to a place among the men.

To Marianne, the wake was almost intolerable. She heard nothing but

---

[4] The stout stick from which no Breton would have been parted.

the old woman's funeral chant, nibbled a little at the customary meal which was served at midnight, and certainly she spared not a thought for the dead who in any case scarcely deserved it. Black Fish's words went round and round in her head, putting her in a fever of apprehension. He had asked her to faint in church but that was a great deal harder than it looked. Marianne had fainted only once before in her whole life and that was at the moment when, swept overboard from the *Seagull* and half drowned, she had been hooked by the wrecker's gaff. Then, pain and suffocation had made her lose consciousness but how did one set about fainting convincingly in cold blood? Occasionally, in England, she had witnessed frail, delicate creatures swooning gracefully at the right moment, while losing none of their fresh complexions, and had guessed readily that it was all put on, but this had to be a really convincing faint, something to create a stir, not a mere gentle swoon. Well, she would do her best and leave the rest to heaven.

She was so deep in her thoughts that it was not until she reached the door of her own room that she saw that Gwen had followed her. Only the men were now keeping up the wake. The women had been given permission to retire to rest. But when the girl seemed about to come in with her, Marianne objected.

'This is my room,' she said curtly.

'It is mine, too, for tonight. And don't think I'm enjoying it. I'm carrying out Morvan's orders, that's all, and I can't say I'm sorry he's got suspicious of you at last!'

The girl's insolent and familiar tone which showed that she no longer felt the need for circumspection, made Marianne's aristocratic blood rise. If Gwen wanted a quarrel, she would get one. Seizing her abruptly by the arm Marianne hustled her into the room more quickly than she might have wished. Then she closed the door carefully behind her.

'Something tells me he would do well to be suspicious of you too, my girl! And since we are to finish the night together, we may as well make the most of it and have it out once and for all!'

This abrupt beginning had at least the advantage of disconcerting Gwen. A shadow of cunning and mistrust spread over her pretty face.

'Have it out? Have what out?'

'Your behaviour! It seems to me there is plenty to say about that. So, you've come to tell me that Morvan does not trust me. And what is the reason? Because Jean Le Dru has escaped? If that is it, he is mistaken. I had nothing to do with it, I cannot say the same for you!'

'And why not, pray?'

'Because you let him go!'

A moment earlier, Marianne had been by no means certain but now that she had spoken the words aloud she saw to her surprise that she had always known it. In fact, the look on Gwen's face was an admission. Marianne went on without giving her time to prepare.

'No use denying it. I know.'

'How do you know?' Gwen said, abandoning contradiction.

'That is my business. I know and that should be enough for you. But what I don't know, is why you did it. And that is something I should be very glad to know.'

Gwen smiled nastily. 'Go and ask Morvan! You'll get nothing out of me.'

'Ask Morvan? That may not be such a bad idea. But don't expect me to believe that he had anything to do with it. But after all, why not appeal to him. I'll tell him —'

'That you are no more the princes' agent than I am! He's begun to suspect already, but I daresay he'd be glad to know for sure. And then tomorrow there'll be a nice meal for the fishes!'

Marianne did not flinch at this. She even permitted herself the luxury of a smile.

'Why not? I have nothing to lose, I have lost it all already. But I can tell him that you were the one that let his prisoner go – a prisoner who served that Surcouf whom he seems to dislike so heartily – and it may be that the fishes will get a double ration. I wish you could have seen him out on the headland when his prisoner sailed past thumbing his nose at him!'

Without bothering to check the effect of her words on Gwen's face, Marianne walked over to the hearth, picked up the tongs and began teasing some life into the still glowing embers. A meditative silence fell between them. Marianne busied herself putting more logs on the fire, waiting patiently for the other girl to make up her mind. At last:

'What do want to know?' Gwen muttered sullenly.

'I told you. Why did you help Jean to escape?'

'Because you needed him! I saw you going out to him and I followed you. I heard what you said – nearly all of it!'

'Well?' Marianne said calmly.

'So I realized you would be lost without him, that you needed him to lie for you. I went in to him after you'd gone. He was asleep and I had quite a job to wake him. But, once he was awake, he was very interested to hear what I had to say.'

'And what had you to say?'

'That you had been lying to him. That you were an English spy on your way to St Malo. That your purpose was to gain an introduction to Surcouf by telling some trumped up hard luck story – everyone knows how soft-hearted he is – and then use your charms on him to make him stop his ships attacking the English. You are quite pretty enough to do it and though the king of the Corsairs may not be very young, he still has an eye for beauty —'

'And he believed you?' Marianne cried, remembering bitterly all she had done to earn the Breton's trust.

'Straight off! Your tale about the duel was a bit hard to swallow too! And he'd seen for himself how far you'd go to get a man on your side. Besides, we are both Bretons after all. We stand up for one another. It wasn't very difficult. Your story was too farfetched. The only piece of luck was in guessing you were going to St Malo when you were wrecked.'

It was all Marianne could do not to give way to utter fury. Everything she had done had been turned against her. Between them, they had made a complete fool of her. So that was all the trust that could be placed in a man's word? No sooner was she out of his arms than Jean was ready to believe everything this girl told him simply because they came from the same land? Or had Gwen paid the same price? But Marianne was making rapid progress in the art of self-control. She merely shrugged and glanced at her companion with contempt.

'Congratulations! You are cleverer than I thought. Now, tell me, what harm have I done you to make you so determined to destroy me? Quite unwittingly, I borrowed your dress. That is a slender grudge!'

'And Morvan? Morvan never took his eyes off you, he cast me aside! You think I would let you take my place?' Gwen flung back savagely.

'Your place? An enviable one to be sure! The mistress of a highway robber, a wrecker who will end his days at a rope's end! It would have been easier for you to help me escape!'

'But not so certain! Only the dead are really safe! And that's why I shall watch you like a hawk until you are unmasked completely and —'

'Much good may it do you!' Marianne sighed irritably. 'Well, guard me if you insist, only let me sleep. I'm going to bed.'

She realized that there was nothing to be gained from Gwen. The girl was too unintelligent and, with her primitive instincts, she knew only one way of getting rid of anyone who was a nuisance to her. They must die. She had released Jean Le Dru in order to cut Marianne off from all help and now she was waiting with cat-like patience for the arrival of the mysterious visitor who, she believed, would finally unmask her enemy and sign the death warrant. Further argument was useless. It was better to try and build up her strength for the next day.

In the great hall the wake was still going on. Even through the thick walls Marianne could hear the slow, mournful chanting. She shivered. The discordant sound of the men's voices might have been the wailing of those very doomed souls which, according to the Breton Legend, emerged at night to haunt the roads and to reproach the living for their selfish pleasures. She did her best to shake off the dismal idea. At this time tomorrow, she hoped to be out of this gloomy place.

The weather, as the funeral procession left the manor, was quite dreadful. Squalls of wind and rain were flattening the gorse and whin bushes and turning the sodden lane into quagmires. The sky was so grey and lowering that it seemed actually to be pressing down on their heads, and the conditions were so bad that the cart which would ordinarily have been used to take the body to the cemetery had to give up. Instead, four strong men carried the coffin on their shoulders, getting what shelter they could from the rough wood. At the head of the procession rode the parish priest on horseback, saying prayers as he went. The household and friends followed as best they could, backs bent against the unceasing wind on which was carried the faint sound of the passing bell. Only the tailor, crouching over his work, was left in the house. But he was not really a man —

Marianne, wrapped in a thick black cloak with the hood pulled well down over her eyes, walked with the other women, hemmed in on one side by Gwen, still plainly showing her dislike, and on the other by old Siozic who was too busy with her beads to notice her at all. But Marianne was not interested in her neighbours. She watched the small grey granite belfry rise above the heath land and thought of Black Fish. Why was he so anxious to help her escape? She had paid him to take her to France and she was in France. His part of the bargain was fulfilled and she was no longer any concern of his. And yet, he had taken still further risks to get her away from Morvan. What had he to gain? And if she went with him, to what new perils might he lead her? It was all getting stranger and stranger! At any rate, she could not well be worse off. She had seen that in the cold glance Morvan had given her as they set out. His demand that she attend the funeral was purely in order to keep her under his eye. She could not be left at the manor and no one could stay with her.

The little church stood beside clumps of dead trees, surrounded by modest graves with, at one side, a charnel-house built like a shrine. On the summit of a nearby hill, a dolmen crouched, like a beast about to spring. It was built of huge stones like a Arc de Triomphe.

The coffin vanished beneath the low porch and the rest of the cortege followed. Marianne shivered as the icy dampness clutched her. It was dark inside. The only illumination was in the sanctuary, where two great candles made of yellow wax and the small red altar lamp seemed to fill the place with shadows. The big black cloaks of the women, the priest's vestments, Morvan's long cape and funereal mask loomed like a ghostly gathering, barely visible in the semi-darkness of the church. What seemed to Marianne sepulchral voices were raised and the service began.

There, in the dark, under that low-arched roof, they might have been already in the tomb. Only the dead man looked at home. The cold was intense. Their breath rose in a cloud as Marianne began to feel increasingly unwell. Her hands and feet were frozen but her forehead under the wet homespun cloth, was burning hot and her heart thudding madly. She knew the time had come but she could not breathe for nerves. She felt suddenly very lonely and helpless. She could not see the reassuring bulk of Black Fish anywhere. Why wasn't he there? Had he changed his mind? She had caught sight of him in the procession earlier but since the entry into the church, he seemed to have vanished into thin air.

The thought that something had happened to him, that perhaps he had abandoned her after all, swept over her with such terrifying certainty that for a second she lost control. She knew she must get it over with, or else go mad. In another moment, she would be capable of any foolishness, anything to fight off the rising panic which was threatening to choke her. She had to take the plunge. Then, taking a deep breath, she swayed on her feet and, uttering a loud shriek, fell flat on her back. She hit her head on the bench and hurt herself so badly that for a moment she thought she was going to faint in good earnest but she retained sufficient presence of mind to make no sound and lay quite still with her eyes closed, breathing slowly.

Around her the solemn boredom of the service was shattered. There was a stir of movement and shocked voices. Marianne felt herself being shaken by an ungentle hand.

'What's the matter with you?' Gwen's voice hissed crossly.

'She's very pale,' Soizic said. 'She needs air.'

The feeling of absurdity and unreality gained on Marianne. She was playing a part, as those in a play. The smell of wet cloaks and unwashed bodies filled her nostrils, overcoming the musty odour of damp and hot wax. The sound of sabots scraping on stone, then Morvan's voice saying curtly: 'Take her outside, see to her – this is too much! Let the service go on! May the soul of the departed not return to blame us! We will sing two more psalms.'

Behind her closed lids, Marianne felt a sudden, quite unexpected gaiety bubble up inside her. Oh, if she could only open her eyes and see their horrified faces! How they must be reaching for their beads and frantically crossing themselves. Such appalling sacrilege! Thanks to her, that scoundrel Vinoc would have a funeral he deserved.

Incredibly she found herself being lifted and carried out. The close air of the church gave way to rain-laden wind and the fresh smell of wet leaves. Nearby, women's voices were muttering in Breton. She was set down roughly on the ground. Someone slapped her face. Then came the sound of two short groans followed by Black Fish's voice.

'Quick, up, and let's be going!'

Marianne opened her eyes and leapt to her feet. She was inside the porch of the tiny charnel-house. Gwen and a sturdy peasant woman whose name she did not know lay motionless close by. But there was no time for surprise. She was seized by Black Fish's huge hands and hurried forward irresistibly. Towed by the giant, she began to run towards the dolmen, slipping and sliding on the muddy grass. But each time, her guide's great hand was there to yank her to her feet.

'Keep going,' Black Fish growled. 'Do you think we've time to waste?'

They rounded the dolmen and Marianne gave a cry of joy as she saw two horses standing ready saddled.

'I hope you can ride!' For answer, Marianne tucked up her skirts, put one foot in the stirrup and was up like a feather.

Black Fish grunted approval. 'A real trooper! Now, come on!'

At that moment, the sound of voices shouting broke out from the church porch. Their flight had been discovered. Marianne could hear Morvan's angry voice shouting to her hopelessly to stop. Laughing wildly, she dug her heels into her horse's sides. The animal leapt forward in the wake of Black Fish who was already galloping headlong down the hill. There was the sound of a shot, and then another, but both went wild. Turning, Marianne saw that the village had disappeared behind the shoulder of the hill. In front was only the empty, whin-covered heath with the roaring wind and here and there massive clumps of rock. But Marianne plunged through the rain with a kind of exaltation. Through a break in the ground, she caught a glimpse of the sea throwing up lofty plumes of spray high in the air and it seemed to her that this great, empty landscape was the most intoxicatingly beautiful place she had ever seen, and the very image of that freedom which she was vaguely aware of having found at last in this land where she had been born.

Spurring on her horse, she caught up with Black Fish and rode level with him.

'Where are we going?'

'To Brest! I have a little house there. Morvan will never think of looking for you there and besides, I have business in the place. Also – I think it's high time you and I had a little talk.'

'Why did you help me get away from Morvan? You don't even know who I am?'

Black Fish chuckled and turned his bearded face towards her. His smile made his face look uglier still.

'For your name, I hope you will tell me that yourself. As for what you are, I'll tell you. You're neither an adventuress, nor an insipid little goose. You're a lass of spirit, running away from some danger or other in England and you've come to France for some reason you don't know yourself, except that you had to go somewhere to stay alive. Am I wrong?'

'No,' Marianne said, 'that's how it is –'

'Besides,' Black Fish added, his voice grown suddenly gruff, 'I used to have a little lass once – she would have been about your age and you've a touch of her.'

'No longer?'

'No. She is dead. Speak no more of it. Ride on! We must find shelter before nightfall.'

Marianne did as she was told but as she urged on her mount, she wondered if it was only the rain that made her strange companion's bearded face so wet. Whatever happened, she was ready to follow where he led. She trusted him.

PART II

The Limping Devil

CHAPTER SEVEN
The Brest Mail

With a thunderous roar the diligence, all four tons of it, swept through the gates of the Hôtel des Postes in the rue Jean Jacques Rousseau and came to a halt in the middle of the courtyard. The rain seemed to come down twice as hard as the postilion jumped down heavily and the grooms ran forward to throw the covers over the steaming horses. The steps were let down to allow the travellers to descend. The brightly lit windows of the inn looked remarkably welcoming in the gathering dusk. The first to emerge was the notary from Rennes followed, almost at once, by the lady from Laval, yawning widely though she had slept three quarters of the way. Marianne came next.

It was Wednesday, the twentieth of December and twelve days since she had left Brest. Twelve exhausting, but thoroughly absorbing days spent with her face pressed close to the window of the diligence gazing out at the passing towns and countryside of this fascinating land of France. All the tales she had heard as a child had painted a grim picture of her father's country as a place delivered up to anarchy, brigandage and murder where no one could expect to be safe unless they spent their life virtually in hiding. She knew of course that the great revolution was over and that a new ruler was in power, but her picture of this ruler was an equally terrifying one, depicting him as a kind of brigand who had picked up the crown from a pool of blood in the market place and then only at the cost of the brutal murder of a romantic young prince betrayed into a hideous trap. And the former revolutionaries, soldiers of fortune, one-time washer-women and unfrocked priests who formed his entourage could not be much better. Marianne had expected a succession of half ruined towns, ravaged countryside, a people cowering under the arrogant despotism of the masters of the hour, and general suffering from the most abject and degrading poverty.

Except in some of the wilder parts of Brittany, what she found all along the diligence's endless journey was cultivated fields, prosperous villages, neat, attractive towns, well-run estates and even a number of handsome private châteaux. She had seen decently clad people, peasant women wearing gold crosses and lace caps, plump cattle and even children playing. Only the roads were in a shocking state but hardly worse than those in England and, just as on the other side of the Channel, there were a fair number of highwaymen to be met with in lonely spots, although the Brest Mail had not met any.

As for Paris, the little she had seen of it through the darkness and the driving rain had made her long to know more. They had entered the city after passing through some bare, leafless woods, by what the notary had told her was the Barrière de l'Étoile, a massive gateway flanked by some very fine buildings with pediments and classical columns. The foundations of some other vast construction were beginning to rise from the ground close by.

'That is to be a monument to the glory of the Grande Armée,' the lawyer had obligingly informed her, 'a gigantic Arc de Triomphe!'

Beyond, a wide, tree-lined avenue with smart carriages moving up and down it ran down towards splendid buildings and gardens and a sea of shining roofs and spires. But instead of proceeding down this thoroughfare, the diligence turned off to the left alongside a high wall.

'The wall of the Fermiers généreaux,' the notary hastened to point out. 'The Paris wall that made Paris wail, as they used to say when it was built, you know. Not so very long ago, but to some of us it feels like a century. This is your first visit to Paris, is it not?'

'Yes. I have lived always in the country,' Marianne had answered. The notary had been practically the only one of all the passengers on the diligence whom she could understand since his familiarity with legal documents had given him a somewhat slow and solemn turn of speech. The others spoke much too quickly for her and employed a number of strange expressions which she, used as she was to the polished and aristocratic French spoken by those she knew in England, found hard to follow. She had therefore taken Black Fish's parting advice and done her best to look as shy and timid as possible.

In the course of her journey, Marianne had looked back with a good deal of affection to the strange companion of her recent adventures. She had found that, beneath his forbidding exterior, Black Fish was kind and brave and the few days she had spent in his little house in the district of Brest known as the Recouvrance, by the banks of the Penfield, had been a time of rest and peace.

It was a very small house built of brine-washed granite with a high, pointed gate and a neat, fenced-in garden. But the stout Bretonne housekeeper kept it as clean as a new pin. From the hearth stoned floor to the copper pans in the kitchen and the lovely old furniture worn soft and smooth with age, everything gleamed and shone. Even Black Fish himself, become once more for a time Nicolas Mallerousse, a retired naval man, took on a completely different air from that he had worn in the tavern at Plymouth. Gone was the piratical appearance and if a certain tang of adventure hung about him still, at least at Recouvrance he acquired a suggestion of honest respectability.

'My house is not large,' he had said, opening the polished oak door for his guest, 'but you are welcome to stay here as long as you wish. I have told you, I have lost my daughter. You can take her place, if you will.'

For a moment, Marianne was speechless. His generosity, springing as it did from genuine affection, went straight to her heart and she had not known what to say but Black Fish had continued:

'I know that when you took ship with me, all you wanted was to put as much space between yourself and England as possible. You've done that. No one will come to look for you at Recouvrance if you should care to stay.'

Marianne knew that she must pluck up her courage and tell him the whole truth. She need not fear his condemnation. That night, over a splendid lobster and a mountain of pancakes and cream provided by the excellent Madame le Guilvinec, she told him of the events at Selton Hall which had led to her flight. She told him, too, how by the merest chance she had learned at Plymouth that she still had some relations living in France.

'It was to my cousin d'Asselnat that I had hoped to go,' she finished up at last 'As my father's first cousin, she is a fairly close relation, while the Empress —'

'I daresay her majesty will welcome you with open arms,' Black Fish said with a hint of new respect. 'She is all that is good and gracious and has strong family feelings. It is to be feared though, that she will not be Empress much longer.'

'What do you mean?'

'That the Emperor has no children, his wife can never give him any and he needs to guarantee his succession. There has been much talk of divorce. Then, Napoleon will marry some foreign princess.'

Marianne had been profoundly shocked at this news although as yet she only half believed it. That the Corsican should wish to part from his wife because she gave him no children did not surprise her. Such behaviour was no more than what was to be expected from a man of his stamp. He was surely without either heart or principles. But as for his marrying a real princess, that would undoubtedly be a very different matter. The usurper must be swollen with pride indeed to think it possible. No princess worthy of the name would deign to sit on such a throne! Moreover, Black Fish-Nicolas seemed to view these events with some displeasure. Marianne thought she caught a hint of disapproval in his voice and, faithful to her old principle of plain speaking, taxed him with it.

'It seems you do not approve of this divorce, Monsieur Mallerousse?'

'You can call me Nicolas! No, I do not approve. Joséphine has meant good fortune to the Emperor, his lucky star, if you like. I am afraid if he sends her packing, his luck may change.'

Marianne forbore to observe that to her way of thinking, the Emperor's luck could not change soon enough, but Nicolas had already reverted to her own future.

'If this is so, child, you've nothing to gain by staying at Recouvrance ; even after a divorce, Joséphine would still be powerful and her protection is not to be ignored. Napoleon has greatly wronged her but I believe truly loved her. The best thing you can do is go to Paris. You won't have any trouble finding your cousin. I'll give you a letter of introduction to the Minister of Police, Citizen Fouché – the Duke of Otranto, I should say. I'm not used to his new title yet, but I'll get round to it.'

'But you, what will you do?'

Nicolas Mallerousse roared with laughter and, still puffing at his long clay pipe, went over to a chest from which he took some garments similar to those he had worn in the tavern on the Barbican.

'I? I shall go back to Plymouth and become Black Fish again, the rogue who'd sell his soul for a sovereign –'

Then, it had been the sailor's turn to make his confession. He admitted that he was an agent of that Fouché of whom he had spoken. His base was at Plymouth where he organized the escape of prisoners from the hulks.

'I was at Portsmouth first of all, and with my help more than one brave lad escaped from that evil hulk the *Crown*. But then an informer was getting on my track so I moved to Plymouth. I can work as well there.'

He did not mention that he also gathered what information he could about English plans and troop movements but Marianne could easily guess.

'Are you a spy, Nicolas?' she asked in a rather shocked voice.

Nicolas pulled a face that made him look uglier than ever but then he laughed.

'It's an ugly word for what are often very brave men. Let us say – a soldier in the shadows, shall we?'

Marianne had spent several quiet days in the little house at Recouvrance . She had viewed the town in the company of Madame Le Guilvinec and the surrounding countryside with Nicolas, discovered that a French port was very much the same as an English one, that the banks of the Penfeld could be very gentle and the wild sea intimately lovely. She had even seen some convicts with their shaven heads and red woollen garments but, her curiosity once satisfied, had preferred to devote her attention to the shops in the rue de Siam where her companion, acting on Black Fish's orders, had seen to it that she was generously provided with new clothes.

On the evening before he was due to return to England, Nicolas had told his temporary charge that a place was reserved for her on the next morning's diligence. He had given her a purse containing some gold pieces and a handful of small change. When Marianne, very red in the face, tried to refuse, he told her:

'It's a loan, no more. You can return it when you are lady-in-waiting to your cousin the Empress.'

'Will you come and see me?'

'Of course I will. I come to Paris now and then to meet Citizen Fouché – the Duke of Otranto I mean.'

'Very well! I accept – but don't forget your promise.'

This bargain sealed, Nicolas had handed Marianne a neatly folded letter addressed to His Grace the Duke of Otranto, Minister of Police, at his house in the quai Malaquis telling her to take great care of it since, after reading the letter, the Minister would certainly give her all the help in his power.

'And his power is very great. The Ci – the Duke that is, is certainly the ablest and most well informed person in the whole world!'

In addition, and just in case she should lose her letter, he had made her learn, by heart some words which she was to be sure to repeat to the minister.

Thus equipped, Marianne bade an affectionate farewell to her friend at the stage coach office in Brest. She was dressed in the height of provincial fashion in a driving coat of mulberry coloured cloth with three capes worn over a dress of the same colour with long, puffed sleeves and a high neck trimmed with a narrow frill of white lace, and kid half-boots laced with velvet ribbon. The whole was set off by a bonnet in the same mulberry shade of velvet lined inside the brim with ruched white silk and trimmed with a saucy curled white feather. It was a cold, bright day and she was excited, although it was a real grief to part from the kind man who had been so good to her. Acting on a sudden impulse, before she climbed into the heavy vehicle, she flung her arms round his neck and kissed him.

'Don't worry,' Nicolas muttered in a gruff voice that did not hide his feelings, 'I'll try and find out how your affairs stand, over there. Perhaps they'll call off the search before very long and one day, maybe, you'll be able to go home.'

But as the Brest Mail rattled on into the heart of the French countryside, Marianne felt her desire to go back to England gradually slipping away from her. Everything she saw was new and interesting. She stared at even the smallest things with wide wondering eyes, serenely unconscious of the surprise and admiration which her own beauty was rousing in her fellow travellers. She was much too busy looking out at this strange land of France which struck a deep and almost unconscious chord in her own heart. It was as though the severed roots were beginning to put out new growth.

All the same, when she had climbed out of the mail coach on that rainy evening, Marianne felt suddenly very much alone and friendless. In the twelve days she had spent travelling in the great coach, she had grown accustomed to it. Now, this huge, unknown city, the bustle all around her, people greeting the relatives and friends who had come to meet them, the unfamiliar faces everywhere all made her the more conscious of her own isolation. The fatigue of the journey added to this feeling of depression and, to make matters worse, she had stepped straight out of the coach into a puddle of water. Unpleasantly cold, wet feet did nothing to make her feel that life was more worth living.

There were a number of porters moving about the vast inn yard and some passengers had already obtained one to carry their bags. The helpful notary, seeing Marianne drifting rather aimlessly, clutching her carpet bag, made a sign to one of them and took him over to her.

'Give your bag to this lad, mademoiselle, and he will carry it to wherever you are going. Where are you bound?'

'I know no one in Paris but I have been recommended to the inn called the Compas d'Or in the rue Montorgueil. The landlord is a friend of my – uncle.' She hesitated a little over the last word, uncertain of the best title to confer on Black Fish. He had recommended the inn as one where his friend Bobois would take good care of her until she could obtain an interview with the Minister of Police.

In the course of their journey, the notary had done his best to discover why so beautiful and reserved a young lady might be travelling alone to Paris but Marianne, with a skill beyond her years, had managed to avoid giving more than vague, generalized answers. She had lost her parents, she said, and was travelling to the city to find the only family she had left. Nicolas had booked her seat in the name of Mademoiselle Mallerousse and had obtained papers for her in that name, leaving it to Fouché to restore her to her real identity as he might see fit. The laws regarding émigrés were severe and it was necessary to find out whether Ellis Selton's niece fell under their prescriptions.

The worthy lawyer agreed that the Compas d'Or was a sound, respectable place. He himself was bound for the Cheval Vert in the rue Geoffroy-Lasnier, famous as the inn where Danton had put up on his arrival from Arcis-sur-Aube. He was expected there, otherwise he would have given himself the honour of escorting Mademoiselle Mallerousse to the Compas d'Or but she might have perfect confidence in the porter who was one he had employed himself many times. He was even conscientious enough to suggest to her how much she ought to pay the man, then, raising his beaver hat, he bowed, expressed the hope that they would meet again before long and disappeared into the crowd. Marianne prepared to follow her guide. 'Is it far to the inn?'

'Ten minutes on foot, mam'zelle! Just down the rue Tiquetonne and we'll be there in no time. Just wait while I put up the heavy brolly for you. In this rain, you'll be sopping wet before we're there.'

Fitting the action to the words, the porter, who was a stocky, red-haired lad with a cheerful countenance and a snub nose, opened an enormous umbrella above his client's head and led her out into the street.

There were few people about, the darkness and the bad weather combining to keep the people of Paris within doors. The big oil lamps slung on wires across the street threw little light and although she was bursting with curiosity, Marianne was obliged to give most of her attention to watching where she put her feet. There were no pavements and the big round cobblestones did not make for easy walking. Without her companion to point out the bad places and show her the planks set like small bridges across the swollen gutters, she would have twisted her ankle time and time again. All the same, some of the shop windows looked enticing and among the passers-by were several well-dressed women, prosperous looking men and lively children.

The porter gave a warning shout and, just in time, he dragged her back against the wall of a building, to avoid a glittering officer on horseback who galloped blindly past and almost rode them down. Marianne had a brief glimpse of a fine black horse, a green coat with white trimmings, white buckskin breeches in long, gleaming boots, a dazzling brass helmet adorned with leopard skin and a long black plume, above a moustached face, red and gold epaulettes and white gloves, a vision at once dashing and colourful.

'Who's that?' she asked, shaken but admiring.

'One of the Empress's dragoons. They're always in a hurry.' Suddenly noticing her dazzled expression he added: 'Handsome fellows, eh? But they're not the best! Anyone can see you're just up from the country, but wait 'till you see a chasseur of the Guard, or a Mameluke, or a Polish lancer or a hussar! Not to mention the marshals with all their gold braid and medals! Oh, the little Corporal knows how to dress his men all right!'

'The little Corporal? Who's that?'

The boy's astonishment as he looked at Marianne was quite genuine. His eyebrows rose until they reached his hair.

'But – the Emperor, of course! Where've you come from, not to know that?'

'A convent!' Marianne retorted crisply, not to lose her dignity. 'You don't meet many dragoons there – or corporals, big or little!'

'Oh, so that's it!'

Very soon they turned into the rue Montorgueil and Marianne forgot all about the dragoon. The chief interest of the street centred on a large, brilliantly lit restaurant with another, more modest establishment close by.

Elegant carriages with gleaming paintwork, drawn by high bred horses with glittering harness, drew up before the doors to disgorge no less exquisite diners, many of them in splendid uniform.

'That's the Rocher de Cancale,' the porter told her with pride. 'They have the best whale pâté in Paris, and the best fish and the best oysters! They come fresh each day by special delivery. For those who can afford it!'

This time, Marianne made no attempt to hide her admiration. Her ideas about the French were having to undergo a certain amount of revision. Through the lighted windows of the famous restaurant, she caught sight of men of stately bearing, shimmering satin, diamonds gleaming on white throats and thought how gorgeous were the uniforms, how rare and precious the fur wraps of the ladies.

'Of course,' the boy went on with a slight sniff, 'it's not the Chord! Company's a bit mixed, for all it's so showy! You don't find many duchesses there but their menfolk like it – it's a great place for birds of paradise!'

The smells wafting out of the great restaurant were none the less titillating to Marianne's nostrils. She realized that she was very hungry.

'Is it far to the Compas d'Or?'

'No. This is it!'

He indicated a handsome renaissance building, now a substantial inn. There was bottled glass in the low, small-paned windows and fine carving on the front. The general air was one of comfort and respectability. A diligence clattered through the wide arch with a great ringing of bells.

'The Creil diligence,' the porter said. 'That and the Gisors both leave from here. Well, this is it, mam'zelle.'

He called out to the landlord, Bobois, who was just turning back indoors after presiding over the departure of the diligence.

'Hey! Landlord! A customer for you!'

The innkeeper's regal bearing unbent considerably at the sight of the well-dressed young woman. At the name of Nicolas Mallerousse a great smile spread over his plump, clean-shaven cheeks, revealing a gleam of gold teeth between thick pepper and salt whiskers.

'Consider yourself at home, little lady! Any niece of Nicolas's is more to me than my own daughter! Hey, Marthon! Come and take mademoiselle's bag!'

A servant girl in a starched cap came running out and Marianne settled her score with the porter, handing a tip which called forth an expression of high delight from the boy.

'Thank you, mam'zelle,' he said, tossing his blue cap in the air. 'If you've any more errands, any time, just say to anyone round here that you want Gracchus-Hannibal Pioche and I'll be right there!'

With this, Gracchus-Hannibal departed whistling, apparently not troubled by his sternly Roman name, while Bobois and the maid escorted

Mademoiselle Mallerousse into the inn. The place was very full and seemed admirably well run. This was the busiest time of the evening and waiters and serving maids were flying in all directions serving those guests who were eating downstairs and carrying food up to others supping in their rooms above. Bobois suggested this latter course to Marianne and she agreed gratefully, feeling somewhat alarmed by such a press of people.

They made their way to the polished oak staircase. Two men were at that moment coming down and Marianne and her escort were obliged to wait until there was room to pass.

One of the men was about forty, of middling height but strong build, elegantly dressed in a blue coat with engraved silver buttons. He had a broad face with strongly marked features framed in dark sideburns, and very bronzed like that of a man who had lived much in the sun. His blue eyes were bright and twinkling and he wore his tall grey hat rakishly on one side. He was twirling a gold knobbed cane idly in one large, ridiculously gloved hand.

Fascinated by the extraordinary impression of power which emanated from this man, Marianne watched him come downstairs without paying much attention to his companion who was, in any case, a little behind. But when she did look at him, it was with a sense of shock. There before her, clad in a severely buttoned dark suit, was Jean Le Dru.

Left alone in the pretty little chamber with its old-fashioned chintz hangings and windows looking out on to the main courtyard of the inn to which Bobois had conducted her, Marianne struggled to put some order into her thoughts. The sight of the young Breton had come as a complete shock to her. She had only just managed not to cry out. It would have been unwise to court recognition, since he knew her real identity. She congratulated herself now that he had certainly not recognized her. She had not been standing directly in the light and the brim of her bonnet had thrown her face into shadow.

Le Dru had followed the man in the blue coat without a glance and Marianne overheard the latter say to Bobois:

'We dine at the Rocher de Cancale, Bobois. You can send word there if anyone should want me.'

'Very well, Monsieur le Baron,' the innkeeper had replied and Marianne was instantly agog with curiosity. Who was this baron her escaped prisoner was following so meekly? However, there was little time for wondering. Marthon brought up a large tray on which was a highly appetising supper and, putting off her quest for information until later, Marianne set to work to satisfy the pangs of hunger.

She was just finishing an agreeable dessert of pineapple and cream when there was a knock at the door.

'Come in,' she called out thinking it was Marthon returning for the tray. But when the door opened it was Jean Le Dru who came in.

Mastering her surprise and alarm at this unexpected visit, she made herself remain seated and merely pushed away the little table which held the remains of her supper.

'Yes?' she said coldly.

Jean closed the door in silence and leaned back against the jamb, looking at her all the while with sparkling eyes.

'So, I was not mistaken! It was you!' he said harshly. 'How did you get away from Morvan?'

'I scarcely think you have the right to ask me that! If I escaped, it was certainly no thanks to you!'

He laughed unpleasantly, almost mechanically, and Marianne saw from his abnormally flushed face that he had been drinking.

'You thought you'd pulled the wool over my eyes, didn't you? You thought you could pop back into bed in your wrecker friend's musty manor house and I would hand myself over meekly to the English, and all for your pretty face? Though I'll admit you paid well!'

'Apparently not enough to make you keep your promise to me! What did Gwen give you to make you change your mind so quickly?'

'The truth about you and your little plots, and the chance to save my own life and ruin your plans! A priceless gift, as you can see – even more precious than your own delectable little person! Oh, don't worry, I've not forgotten that night! Do you know how often I've dreamed about you?'

'What should I care! You betrayed me, deceived me! You preferred to listen to the first stupid story you were told, when you knew, better than anyone, that I was forced to get away from England to save my life, that I needed help, support – and you abandoned me like the coward you are, and killed a man besides!'

'You cannot blame me for the death of that vermin? He was a wrecker! I ought to get a medal! As for you, you won't make me believe any more of your stories. I know who you are, and what you've come to France to do!'

'And I know that the story you did believe was a hundred times more unlikely. I know what Gwen told you, that I meant to seduce your wonderful Surcouf until he abandoned all his most cherished convictions. That was it, wasn't it? A likely story! I don't even know the man!'

Jean jerked himself away from the door and strode towards her, sudden anger flaming in eyes that already glittered unnaturally.

'You don't know him. You dare to tell me that you don't know him when you have followed him here, to Paris, to this very inn? Can't you see that everything proves you guilty? You slut, you had no need to escape from Morvan! He let you go himself, he even paid you, set you up in clothes and packed you off to find your prey! You've had plenty of time to go to St Malo, find out that he was in Paris and now, like a good bloodhound, follow the trail as far as here!'

For a moment, this tirade left Marianne numb with shock. Was he too drunk to know what he was saying? Or was she really dealing with a madman? She began to be afraid of this almost uncontrollable rage but even so, she had to get to the bottom of his strange words. She determined to shout back.

'I don't understand a word of what you are saying! I did not go to St Malo and I have never had anything to do with your Surcouf. I have never set eyes on him, I tell you, and if he is in Paris —'

A ringing slap stopped her words and almost her breath. She tried to run to the door and call for help but Jean was after her and, twisting both arms behind her back, held her fast with one hand while with the other, he hit her again a second time, so hard that she thought her head must burst. He bent over her, his face so close she could smell the reek of wine on his breath.

'Liar! You dirty little liar! You have the nerve to tell me you don't know him, that you've never seen him? And what about this evening, on the stairs, didn't you see him then? Didn't you know him then, when all France knows his face almost as well as the Emperor's!'

Marianne struggled furiously to escape from the iron fist that held her.

'Let me go!' she muttered through her teeth. 'Let me go at once or I'll scream! You are mad or drunk, or both! Let me go, I tell you, or I'll scream!'

'Scream? Go on then if you want to! Try!'

Twisting her arm to force her to be still, he pulled her roughly to him and stopped her scream with a savage kiss. Marianne half fainted for a moment, but she recovered quickly. In order to escape his hateful kiss, she bit hard at the mouth crushed against hers. An instant later, she was free.

She saw, with a quick surge of triumph, her late attacker whip out a handkerchief and dab at his bleeding lips. He looked so foolish that she could almost have laughed in his face. But for the moment, it seemed to her that nothing mattered so much as getting rid of this horrid person. How could she ever have liked him, even for a moment? With his vigorous, outdoor frame crammed into that dark suit he looked like a peasant in his Sunday best. He was almost ridiculous. With a contemptuous toss of her head, she turned on her heel and again made for the door, intending to fling it wide, but he caught her half-way and picking her up as though she had been a parcel, he strode with her to the bed, flung her down and held her there, both hands gripping her arms, while he seated himself on the edge.

'Not so fast! You'll not escape so easily, my pretty one!'

Marianne saw to her surprise that his anger had quite gone. He was even laughing, careless of his lip which was already beginning to swell.

'I have told you to leave me alone,' she said calmly, but he seemed not to have heard. He was bending over her, studying her with the intensity of a collector presented with some rare item.

'How lovely you can be!' he said softly. 'It suits you to be angry. If you could see your eyes! They flash like emeralds in the light! I know you're worthless, a filthy little royalist spy, but it makes no difference – I can't help loving you—'

'Loving me?' Marianne said, flabbergasted by this unexpected declaration.

'Yes. It's true, you know, that I have not been able to forget you. You have haunted my days, and my nights – I kept seeing you, lying there in the straw, with your hair all about you, I could feel your soft skin under my hands – and now, I can think of nothing else except that you are here, that I have found you again! I have hungered for you, Marianne, and if you will forget all that lies between us, we will stay together always!'

It could not be true, he must be raving! He had stopped shouting at her, stopped hitting her. Quite suddenly, he had become all gentleness and tenderness. His hands were moving to caress her. He was bending down, slowly, inexorably, towards her lips, as though they held some fascination for him. In a flash, Marianne realized that he was on the point of subjecting her to a repetition of her unpleasant experience in the barn. At once, with an instinctive reaction of her whole body, she thrust him away with all her strength and screamed.

'No!—'

With a quick jerk, she was on her feet while Jean clutched at the bed to prevent himself falling. Smoothing out the disordered folds of her dress, Marianne folded her arms and stared defiantly at her attacker.

'Who do you take me for? You come in here, insult me, strike me and then on top of that, you think you only have to babble a few words of love and I'll fall into your arms! You love me? I am much obliged, and now, sir, do me the favour of leaving this room instantly! I have no wish to renew our – converse of the other night!'

By now, he too was on his feet, automatically brushing down his clothes with one hand. The expression of his face was heavy with chagrin.

'And once, there in Brittany, just for a moment, I could have thought you loved me—'

A rush of childish anger made her answer in words full of scorn.

'Me? Love you? You must be mad, I think! I needed you, that was all.'

The name he called her was too base not to betray the depths of his disappointment. With a look of hatred, he went to the door and opened it at last. But on the threshold, he turned.

'You have rejected me, well, it will be the worse for you, Marianne! You shall be sorry!'

'I doubt it! Goodbye!'

She heard him go downstairs and, dropping into a chair, poured herself a few drops of wine to calm her. As her anger left her, she tried to think sensibly about the threat he had uttered but she finally came to the conclusion that there was nothing in it beyond the venom of a child that has failed to get its own way. He loved her, and therefore would do nothing to hurt her! In which she showed very little understanding of masculine vanity.

Marianne was still nursing these optimistic thoughts and wondering which novel it was where the heroine had been obliged to deal with a similar situation, when the door of her room was flung violently open from outside. Jean Le Dru burst in, followed by two gendarmes and pointed at the girl who sat there thunder-struck.

'There she is! She's an émigrée and has entered the country illegally. Her name is Marianne d'Asselnat and she is a royalist agent!'

Before Marianne could think of resistance, the two representatives of the law had seized her, each by one arm, and dragged her out of the room. Under the horrified gaze of the worthy Bobois and those, infinitely less agitated but still highly interested, of the other customers of the inn, she was hustled ignominiously down the stairs, thrust into a waiting cab and driven off.

She found herself inside a small black box with lowered blinds, beside a heavily moustached gendarme. Her first impulse was to scream aloud in a frenzy of rage and indignation, in the vain hope that someone would come to her rescue.

The gendarme tucked himself into his corner, and merely observed quietly: 'I shouldn't shout like that, if I were you, little lady. Or I'll have to gag you and truss you like a chicken! Be good now, it'll be best for everybody.'

Defeated, Marianne gave up the struggle and huddled as far as she could away from her guard. If ever she got her hands on that wretch Le Dru, she vowed, he would see what she was made of! To have her arrested like a common criminal! How could he—

Anger soon gave way to tears and then, because she was, after all, very tired and the swaying of the coach was soporific, Marianne fell asleep at last with the tears still wet on her pretty face.

CHAPTER EIGHT
A Police Duke and a Corsair Baron

Waking in the middle of the night to find herself in a cell of the prison of St. Lazare, Marianne thought at first she must be dreaming. She had been snatched from her pretty little room so suddenly that, still half asleep, she could not help trying to shake off the nightmare but, little by little, it dawned on her that it was real.

The candle which had been left on a rickety table showed her a high, narrow room into which, during the day, the light must filter from a barred window set high up in the wall. The damp had made strange maps on the grey walls while broken flagstones and rusty locks revealed the antiquity of this one-time convent. The only furniture, apart from the table and a stool, was a narrow bed on which was a straw mattress and a blanket. It was, as Marianne discovered by sitting on it, very hard. It was also extremely cold, since no fire was provided for the comfort of the prisoners. They had given her no time to snatch up her coat or carpet bag and, with nothing but her dress, Marianne could only hug herself in a desperate attempt to keep warm.

Her situation was a highly critical one. Nicolas Mallerousse had explained to her the perils awaiting the émigrés who returned to France illegally and, what was worse, the precious letter had been left behind in her bag. Marianne's feelings wavered between despair, when she thought of herself, and fury when she thought of the dastardly Le Dru who had denounced her because she refused to submit to his embraces. Finding this second state infinitely more stimulating than the first, she concentrated on it and even managed to extract a certain additional warmth from the anger that made her blood boil.

Dragging the blanket off the bed, she draped it round her shoulders and began striding furiously up and down the narrow space allotted to her, becoming increasingly wide awake as she grew warmer. She had to think, and think clearly, if she did not mean to moulder in this prison until it pleased Napoleon's police either to incarcerate her in some yet deeper dungeon, execute her or send her back to England under a strong guard. She was not altogether sure what happened to exiles who returned illegally since Nicolas had not seen fit to tell her, probably to avoid frightening her, but she guessed that it was bound to be unpleasant.

Nor did she know precisely where she was. The gendarme had told her on arrival that it was the prison of St. Lazare but that meant nothing to her, the only prisons she was at all acquainted with being the Tower of London and the Plymouth hulks. However, since prisons were the department of the Minister of Police, the important thing was to see him as quickly as possible. She no longer had her letter, it was true, but she still had in her head the words which Nicolas had made her learn by heart and told her to repeat to him.

She must therefore see this lofty personage as soon as possible, and that meant drawing as much attention to herself as possible. The silence all about her was unendurable. To keep her spirits up, she thought of Jean Le Dru and of what she would do to him were fate ever good enough to deliver him up to her bound hand and foot. The method worked. Wide awake and stirred to a fine rage, Marianne flung herself on the door and began pounding on it and screaming at the top of her voice.

'I want to see the Minister of Police! I demand to see the Minister of Police!'

Nothing happened at first but she went on shouting still more loudly without losing heart. In a little while, there was a pattering of footsteps in the passage and a nun's austere face appeared at the barred peep-hole in the door.

'What is the meaning of this disturbance! Be quiet at once! You will wake everyone!'

'I don't care if I do. I have been wrongfully arrested. I am not an émigrée, I am Marianne Mallerousse and it says so in my papers if they had given me a chance to bring them. I want to see the Minister!'

'Ministers cannot be woken up in the middle of the night for the sake of little girls who lose their temper. Go to sleep! No doubt your case will be dealt with in the morning.'

'If it can wait till morning, I can't see why I wasn't allowed to sleep peacefully in my own bed. The rate your gendarmes moved, you'd have thought there was a fire on!'

'They had to make sure of you. You might have given them the slip.'

'I'm sorry to have to tell you, sister, but you're talking nonsense. I had just taken a room at the inn after a long and tiring journey. Can you tell me why I should have run away again, or where?'

The few square inches of face framed in the black and white headdress seemed to become still more withdrawn.

'I am not here to argue with you about the method of your arrest, my girl. You are in prison. And I am under orders to guard you. Be quiet and try to sleep!'

'Sleep? Could anyone sleep with such a sense of injustice!' Marianne cried in ringing, melodramatic tones. 'I shall not sleep until my cries are heard! Go and fetch the Minister. He must listen to me!'

'He can listen to you just as well tomorrow. Be quiet, now. If you persist in this disturbance, I shall have you transferred to a punishment cell where you will be no better off—'

The words carried conviction and since she was by no means anxious to find herself thrown into an even gloomier dungeon, Marianne thought it wisest to lower her voice. But she did not admit defeat.

'Very well! I will be quiet. But mind this, sister. I have something important to communicate to the Minister, something very important indeed – and he may not be best pleased if you prevent me reaching him in time. However, if the Minister's displeasure means nothing to you—'

Marianne could see from the sudden alarm reflected on the nun's face which, she could have sworn changed colour, that it did mean a good deal,. The Citizen Fouché, so recently elevated to a dukedom, could not be an easy man.

'Very well,' the sister said quietly. 'I will inform our Mother Superior and she will take the necessary steps tomorrow morning. But, for God's sake, make no more noise!'

She looked round anxiously. In fact, the inmates of the neighbouring cells were awake and the murmur of grumbling voices could be heard on all sides. The silence was peopled and the desert lived, to all appearances much to the wardress's annoyance.

'There!' she said crossly. 'You have woken the whole floor. It will take me a good quarter of an hour to get them quiet again. You deserve punishment.'

'Don't upset yourself,' Marianne said kindly. 'I'll be quiet. But you be sure to keep your promise!'

'I have promised nothing. But I do promise. Now, be quiet.'

The face vanished and the hatch snapped shut. The prisoner heard the nun's voice, loud and firm now, moving along the corridor telling each one to be quiet.

Satisfied with her progress, Marianne returned to her mattress, her ears alert for the various noises around her. Who were they, these women whose sleep she had disturbed, whose dreams she had unwittingly entered? Were they real malefactors, thieves and prostitutes or, like herself, innocent victims of the terrible police machine? She felt an instinctive sympathy for these faceless, complaining voices, simply because they were women. How many of them had suffered, like herself, at the hands of one or more men. In all the books she had read, excepting possibly the frightful story of Lady Macbeth, every wretched woman who came to a bad end was always driven to it by a man.

And so, pondering on these other women, invisible yet ever-present, with whom fate had thrown her, Marianne fell asleep at last without realizing it. When she woke, it was broad daylight, as broad, that is, as daylight could be in a cell in St. Lazare, and the sister wardress was standing beside her with a bundle under her arm. Dumped on the bed, this bundle proved to contain a plain grey woollen dress, a cap and fichu of unbleached linen, a coarse shift, thick, black woollen stockings and a pair of clogs.

'Take off your clothes,' the sister commanded sternly, 'and put these on.'

It was a different nun from the night before and suddenly Marianne lost her temper.

'Put on these hideous things? Certainly not! To begin with, I am not staying here. I am to see the Minister of Police this morning and –'

The newcomer's face was expressionless as her voice. It was so large and pale as to be almost indistinguishable from her veil, so that the total effect was something like a full moon, utterly devoid of character. Apparently, however, its owner knew how to obey orders. In exactly the same tone, she repeated: 'Get undressed and put these on.'

'Never!'

The nun showed no sign of anger. Going out into the passage, she took a clapper from her pocket and banged three times. Not more than a few seconds later, two strapping creatures whose uniforms told Marianne they must be two of her fellow prisoners, burst into the cell. In fact, they were so large and strong that but for their petticoats and a certain sparseness of moustache, they might easily have been mistaken for a pair of grenadiers. Moreover, the identical vivid scarlet and high polish of their cheeks showed that the prison diet was by no means as debilitating as might have been imagined and that, for these two at any rate, it certainly included a fair ration of wine.

In no time at all, Marianne, speechless with horror, was stripped of her own clothes and dressed in the prison uniform, receiving a resounding slap on the buttocks from one of her impromptu tirewomen in the process – a pleasantry which called down a severe rebuke on the head of its author.

'It was so tempting,' was the woman's excuse. 'Pity to lock up such a jolly little piece!'

Marianne's indignation was such that it almost robbed her of her voice but disdaining the two slatterns as unworthy of her notice, she turned her attention to the wardress.

'I wish to see the Mother Superior,' she announced. 'It is very urgent.'

'Our Mother Superior has let it be understood that she will see you today. Until then, you will wait quietly. For the present, go with the others to the chapel—'

Marianne had no choice but to leave the cell, stumbling in the clogs that were too big for her, and join the shuffling file of the other prisoners. About a score of women were moving in single file down the high, narrow corridor amid a great deal of coughing, sniffing and muttering and a strong smell of unwashed bodies. The general impression was of a herd rather than a file. The faces of all wore the same expression of dumb apathy. All their feet dragged on the uneven flagstones, all their shoulders were bowed. Only by their height and the hair, blonde, black, brown or grey escaping from the coarse linen caps, could the female prisoners of St. Lazare be told apart.

Swallowing her impatience and resentment, Marianne took her place in the line but it was not long before she realized that the woman behind her was amusing herself by systematically treading on her heels. The first time it happened, she only turned round, thinking it was an accident. Coming after her was a dumpy little blonde person, her eyes hidden by pale, drooping lids that made her look half asleep. Her clothes were clean but the vacant grin on her slack lips made Marianne suddenly long to slap her face. The next time the rough wooden shoe scraped her ankle, she muttered under her breath: 'Watch what you're doing, you're hurting me—'

No answer. The other girl kept her eyes lowered, the same stupid smile on her pasty face. Then, for the third time, the sabot ground into Marianne's heel, so hard that she could not help giving out a sharp cry of pain.

Patience was not one of Marianne's chief virtues and the last few hours had used up what little she had left. She swung round instantly and dealt the offender a ringing blow on her plump cheek. This time, she found herself gazing into a pair of almost colourless eyes that reminded her oddly of an adder which her favourite horse, Sea Bird, had crushed beneath his hoof one day out hunting. The other girl said nothing, she simply bared her yellow teeth and hurled herself straight at her enemy's stomach. Immediately, all those round the two women stopped to watch, instinctively forming a circle to leave room for the two who were fighting. There were shouts of encouragement, all addressed to Marianne's opponent.

'Go it, la Tricoteuse! Hit her!'

'Thump her hard! Stuck-up little madam! An *aristo*!'

'Smash her! Hear the bloody racket she kicked up last night? Asking for the Minister of Police!'

'She's an informer! Do her good to cool her off!'

Marianne avoided the blow aimed at her stomach but she was appalled at this unexpected overflow of hatred. La Tricoteuse, apparently meaning to do her best to satisfy her supporters, drew off for a fresh attack. Her jaw worked spasmodically, betraying only a mindless lust to kill. The colourless eyes gleamed dangerously and all at once, Marianne saw a short, sharp knife

140

glinting in the woman's hand. The head of the column of women had already reached the staircase and Marianne knew that she was lost. The way to the end of the corridor was blocked by several prisoners, among them, she saw with horror, the two dragoons who had dressed her. All of them seemed united against the newcomer in their midst and determined to give her short shrift. If she escaped la Tricoteuse's knife, she would not escape the clogs of the others. Already, she could see two or three of those closest to her had taken off their wooden shoes and were brandishing them threateningly, ready to batter her to death if she refused to succumb meekly to the knife. One shoe, she noticed, had been filed to a murderously sharp point.

Marianne cast an anguished glance at the staircase but the nun leading the column must by now have been at the bottom. It was all happening with such dreadful speed. In another instant, she would be dead, pointlessly murdered by a gang of semi-lunatics. All these women were strangers to her and yet they seemed to be looking forward to her death as though to a special treat. As la Tricoteuse bore down on her, the knife held high, Marianne gave one terrified scream.

'Help!'

Her cry pierced through the blanket of muffled, whispering voices which surrounded her like a sickening wall of hatred. The knife passed within a hair's-breadth of her head. But her efforts to avoid it brought her close to one of the other prisoners and the raised sabot all but caught her full on the forehead. As it was, she received only a glancing blow on the head and owed it to her cap and the thickness of her hair that she was not stunned. Still there seemed no escape. La Tricoteuse was coming for her again with an idiot giggle that terrified Marianne, while all around her were grinning faces twisted into grotesque masks of bestial cruelty. How could human beings sink so low?

But her cry for help had been heard. Before la Tricoteuse could attack for the third time, the sister-wardress returned, flanked by another bearing a massive cudgel. The circle of viragos was broken up and, thrusting her way through, the nun seized la Tricoteuse by the arm and twisted the knife out of her grasp. Meanwhile, her companion, dealing out some well-timed blows ill-suited to the sanctity of her calling but very much to the credit of her muscles, was getting the other women back into line. Marianne, who had flung herself to the ground for safety, found herself yanked to her feet more quickly than she could have wished. Then, almost immediately, the accusations broke out.

'La Tricoteuse was only defending herself, sister! This little sneak half throttled her!'

'It's not true,' Marianne protested. 'I only slapped her because she kept treading on my heels.'

'Ho, indeed! Dirty liar! You tried to finish us.'

'Then what about the knife?' Marianne cried furiously. 'I suppose that was mine, too!'

'Sure it was!' screeched a tall, thin girl whose unnaturally red cheeks proclaimed consumption. 'It was all she could do to get it away from you!'

These bare-faced falsehoods inflamed Marianne to such a pitch that she forgot even the most elementary rules of caution. These women were like dangerous animals and instinctively she reacted to them as such. She was about to turn and rend the worst of them, while la Tricoteuse snivelled realistically and whined that the *aristo* had tried to kill her, but before she could move she felt herself firmly grasped round the waist and forced to stay where she was.

'That's enough!' the sister's voice said sternly. 'To chapel, everyone! And try and ask God to forgive you. As for you, the new one, Mother Superior will deal with you after mass! We have punishment cells for troublemakers.'

Satisfied with the thought that 'the new one' could pay for all, the prisoners went quietly to their places while Marianne, to her intense fury and indignation, found herself marched after them, held firmly in the sister-wardress's strong grip. She was not released until they reached the big, cold grey chapel where she was safely shut up in one of the small box-like stalls filling the nave, each of which contained room for only one person and commanded a view of nothing but the altar. Each prisoner was locked into one of these contraptions with no communication with any other, thus avoiding the possibility of any disturbance and allowing the nuns to gather peaceably in their appointed places in the choir.

Marianne heard nothing of the mass. She was burning with rebellious indignation, having concluded from the wardress's attitude that she, and she alone, was to be held responsible for what had happened. She forgot even the hideous fear she had endured and was far too angry to have any thought of humbling herself, even to the Almighty, and too certain of the justice of her own cause to ask for help. Ever since that dreadful wedding night, Marianne's ideas of justice, human and divine, had been very well defined. In a world where wrong invariably triumphed, it was necessary to fight tooth and claw in order to survive. Christian resignation had never been her strong point but from now on, she meant to have nothing more to do with it.

'Oh Lord,' was her only prayer, 'don't help those who want to hurt me when I have done no harm to them! If you are really the God of justice, now is the time to show it. Or if not, in a few minutes they will drag me down into some horrid, black dungeon and you alone know when I shall get out.'

Strong in this injunction to the Almighty and determined to defend herself to her last ounce of strength, Marianne admitted to being hustled out of her box, the last of all the prisoners, and, with a sister-wardress on either side of her, led off to see the Mother Superior. Outside a lofty door with peeling chocolate coloured paint, they came to a halt and one of the wardresses knocked.

'Come in,' said a sharp voice which to Marianne boded no good. The door was opened. One of the sisters gave Marianne a gentle push and closed it again behind her. She was then able to discover that although, as the number of holy pictures and objects scattered about the room indicated, she was certainly in the Superior's office, it was no nun she had to deal with. The owner of the sharp voice was a man of medium height and slim build who stood by the window with his hands clasped behind his back.

'Come in,' he said again as Marianne paused at the edge of the big, worn carpet that covered the floor, 'and sit down.'

'I was told I was to see the Mother Superior,' she said with as much confidence as she could muster.

'I am not she, as you have no doubt realized. I trust however, you will have no complaint to make about the change since you appear to have been demanding me all night.'

A wave of gladness brought a sudden flush to the girl's cheeks.

'Oh! You are—'

'The Minister of Police, precisely. And now, since I am here to listen to you, suppose you tell me what you have to say.'

To Marianne, her spirits already lowered by previous events, this, spoken in a harsh, dry voice, seemed an unpromising beginning. There was something about this man in the green coat with a red ribbon which made a complexion the colour of old ivory look paler still, something unbending and self-contained which impressed her. His hatchet face with the thin lips and heavy, drooping eyelids, was a curious mixture of alertness and imperturbability. The chin that rested on the abundant folds of a silk neckcloth was resolute but the expression in the eyes beneath the fringe of grey, almost white hair clustered in short curls about his brow, was quite unreadable. The length of his body and narrowness of his shoulders, which not even admirable tailoring could disguise, gave to his appearance a curious fluidity which was not without its own indefinable charm. And Marianne, whose idea of a policeman was of some kind of half-educated lout, an idea based largely on the novels of Tobias Smollett, decided inwardly that here was a person worthy of the name, one who might well be dangerous but who as an erstwhile revolutionary carried his ducal title with a certain air.

Fouché had begun to stroll slowly up and down the room, his hands still clasped behind his back, waiting to hear the girl's story. When nothing happened, he paused before her, inclining a little forward.

'Well?' he enquired sardonically. 'What have you to say for yourself? You would have had the good sisters chasing through the streets in the middle of the night to find me and now that I am here you can't open your mouth. Must I help you?'

Marianne looked a little fearfully up into his face.

'I should be very glad, if you would not dislike it too much,' she said sincerely. 'I don't know where to begin—'

This innocent avowal extracted a smile from the Minister. He drew up a chair facing the prisoner and sat down.

'Very well. I am willing to admit that to one of your age police interrogations may be something of a novelty. What is your name?'

'Marianne, Anne, Elizabeth d'Asselnat de Villeneuve —'

'So, you are an émigrée. That is serious.'

'I was only a few months old when I was taken to England, after my parents went to the guillotine, to my aunt, who was the only close relative left to me. Does that really make me an émigrée?'

'The least one can say is that you did not become one of your own free will. Go on. Tell me your whole story.'

This time, Marianne did not hesitate at all. Nicolas had advised her to be completely frank with the Duke of Otranto. He himself had given the gist of the situation in his letter but since this letter had been left at the Compas d'Or and might well be lost altogether, it was better to make a complete confession. This she did.

When she finished, she was surprised to see her interrogator put his hand into his pocket and take out a piece of paper which she recognized at once. It was Black Fish's letter. Smiling faintly, Fouché dangled it in his long, slender fingers.

'But—' Marianne almost choked. 'That is my letter! Why did you make me tell it all when you knew already?'

'To see if you would tell the truth. Having read this, young lady, I am entirely satisfied with the examination.'

'Oh,' said Marianne. 'I see. The gendarmes must have searched my room. They found that letter and gave it to you.'

'By no means! It did not occur to them. But don't blame them. No, simpler than that, your baggage was brought to me at the ministry at daybreak this morning by someone who was present at your arrest and appeared to feel strongly about it.'

'Monsieur Bobois! Oh, how good of him! He cannot have understood at all and—'

'Don't jump to conclusions, young woman! Who said anything about Bobois? He would certainly never have contemplated the liberty indulged in by your cavalier. The devilish fellow actually burst into my bedchamber, almost had me out of bed! Admittedly, he felt somewhat responsible for your arrest.'

Marianne's curiosity was not proof against these wholly bewildering observations. Forgetting that she was a prisoner and to whom she was talking, she exclaimed 'For the love of heaven, sir, stop playing at riddles with me. I do not understand a single word of this. Who has spoken for me? Who has taken liberties? Who would have hauled you from your bed?'

Fouché extracted a snuffbox from his waistcoat pocket and took a leisurely pinch before finally observing pleasantly:

'Who? But Surcouf, of course! It takes a Corsair to dare to grapple with a minister.'

'But – I am not acquainted with him!' Marianne said desperately, quite overcome at this reappearance in her life of a stranger who certainly seemed a person of no mean importance.

'No, but you seem to have made some impression on him, the more so in that, so far as I can understand it, it was one of his men who denounced you.'

'That is true. The man escaped from the hulks at Plymouth and shared the crossing – and the shipwreck with me and would never believe that I was not an agent of the prince's.'

Whatever promises she might have made to Black Fish, she refrained from any mention of the episode in the barn, thinking with some justification that it was not a matter for the police.

'There are people like that, with fixed ideas,' Fouché agreed pleasantly. He helped himself to another pinch of snuff and sighed.

'Good. Now, all that remains is for you to give me the verbal message sent by Mallerousse. I hope you still remember it?'

'Word for word! He said: 'The former accomplices of Saint Hilaire, Guillevic, Thomas and La Bonté, have landed in the Morbihan and made their way to Ploermel. The general opinion is that they have come to get the money hidden by Saint Hilaire, but that may not be their real objective.'

As she spoke Marianne saw Fouché begin to frown. He got up and resumed his pacing up and down the room. From the things he was muttering under his breath, she gathered with some anxiety that he was displeased. At last, he said irritably:

'Mallerousse must have great faith in you to trust you with such important information. I tremble to think what might have happened to you on the way.'

'Is it so important?'

The Minister's keen eyes fastened on her as though to sound her very depths.

'Much more than you can have any idea of – and your question shows me that you cannot be in any way connected with the committee in London, or you would know the persons concerned. At all events, I thank you. You may go and get dressed.'

'Get dressed? But where are my clothes? And what for?'

'Your clothes are over there behind that screen. I need not tell you that you are free. But I should prefer your departure from the prison to go unnoticed as far as possible. So get dressed quickly, and come with me. I am going to the Mother Superior now.'

Marianne did not need telling twice. She hurried behind the screen, a big studded leather affair, green with age, and wriggled out of her prison clothes with joyful speed. She had not worn them long, but it had been long enough to give her a lively distaste for them and it was with a great feeling of relief and wellbeing that she slipped back into her soft petticoat, mulberry-coloured dress, warm coat and pretty hat. The shabby room contained nothing in the way of a mirror but Marianne did not care. What mattered was to be herself again as quickly as possible.

When she emerged, fully dressed, she found herself face to face with a large, authoritative-looking woman in a nun's habit whose face, despite the ravages of fat, still showed the remnants of great beauty. The Superior smiled kindly at her former prisoner.

'I am glad you are to stay no longer with us. I fear the time you have spent here can have left you with no pleasant memories.'

'The time was so short, Mother, that the memory will quickly fade.'

A few more courtesies and Marianne found herself out in the passage again with Fouché, following a nun who showed them to a small staircase leading straight down to the entrance where the Minister's carriage waited. The Mother Superior deemed it best that the other prisoners should know nothing of Marianne's departure. They would merely suppose that she had been put in solitary confinement.

'Where are you taking me?' Marianne asked her companion.

'I have not yet decided. You landed on me somewhat out of the blue. I need time to think.'

'Then, if it is all the same to you, please take me where I can get something to eat. I have had nothing since last night and I am dying of hunger!'

Fouché smiled at this youthful appetite.

'I believe it may be possible to feed you. In you get,' he added, putting on his hat as he spoke. A hand, elegantly gloved in pale kid, reached out from the interior of the vehicle to help her up and a deep voice exclaimed: 'Ah! I am glad to see you at liberty again.'

A powerful arm almost lifted Marianne into the carriage and she found herself sitting on velvet cushions facing a smiling man whom she instantly recognized as Baron Surcouf.

The worthy Bobois's sensations of relief at seeing her return escorted by the Minister of Police in person and by his own best customer found their expression in the rapidity with which he set about producing the meal which Surcouf ordered. The morning was far advanced and as it was growing somewhat late for breakfast even at the Compas d'Or, Marianne had just time for some small attention to her appearance before sitting down.

Fouché excused himself, saying he had business at the Ministry but that he would expect Marianne at four o'clock in his house in the quai Voltaire when he would inform her of his decision regarding her future. Meanwhile, Marianne and her new friend sat down to a table spread with a clean white cloth and a variety of dishes calculated to satisfy even the most demanding appetite.

Understanding between Surcouf and Marianne had been instant and complete. There was a vigour about the Corsair's square, leonine face which inspired trust while the steady gaze of his blue eyes compelled honesty. His vivid personality exuded energy, enthusiasm and authority. The landlord and his staff hovered around him, anticipating his slightest whim, as eagerly as if they had been the crew of a ship under his command. As she did ample justice to her breakfast, Marianne reflected that, more than anything else, it showed the change which had taken place in her life. This smiling man was a corsair, the very king of corsairs from what people said, and England had no more formidable and determined enemy. And yet, here she was, she, the one-time mistress of Selton Hall, sitting down and breaking bread with him as though they had known each other all their lives. What would Aunt Ellis have said?

She could not have said herself exactly what she was doing there and why this stranger should have interested himself in her affairs to the extent of pursuing a Minister in his own home. Had he some ulterior motive? The truth was that when Surcouf looked at Marianne his face had the dazzled expression of a child who has been given a particularly lovely toy, eyes full of stars yet hardly daring to touch. He blushed beneath his tan when Marianne smiled at him and if, by chance, her hand touched his on the table, he would draw back awkwardly. Marianne was too much a woman already not to find the game amusing, though it in no way interfered with her enjoyment of master Bobois's excellent cooking.

But sharp as Marianne's appetite was, it could not compare with Surcouf's. Dish after dish vanished with a remorseless regularity that was little short of prodigious. Filled with admiration for such capacity, Marianne waited for a break before putting the question that burned on her lips.

'May I – may I ask what has become of Jean Le Dru?'

'Gone!' Surcouf said laconically.

'What? You have dismissed him? But – what for?'

'Anyone capable of handing over a woman, worse a young girl, into the clutches of the police cannot continue to serve under me. War is a matter for men, Mademoiselle Marianne. It is fought by men, with men's weapons. Laying information is not one of them. There are some things for which even love is no excuse.'

The word sent the colour flooding into Marianne's cheeks.

'Love? Do you believe then—'

'That he loves you? Stands out a mile. He would not seem to hate you so much if he were not mad for you. But, as I say, that does not excuse him in my eyes. Have some of this lettuce, it's delicious.'

Marianne reflected inwardly as she helped herself to salad that this dismissal was unlikely to make Jean Le Dru any more her friend. He must certainly resent it bitterly and his love, if love there was, was almost bound to be transformed into an implacable hatred. She knew, better than anyone, that he could be a dangerous enemy. The prospect of ever coming face to face with him again was uninviting.

The Corsair had stopped eating and was watching her.

'What are you thinking?' he asked.

'About that boy still. What will become of him? You are his god—'

'There are other ships and other men even in St Malo! He can go to my brother Nicolas. Besides, if you think Le Dru worships me, you're mistaken. He has a god, certainly, but it is not myself. It is the Emperor. There is no lack of régime nts to serve him in, under his very eyes even.'

The subject was closed, not to be reopened. Marianne turned the conversation instead to draw out her host to talk about himself. He both attracted and intrigued her. However, it was not easy. Surcouf was a modest man but Marianne had realized that mention of the sea was enough to make him open out. The sea was Surcouf's very life, the air he breathed and the blood in his veins. The reason that he had not set out again immediately on his return from Madagascar was that, instead of commanding only his own vessel, he was now fitting out a regular fleet for the service of France and her master on all the seas of the world. At the age of thirty-six, Surcouf was a rich man, powerful in his own land, a baron of the empire and the father of a growing family.

It seemed odd to Marianne to hear him abusing those 'damned English'. He certainly had no love for them but then, he too had tried the dreadful hulks and, from a child, the mere sight of the Union Jack floating at a masthead had been enough to send him into a fury. But it did not make him blind.

'Nelson was a fine fellow,' he declared, 'a first-rate sailor. But had I commanded the French Fleet instead of that half-wit Villeneuve, we shouldn't have been beaten at Trafalgar and perhaps that one-eyed genius might still be living. However, for his death alone I cannot regard the battle as a total loss. That Englishman was worth a fleet in himself.'

The cup of coffee which concluded the meal finally reconciled Marianne to the idea that life was, after all, worth living. She loved coffee although, until now, she had not drunk very much of it. Aunt Ellis had drunk only tea but the only neighbour with whom she was on any terms, an elderly eccentric called Sir David Trent, indulged in large quantities of coffee. At his house, Marianne had first made the acquaintance of this fragrant beverage, and she adored it. Now, she drained her cup with such evident enjoyment that she was immediately pressed to take another. While she drank it, as slowly as the first, Surcouf watched her closely.

'What will you do now?'

'I do not know. Monsieur Fouché has told me he will make arrangements.'

'The best solution, certainly, will be for you to join the former Empress at Malmaison.'

'*Former*? Has the divorce gone through?'

'Joséphine left the Tuileries five days ago, never to return. She is now at her house at Malmaison with those members of her court who have remained faithful to her. Her daughter, the Queen of Holland, scarcely leaves her side, but I fear you may find yourself in a sad place. From what I hear, they seem to weep a good deal.'

The look on the Corsair's face was enough to demonstrate to his companion his horror of tears.

'I do not fear that,' Marianne said quietly. 'I have little enough for gaiety myself, you see.'

'Fouché will decide. I think he will do what is best for you. I would offer you the hospitality of my house near St Malo where you would be treated with the consideration that is your due but your beauty is such that I fear –'

He became suddenly very red and busied himself with pouring out more coffee leaving the sentence unfinished Marianne understood. The baron's wife might not be overjoyed at her husband's inviting a young girl of her age into his house. But she did not take offence. Rather she was amused by her companion's embarrassment. It was funny to see this man of action caught between his desire to be of use to her and fear of being scolded by his wife. But she hastened to reassure him.

'Thank you. It is good of you to wish to offer me a roof, but I should, in any case, prefer to remain in Paris where I still have some family.'

He sighed, clearly showing his disappointment at being unable to take her with him, and could not help adding softly: 'A pity. It would have made me very happy –'

Then, as though ashamed of what he had said, he began shouting that the coffee was cold, making the honest Bobois pay for the relief of his feelings.

When the time came to go to the Ministry of Police, Surcouf called her a cab. Once inside, Marianne saw to her surprise that her travelling bag had been placed there also. Deciding that Fouché must have given instructions to the landlord, she refrained from asking any further questions.

The cab moved off slowly on account of the almost permanent traffic block in the rue MMontorgueil. It was used by the market gardeners returning from les Halles with their empty carts and stacks of empty baskets on their way home to Saint Denis or Argentueil. The street was clamorous with men shouting and calling to one another to have a drink before setting out. Outside the Rocher de Cancale, were only two or three carriages. The restaurant's busiest time was in the evening. But in the midst of all this activity, Marianne, looking eagerly out of the window, caught sight of one face, a figure quickly lost in the crowd, and drew back instinctively into her corner. Why should Jean Le Dru be lurking there? What was he doing in this street at all? Was he hoping for an opportunity to restore himself to Surcouf's good graces – or was his object Marianne herself? The brooding anger in the eyes that met hers told her all she needed to know. Jean Le Dru was her bitter enemy. She turned and looked the other way, trying to throw off the disagreeable feeling this gave her. Surcouf was occupied with watching her and noticed nothing.

Police headquarters in the quai Malaquais was a handsome seventeenth century mansion whose lawful owners, the Juigné family, had been dispossessed at the time of the Revolution. Since then, it had endured many vicissitudes. The Commissions for arms and ammunition and that for education, housed successively within its walls, had done nothing to improve it. Since 1796, Citizen Joseph Fouché, later Monsieur Fouché and later still his grace the Duke of Otranto, had made it the focus of his home and offices, but the minister was a man of simple tastes, at least so far as his residence in Paris was concerned. He preferred to keep his splendours for his magnificent country house at Ferrières. Consequently, the Hôtel de Juigné had not had so much as a wash from him and the patina of age lay heavily on its venerable walls.

If the domestic apartment ruled over by Bonne-Jeanne, the plain and uncompromising Madame Fouché, and the chief reception rooms still retained something of their splendour, this was a tribute to the quality of their original decoration and the housewifely virtues of the mistress of the establishment, since Fouché saw no reason to spend good money on his ministry.

This ministry was a world in itself. The maze of offices, crammed with files and card indexes presided over by a race of overworked clerks, extended at the back from the rue des Augustins[5] to the rue des Saints Pères, joined to the ministry itself by covered wooden passages. The place was filled with a strange and motley assortment of people, and with a mixture of smells that ran the gamut from the expensive perfume of the woman of fashion to the more plebeian effluvia of informers and police spies of all

---

[5] The present Rue Bonaparte

kinds.

When Marianne, still dazed from her short drive across Paris, found herself plunged into this unlikely setting, she was glad of Surcouf's strong arm and reassuringly broad shoulders. With him beside her, she felt better able to confront the shifty glances and startling appearance of some of those who came and went round the many corners of the Hôtel de Juigné. They had, in fact, been obliged to enter the building by a side entrance in the rue des Pères. Marianne's cab had to take another way round because the quai Malaquais was hopelessly jammed by a crowd of vehicles of all descriptions struggling in and out of the forecourt of a large private house directly opposite the ministry.

'Big party at Princess d'Aremberg's!' the coachman growled. 'Have to go round the other way —'

Because of this, Marianne was able to get a general impression of the minister's lair, and it was by no means an agreeable one. There was a dusty, hole and corner smell about it, and she was glad when they came to the ministerial antechamber which was presided over by an usher in plain livery. This lofty personage regarded Marianne with an impassive eye.

'His grace is expecting Mam'zelle Mallerousse,' he announced, 'but no one else.'

'And what may that mean?' the Corsair exclaimed with quick annoyance.

'That my orders are to admit the young lady, and the young lady alone.'

'Indeed? We shall see!'

Taking Marianne firmly by the arm, Surcouf flung open the double doors guarding Fouché's office.

It was a small room, its simplicity in strong contrast to the importance of its occupant. The only furniture was an enormous desk, cluttered with documents and files, three or four straight backed chairs and a cupboard. Fouché himself was sitting, sipping from a cup of some infusion just handed to him by a servant. Beside him was a crowned bust, representing, or so Marianne assumed, some Roman Emperor. He jumped at Surcouf's entry.

'I wasn't to be let in, it seems, citizen minister,' the Corsair grumbled loudly leading Marianne to one of the unprepossessing chairs. 'Care to tell my why?'

Fouché choked, spilling his scalding tisane over his fingers. It was several moments before he was able to speak. While the servant hastened to mop him down, he pushed the cup irritably from him.

'For the love of heaven, my dear baron, when will you lose this detestable habit of bursting in on people like a tidal wave?'

'When people learn to treat me with courtesy! Why did you see fit to deny me entry?'

'But I have not denied you entry. I was expecting Mademoiselle

Mallerousse and I gave orders accordingly. I had no idea you would escort her here. Do I take it you've turned nursery maid?'

'By no means, but when I undertake something, I see it through. I want to know what you are going to do with her. And I shall not go away until I do.'

With that, demonstrating his firm resolve to miss nothing of what was to come, Surcouf sat down on another of the hard chairs, folded his hands on top of his cane and waited. Marianne repressed a smile. The man was irresistible! And, certainly a great comfort. One could follow him to the ends of the earth with absolute confidence. Fouché, however, sighed elaborately.

'Anyone would think I was some kind of ogre! What do you think I'm going to do? Send her back to St. Lazare? Shut her up in a convent or send her off as a camp follower with the Guard? Can't you trust me just a little?'

Surcouf said nothing but his expression left his trustfulness in some doubt. Fouché raised one eyebrow, took a pinch of snuff and then continued silkily:

'Have you anything against the Duchess of Otranto? I would remind you that having four children of her own, my wife is a perfectly proper person to have the care of a young woman. For, to cut a long story short, I intend to give our young friend who comes to me with a strong recommendation of an old comrade of my own, into her charge. Are you satisfied?'

Whether he was or not, the Corsair said nothing but Marianne repressed a look of distaste. The idea of living in this house with its police court atmosphere did not appeal to her at all, especially since, apart from Black Fish's recommendation, she could not understand why Fouché should show such interest in her. Perhaps she was being highly honoured and no doubt she should be very grateful but this was not what she had come to Paris for.

'I thought,' she began timidly, 'that I might go to live with my cousin d'Asselnat—'

'And even last week, that might have been possible. Unfortunately, since then, your cousin has brought some trouble on herself. She is no longer in a position to take care of you.'

'What does that mean?'

'That she set out five days ago for Auvergne where she will remain under house arrest. Before that, I may add, she had been for three days a guest of the police in the Madelonettes prison.'

'In prison? My cousin?' Marianne exclaimed, startled that fate should apparently be leading all the last bearers of her name into dungeons. 'But what for?'

'For throwing a letter reflecting upon the conduct of the Emperor's private life into his majesty's carriage. Considering the somewhat violent tenor of this missive, we deemed it best, for her good as much as for our own, that Mademoiselle Adélaïde should be sent to recover her temper in the peace of the countryside.'

'Then, I will join her there!' Marianne announced firmly.

'I should not advise it. Do not forget that you are at present, under your real name, an émigrée entering the country illegally and therefore subject to severe penalties. It is best that you should remain Mademoiselle Mallerousse – and so quite unconnected with your cousin. Moreover, her opinions are not such as I would wish you, for your own safety, to share.'

With this, Fouché appeared to consider the subject closed. Turning to Surcouf, who had been awaiting the end of this dialogue with furrowed brow, he gave him his most attractive smile.

'I think, my dear baron,' he purred, 'that you may now make your farewells to our young friend before I present her to the duchess.'

But Surcouf did not budge from his chair.

'So the cousin's in disfavour, very well,' he said distinctly, 'but there is another member of the family. You have not, I think, placed the Empress under arrest?'

'Poor soul!' Fouché's sigh told the extent of his compassion for Joséphine. 'I did think of her, but to be honest with you, the reports I am receiving from Malmaison are not encouraging. The poor Empress weeps day and night and will receive no one but her particular friends. She is really in no state to be burdened with anyone else, especially a distant connection she has never seen. I believe we must let a little time elapse. Later, when her majesty is more herself, I shall certainly inform her. Until then, mademoiselle Marianne must be content with our protection –'

Fouché rose, seeming to indicate that the interview was at an end, but continued to forage among the papers on his desk. He soon found the letter he was looking for and, after a glance at its contents, he remarked:

'In any case, my dear baron, I think that your own stay in Paris will not be prolonged. You will be anxious to return to St Malo. I have here a report of a pretty feat carried out by one of your men. Gauthier, captain of the *Hirondelle*, has been to Guernsey and recovered your brig the *Incomparable*, captured in November, from under the very noses of the English.'

'Is that true?'

This time, Surcouf was on his feet in an instant, his eyes shining with joy. His face was flushed and the suspicion which could have been read openly on it a moment before had vanished as by a miracle. Marianne thought, a little sadly, that he was looking at the minister as if he were a messenger from heaven, and that she herself was almost forgotten. But, to a sailor, what was the passing attraction he had felt for her compared to what was the very essence of his soul, his ship and his men? Already, he was picking up the hat he had placed on the cupboard.

'I'll take the night mail! Thank you, my dear minister. You have given me the best possible news. It remains only for me to bid you farewell —' He turned to Marianne and bowed. 'And you also, mademoiselle,' he said in a soft voice. 'I leave you in good hands and wish you the very best of luck. Do not forget me!'

He was going away, he was leaving Paris, leaving her in this disagreeable place! A little bitterness crept over Marianne. She discovered that she had grown used, astonishingly quickly, to this solid, reassuring and utterly reliable friend. Perhaps because he reminded her of Black Fish. Now, he was going back to his own affairs, leaving her to her fate, and tomorrow, perhaps sooner, he would have forgotten her completely. She realized, instinctively, that this man was a rare beast. There was a scent about him of fresh air, freedom, of *joie de vivre*, while when she looked at Fouché's pale, narrow face she found herself thinking, she could not have said why, of dimly lit chapels, whispering voices, the reek of incense and secret confidences. Later, learning that Fouché had been destined for the church and educated at the Oratory in Nantes, she would recall this impression and understand it better.

Forcing back the disappointed tears, she held out both hands in a spontaneous gesture to the friend who was leaving her.

'Thank you for everything! And write to me, please.'

He gave her a quick smile and caught her outstretched hands in a grip that almost made her cry out.

'I promise! Only, you must forgive me if I write badly. I am no man of letters but, for your sake, I would do things still more difficult. If you are ever in need of anything, call on me. I will come running.'

Dropping a quick kiss on Marianne's suddenly icy fingers, he picked up his cane and left the room without a backward glance. Fouché's eyes followed him inscrutably. As the door closed behind him, the minister sighed.

'Well, there is pure, disinterested devotion for you. I congratulate you. Surcouf is a big fish and by no means an easy one to unhook. I thought I should never manage to get him away from you. But, now that it is done at last, we can have a serious talk, you and I.'

'Were we not talking seriously before?'

'Yes and no —'

As he spoke, Fouché rang a small bell on his desk. A little, yellow-complexioned, hollow chested man all dressed in black came in, bearing a portfolio under his arm, and murmured something in the minister's ear. This was Maillocheau, his secretary.

'Very well,' Fouché said. 'Take him in the other way. I'll come at once.'

With a courteous apology for the fact that he was obliged to desert his visitor for a few moments, Fouché stepped into an adjoining room, leaving the door sufficiently wide open for Marianne to see something of the room beyond. It was a small room, simply furnished, and at first Marianne gave little attention to it. She had no particular interest in Fouché's sudden visitor, assuming it to be some police matter. A criminal to interrogate, perhaps. Yes, for she heard dragging footsteps and also the clink of chains. The man must be in fetters. Marianne shivered and made an effort to turn her eyes away from the door and look at the window. But Fouché was speaking and what he said soon forced itself on the girl's attention.

'You are the Baron Hervé de Keriovas, are you not?'

'I am.'

'You are also a Chouan known by the name of Morvan. Your manor in Brittany has been used before now as a link between the insurgents and the committee in London. More recently, you have sheltered Armand de Châteaubriant—'

There was no answer. The man was maintaining an obstinate silence. But Marianne had risen and gone quietly to the door. Two steps were enough to show her the prisoner standing full in the light. The figure was certainly Morvan's although this time it was moulded by green coat and light grey kerseymere pantaloons tucked into top boots. But now, for the first time, she saw his face.

It was a dreadful sight, disfigured all down one side by a great scar that made a ruin of one cheek, dragged at the eye and disappeared into the hair that Marianne now saw to her surprise was short, fair and curly. The dark lovelocks she remembered must have been a wig. Only the unnatural brilliance of his eyes and the strong, mocking lines of his mouth did she recognize the man who had held her captive.

Morvan seemed perfectly at ease. He stood before Fouché, his fettered wrists held before him, contemplating his interrogator with an air of utter boredom, as though he were merely obliged to be present at some scene which did not concern him.

Fouché continued. 'It is not, however, for your activities as a Chouan that you have been arrested and taken to Vincennes where you have been, I believe, for four days now.'

Morvan bowed in silence.

'Information has been laid to the effect that you are the leader of the band of wreckers operating in that region. Have you anything to say?'

Still no answer. Morvan merely shrugged. The silence that followed weighed heavily on Marianne. Outside, a carriage rumbled along the quai but she scarcely heard it. She was looking at the wrecker's ravaged face, amazed to see the pride in it. Morvan seemed to her a nobler figure standing there, with fettered hands, flanked by the two gendarmes than in his black mask on the shore amid the raging storm. Again, came the minister's chill voice.

'You prefer to say nothing? As you like. Take him away. The magistrates may get something out of him.'

Marianne did not see Morvan go. She had only just time to regain her seat before Fouché came back into the room and shut the door behind him. He took snuff leisurely. Marianne, struggling to appear calm, was uncomfortably conscious of his eyes resting heavily on her, yet she dared not meet his gaze. Ever since Surcouf had left the room she had felt alone and defenceless. The sight of Morvan had completed her sense of bewilderment. She heard Fouché say:

'Good. Now we are alone. First, let me restore these to you.'

His hand felt for a moment in one of the drawers of his desk and emerged holding something glittering which he placed on the table. To her amazement, Marianne saw her pearl necklace and the locket containing the Queen's hair.

She made no move to take them, only stared at them in silence. Fouché laughed.

'Wake up! They are yours, aren't they?'

'Yes – but – how did you get them?'

'Off the gentleman you saw in there between the two gendarmes. You did see him, I suppose? I had him out of his cell at Vincennes on purpose to let you see him. I was well aware I should get nothing out of him. He will, I may say, not be going back to Vincennes.'

'Why not?'

'Because on the way back he is going to escape – with some little assistance on our part.'

This time, Marianne was utterly at a loss. Fouché's face was half hidden from her by the gathering dusk but she could feel his eyes on her and knew he was smiling. His smile only added to the fear that was mounting in her and when she spoke it was in a voice devoid of colour.

'You are going to let him escape? That wrecker? But why?'

'Because he is more use to me free. It would, by the by, be best for you to avoid an encounter with him. He believes he owes his arrest to a young woman sent from London by the royalist committee –'

Marianne felt the colour drain from her face. Fouché gave her a moment or two to assimilate this information before adding smoothly:

'I should not let it worry you too much. You have nothing to fear while I'm here. I know everything – and nothing is impossible for me. You will be quite safe, provided you are careful – and do exactly as I tell you.'

The last words were spoken very slowly and distinctly and now, at last, Marianne understood. Her fate, her future and her very life were in the hands of this cold, pale man; beneath his kindly manner, he was playing with her as a cat plays with a mouse. She cast one anguished glance towards the door. It was shut and Surcouf had gone. She was alone, more alone even than she had been in her prison cell in St. Lazare. A servant came in to light the candles on the desk and a golden light sprang up in the lofty room, softening the heavy green curtains. Marianne knew that she was helpless. She had no choice but to do as this man willed because she could not resume her own identity without exposing herself to the penalties of the law, or try to escape without the risk of coming face to face with either Jean Le Dru or Morvan, two men who were her deadly enemies. The trap had been well sprung! She understood now what it was to be a great policeman, it meant someone completely unscrupulous.

She felt suddenly tired and almost cold. She put a trembling hand up to her eyes in a pathetic, childish gesture as though to brush away a veil of mist that obscured her sight. Fouché's voice came to her from an immense distance.

'Come now! Don't upset yourself. Whatever you may imagine, I wish you no harm. Merely, I need someone like you.'

'Politics is a tricky business, full of traps for the unwary. By trusting you with a message of such importance, Nicolas involved you, perhaps without being fully aware of it. You are just the person I need and you have within you all you need to win your battle with life. Listen to me. Do as I say and I promise you that you will not only have nothing more to fear from the law in England, but will also rise to the most enviable position. Here, fortunes are made and lost very quickly. Will you serve me and try your luck?'

There was a hypnotic quality in Fouché's voice which both allayed Marianne's physical terror and, at the same time, chilled something within her. There was no mistaking the real meaning to his words. It was blackmail, pure and simple. Either she did as Fouché wished, and she was well aware that he had only helped and comforted her in order the better to bend her to his will, or she could reject his proposals and perhaps find herself abandoned to the snares and dangers of these unknown streets. Unless, of course, she was simply sent straight back to St. Lazare to heaven knew what fate! In any case her choice was very limited. She could hardly go on plunging blithely forward to a fate she could not even guess. Perhaps, after all, it might be best to let herself be guided by this man who, dangerous as she guessed him to be, was still the person to whom Black Fish had sent her. There remained to be discovered precisely what it was he wanted of her.

Marianne looked up. Her green eyes sparkled through a veil of tears as she met the minister's opaque gaze.

'What must I do?'

Fouché leaned back in his chair, placed his fingertips together and crossed his thin legs.

'I told our friend Surcouf that I meant to entrust you to my wife's keeping merely in order to get rid of him. In fact, I have already found you a situation.'

'A situation? Where?'

'With the Prince of Benevento otherwise vice-grand-elector of the Empire, Charles-Maurice de Talleyrand-Périgord. His wife has need of a reader – and his house is one of the greatest in Paris, perhaps the greatest. For me, at any rate. You cannot conceive how much I like to know of what goes on in such houses.'

Marianne's cheeks flushed with anger and she sprang to her feet, trembling.

'A spy! No, indeed! I will never stoop to that!' Fouché appeared quite unaffected by her excitement. Without even looking at her, he jotted something down on a piece of paper then picked up a spoon from a small silver-gilt tray on which was also a carafe and a glass. He tipped some white powder from a small envelope into the spoon and swallowed it, with a mouthful of water. Then he coughed.

'Ahem! It is up to you, child. I have no wish to force your hand but you should remember, I think, that if St. Lazare is no very agreeable dwelling place for a young girl, the English prisons are on the whole rather worse – especially when there is a noose at the end.'

The words fell as inexorably as a sentence.

Marianne sat down again, feeling as though her legs had been cut from under her.

'You would not do that?' she murmured in a choked voice.

'What? Hand you over to the English police? No. But, just supposing Mademoiselle Mallerousse were unwise enough to behave as though she were Mademoiselle d'Asselnat, I should have no choice but to carry out the law. Now, the law gives me two alternatives: to imprison you or to put you back on a boat –'

Marianne pointed silently to the carafe.

'A little water, if you please –'

As she sipped it, she forced herself to think. Fouché had put his cards on the table and she realized that it was useless to hope that he might change his mind. Her best course was to agree, or appear to agree. Afterwards she could try and escape. But where to? She had no idea as yet but it would be time to think of that later, at more leisure. Meanwhile, first things first. At all events, she did not intend to give in without an argument. Putting the glass back on the tray, she said loftily:

'You offer me a situation as a reader? It is not very grand. I am more ambitious.'

'Princess Talleyrand's last reader was a countess fallen on hard times. You cannot expect me to do better than offer you the best house in Paris. But if you prefer to be a scullery maid –'

'I am not amused. Let me remind you that I have no talent for the – the profession you propose, that it is altogether strange to me. I do not even know what I shall have to do.'

'Listen. Keep your ears open and make a note of everything you hear, absolutely everything.'

'I cannot go about with notes in my hand —'

'Don't play the fool with me!' Fouché snapped. 'Your memory is perfect. I saw that from the way you repeated Nicolas's message. Moreover, you speak several languages. That is a valuable asset in the house of a diplomat – even one in disgrace.'

'What do you mean?'

'That the Prince of Benevento is out of favour with the Emperor. He is no longer Minister of Foreign Affairs and his title of vice-grand-elector is no more than a high-sounding sinecure. But that only makes Talleyrand more dangerous. He has vast contacts, formidable intelligence – and —'

' — and you are his enemy!'

'I? No, you mistake me! We have been enemies in the past. But that is ancient history and in politics one forgets quickly. For some time now, we have been the best of friends, do not forget that. But that does not mean I would not like to know the little day to day details in the rue de Varennes. As the princess's reader, you will be present at all large gatherings, you will live in the midst of the household. As I have said, all you will have to do is keep a kind of journal. Every night, before going to bed, you will write a little report on the day.'

'And how will it reach you?'

'Don't worry about that. Each morning, a servant will come into your room to light the fire. He will say: "I hope this wood will burn well". You will give him your report. He will see that it reaches me.'

'How will you know it is mine? Should I sign my name?'

'Certainly not. You will sign it, let me see – yes, with a star like this.'

Fouché drew a quick sketch of a six-pointed star on a piece of paper.

'There! That shall be your emblem – and your name. Here, you will draw the star. That will provide a cover for your real identity. For you will have to take care not to arouse any suspicions in the master of the house. He is perhaps the most intelligent man in Europe. Certainly, the most artful! I would not give much for your chances should he unmask you. So, you have every reason to take care. And, let me say again, that you will not regret working with me. I can reward good service – royally!'

The atmosphere of the office was beginning to weigh on Marianne. She was tired and her head was aching. Exhaustion was taking its own toll. She had slept little on her truckle bed in St. Lazare. She rose and going to the window pulled aside the curtain and stood looking out. It was quite dark now but two lanterns burned in the courtyard, revealing the figures of the sentries. Everywhere was strangely quiet. The river Seine glimmered faintly beyond the curtain of trees. From somewhere, came the muffled sound of a harp. The notes came a little discordantly, as though the hands on the strings were clumsy and inexperienced, but this only added to the air of unreality belonging to this evening.

'I must escape!' she thought desperately. 'I must escape -- I must get away to Auvergne, to find my cousin. But, for the present, I can do nothing except obey.' Aloud, she sighed, 'I hope you will not be disappointed. I know no one here. How can I know what will interest you?'

Fouché, too, rose and came to stand behind her. She saw his reflection in the glass and smelled the faint odour of snuff which hung about him. When he spoke, his voice was kind and reassuring.

'That is for me to judge. I have need of a fresh eye, of unprejudiced ears. You know nothing and therefore, since you will not know what is important, you will have no temptation to hide anything. Come, now, we will go up and see my wife. What you need is a good supper and a good bed. Tomorrow, I will tell you all you need to know if you are to move safely in your new environment.'

Marianne only nodded, defeated but not resigned. As she followed her persecutor up the narrow private staircase leading from the next room which connected the office with the duchess's apartment, she was thinking already that she would take the first opportunity that offered to run away from this house where she was being sent. After that the choice would be hers. She could either throw herself at the feet of the divorced Empress and beg for her protection, or she could take the first diligence into Auvergne to find her cousin, even if she did turn out to be mad. Better a well-disposed mad woman than an over-intelligent man. Marianne was beginning to feel a hearty dislike for the world of men. It was a selfish, ruthless and cruel world. Woe to her who tried to fight it.

CHAPTER NINE
The Ladies of the Hôtel Matignon

As she followed the imposing servant in white wig and livery of mulberry and grey up the great white marble staircase, Marianne looked dazedly about her and wondered if she had not been brought to some royal palace by mistake. Never, in all her life, had she seen a house like this. It left the ponderous magnificence of Selton Hall far behind, and seemed stern, almost rustic in comparison with the light, graceful elegance of eighteenth-century France.

Here, it was all tall mirrors, delicate, gilded scroll work, pale, heavy silks, exquisite Chinese porcelain and thick carpets, softer than smooth lawns underfoot. Outside, the dismal, grey December rain was still deluging Paris persistently. But in here one could forget the dreadful weather. It was as though the house had its own private source of light. And how pleasantly warm it was.

They mounted the stairs slowly, with the dignity befitting a noble household. Marianne's eyes riveted themselves on the solemn workings of the servant's large white calves but her mind was busy going over Fouché's last advice. Now and then, her hand went to her reticule to feel the letter he had given her, a letter written by a woman whom she had never seen but who had written a most moving letter to her dear friend the Princess of Benevento, praising her young friend Marianne Mallerousse's talent as a reader in the most affecting terms. This seemed to be just one example of the magic that could be worked by a Minister of Police.

You will be sure of a welcome, Fouché had told her. The Countess Sainte-Croix is an old friend of Madame de Talleyrand. They have known one another since the days when she was still Madame Grand with a reputation somewhat less – er, impeccable than it is today. Indeed, your own birth is considerably higher than that of the princess who, however, now bears one of the greatest names in France. This was said no doubt to reassure her. But it did not prevent Marianne from feeling an icy prickle of sweat run down her spine as the great doors, bearing above them the legend *Hôtel de Matignon*, swung open to reveal the vast forecourt, surrounded by elegant buildings. The army of lackeys in powdered wigs and maid servants in starched caps of whom she caught glimpses, did not improve matters. Marianne felt as though she had been thrust, quite alone and wearing an unconvincing false nose, into the midst of a human sea with snares and ambushes lying in wait on all sides. It seemed to her that everyone must be able to read on her face what she had come to do.

A wave of moist, scented air hit her in the face. Roused from her thoughts, Marianne became aware that the large, purple lackey had given way to a lady's maid in a pink and grey striped dress and lace cap and that she had been introduced into an elegant bathroom with windows giving on to extensive gardens.

A great cloud of fragrant steam was rising from an enormous bath, like a sarcophagus of pink marble, with solid gold taps in the shape of swans' necks. Emerging from the steam, was a woman's head, enveloped in an immense turban and resting on a cushion. Two lady's maids glided like shadows about the exquisite mosaic floor representing the Rape of Europa, bearing armfuls of linen and an assortment of vessels. The walls were lined with mirrors which multiplied to infinity the slender, pink marble columns supporting the ceiling with its painted design of cupids and scenes from mythology. In a corner, beside an enormous vase of flowers standing on the floor itself, a small day-bed upholstered in the same gold shot taffeta as the curtains, awaited the bather. Marianne felt as though she had been suddenly transported inside a large pale pink shell but, in her walking dress, she was instantly far too hot.

She blinked at the extravagance and unaccustomed luxury. Nothing could have been less like the small and primitive toilet arrangements of Madame Fouché.

The woman in the turban, whose face was invisible under a thick mask of greenish jelly, said something Marianne did not catch and pointed languidly to a low stool. Marianne sat down nervously.

'Her highness the princess begs you to wait a moment,' one of the maids said in a whisper. 'She will not be long.'

Marianne turned her eyes away modestly while the waiting women fussed about the bath tub with a great white linen bath sheet and countless small towels. A few moments later, minus her herbal mask and wrapped in a dressing gown of white satin deeply frilled with lace, Madame de Talleyrand came to meet Marianne.

'You must be the young person Madame Sainte-Croix was speaking about last evening? Have you her letter?'

With a little curtsey, Marianne held out the paper sealed with green wax that Fouché had given her. The princess opened it and began to read while Marianne studied her new mistress curiously. Fouché, in describing the wife of the former bishop of Autun, had revealed her age, which was forty-seven. But there was no denying that she did not look it. Catherine de Talleyrand-Périgord was still a very beautiful woman. Tall and Junoesque, with wide, artless blue eyes under thick dark lashes, a mass of warm gold, naturally curly hair, plump lips, parted to show small perfect teeth, a prettily arched nose and charming smile, she had everything a woman could ask for, in a physical sense at least, for her mind was by no means equal to her looks. Without being as stupid as her numerous rivals claimed, she had a kind of naivety which, joined to great depths of vanity, made her an easy target for ill-natured criticism. If she had not been so lovely, no one would have understood why Talleyrand, the most subtle and accomplished man of his time, should have burdened himself with her and there were few women in Paris more derided. Napoleon himself openly detested her and her husband, tired of her childish prattle, barely spoke to her, although this did not prevent him making quite sure that she was treated with proper respect.

The princess's reading of the letter and Marianne's examination of her finished at the same time. The princess glanced up at the girl and smiled.

'I am told that you are of good family, although not bearing a noble name, and that you have received an excellent education. Madame Sainte-Croix says that you read well, sing and speak several languages. Altogether, you must certainly do credit to my house. I can see for myself that you are pretty and have considerable natural elegance, I am pleased to say. Your duties here will be very light. I read little but I am fond of music. You will generally bear me company but, when we are together, you will take care to keep always five paces behind me. My name and rank are of the highest and I make it a point to insist on proper respect.'

'Very natural, I am sure.' Marianne smiled, amused by the innocent anarchy of this speech. Fouché had not exaggerated.

Madame de Talleyrand might be an excellent creature but she was inordinately proud of being a princess.

'You may go now,' the princess told her graciously. 'I will send for you later. My maid, Fanny, will show you your room.'

Marianne was dismissed with an aristocratic wave of her hand, but the haughtiness of the gesture was softened by the kindness of the smile that accompanied it. Marianne decided that the princess seemed on the whole good natured as well as pretty and this only added to her discomfort. If Madame de Talleyrand could only have guessed what the person she welcomed so readily had come to do! No, Marianne felt that she was by no means suited to her employment and, if she could not manage to make her escape as quickly as she should like, she would take care to say as little as possible to her dangerous employer, if anything at all. She was about to withdraw when the princess called her back.

'Wait, child! I must have some idea of your wardrobe. We have company to dine four times a week and entertain most evenings, to say nothing of the Christmas festivities that will soon be on us. I cannot tolerate anything unsuitable in your appearance.' Marianne blushed. The neat clothes she had bought in Brest with the help of Madame de Guilvinec had seemed to her very elegant until today, but, since setting foot in this princely mansion, she had been conscious that she must look very simple.

'I have what I'm wearing, your highness, and two other dresses, one of black velvet, the other green wool —'

'That will not do at all! Especially since the one you are wearing makes you look as though you were dressed in the livery of the house, which is the same colour. Come with me to my bedroom.'

Leaning on the arm of Marianne, who was both amused and embarrassed by this sudden familiarity, the princess swept majestically into a vast chamber adjoining the bathroom. Here, as in the temple of beauty next door, all was pink and gold and the swan reigned supreme, in gilded bronze, on the arms of the chairs and in allegorical paintings. A handsome canopied bed shared pride of place with an enormous cheval mirror flanked by a pair of gilded lamp brackets. All else was buried under an endless sea of open or closed boxes of all sizes and every conceivable colour. Among them, four people stood to attention. Three were women, the first two evidently shopkeeper's assistants, the third a massive female compressed into a garment of apple green quilting with gold frogs, and crowned with a towering edifice of green taffeta and white Mechlin lace.

The fourth person was a chubby little man, rather like a perky sparrow, though at present his chest was puffed out like a pouter pigeon with his own importance. His face was rouged and powdered and he wore an elaborately curled wig that was clearly meant to increase his height. His bow at the princess's entrance would have done no discredit to a dancing master and his capers appeared to Marianne irresistibly funny. The princess, however, instantly released her hold on Marianne's arm and descended on the ludicrous little creature with outstretched hands.

'Ah, my dear, dear Leroy! You have come! And in this appalling weather! How can I ever thank you.'

'I could not fail to deliver your highness's gowns for the Christmas season in person – and I can confidently say we have performed miracles.'

With the air of a conjurer producing rabbits out of a hat, he drew from the various boxes a succession of dazzling gowns, cashmere shawls, scarfs and sashes, while the large green lady, who was none other than Mademoiselle Minette, famous as the purveyor of exquisite lingerie, released a cascade of gossamer shifts, embroidered and lace-trimmed underskirts, veils and the rest. Suddenly, Marianne forgot her private griefs and found

164

herself enjoying this refreshingly frivolous scene with wholly feminine pleasure. Besides, the little Leroy was really very funny.

For a while, Madame de Talleyrand forgot her new reader in overwhelming the little man in a quite incredible flood of compliments and civilities, compliments that were very well deserved because the contents of the boxes were marvellous indeed. Gazing in open-eyed wonderment, Marianne forgot the absurdity of his person. Ignorant as yet that the little man was in fact the great Leroy, couturier to the Empress herself, and whose creations were sought avidly by the entire court and even by the whole of Napoleonic Europe, she was amazed that such a person should be capable of creating these fragile works of art. There was one dress in particular, of almond green satin oversown with crystal drops in strange, underwater patterns, that dazzled her utterly. It seemed to shimmer all over, as though with dew, and Marianne found herself dreaming of how wonderful it would be if she were one day to own such a dress. She was just putting out a timid hand to touch the shimmering stuff when she was startled by a loud indignant exclamation from the couturier.

'Her highness wishes me to dress her reader? Me? Leroy? Oh – I'd die!'

Before Marianne had time to feel wounded by the little man's protests, peremptory hands had swung her round on her heels, her bonnet strings were untied and the bonnet itself sent flying into a corner. The young lady assistants hurried to the rescue and whipped off her coat, while Madame de Talleyrand expostulated with an indignation at least equal to Leroy's:

'She is *my* reader, Leroy. And so worth quite as much as all your twopenny duchesses and countesses! Only look at her! I mean to see this beauty properly displayed. It will serve to set off my own.'

There was a thoughtfulness in the couturier's Olympian eye as he came and stood before Marianne. He studied her from all angles, walking slowly round her as though observing a monument.

'Take off that frightful dress!' he commanded finally. 'It positively reeks of the provinces.'

Before she could utter so much as a gasp, Marianne found herself standing in her shift and petticoat. Instinctively, she brought up her arms to cover her breast but let them fall again at a sharp tap from Leroy.

'When one has a bosom like yours, mam'zelle, not merely does one not hide it, one displays it, one sets it like a rich jewel! Her highness is right. You are ravishing, even though unfinished as yet. But I can predict that you will be more than beautiful – such a figure! Such hair! Such legs! Ah, the legs, in the present fashion the legs are everything. The gowns reveal them in a way that is almost indiscreet – which reminds me,' turning to the princess, 'has your highness heard? The marquise Visconti, believing her thighs somewhat too well-developed, has got Coutaud to make her a pair of laced stays which she wears one on each leg like corsets! Too absurd! Everyone will think she has wooden legs! But there, she is the most obstinate woman of my acquaintance.'

The princess and the couturier embarked on an exchange of gossip while Mam'zelle Minette shook out a wrap trimmed with broderie anglaise and narrow lavender blue ribbon and laid it over her armchair. But, though he chattered on, Leroy was by no means idle. He took careful note of Marianne's measurements and in the interval of a particularly scandalous story, called out the figures to one of his assistants who copied them gravely into a note book. When it was done and Marianne was still dazed by his flow of words, he told her sharply to get dressed and then asked:

'What should I make for mademoiselle?'

'A complete wardrobe – and you too, Mademoiselle Minette. She has nothing! And I would have something sent round for this evening. There will be a dinner and an evening party.'

Leroy raised his arms to heaven.

'This evening? But it is quite impossible!'

'I thought there was no such word in your vocabulary, Leroy.'

'No, indeed, in the general way, your highness. But if your highness would care to remember, I am overwhelmed with orders and –'

'I want a dress this evening.'

For a moment, it seemed to Marianne that the couturier would burst into tears but then one of the young ladies bent forward and murmured something into his ear. His face cleared.

'Ah! Perhaps! Mam'zelle Palmyre reminds me that we have one little white dress, simple but utterly charming, that has been ordered by her grace the Duchess of Rovigo but which perhaps –'

'Have the white dress sent round,' the princess ordered without more ado. 'I hope you would not hesitate between that woman and myself! Now, let us see your new creations. Fanny, take Mademoiselle Marianne to her room.'

Marianne found herself trotting breathless and astonished behind the maid, having had no time even to thank the eccentric princess who five minutes after engaging her, was ordering her a complete wardrobe from the most fashionable designer in Paris as though it was the most natural thing in the world. She actually wondered if she could be dreaming and very nearly pinched herself to make sure. But, since the dream was on the whole an agreeable one, she decided to make it last as long as possible. It was all very strange! She had come here, full of shame and dark suspicions, almost fearful of finding herself in the midst of some horrid adventure like those recounted by another of her favourite authors, Mrs Radcliffe, and so far, the talk had been of nothing but satins and lace!

She thought suddenly of the report she was to write for Fouché that very night. A beginning full of vain gossip and furbelows. She wished she could see his face when he read Monsieur Leroy's story about the Marquise Visconti's leg corsets! But, in the long run, if she could make him believe that she was good for nothing but retailing useless patter, it would be all for the best. In that way, she would be betraying no one and Fouché might eventually tire.

Fanny had gone away, closing the door behind her, and Marianne was left in a small, bright room in a corner of the main building to which her few belongings had already preceded her. As she took possession of her new apartment, she surprised herself by humming a tune which she had heard whistled by a boy in the street that morning. She paused, amazed that all at once she should feel so light-hearted. It was the first time she had sung at all since Aunt Ellis's death. In fact, though, this sudden new euphoria was no more than the normal reaction of a healthy young person, a faithful reflection of the situation of finding herself comfortably settled in this elegant household after the terrors she had lived through and the dreadful places in which she had found herself. After the furies of the Channel, Morvan's decaying manor house, the rattling of the diligence and the horrors of St. Lazare, these dainty furnishings, painted blue and grey in the style made fashionable by the late Directory, and the walls hung with one of the brand-new figured designs from M. Oberkampf's establishment at Jouy-en-Josas, were restfulness itself. Marianne resumed her singing with a clear conscience.

Outside were the cold, the wet and the mud, and outside also the perilous shades of Morvan and Jean Le Dru. But neither would come to seek her beneath the roof of the vice-grand-elector of the Empire and for that Marianne said a mental word of thanks to Joseph Fouché. Now, of the two of them, it remained to be seen who would prove the shrewder. Since he meant to make use of her, it seemed to Marianne quite fair to pay him back in his own coin. He could hardly force her to pick locks or steam open letters and by the time he finally discovered she was no use to him; she would be far away.

'Quanto é bella giovinezza
    Che sen fugge tuttavia
    Di doman non v'a certezza…'

The last words died away from Marianne's lips while the solemn person accompanying her on the pianoforte vigorously attacked the final chords. There followed what seemed to her a frightening silence. The music room was vast. The gathering dusk hid its remoter reaches and all the light was concentrated on the instrument, gilded and illuminated by the lustre of the great silver candelabra which stood upon it. Marianne's audience was invisible to her. She knew that in the room were Madame de Talleyrand and Charlotte, her adopted daughter, a child of eleven whose features were as yet unformed but whose smile held no mysteries, as well as Charlotte's tutor, M. Fercoc. But she could not see where they were sitting. The only one she could see clearly was the sober old gentleman in the white wig to whom she had been presented with such ceremony. He was Charlotte's music teacher but he was also a famous musician, and Director of the Conservatoire. His name was M. Gossec. But this was not particularly comforting since it was his verdict which the princess waited to hear.

The princess had been anxious to lose no time in trying out her new reader's voice and manner of singing. M. Gossec was to come and give Charlotte her lesson. Advantage had been taken of it to let him hear Marianne. So now, here she was, palms moist with an anxiety that she could not help condemning as idiotic, waiting to hear what would fall from those pursed lips.

The whole thing was utterly ridiculous! She had sung just as she had been used to do at Selton and quite as naturally. Yet, here she was waiting for the verdict as if her life depended on it.

Gossec, indeed, seemed in no hurry to deliver his opinion. He was sitting, round-shouldered at his instrument in a pool of yellow light, hands resting lightly on his knees. The others must be holding their breath because they could not be heard any more than they could be seen. Perhaps they were afraid to hazard an opinion before the master had given his.

Marianne's nerves were stretched to such a point that she was ready to forget her place and break the holy silence herself when Gossec swung round suddenly. His broad face with its roman nose, looked up at her.

'I do not know what to say to you, mademoiselle. Words fail me! I am an old man and I have heard many singers in my time – but never one with such a quality as yours. You have the finest voice that I have ever heard. Such rare beauty! Especially in the lower registers. Already, you sing contralto and you are just how old?'

'Seventeen,' Marianne murmured dazedly.

'Seventeen!' He sighed ecstatically. 'And such depth already! Do you know, mademoiselle, that you have a fortune in your throat?'

'A fortune? You mean that –'

'That should you decide to sing for the theatre, I can procure you an engagement on any of the greatest stages of Europe! Say the word and you shall become the greatest singer of the age – with a little work, of course, for your voice is not yet used to capacity.'

The northerner, who was ordinarily so cold and measured in his speech, was clearly transported by love of his art. Marianne was too dumbfounded to believe her ears. She was used to hearing her voice praised but had always assumed that this was common politeness. Now, here was this man telling her that she could become the greatest singer of her time! A deep and almost overwhelming joy surged up in her. If the musician spoke the truth, if he could really procure her engagements in the theatre, this would be her chance to escape from the somewhat degrading position of dependence forced on her by Fouché. She would be able to live her own life, free and independent. It was not usual, of course, for young women of noble family to tread the boards but she was no longer an aristocrat, merely a fugitive, and what was forbidden for Marianne d'Asselnat was not so for Marianne Mallerousse. In an instant Gossec had ripped apart the misty curtain which had hidden the future from her eyes. She gave him a look brimming with gratitude.

'I should like to work, if that were possible. And sing too, since you tell me I can.'

'Tell you you can! My child, you should say rather that it would be a crime not to sing. You owe to the world the pleasures your voice holds and it will make me very happy to be the one who should discover you. I am prepared to make you work every day!'

Both of them had forgotten everything in the world but their glorious dream. Then, suddenly the dream was broken by the gushing voice of Madame de Talleyrand and her purple cashmere dress appeared suddenly in the candlelight beside the instrument. The rings on her fingers glittered as she clapped her hands, all the more enthusiastically from having waited rather a long time to begin.

'Exquisite,' she exclaimed, 'quite exquisite! I must write to Madame Sainte-Croix to thank her for sending us such a treasure. The dear child shall lack no occasion of being heard here. The prince is devoted to music and we shall have much pleasure in presenting so charming a voice to our guests.'

'I understand your feelings, madame,' Gossec demurred. 'But this is too great a voice for the confined space of a drawing room or for light, fashionable songs. This is a voice worthy of a cathedral! She can, she must sing opera—'

'Very well, and so she shall! You shall come every day, my dear friend, and give her as many lessons as you like. Then, she shall sing in our little theatre and in the chapel at Valençay! It will be quite charming, for she is much prettier than that fat Grassini the Emperor was so infatuated with.'

Gossec was beside himself at the princess's evident incomprehension. Marianne, highly amused, saw him turn gradually brick red with the force of his passion.

'Your serene highness!' he cried. 'It would be a crime unprecedented—'

But her serene highness clung firmly to her idea.

'No, no. You shall see, we will perform wonders! We might present a Spanish entertainment to amuse those poor infantes. They are so dreadfully bored. We'll discuss it later. Now, you must come and let me show you the wonderful flower pieces I have ordered for tonight. You will be enchanted —'

'Madame!' Gossec protested stiffly. 'I am a musician, not a florist.'

The princess gave him a bewitching smile and, slipping her arm affectionately into his, bore the old man irresistibly to the door.

'I know, I know! But you have such taste! Come with me, Charlotte, and you too, M. Fercoc. Put away the music, child, and then you may go up and prepare for this evening. I will arrange the matter of lessons with M. Gossec.'

The latter part of this short speech was clearly addressed to Marianne, bringing her down abruptly from the heights of music to her position as a mere dependant. It hurt, like a small but irritating scratch. The little girl, Charlotte, emerging from the shadows where she had been sitting quietly, made a move as though she would speak to her but instead, docile and obedient, she followed her mother in silence. The tutor's rather solemn figure wound up the procession. Marianne found herself alone in the big room, feeling a little dazed by all that had just happened. Was this fate's answer to her desperate questioning?

The servants had drawn the gold damask curtains. For all its great size, the room seemed close and intimate. The great gilded harp slumbering by a window, the richly glowing music stand, the gold of the piano, lay like precious jewels in a casket. The whole house had taken on a magical, unreal atmosphere. Still somewhat bewildered, Marianne began thinking of the man who had commanded and inspired all this. The princess was only a beautiful goose cap, kind and generous but empty headed. She liked splendour and pretty clothes but she was hardly capable of appreciating the grace of that translucent alabaster figure, the youthful form draped modestly by the sculptor's art in what seemed diaphanous draperies, or of displaying it to such perfection against just that background of dark velvet. Everywhere, the decorations had a kind of sober magnificence, revealing the presence of one guiding hand which Marianne was conscious of a sudden wish to know. Perhaps the owner of that hand would also like her voice and help her to put it to its proper use.

Drawing out this moment of quiet and solitude, Marianne did not hurry to gather up the music. Instead, she went slowly over to the piano and stroked its polished wood, softer than satin. At Selton Hall she had had her own pianoforte, not as beautiful as this one, but she had loved it and had much pleasure from it. An unexpected pain smote her heart suddenly. She saw herself again sitting at that piano, singing to Francis an Irish ballad which had been his favourite. She had learned it especially for him. How did it go?

Slipping on to the stool, Marianne let her fingers roam over the keys, seeking out the notes which her memory at first refused to give up. The ache in her heart became more than she could bear. She had loved Francis then, and had longed with her whole being to win his love. Memory claimed her.

She closed her eyes and instantly Francis' face appeared on the screen of her closed lids with such terrifying clarity that Marianne found herself trembling. She had tried so hard to wipe out Francis from her memory as she had wiped him from her heart. She had hoped that his very features would have become strange to her. But no, she remembered too well not to be conscious of the pain.

She saw again the grey eyes with their eternal weariness, the handsome, disdainful mouth that could yet smile with such bewitching charm, the thick fair hair and perfect features – the picture was so clear that Marianne opened her eyes to make it go away but they were misted with tears and she seemed to see him still in the shimmering candlelight, she even thought she heard him laugh as though, having sent him to his death, he still returned defying her to drive him from her mind. Yet Marianne felt no remorse for having killed him. She would do it again if she had to because she could not bear the shame he had brought on her, but she had loved him as a child loves and her heart would not forget.

'You must not cry.' A cool, drawling voice spoke suddenly. 'No one here will hurt you.'

It came to Marianne then that the face she had half glimpsed in the light and taken for the ghost of Francis was quite real. She brushed the tears quickly from her eyes and was able to see him more clearly. He was a man with light-coloured hair which he wore rather long, making a frame for his face. He was very tall with a strong chin and a scornful curl to his lip which gave him a somewhat proud and insolent appearance. High cheek-bones, an impudent retrousse nose and strongly sensual mouth added to the enigmatic character of his face. His skin was very pale and so were the hard, sapphire eyes, seemingly half asleep beneath heavy lids. He was dressed in black which threw up the whiteness of his high cravat and had about him an extraordinary air of quiet power.

Marianne sprang to her feet so quickly that she almost knocked over the candelabra. The man came forward, leaning on the gold-knobbed cane he held. Marianne saw that he walked with a limp and knew, at last, who was before her.

'My lord!' she stammered and then stopped, unable to think of anything to add to this ceremonious beginning.

'You know me then? That is more than I can say of you, eh, mademoiselle?'

He spoke in a slow, deep voice essentially undramatic. It was a voice that seemed to remain always on one level and that, more than anything else, conveyed the perfect measure of its owner's self-control.

'Marianne, my lord, Marianne Mallerousse.'

'Marianne? A pretty name, and one that suits you. But with your face – and your voice, one is not called Mallerousse, eh?'

Talleyrand had a habit of punctuating his remarks with this interjection. It was not so much a question as a little trick acquired in the course of his long career as a diplomat, and one which had the advantage of provoking in his unsuspecting listener a disposition to agree with his previous remark.

'My voice?' Marianne said in a low voice, feeling her heart beating fast.

A wave of the gold-knobbed cane towards a pillar at the shadowy end of the room.

'I have been standing there for some time, listening. As I was passing, just now, I heard you singing but was careful not to show myself. I like to be alone to indulge my admiration.'

He had come very close now and stood a head taller than she, bending on her the hypnotic glance whose power had been felt by so many women. Marianne sank respectfully into a deep curtsey, deliberately pointing the distance that lay between the prince and herself.

'Your serene highness is too kind.'

Her confidence was slowly returning. Far from being overawed by Talleyrand's presence and by the danger which lay in wait for her each moment, Marianne was aware of a sensation of release and a relaxation of tension in finding herself at last face to face with him. He was very much the *grand seigneur*, a true nobleman. With all due allowances, he belonged to her own class and her own kind, in whose veins ran the best blood of France and England. All the rest, his wife included, were mere puppets dressed in the trappings of nobility, but he was different. Behind that mild hauteur and simple elegance lay centuries of history. What was Fouché next to him? A backstairs spy seeking to drag her down to the same level as himself. And now, this man too had been struck by her voice, although expressing his delight with less outward enthusiasm than Gossec.

He did not bow but gave her his hand to rise before asking softly:

'You are quite sure your name is Mallerousse, eh?'

'Quite sure, my lord. It grieves me if it is not to your Highness's liking.'

'Bah! A name may be changed. A simple accident of birth. One would expect you rather to be a duchess, my dear. But what is such a lovely, unknown nightingale doing in my house?'

'Madame Sainte-Croix sent me. I am her Highness's new reader.'

Talleyrand laughed at that.

'It is the world upside down! Old crows associate with birds of paradise! That means you are from Brittany, eh?'

'Indeed. I came by the Brest mail, yesterday.'

'Astonishing! Brittany must have changed a great deal to produce such blooms. I had thought there was nothing there but heather and broom – but their roses are finer than our own. One day, child, you shall tell me your story. I think it would amuse me. Such eyes!'

Pinching Marianne's chin casually between thumb and forefinger, he tilted up her face and gazed earnestly at the light reflected in her green eyes.

'Just like the sea,' he murmured in a soft, dreamy voice. 'The sea has just that colour and sparkle when sunlight plays on it. And such lips—'

The insolent face hovered close to them and Marianne recoiled instinctively flushing with shame at the familiarity which told her clearly just how far she had sunk.

'My lord,' she said sharply, 'Bretonne I may be, but that does not mean—'

He gave a low, sardonic chuckle.

'Wise too? And witty? Surely, Mam'zelle Mallerousse, you have too many talents for a mere reader?'

Marianne bit her lip. She had spoken to him as an equal and regretted it. Fouché had warned her, this man had probably the subtlest mind in the whole Empire. It was perilous to arouse his suspicions. She must be careful not to step outside her part. Yet what if in permitting one kiss, she was to give the prince a title to yet further liberties? The Minister of Police had made no secret of the fact that Talleyrand liked women and had loved many in his time.

'For the present, I kiss your hand, Mam'zelle Mallerousse,' the prince said, deliberately placing a slight emphasis on the name. 'We shall meet again.'

He turned abruptly and Marianne watched him limp away into the shadows. Curiously, that uneven gait gave to his progress a touch of something slow and hesitant that was not ungraceful. Even in his infirmity, the man had charm.

Suddenly, an idea came to her. Had Fouché the Fox really sent her here simply to play her humble part as reader to the princess – or, knowing the prince's fondness for pretty women and confident of the effect of his protégée's beauty, had he intended her for a more intimate role, and one of infinitely greater interest to himself? If that were true, the Minister was more vile than she had thought. A shudder of disgust ran through her.

Her reflections were cut short by the entry of a lackey bearing two candelabra whose clusters of lighted candles drove away the shadows. Hurriedly putting away the sheets of music, she left the room and made her way upstairs, leaving her gloomy meditations behind her and carrying away like a precious treasure the brand-new hope which the old musician had illumined in her heart, the hope of becoming a singer.

The hours slipped away and it was long past midnight before Marianne, wearing a flowing wrapper of white wool with wide sleeves worked in several shades of green which Mademoiselle Minette had delivered to her in the course of the day, seated herself at the small writing table between the window and the fireplace. In one of its drawers, she had found a good supply of paper, pens and ink, a sand box and sealing wax. Now, she had to get down to the first of those daily reports which the man who mended the fire was to take away each morning.

It was an uninviting task, quite apart from the revulsion Marianne still felt for the role of spy which had been thrust upon her. She was tired and the white bed with its fine linen sheets, on which some attentive hand had laid out a soft batiste nightgown, was terribly inviting. She longed to get into it and be free to dream her own dreams.

To help clear her thoughts, Marianne drank a glass of water and gazed for a moment at the rose blooming in a crystal vase on the corner of her table, then, with a sigh, she set to work. It was time to close the little window that had opened on the future and address herself to disagreeable reality.

She began with a short description of her arrival in the house and then went on, as she had made up her mind to do, to swamp Fouché in a merciless flood of frills and flounces. Even so, she was obliged to come to the evening at last. The party was not yet over and now and then, the distant strains of a Haydn waltz came floating into the room, reminding her irresistibly of all the wonderful things that she had seen. It was all so beautiful! But how to convey such splendour in a dry police report, even one written to the sound of such divine music?

She recalled the Minister's advice: 'Forget that you are making a report. Write as you would write in your own journal, no more no less –'

After that, it was easy.

'I was not present at the dinner given in honour of the Viceroy and Vicereine of Italy,' Marianne began. 'A mere reader has no place among such exalted persons. All I got was the menu – containing such dishes as I could scarcely even imagine: *'Duchesse de volaille à la crème, Épigrammes d'Agneau à la Tourville, Chauds-Froids de mauviettes, Délices de homard à la Richelieu'*. One would think they had no use for their great men but to cook for them! I confess I find it a trifle lacking in respect. I was served in my own room but what it was I ate, apart from a roast chicken, I have no idea; however, it was all delicious. The maidservant, Fanny, told me that the prince was very particular in the matter of his table. It seems his chef is a person of the utmost importance ... he is called Monsieur Carême and I had the honour to meet him a little earlier when the princess asked me to go with her to the dining room to make sure of the arrangements of the flowers. I am sorry to say he barely glanced at me. He is a choleric little man dressed in starched white garments with the face of a discontented cherub and carrying a large knife prominently displayed across his ample paunch. I was amazed to see with what respect Madame de Talleyrand spoke to him. It is said that even the prince himself is careful how he addresses him.

'I shall not describe the magnificence of the table, the service being entirely of silver-gilt and all ablaze with flowers, black iris and yellow roses, but I will just add that musicians played Mozart throughout the meal.

'The chief part of the evening had already begun when the princess sent for me, upon the excuse of fetching her a scarf, out of pure goodness I am sure, for she had no need for one—'

Marianne's pen remained poised while she closed her eyes briefly. How could she convey her sensations of dazed wonderment on entering the great white and gold salon, ablaze with light? How could she describe the dazzling appearance of the women, many of them young and beautiful, their satins and diamonds, flowers and plumes, glittering against a background of gorgeous uniforms. There were many officers present, wearing magnificent dress uniforms that reminded Marianne of the lancer she had seen in the rue MMontorgueil. She could almost hear Gracchus-Hannibal Pioche telling her with simple pride in his voice: 'Wait until you've seen the rest!' It hardly seemed possible that real soldiers could be arrayed with such dazzling splendour. There were uniforms of blue, red and green, all glittering with gold and, merciful heavens, the pelisse which that blue hussar wore draped with such a casual air from his right shoulder was actually lined with sable!

'The princess looked very handsome in periwinkle blue velvet sewn with stars,' Marianne went on. 'I, standing behind her chair, endeavoured to keep my eyes lowered not to appear too dazzled and provincial. But the temptation was too great! After a while, I began to notice that the guests showed little inclination to gather round the mistress of the house. They would greet her courteously but afterwards move away to join groups here or there. One woman only seated herself by Madame de Talleyrand. This person, a stout lady with rather short, thick legs and a large bosom draped in lemon yellow satin, surprised me greatly by flinging herself upon my neck when I entered the salon with the scarf and embracing me with great enthusiasm. Realizing, from the description I had been given, that this must be Madame Sainte-Croix I responded with a proper show of respectful gratitude. I think the lady was pleased with my behaviour. At all events, she very soon turned the princess's attention away from me and I was able to continue my observation of those present.

'Sitting on a small sofa close by, were two women who seemed much in demand. One was short, dark and slim with thick dark curls, almost in the Arabian style, and very elegant in a dress of black lace over pink. A set of enormous rubies glittered at her throat, in her hair and on her slender, pink-gloved arms. The other was also dark but her hair was cloudier and her features somewhat Asiatic, rather flat with high cheek-bones and black eyes. But those eyes held such a brilliance and sparkled with such wit and intelligence, while her figure, though almost too thin, had breeding and altogether a quite extraordinary charm. In a dress of purple silk with a turban and heavy gold ornaments of barbaric splendour, she had something of the air of a pagan idol, although her bearing was certainly royal.

'I learned, from the conversation of the princess and a friend, that the little dark, arrogant-looking woman was Madame Junot, Duchess of

Abrantes and that the marvellous rubies she was wearing had been 'plundered by Junot in Portugal quite recently'. The other, the lady in the barbaric jewellery, was Countess Metternich, whose husband, the Austrian ambassador, seemed to have been obliged to return to Vienna after the battle of the Wagram, leaving his wife virtually a hostage. According to Madame Sainte-Croix, who professed herself to be very shocked, the friendship between these two ladies has no other source than the attractions of the second's husband, the first having had a great *timbre* for him last summer —'

Here, Marianne paused for a moment to correct a small mistake and sighed. Was Fouché really interested in all this fashionable gossip which he must surely know as well as she? To be sure, it was by no means tedious to relate, except when one was so terribly sleepy ... with another sigh, Marianne dipped her pen in the ink and resumed.

'After this, the ladies turned their attention to a very pretty, blonde woman in mauve muslin with a large diamond tiara in her hair, who had gathered a kind of little court about her chair. She was the Duchess Anna de Courlande whose youngest daughter, Dorothée, has lately married the Prince of Benevento's nephew, Count Edmond de Périgord. Neither lady seemed to like her very much. The prince, however, would seem to have a much higher estimation of the foreigner's charms since he scarcely quitted her chair. The two ladies then began to talk in a lower tone and I heard nothing more. I was obliged to be content with overhearing a few scraps of conversation in a general way. 'The Emperor remains shut up in the Trianon... Since the divorce, he never leaves it, except to go to Malmaison ... Poor Joséphine is inconsolable. Madame de Rémusat says she weeps endlessly and that she dare not leave her alone ... It seems that the famous castrato Crescentini goes every night to sing for Napoleon. Music is the only thing which can soothe him ... Do you think he will marry the Tsar's sister? ... Have you heard that Junot's aide-de-camp caused a great scandal yesterday at the Palais-Royal trying to seduce a milliner? ... The King and Queen of Bavaria are here. They are with King Joseph at the Hôtel Marbeuf ...' A log collapsed in the hearth amid a shower of sparks. Marianne woke with a start. She must have dozed off as she wrote. The pen had fallen from her fingers and left a long trail of ink. Glancing up at the clock on the mantelpiece, she saw that it was two o'clock in the morning. The music had stopped but a hum of conversation could still be heard, muffled by distance. The whist players must still be at the tables. Marianne knew from experience that time meant nothing to those absorbed in their passion for the game. Even the sight of the cards was painful to her and she had preferred to retire rather than risk being asked to play.

She rose with an effort, yawned and stretched herself. Lord but she was sleepy! It was no good, bed was too tempting. She scowled at the unfinished report. She was much too tired to go on. With sudden decision, she picked up the pen and wrote quickly: 'I am too tired now. I will finish tomorrow.' Quickly sketching the star which was to serve as her signature, she folded the paper and sealed it with wax and a plain seal which she found in one of the drawers, then slipped it under her pillow. After all, she had nothing really exciting to report. She might as well go to bed.

She was just undoing the ribbons which fastened her wrapper when she was arrested by hearing a quite unexpected sound. Cutting through the muted hum of conversation, she had distinctly heard a cry of anger, followed at once by the sound of sobbing.

She listened intently but, although she heard nothing more, she was certain that she had not been dreaming. She went quietly to the window which she had left open, in spite of the weather, for the sake of fresh air. At Selton Hall she had always been used to sleeping with her window open. Now, leaning out, she saw lights in two windows, one of which was directly beneath her own. She knew already that this was the room in which the prince was accustomed to work. There must have been a window open there too because she could now hear the sobs quite clearly. Then came the smooth tones of the prince himself.

'Really, you are being quite unreasonable! Why must you upset yourself like this, eh?'

But almost immediately there came the sound of the window being shut and Marianne heard nothing more. But she could have sworn it was a woman crying, and she sounded desperate. Marianne went slowly back to her bed. Her curiosity was wide awake now but still training held her back. She could not go listening at keyholes, like any servant, or like a spy – which, of course, was precisely what she was. On the other hand, there was the chance of being able to help someone in trouble. The woman who was crying had sounded dreadfully unhappy.

Her curiosity now decently cloaked in human kindness, Marianne quickly exchanged her wrapper for her mulberry-coloured dress and slipped out of the room. A small service staircase at the far end of the gallery led directly to the floor below, emerging not far from Talleyrand's office.

As she reached the bottom of the stairs, Marianne saw a long spear of light stretching across the floor, coming from the office door. It must have been left ajar. At the same time, she heard the sobs once again and then a youthful voice with a strong German accent.

'Your behaviour with my mother is abominable, unspeakable. Surely you must understand that I cannot endure the knowledge that she is your mistress?'

'Aren't you a little young to upset yourself about such matters, my dear Dorothée? The affairs of adults are no concern of children and, despite your marriage, you are still a child to me. I am very fond of your mother –'

'Too fond! You are too fond of her and all the world knows it. There are those old women who are forever hanging round you, with their squabbling and tittle-tattling. Now they are trying to make Mama one of them, forcing her to join their little club, what one might call Monsieur de Talleyrand's harem! When I see Mama surrounded by Madame Laval, Madame de Luynes and the Duchess of Fitz-James it makes me feel like weeping—'

The young voice rose angrily, reaching a note of shrill, high-pitched fury that was only increased by the imperfect French which made its owner stumble over some of the words.

Marianne knew now who it was in the room with the prince, whose the sobbing and the cries of anger. She had seen her in the salon only a little while before. It was the prince's niece, Madame Edmond de Périgord, formerly Princess Dorothée de Courlande, a young and very wealthy heiress whom Talleyrand had succeeded, with the Tsar's help, in marrying off to his nephew a few months previously. She was very young, sixteen at the most, and Marianne had thought her on the whole rather plain, thin, sallow and gauche, although dressed in a style of elegance that betrayed the hand of Leroy. Her one beauty, but that quite remarkable, was her enormous eyes which seemed to fill the whole of her small face. They were of a strange colour which seemed at first to be black but was in fact dark blue merging into brown. But Marianne had been struck by the little princess's air of breeding and the wilful, slightly arrogant way she had of throwing back her head as children did when they were determined not to show that they were frightened or unhappy. Of the husband, she could recall very little; a personable but undistinguished youth in the splendid uniform of a hussar officer.

Monsieur Fercoc, the tutor, who had chatted to her for a while, had also remarked, in discreetly veiled terms, on the relations existing between Talleyrand and the Duchess of Courlandee, Dorothée's mother. He had pointed out the blonde duchess, sitting with three other women; they were no longer young, but their air of assurance, verging on insolence, clearly recalled the old court of Versailles. All three had been Talleyrand's mistresses and remained his most devoted admirers. Their loyalty to him was limitless and very nearly blind.

'The three Fates!' Marianne had thought with the unconscious cruelty of seventeen, ignoring the fact that these women retained the traces of great beauty. However, there were too many people in the room for her to dwell on them for long.

On the other side of the door, Talleyrand was still endeavouring to soothe the angry girl.

'I am surprised at you, Dorothée. I should never have believed you capable of listening to every piece of gossip that circulates in Paris. To most of these busybodies, a friendship between a man and a woman can mean only one thing—'

'Why do you have to lie to me?' the young woman burst out furiously. 'You know quite well it is not gossip but pure truth! Gossip may be all very well but I know, I know I tell you! And I am ashamed, so terribly ashamed when I see two heads getting together behind a fan and eyes looking first at me, and then at my mother! And this is a shame that I will not endure. I am a Courlande!'

The last words rose almost to a scream. Marianne, standing stock-still in the darkened gallery, heard the prince cough dryly but when he spoke again, she noticed that his voice had taken on an icy hardness.

'If you are so fond of gossip, my child, you should take more note of the old rumours concerning your forebear, Jean Biren – made Duke of Courlande by the whim of a Tsarina. Was it really true that he was a groom? Certainly, hearing your language tonight, I should be tempted to believe it! You must learn to control yourself. It really will not do to shout in this way in Paris, or indeed in any civilized society. If you are so sensitive to gossip, you should have chosen a convent, my child, rather than marriage—'

'As though I had chosen it!' the girl said bitterly. 'As though you had not forced your nephew on me, knowing I loved another!'

'Another whom you never saw and who thought little enough of you. If Prince Adam Czartorisky had been so anxious to marry you, he might have behaved in a less distant fashion, eh?'

'How you enjoy hurting people! Oh, I hate you!'

'No, you don't. There are times when I think you love me more than you will admit, even to yourself. Do you know, your little outburst smacks a good deal of jealousy? Now, don't get on your high horse again. Calm down, smile and let me tell you something. I know of no one in this world we live in who does not love and respect your mother. She is a woman born to be loved. So, be like everyone else, my child. This world hangs in a very delicate balance. Take care your tantrums do not shake it.'

The sobs had begun again. Marianne listened, unable to tear herself away. She had only just time to spring back into the shadows of the staircase when the door was thrown wide open and the prince's tall figure appeared in the doorway. He stepped outside, seemed to hesitate for a moment then shrugged and moved away. The regular click of his stick and the more irregular sound of his footsteps on the tiled floor quickly died away. But, inside the room, Dorothée de Périgord was still crying.

Again, Marianne hesitated. What she had overheard was a private matter which did not concern her but she felt drawn to the little sad-eyed princess and wished she could help her. Surely, it was quite natural for the child to feel revulsion at the spectacle of a liaison between her mother and her uncle by marriage? Such adventures might be all very well for the fashionable world but no truly pure and principled mind could fail to be hurt by them.

Marianne sighed and turned regretfully to make her way upstairs. She felt very close to the girl weeping in there. Dorothée was suffering from an unhappy love, as she herself had suffered, but there seemed nothing she could do for her. Better to go back to her room and try to forget, for not for anything in the world would Marianne have reported what she had just heard to Fouché. She was just turning away when, through the now closed door, she heard the girl speak again.

'I loathe this hateful country! There is no one who understands me! No one! If there were just one person —'

This time, she spoke in German and with such a mixture of rage and pain in her voice that Marianne could no longer resist the urge to fly to her assistance. Before she realized what she was doing, she had pushed open the door and walked in. It was a large room, rather plainly furnished in mahogany with dark green hangings. Dorothée was walking agitatedly up and down, her arms folded and her cheeks streaked with tears she had not bothered to wipe away. She stood facing Marianne who murmured in a soft voice:

'If there is anything I can do to help you, please command me —'

She had spoken in German. The little countess's huge eyes seemed to grow larger still.

'You speak my language? But who are you?'

Then she seemed to remember suddenly and the joy which had shone for a moment in her eyes went out like a snuffed candle flame.

'Oh! I know! You are reader to Madame de Talleyrand! I thank you for your solicitude, but I do not need anything.'

The cool voice reminded Marianne that she was scarcely more than a servant here, but she smiled without taking offence.

'You think that so humble a person as myself is not worthy to offer help to a princess of Courlande? You long to find someone here who will understand, yet in me you see a mere servant. What is a servant to you who have hundreds —'

'My only friend is a servant,' the girl burst out quickly as though in spite of herself. 'That is Anja, my nurse – she is the one person I trust. But you! Were you not recommended here by Madame Sainte-Croix? A go between! She may have sent you to the princess but I think the prince was more in her mind!'

Marianne saw wearily that she would find this suspicion not easy to outlive, especially since she herself, after her first interview with Talleyrand, had been the first to leap to it. Suddenly she wanted more than anything else to clear herself, to take off the mask which Fouché had forced on her.

'Madame de Sainte-Croix did recommend me but I am not really known to her. She does not even know who I am.'

'Who are you then?'

'An émigrée – hiding, trying to live –'

'If that is so, then why tell me? I could call someone and denounce you, have you dismissed, thrown into prison.'

Marianne smiled again and nodded.

'Denounce is not a word that comes well from your lips, madame. To gain someone's confidence, one must first give one's own. I am in your hands. Very well, denounce me –'

There was a pause while Dorothée de Périgord looked more intensely at this girl, scarcely older than herself. The chance to speak her native language gave her a childish pleasure which, with the softening of her glance, was not lost on Marianne. Lowering her voice instinctively, Dorothée asked in a much gentler tone: 'What is your name – your real name?'

Determined to win this odd child's friendship at all costs, Marianne was on the point of telling her when the door opened again. Glittering in the doorway was the splendid but uninspiring figure of the hussar officer who was the young countess's husband.

'Dorothée, what are you doing? Your mother is looking everywhere for you. She is tired and wishes to go home.'

'I felt unwell. It must have been the heat. Mam'zelle – Mallerousse very kindly came to my rescue –'

Marianne trembled to see how well her borrowed name had been noted. When Dorothée turned to her it was with a smile of real pleasure in her eyes. She held out her hand.

'Thank you,' she said, reverting once more to German. 'You have helped me more than you know. Come and visit me. I live at number two, rue de la Grange Batelière and I am always at home in the mornings. Will you come?'

'I will come,' Marianne promised with the slight, respectful bow over the proffered hand, which her role demanded. It seemed to judge from his look of bored impatience, that Edmond de Périgord did not understand German.

'Come along now –'

Marianne followed them out of the room. She had no wish to be found there by the prince. She ran swiftly upstairs, slipped off her dress and, putting on her nightgown and nightcap, jumped into bed and put out her candle. In the light of the dying fire, she could see the report she had written lying on the table and smiled. These precious beginnings of friendship were something of which the inquisitive Minister of Police should know nothing. Nor should he learn of the little countess's unhappiness. Marianne found herself thinking of her with an almost sisterly affection due to the discovery that she too, in spite of her princely birth, her brilliant marriage, her fortune and the honours with which she was surrounded, in spite of all that she possessed which Marianne had lost, she too was made miserable and unhappy by the ruthless world of men. The little princess of Courlande had been torn from her own land and life and dreams of love to be used as a pawn on the chess board of politics. She had been taken from the man she loved and forced to accept another, and that other an enemy whom she could not but dislike. And then, to crown all, she was obliged to sit by and witness a liaison between her own mother and another of her enemies! How cynically Talleyrand had informed her that she was merely a child of no importance, not yet wise enough to bow to worldly expediency.

Poor, angry little Dorothée, trying to fight with her bare hands the whole united force of men and their appetites. What were these people made of that the Emperor of the French and Talleyrand should join together with the Tsar himself to break the will of a fifteen-year-old child? Did they feel no shame? What were these policies that still demanded human sacrifice?

Thinking of her new friend, Marianne gradually forgot her own problems and experienced a certain lightening of her heart. She was discovering that she was by no means the only one to suffer and, in doing so, was realizing her own strength. More than ever now, she was determined to fight the overbearing power of men, their sordid passions and lying words of love. And at the same time, she meant to do all she could to help her sisters in distress. And God knew they existed! For one Ivy St Albans, serving men and fighting on their side, she had seen a Dorothée de Courlande sold like so much merchandise, an Adélaïde d'Asselnat flung into prison and exiled for daring to say what she thought, an Empress dethroned for failing to provide a tyrant with an heir, a princess of Benevento flouted and ignored in her own house and a countess Metternich abandoned as a hostage. Someday, she, Marianne would show that a woman could beat them at their own game!

That night, Marianne declared war on men.

When the servant whose duty it was to attend to her fire came into her room next morning, Marianne was sitting by the window reading. She did not look up from her book.

The man cleaned the hearth, piled up the new logs, and revived the still glowing embers with a large pair of bellows. When he had done, there was silence. Marianne could hear him breathing loudly and guessed that her air of indifference made him uncomfortable. Rather cruelly she decided to enjoy his discomfiture. Not for anything would she have spoken first. Either he would speak or he would go. At last, she heard him cough.

'I think this wood will burn well.'

Only then did she raise her eyes and saw a man neither young nor old, of average build and unremarkable features. In fact, he was a man who, but for his braided livery would have passed absolutely unnoticed anywhere, blended into any background. The perfect spy. She nodded to the report lying on the corner of the desk.

'The paper – there on the table,' was all she said.

The man took the letter and slipped it into his capacious pocket before glancing sideways at Marianne.

'My name's Floquet,' he said. 'Célestin Floquet. What's yours?'

'I am Mademoiselle Mallerousse,' Marianne said coldly, taking up her book once more. 'You should know that.'

'Oh yes, I know that! But that's not what I asked. What's your first name? Between colleagues –'

Marianne had vowed to keep quite calm but the impertinence of the man stung her to instant anger. If she were to be obliged to endure familiarities from this backstairs spy –

'I have no first name. And I am not your colleague.'

Her fingers tightened on the book's leather binding but she made herself keep her eyes firmly on the page rather than look at Floquet's commonplace features. But she could not shut out his mocking laugh.

'Hoity-toity! Proud, 'aint we! And what do you t'ink you are, my pretty? Just don't you forget that I'm the boss here, see! Who'll bring you your pickings from papa Fouché come pay-day?'

It was too much! Forgetting all caution, as well as all her good resolutions, Marianne sprang to her feet and pointed to the door.

'Do what you have to do but let that be all!' she exclaimed. 'We have nothing to say to one another and we never will have. Now go!'

Floquet shrugged but he picked up his wood basket and the pan of ashes.

'All right!' he muttered rudely. 'Have it your own way. There's no harm in old Floquet but he's not one to let folk tread on his toes!'

The moment he had gone, Marianne almost ran to the bedside table, poured herself a glass of water and drank it with one gulp. Her hands were shaking so violently that the glass knocked against the carafe as she poured. Never until that moment had she been so dearly aware of her degradation. That one tiny incident opened her eyes. That a lackey, a common informer should think himself entitled to address her as an equal! She could bear anything but not that – not that!

Tomorrow, in her report, she would demand, even at the risk of rousing his anger, that Fouché compelled this Floquet to keep his distance. If he did not, she would never write another word –

She heard the distant rumble of a carriage in the street and once again the longing to escape swept over her, irritated as she was by this fresh encounter with the male sex. After all, what was there to prevent her slipping on her cloak, packing her few possessions and hurrying to the stage coach office? She could go back to Brest. Nicolas had returned to England but Madame de Guilvinec would be only too happy to look after her. Or she could go to Auvergne and find her turbulent cousin who might take her in.

No, she could not do that. If Mademoiselle d'Asselnat were being watched, the arrival of a suspicious, fugitive cousin was bound to cause trouble for her. As for Madame de Guilvinec, Marianne remembered now that she must already have left Recouvrance for Hennebont, where her daughter was ill and had sent for her to take care of her children.

Then, she had another idea. Why not go to Rome and look for her godfather? The Abbé Gauthier de Chazay had as yet no idea of the series of disasters which had fallen on his god-daughter. He imagined her living quietly, if not happily, on her country estate in England. Seeing her in such distress, he would naturally feel bound to help her, but what would this good, kind but unswervingly upright man think in his heart of a Marianne who was guilty of two murders, arson and hunted by the law of two countries? The mere thought that he might turn from her in disgust was enough to send a thrill of horror through Marianne. No, there was nothing to be done. She would have to stay, for a little while at least. There was her music and the worthy M. Gossec, in whom she had placed such hopes, would be coming soon to give her the first lesson. She prayed to God that He too would not fail her.

Quite suddenly, Marianne's nerves gave way. She threw herself on her bed and burst into tears. She cried bitterly for a long time, swamped by a great wave of misery which for the moment overwhelmed her. To think that in those far off days when she sat poring over her beloved novels, she used to dream of being one of those fantastic heroines who sailed through the direst perils and the blackest tragedies without so much as a crease in their gowns, much less in their pure souls! Her own life was not even a bad novel! It was a farce, a grotesque and degrading farce, a slow and terrifying descent through the mud towards some dreadful and inevitable but as yet unseen abyss.

Little by little, her sobs died away. She began to feel calm again. She seemed to hear from far back in her childhood the deep voice of old Dobbs who had first put her in the saddle and taught her to handle arms. There was a day when she fell in the river and was screaming at the top of her voice, when he had called to her: 'Swim, Miss Marianne! Don't waste your strength yelling! When you're in the water, you've got to swim.'

It was true that Dobbs had promptly jumped in too to help her but her own instincts had already come to her rescue. She had paddled wildly, like a puppy, and it was after that she had learned to swim. Well, she supposed it was much the same now. The water was dirty but she could only paddle along, hoping she would soon learn the proper movements and with their help come at last into clearer and more wholesome water. All the same, that very evening, she appended her ultimatum to Fouché to her report. Floquet, coming to light the fire, placed a heavily sealed letter on her writing desk. He neither spoke nor looked at her.

Inside, Marianne found a note. 'Never fear. You will suffer no further importunities.' It was unsigned. There was something else, too, which made her blush to the roots of her hair. This was a draft on the bank of France to the value of fifty napoleons.

Torn between relief at knowing that she was safe from Floquet's advances and the shame of receiving money, which in her eyes was dirty and dishonestly come by, Marianne nearly threw the whole lot in the fire. However, she thought better of it and pushed the note into her pocket before putting on her outdoor clothes in preparation for going with the princess to the church of Saint-Thomas-d'Aquin.

Stubbornly ignoring the minor uproar which her arrival never failed to provoke, the wife of the former bishop of Autun persisted in regularly attending mass in some state and endeavouring to earn forgiveness by the generosity of her donations.

Today being Christmas day, Madame de Talleyrand-Périgord was exceptionally munificent. As for Marianne, before leaving the church she made sure of slipping Fouché's note unobtrusively into the poor box. That done, she went with a lighter heart and a little smile on her lips at the thought that Fouché's tainted money would do some good in the end, to join her mistress, she was lingering under the bare trees in the square and clearly enjoying the somewhat embarrassed but none the less sincere thanks of the Superior of the Dominicans, to whom the church of Saint-Thomas-d'Aquin belonged.

CHAPTER TEN
The Unexpected Guest

It was a bright cold morning early in January. A pale sun was bravely striking sparks off the stalactites hanging from the roofs and some reflected rays off the ice in the gutters. The keen air reddened the noses of the people in the street but they hurried on cheerfully, hopping up and down the kerb at every break in the pavement occasioned by the carriage entrances of some great houses.

The rue de la Loi[6] presented a scene of great activity. There were few carriages to be seen apart from three standing outside the door of the couturier Leroy and a hired cab outside his neighbour, the Hôtel du Nord, but the street traders were in full cry. A man strolled by pushing a barrow and offering bundles of firewood for sale. Nearby, an old woman with a thick blue woollen shawl over her head was heaving along a great bucket, calling: 'Dried plums! Fat dried plums!' On the other side of the street, a pretty girl in a red and yellow striped dress was crying 'Hot chestnuts!' Not far away, a little knife-grinder was busy on a heap of knives while a haughty looking servant waited.

Marianne, coming out of Leroy's, paused for a moment to breath in the fresh air. Inside, the famous couturier's salons were in a state of continuous frenzy and the atmosphere stifling. Besides, she had learned to love the lively, colourful streets of Paris with all their passers-by, rich and elegant and poor and wretched, and the host of different street traders crying their wares. She smiled at the little chimney sweep as he went whistling by; he immediately whistled louder than ever, eyeing her with frank approval.

While Fanny, the maid who was with her, was handing the huge pink box she carried to the coachman, Marianne took from her reticule the list of errands given her by Madame de Talleyrand. She had already been to

---

[6] The present Rue de Richelieu

Madame Bonjour for a set of artificial flowers, to Jacques, the bootmaker, and Nitot the jeweller about the re-setting of two stones in a parure of cameos and outsize turquoises, of which the princess was particularly fond, and then to Leroy to inquire about the ball dress which the princess was to wear on the eighteenth at the Prince of Neuchatel's ball. Now, she saw with satisfaction that she had only to call at 'La Reine d' Espagne', to hurry the progress of an ermine tippet which her mistress was awaiting impatiently, and finally at the post office.

Marianne smiled, remembering the mysterious air with which Madame de Talleyrand had given her the letter, prettily but discreetly sealed and delicately perfumed on the start of its long journey over the bad French roads to the Jura mountains – where it was to bring some consolation in exile to the handsome Duke of San Carlos, who had been guilty of somewhat too public an intrigue with his hostess while staying at the Château de Valençay. Marianne was amused and a little touched to find herself carrying messages of love. It was certainly a proof of trust which that excellent woman placed in her.

The coachman was holding the door. Marianne folded her list and was about to climb into the carriage where Fanny was waiting for her when she felt a light touch on her arm and a cheerful voice cried:

'Good day to you, mam'zelle! Remember me?'

'But of course! You are Gracchus-Hannibal Pioche, are you not?'

'I am indeed!' The boy beamed delightedly. 'Nice to see you again, mam'zelle!'

Marianne could not help laughing at the sight of that round, amiable face with its mop of red hair under a blue cap and the big red umbrella. He had been the first person to welcome her to Paris and she was glad to see him again. Gracchus-Hannibal, infected by her laughter, followed suit and for a moment, the two of them stood there beaming at one another to the not inconsiderable horror of the coachman.

'But what are you doing here?' Marianne asked.

'Working, as you see. I wasn't sure at first whether I ought to speak to you. With this fine carriage and you so well turned out –'

His eyes rested for a moment on her dark green velvet pelisse, trimmed and lined with miniver, and her *toque à la Polonaise* with its deep gold tassels. He lowered his voice.

'It's just that there's something I had to tell you –'

Something in Gracchus-Hannibal's expression warned Marianne that this was serious. She moved away from the carriage and into the shelter of the doorway she had just left.

'What is it?'

The boy peered carefully about, paying particular attention to the corner of the rue de la Loi where it joined the boulevard.

'See that *sapin* standing at the corner, outside La Petite Jeannette?'

'The sapin?'

'The four-wheeler! See it?'

'Yes. But what of it?'

'Party inside's been following you all morning. Can't tell you what he looks like altogether, seeing as he's got a coat collar comes up to his ears and a hat pulled down to same.'

'Someone following me? Are you sure?' Marianne asked with sudden uneasiness. 'How do you know?'

'Cos I've been following you myself, of course. Caught sight of you going into Madame Bonjour's, and waited – only I didn't dare speak to you. Then I followed you. I wanted to see where you lived.' He blushed so hard at this admission that in spite of her alarm, Marianne could not help smiling. 'I kept on the trail of your horses. And you gave me a run for it! If it wasn't for the traffic – I was with you at Jacques, and then Nitot and then here – that's how I came to notice the black cab sticking to your tail.'

'But – he did not see you?'

Gracchus-Hannibal gave a shrug.

'Who notices an errand boy? Paris is full of us. And we all look much the same. As for the party in the *sapin*, you can find out for yourself, if you don't believe me.'

'How?'

'Have you other calls to make, or are you going home?'

'Only to "La Reine d'Espagne" and then to the post. After that I am going home.'

'Then you can easily see with your own eyes. And with eyes like yours, you ought to see all right!' Gracchus-Hannibal blushed more furiously than ever. 'I mean to keep with you myself, only, if you wouldn't mind telling me where you live? You see, if it's at Auteuil or Vaugirard –'

Eloquent miming told Marianne that, if that was so, his legs would not stay the course.

'I live at Prince de Talleyrand's in the rue de Varennes –'

'Oh, then I'm not surprised you're being followed! It's all intrigue where the limping devil's concerned! It may be one of Fouché's men. But here –' He looked suddenly anxious, 'you aren't family, are you?'

'Because you spoke of him so? No, don't worry. I am merely reader to the princess.'

'I'm glad, in a way – but then, in another, I don't see why the minister of police should want to know about you?'

Neither did Marianne and this made it all the more necessary to check on the boy's observation for herself. Each morning, reluctantly but without fail she had delivered the previous night's report to the servant, Floquet.

'I'll take your advice,' she said, 'and see if this carriage is really watching me. Whatever the truth, thank you for telling me. Will you come and see me one day?'

'At the prince's house? Not on your life! I'd be lucky if I got as far as the butler in a place like that. But I'll find you, if I need to. Just tell me your name, in case I should have anything to report. I can write, you see,' he added proudly.

'Excellent. I am Mademoiselle Mallerousse.'

There was no mistaking the disappointment on the boy's face.

'Is that all? You've such a look about you, you ought to be called Conde or Montmorency at the least! But there, one doesn't choose one's name. Good day to you mam'zelle!'

Gracchus-Hannibal settled his blue cap firmly on his head, tucked his umbrella underneath his arm and strolled off whistling with his hands in his pockets, leaving Marianne feeling slightly dazed at what she had just heard. As she walked slowly back to her own carriage, she glanced at that standing outside La Petite Jeannette. The man inside could not have seen her talking in the shadow of the doorway. He must think she had forgotten something and gone back inside. Climbing into the carriage as though nothing had happened, she called out to Lambert, the coachman, while Fanny was busy wrapping a fur rug round her knee: 'Now to "La Reine d'Espagne" —'

'Very good, mademoiselle.'

The smart brougham drawn by a fine pair of Irish greys moved off in the direction of the boulevard, passing the stationary vehicle and allowing Marianne a glimpse of a dark figure inside, then turned the corner by the café Dangest and passed under the trees of the boulevard Italienes. Marianne waited a few moments and then turned round just in time to see the black cab also turn into the boulevard. She turned again as they drew up outside the famous furriers and saw the cab pull in behind a large delivery cart. It was there again at the post office and was still in sight when the brougham finally turned into the rue de Varennes.

I don't like it, Marianne thought while Joris the porter was opening the gates for the horses. Who are these people, and why are they following me?

She had no means of finding out except the one possible way of mentioning it in her report. If Fouché were responsible, he would not admit it but if the man in the black cab were not one of his he would certainly give her some instructions.

Somewhat comforted by this decision, Marianne jumped down from the carriage and leaving Fanny to take care of her parcel made her way into the great hall and up the marble staircase to render an account of her morning's errands.

She was in a hurry since M. Gossec was due to arrive for her daily lesson in a few minutes time. These lessons had become the great joy of her life. She felt her own excitement warmed by that of the old teacher and worked hard in the hope of soon earning her freedom.

She had just put her foot on the bottom step when Courtiade, the prince's valet, appeared at her elbow.

'His serene highness awaits mademoiselle in his study,' he said in the measured tones which never varied and were the very essence of the model servant he was.

After almost thirty years in the Prince's service, he had come in some degree to identify himself with his master, even to adopting certain of his more innocent mannerisms. Courtiade's sole function in the household was to wait upon the prince and he was both respected and feared by the other servants, in whose eyes he possessed something of the powers of an *éminence grise* . Consequently, the pretended Mademoiselle Mallerousse looked at him in some surprise.

'His highness, you mean – the prince.'

'His serene highness,' Courtiade repeated with a bow and that slight pursing of his lips which marked his disapproval of such lack of respect, 'has instructed me to inform mademoiselle that he has been awaiting her return. If mademoiselle will follow me.'

Suppressing a faint expression of annoyance as she thought of her singing lesson, Marianne followed the valet to the door of the room with which she was more familiar than Talleyrand knew.

Courtiade tapped discreetly, entered and announced: 'Mademoiselle Mallerousse, my lord.'

'Let her come in, Courtiade. Then go and inform Madame de Périgord that I shall have the honour to wait on her at five o'clock.'

Talleyrand was seated at his desk but at Marianne's entry he rose and bowed briefly before resuming his seat and motioning his visitor to a chair. He was dressed, as usual, in black, but the star of the order of St George glittering on his breast reminded Marianne that he was to dine that day with the Russian ambassador, the aged Prince Kurakin. On one corner of the desk stood an antique vase of translucent alabaster, filled with exquisite roses of a red so dark as to be almost black but wholly without scent. The only fragrance in the room was a faint smell of verbena which Talleyrand liked. Cheered by a ray of sunshine which took away some of the austerity from the dark curtains, the room breathed an atmosphere of privacy and peace.

Marianne sat on the edge of her chair, hardly daring to breathe for fear of disturbing the silence, broken only by the faint scratching of the prince's pen on the paper. Talleyrand finished his letter, then, throwing down his pen, raised his pale eyes to look at her. There was something cold and enigmatic in his expression which made Marianne uneasy without quite knowing why.

'The Countess de Périgord seems to hold you in great esteem, Mademoiselle Mallerousse. That is no mean achievement, you know. What witchcraft did you employ to gain that victory? Madame de Périgord is too young to give her friendship by halves. Is it – your voice?'

'That may be so, my lord, but I do not think so. It is simply, that I speak German. It is not only the sound of my voice but that of her native town which pleases the countess.'

'I can believe that. You speak several languages, I believe?'

'Four, my lord, not counting French.'

'Indeed! Girls are well taught – in Brittany. I should never have believed it. However, that decides me to ask you whether, in view of your education, you would agree to act as my secretary from time to time. I need someone to translate certain of my letters. You could be very useful to me and the princess would be quite willing to lend you.'

The proposal took Marianne by surprise and she felt the colour flood into her cheeks. What Talleyrand was suggesting to her was quite impossible. If she were to become his secretary Fouché would know of it at once. He would be delighted and instantly demand vastly more detailed and interesting reports. Marianne had absolutely no desire to record anything beyond the society gossips and small, day to day, household items to which she had prudently confined herself so far. Fouché had been satisfied with that and that was how it must go on. But if she were to be admitted to a sight of the prince's correspondence, Fouché would no longer be satisfied with it and then Marianne would be obliged to become the one thing she was determined not to be and believed at present she was not, which was a real spy. She stood up.

'My lord,' she said, 'I am deeply sensible of the honour your serene highness does me, but I cannot accept.'

'And why not, if you please?' Talleyrand said sharply.

'I – I am not a fit person. Your highness is a statesman, a diplomat, I am fresh from the country and in no way fitted for a post of such importance. Even my handwriting—'

'You write an excellent hand, I believe. At least, if this is anything to go by, eh?'

He took some sheets of paper from a drawer as he spoke and, to her horror, Marianne saw that what he held in his hand was the report she had given Floquet that morning. She knew then that she was lost. For an instant, the mahogany furniture seemed to dance before her eyes as though the house itself were falling and she had a momentary impression that the bronze lustre had fallen on her head. But it wasn't in Marianne's nature to go to pieces in a crisis. All her instincts were to stand up and fight. The blood drained from her face with the effort it cost her but she managed to show nothing of the desperate fear which possessed her. With a little curtsey to the prince, she turned on her heel and walked collectedly towards the door.

'In that case,' she said calmly, 'I have nothing more to do here. I am your most serene highness's servant!'

Talleyrand had a long familiarity with the ways of women but it had not prepared him for this.

'Where do you think you're going?'

'To pack,' Marianne answered frigidly. 'I shall then take myself off before your most serene highness decides how to punish me.'

Talleyrand could not help laughing.

'Good God, how should I punish you? I can't even ask my friend Fouché to have you arrested, since it was he who sent you. And I can scarcely see myself doing away with you discreetly in my own library or calling the world to witness the frightful blackness of your little heart. Come back here and sit down and listen to me.'

Marianne obeyed reluctantly. The steady gaze of the prince's pale eyes made her uncomfortable. There was a kind of humorous penetration in them which made her feel as though they could pierce through her clothes, and even her skin, to lay bare her very heart and soul. She was also slightly apprehensive about what was to follow. But, when she was seated once more, Talleyrand smiled.

'My dear child,' he began, 'I have known our Minister of Police, and his methods, for too long not to have learned to beware. We have cordially detested one another for years and our – mutual affection is much too recent, and a great deal too interesting, not to require handling with some degree of caution. So you see, Mademoiselle Mallerousse – by the way, are you really called Mallerousse?'

'No,' Marianne replied shortly. 'But you will gain nothing by questioning me further. I shall not soil my true name by dragging it into this business. You may do what you like with me!'

'A tempting offer, eh? Never mind. I am glad to see I was not mistaken in my judgement of you. As for your real name, that does not greatly concern me. You are undoubtedly an Émigrée who has re-entered the country illegally and been obliged to accept our dear Fouché's – er – protection. He has a gift for making such bargains. Keep your secret, then, you will tell me of your own accord someday. Now, what are we going to do with you?'

He rose and began walking slowly about the room. Marianne stared down at her green velvet reticule, partly to conceal what was passing in her mind and partly to avoid having to look at the tall black figure moving to and fro across a patch of sunlight. From time to time, the figure would move out of sight and then Marianne was acutely conscious of the eyes resting on her. She controlled her nervousness with an effort. What was he waiting for? What, precisely, did he want with her? Why did he not speak?

She realized suddenly that he had come to a halt behind her. A hand, light yet commanding, rested on her shoulder, almost brushing her cheek.

'I think,' he said at last, 'We shall continue with our plan. There are certain things in which you can be of invaluable assistance to me. As for those services required of you by his grace the Duke of Otranto - well, you will simply go on as though nothing had happened.'

Marianne gave a start.

'What? You - your highness, I mean, wishes me to go on —'

'Most certainly! You will, naturally, show me your letters before giving them to Floquet. It is most desirable from my own point of view that certain exalted circles should be well informed of what takes place in my house. It shows the Emperor is still interested, whatever he may think. Go on, my dear, go on. One way and another, I think, you will be kept very busy. All the same —'

He paused. The hand on Marianne's shoulder seemed to grow a shade heavier, almost threatening. But only for an instant. The next second it had become gentle and caressing, running lightly over the girl's slender neck to the warm nape. Marianne held her breath.

'All the same, I may perhaps request some services - of another kind.'

Instantly, Marianne had torn herself free of the caressing hand and sprung to her feet to face the prince, scarlet with anger. She understood now what he wanted of her, the kind of services he expected in exchange for his promised silence. It was blackmail worse than Fouché's!

'Do not count on me for services of that kind!' she cried fiercely. 'I have spied on you, yes, although my reports contained nothing worth reading! But I will not buy my freedom in your bed!'

Talleyrand's lips quivered, then he laughed outright.

'Are you not, as the princess would say, a little lacking in respect? For shame, Mademoiselle Mallerousse! These are notions and expressions, that go only too well with your foreign name! I meant merely - to ask you to sing, for one or more of my friends, when and where I shall request.'

'Oh. Is that —'

'All? Certainly. Nothing more. My dear Marianne - may I call you by that charming name that suits you so well? - you are very lovely, but I have never enjoyed making love to a woman who yielded to anything but her own desires. Love is like music, an ineffable harmony, and the body merely an instrument, although the most wonderful of all instruments beyond a doubt. If one of the two is out of tune, then that harmony is broken. I dislike false notes - as much as you do yourself.'

'May - may your highness forgive me,' Marianne said in a low voice, feeling horribly ashamed. 'I behaved foolishly and I beg your pardon. Naturally, I should be glad to be of service.'

'So I should hope. And now, since we are agreed, give me your hand. We'll shake hands on it like our American friends, as befits two people who understand one another. There is a great deal of good in these American fashions, and on the whole, I approve of them although they are often somewhat direct for my taste.'

His smile was disarming and Marianne returned it frankly. Her fingers shook a little as she placed them timidly in the prince's hand but his grip was quick and firm.

'I shall send for you tomorrow morning, if the princess does not need you.'

'Your most serene highness's to command – '

A brief curtsey and Marianne found herself out in the corridor feeling rather dazed and bewildered but extraordinarily relieved. She had rebelled too much against her position and her resentment against Fouché was too strong for her not to feel inwardly delighted at this reversal of the situation, especially since she could not help liking the aristocrat, Talleyrand, much more than the wily Fouché. Her nightmare was at an end. She was no longer a spy. In future she would not be betraying the roof that sheltered her and could enjoy the comfort and luxury she had found there with a quiet mind, devoting herself wholly to her music until such time as Gossec should help her make her debut as a singer.

It was too late for her lesson. A glance into the music room showed her that Gossec had gone but Marianne was too happy to let that worry her. She was on her way up to her own room humming a little tune when her thoughts turned suddenly to the vehicle which had followed her all morning and she had a sudden impulse to see if it was still there. She turned and ran back down the stairs, across the hall and out into the courtyard. Beside the main portico, with its double row of ionic columns giving on to the impressive stone sweep that formed the main approach to the mansion, there was a small postern which was never closed during the day. This, Marianne opened and, slipping outside, hurried along the wall to the corner. Her newly acquired spirits fell a little when she saw that the black carriage was still there.

It was still there later in the afternoon when Marianne went out with the princess and little Charlotte for a drive along the new embankments which the imperial government was constructing along the Seine.

There was a change. Marianne noticed it first that evening, when, on their return from their drive, Madame de Talleyrand asked her to go with her to her room. When they got there, she flung herself on a sofa with a weary sigh and announced:

'There will be company tonight, as you know, child, but I am too tired to go down. I shall stay in my room.'

'But – what will his most serene highness say should your highness not be there to receive your guests?'

The erstwhile Madame Grand smiled sadly.

'Nothing. His highness will do very well without me. I daresay he may even be thankful.'

Suddenly, Marianne felt very sorry for her. This was the first time the princess had shown any signs of bitterness but since her entry into the household, Marianne had had daily opportunities to observe the purely decorative and useless role she filled in her husband's house. Talleyrand was polite to his wife, but that was all. He scarcely spoke to her except to inquire for her health or to make some other commonplace remark. Apart from this, his charm was reserved for the numerous women who buzzed around him constantly in a rustling, scented swarm. Madame de Talleyrand seemed to accept this state of affairs with equanimity, hence Marianne's surprise at her melancholy mood on this occasion. She wondered whether the indifference was merely a well-mannered cloak for a real wound. Her surprise was still greater when the princess added that she would not need her that evening and that instead she should be ready to make her appearance in the salon after dinner.

'Without your highness?'

'Yes, without me – the prince desires that you shall sing. The great Czech, Dussek, is to play, with Niedermannthe harpist and the violinist Libon. You are to complete the concert.'

Marianne felt slightly daunted at the prospect of appearing in the company of three such brilliant performers. In spite of Gossec's daily lessons and his warm encouragement and praise, she was not yet sufficiently sure of her voice and talent. On the other hand, the fact of singing before such a splendid gathering could be important for her. But she must speak to Gossec first and agree with him what she was to sing. Whatever happened, she was well aware that the order came from a higher authority and that there could be no question of declining. This was all part of the new agreement between herself and Talleyrand. She could only obey even if, privately, she considered that the prince had lost little enough time in making her perform her part.

A little before eleven that evening, Marianne emerged from her room and made her way to the great salon. The guests who had not been present at the dinner were beginning to arrive and the party about to begin. The courtyard and the street had been filled for several minutes with the rattle of carriages and the jingle of harness, accompanied by the shouts of coachmen and lackeys, almost drowning the strains of violins rising from below.

Passing a long mirror, Marianne paused. However little enthusiasm she felt for the evening, she knew she looked her best. Her dress of almond green tulle suited her to perfection, although she acknowledged some doubts about the deep décolleté. Despite the small spray of lilac at its lowest point, it was cut to the very limits of decency, displaying to advantage the golden skin and full, rich curves of her breasts and shoulders. The hands that held the music of the song she was to sing were clad in long, lilac mittens and there were a few sprays of lilac caught up with ribbons of green tulle among the crown of glossy, dark ringlets piled high on her head. Marianne decided she looked very nice. This was a discovery she owed to Paris, to Leroy and to this elegant household who had taught her to understand her own beauty. Until then, she had not really been aware of it, although she had already discovered her power to arouse desire in men. But now, she was sure of it. Perhaps because a man like Talleyrand had told her. He had taught her, in a way, to look at herself and she was not yet tired of the novel enjoyment.

She lingered a moment before the glass, enjoying her own radiant reflection enhanced by the soft candlelight. Her green eyes were sparkling and there was a moist sheen on her lips, and suddenly, Marianne sighed. How she would have loved to look as beautiful as this a year ago! Then, perhaps Francis would have loved her for herself and not for her fortune. Perhaps they might really have been happy together! But Francis was dead and this dazzling reflection was only the ghost of Marianne d'Asselnat inhabiting the body of a stranger, a homeless wanderer whose flesh was already a woman's flesh but whose heart held nothing now but emptiness. And yet, it would have been good to love and be loved, to make of this useless beauty a gift for the eyes of a man in love.

She saw her reflected image part its lips and shape them into a kiss and closed her eyes, overcome by a sudden languor. She opened them again almost at once with a little cry. A pair of arms were round her and a pair of warm lips pressed hungrily against the nape of her neck. She saw herself in the glass, held prisoner by two anonymous but trembling hands. A head of which she could make out nothing at first beyond dark, curly hair, was buried in her shoulder. She struggled as hard as she could, lips tight closed to prevent herself crying out, and finally succeeded in breaking her attacker's grip and sending him reeling from a blow that would have done credit to a washerwoman. He staggered back against the wrought iron balusters and only luck saved him from plunging head-first down the stairs. Not until then did Marianne recognize Charlotte's tutor, Monsieur Fercoc.

'You? But what possessed you? Are you mad?'

'I believe – oh, I daresay I may be! I lost my head – and my spectacles. Oh, Lord! I suppose you can't see them anywhere? All I can see of you is a green mist – I am a fool, indeed!'

'Indeed, you are!' Marianne agreed. Her anger had vanished entirely and she felt only an overwhelming urge to laugh. Fercoc, blinking and groping blindly at the empty air, was more comical than alarming. He seemed dreadfully upset and perfectly harmless.

Catching the gleam of his spectacles from the floor beneath a gilded console table, she picked them up and having first assured herself that they had suffered no damage in their fall, replaced them on the tutor's nose, inquiring wickedly:

'And can you see better now?'

'Oh! Yes – oh! Thank you! How kind you are, how very –'

'How very foolish you should say. My dear sir, I have returned good for ill. Will you be good enough to tell me what this assault might signify?'

With the recovery of his spectacles, Fercoc had also recovered both his manners and his confusion. He hung his head.

'I ask your pardon, Mademoiselle Marianne. As I said, I lost my head. You were looking at yourself in the mirror and you were so lovely, so luminous, so exactly the way I see you in my dreams –'

'You dream about me?' She asked with instinctive coquetry.

'Very often – but not as much as I should like! I wish that I could dream of you every night because at night you notice me, you come to me – and then I dare such things, in my dreams. I thought I was still dreaming.'

There was such warmth and fervour in his voice that Marianne was quite disarmed. She smiled and looked at him with more attention. If he did not look always so timid and down-trodden, she thought, he would be quite a nice-looking boy. His eyes behind his spectacles were kind and gentle, too gentle. The eyes of a devoted dog, not of a lover! All the other eyes she had seen bent on her had been masterful and demanding. Francis' eyes had been cold, Jean Le Dru's hot and fierce, while that other, the impudent American who thought that he had bought her, had had eyes like a bird of prey; not one of them had had eyes like these, soft and heavy with untold tenderness which went some way to banish her distrust of men.

'Do you forgive me?' he asked timidly. 'You are not angry with me?'

'No, I am not angry. It is not your fault – if you love me.'

It was a statement rather than a question. She knew that this boy loved her. He would not have looked at her like that had it been simple desire. It was a new and rather refreshing experience. The young man's eyes lit up at her words.

'Oh! You understand? You know I love you.'

'It was not hard to guess. And I have only just found out.'

'And – do you think that, one day, you –'

'That one day I might love you?' Marianne's smile was sad. 'How can you ask me that? I like you and I think we can be friends – but as for love! I do not know if I can love again.'

'Then, you have been in love?' he said in a low voice.

'Yes. And my life has been one long regret ever since. So, please, be kind and never speak to me of love.'

'And he?' Fercoc muttered with sudden violence. 'Does he never speak to you of love?'

'He? Who is he?'

'The prince. I may be short-sighted but with my spectacles I can see clearly enough. I have seen him look at you with his cold snake's eyes.'

Marianne stepped closer and gave the tutor's cheek a gentle, sisterly pat.

'I should not think a snake's eyes so very ardent! So let us have no more nonsense, my friend. The prince's looks mean nothing, to me of all people.'

'And yet I thought – that she had sent you here for him more than for her.'

There was a rustle of tulle as Marianne's hands dropped heavily to her side. It seemed that once again she had fallen into a trap. But now, the boy's innocence annoyed her. Perhaps because it echoed too clearly her own suspicions as to Fouché's private intentions regarding her. She saw that apart from the Countess de Périgord, who knew the truth more or less, everyone she met in this house with some knowledge of its master could have but one idea, that although she might spend her days with the princess her nights must belong to the prince. She had had more than enough of being taken for something she was not. It was insufferable! And this boy was no better than all the rest!

Alarmed by her silence, Fercoc was about to say something more but she silenced him with a gesture.

'No. Don't say any more. I have no time. I must go down. But let me tell you one thing, that whatever you may believe, I am not here for the prince. Good evening to you, Monsieur Fercoc.'

He tried to detain her.

'Mademoiselle – one moment – if I have annoyed you –'

But Marianne was no longer listening. The moment's gentleness had passed. He leaned over the baluster and watched her glide swiftly down the stairs, light as an iridescent shade, unaware that her irritation was directed more against herself than him. She was running away from her own weakness as well as from the image that others seemed determined to make of her. The love that he had offered her might have been sweet and soothing. Why did he have to spoil its freshness with his clumsy suspicions? They were insulting and irrelevant. Were there really only three kinds of men, cynics, brutes and fools? Would there never be one who was different?

At her approach, the footman's white-gloved hand pushed open the small door in the panelling of the great salon, which enabled her to avoid entering by the main double doors. She was met by a wave of light and heat, perfume and music. The great white and gold room, adorned with huge banks of pale pink tulips sent that very morning from the hot houses of Valençay, glittered at its most brilliant in the light of immense crystal chandeliers ablaze with innumerable candles. It was filled with a cheerful hubbub of conversation, punctuated by the flutter of fans, the silky swish of trains brushing the carpets, almost drowning invisible violins. Gowns shimmered, diamonds glittered and against a background of white uniforms, Russian or Austrian, that proclaimed the prince's cosmopolitan hospitality, Marianne beheld the gorgeous purple and gold of a marshal of the Empire and recognized the features of Léonine de Ney, Duke of Elchingen. She saw the Duchess of Courlande reclining on a sofa wearing a plumed pink turban. Dorothée de Périgord, who was seated next to a tall, thin, talkative woman, Countess Kielmannsegge, smiled and beckoned to her. Last of all, she saw Talleyrand standing watching her. Her eye, at first drawn by the prince, a sombre and magnificent figure in a plain but perfectly cut black coat studded with foreign decorations, moved on insensibly to the other and still taller figure, also in black, standing beside him.

He too was watching her entrance. He had a thin, hawk-like face, a bronzed complexion and blue eyes that were very bright. Marianne felt an iron band tighten suddenly around her forehead and there was a taste of ashes in her mouth. Her fingers tightened on the roll of music. The man was Jason Beaufort.

Marianne's first instinct was to turn on her heels and run, but in a moment, common sense prevailed over the terror which had taken hold of her. She could not run away. It might have been possible if Beaufort or the prince had not seen her, but both were looking at her fixedly. She had to stay.

Unable, however, to bring herself to approach the two men directly, Marianne veered off towards the corner where the Countess de Périgord was still sitting and beckoning to her. She felt in desperate need of a breathing space in which to try and think.

Dorothée greeted her with the rather exaggerated friendliness she tended to show partly for the pleasure of disconcerting those around her.

'Come and sit with us, Marianne, we are busy tearing everyone to pieces. It is great fun.'

Marianne forced a somewhat absent-minded smile and answered automatically: 'Heaven preserve me from providing you with a target, my lady. Who is your present victim?'

'Why, the Emperor himself. The rumour is spreading that he means to marry an arch-duchess. He has her household in hand already and I have been suggested for lady-in-waiting. What do you think?'

'I think, countess, that your birth makes you equal to the most exalted positions. This does not surprise me ... should you like it?'

The conversation dragged on agonizingly, but she had to gain time, time to think!

Dorothée de Périgord gave her great childish whoop of laughter.

199

'To be honest, no! Oh, not that I have any objection to serving a Habsburg if she should be fool enough to marry the ogre, but I have no desire to live in Napoleon's immediate circle. There are quite enough of those dreadful, unavoidable evenings at the Tuileries as it is.'

The Countess Kielmannsegge had so far been content to listen but now she apparently felt that her young friend had been expending too much politeness on someone of no importance and that it was time for her to recover the initiative.

'Do you know what he said to Madame de Montmorency the other day? It was rather good, I must admit.'

'Good heavens, no! Do tell us!'

'You know the Emperor wanted to make Montmorency a count and his wife objected on the score that it was by no means good enough for his illustrious family. "Sire," she said, "we are the first barons of Christendom." But the Emperor only laughed and told her: "I know that, madame, but you do not seem to me a good enough Christian."'

'He can be witty when he likes,' Dorothée said thoughtfully. 'Even so, I should prefer not to be obliged to serve his wife. Fortunately, it has not happened yet.'

The words reached Marianne only faintly through the mist of anxiety which beset her. She was scarcely listening, but Madame Kielmannsegge had won her point and recovered Madame de Périgord's attention. In any case, two other guests, the Canoness de Chastenay and M. de la Tour du Pin had joined the group and Marianne was sufficiently recovered to try and examine her situation. Such was her fear of what might happen that she scarcely dared to turn her eyes in the direction where she had seen the American. For Talleyrand knew already that she was an émigrée returned illegally to France but now he would discover her real identity, and that she was a murderess. Marianne felt her heart sink within her at the memory of those words heard through the mist that night on the Barbican at Plymouth. She could hear them still: 'She'll not escape the gallows for long –' And the shudder which had run through her then seized her once more. The old fear that had been with her for so long and which she had thought herself free at last returned as sickeningly as ever. This Beaufort hated her. She had refused to submit to his whim after he had possessed himself of her fortune, instead, she had rejected him with horror and he meant to avenge himself by delivering her up to the hangman.

Suddenly, the splendid room, the fashionable throng, even the music seemed to melt away and Marianne was as cold as if she had been miraculously transported out of doors into the snow that was beginning to fall. Tears pricked at her eyes. It was no good. She had thought in vain to escape from that dreadful night which had destroyed her life but, mercilessly, inexorably, the night had overtaken her again. The brief, cherished dream of devoting her whole life to singing, of living for herself and doing with her life exactly what she liked, was melting away just when it was almost within her grasp. She had such high hopes of this evening and now, once again, it was a man who would bring it all to ruin. What should she do, she wondered. Throw herself at Talleyrand's feet and tell him her story, her whole story, then beg him to protect her and help her stay in France? Remembering the effect her story had produced on the old Duc d'Avaray, Marianne had no great wish to repeat the experience. She could never find a man to believe her because the truth of her story was an affront to their image of themselves.

She cast a fearful glance around, looking for Beaufort's tall figure but did not see him. She did hear Talleyrand's slow drawl, however, not far away in a group which had formed round the university Grand Master, M. de Fontanes, who was once more holding forth upon his favourite subject, M. de Châteauxbriand and all his works, and, especially, his most recent publication, *Les Martyrs*. The book had met with considerable public success and, at the same time some violent opposition. Attracted by his gentle, academic tones, Marianne drew nearer with some idea of exchanging a quiet word with Talleyrand, who was standing quite close to the speaker watching him with a faint, mocking smile. The prince was accused of being an amoral cynic, with a strong disregard of convention. Perhaps he would be less shocked than she had imagined by the idea that she had killed a man.

'I maintain that *Les Martyrs* is a fine book and I cannot understand, my dear prince,' Fontanes was saying, 'why you should pour scorn on one of the most remarkable works of our time.'

'My dear Fontanes, M. de Châteauxbriand bores me,' Talleyrand drawled. 'The hermit of the Valley of the Wolves seems very much inclined to regard himself as God, or possibly Moses. One would think him the only man capable of telling the world what a martyr was.'

'That is a little hard. I confess to being much moved myself by the beauty and imagery of sentiments. I am particularly fond of the excellent scene where Eudora and Cymodocée are to be devoured by the wild beasts.'

'So is the book,' Talleyrand said dryly. 'But now, forget your idol for a while, my friend, and come and listen to a little music. Myself, I think it soothes the savage beasts infinitely better than M. Châteauxbriand, eh?'

At once a general drift began towards the music room and Marianne was obliged to give up her hope of speaking to the prince. She had no choice but to follow the rest, since she was to sing, but she had the unpleasant conviction that she would not be able to produce a single note. She was bound for irrevocable disaster. But then, since all was in any case lost, perhaps there was no need to add to her troubles with a public execution, and cover herself with ignominy before all these people? Standing by the big double doors, she allowed the crowd to flow past her and then turned away.

She would go up to her room first and fetch a cloak, then get someone to call her a cab and order it to take her to the rue de la Grange Batelière. She would wait there for Dorothée de Périgord, who seemed the one person able to protect her.

But the movement was never finished. The tall figure of the American rose suddenly before her, barring her way to the door.

'And where are you off to?' he said, taking her arm. 'The music room is this way. And it seems you are to sing for us?'

The tone was as natural as if they had met the day before but its very ordinariness struck terror into Marianne, who thought she read into it the direst of threats. She sought to release her arm and tried to bluff her way out.

'I beg you will release me, sir. I do not know you —'

He laughed, showing a glimpse of dazzling white teeth, but his grip on his prey did not slacken.

'My dear Mademoiselle Mallerousse - is it? - where did you learn such falsehoods? And, by the way, where did you pick up that name? It is really quite appalling.'

'Appalling or no, it suits me and I beg you again to release me. We have nothing to say to one another —'

'You think not? It seems to me we have a great deal to say to one another. And so, my dear Marianne, I shall not let you go. And while I think of it, if you did not wish to be recognized, there were one or two little things you should have changed, your eyes, your hair, your face, your figure - as I said, I will not let you go except to the pianoforte which awaits you and not even then unless you will give me your solemn promise of a few minutes' private conversation.'

'See you alone? Here? But where? That is quite impossible.'

'You have a room —'

'The princess's apartments are close by. My reputation —'

'Ah, yes, to be sure, you cherish it do you not?' Beaufort said with irony. He gave her a wolfish grin. 'Then think of somewhere else. But think fast. People will start to wonder why I'm holding on to you as though I'd caught you picking my pocket.'

Marianne cast desperate eyes at the window. Never had she felt so helpless. The man was a devil! Suddenly, she remembered the little summer-house at the end of the garden. It was known as M. de Matignon's Petit Trianon and was hardly ever used.

'After supper, when the gaming tables are set up,' she murmured quickly. 'Meet me at the bottom of the garden.'

'In this weather? You know it's snowing?'

'I thought you were a sailor,' Marianne retorted scornfully. 'Are you afraid of snow?'

'Not for myself, only for your pretty feet, my dear,' he answered with a slight bow. 'But if you are prepared to brave the elements—'

'Unless you prefer cards,' Marianne sneered. 'You are a whist player of some skill, I believe.'

She found it gave her courage to be rude to him, although the worst of her terror had already left her. She was beginning to think that all might not be lost. The fact that he should wish to see her alone suggested that he had something more to say. Now, everything would depend upon the price of his silence and what that price might be, Marianne preferred not to think.

But Jason Beaufort had no mind to let her off so lightly. Releasing his grip on her arm, he nicked the ruffles at his throat with a faintly old-world gesture.

'There's a time for everything,' he observed coolly. 'Very well then, we shall meet again after supper, try not to fail. You don't know how much I can enjoy starting off a really good scandal.'

Marianne flushed angrily. He was mocking her. A hateful little spark of mischief danced in his blue eyes.

'Never fear,' she said shortly. 'I'll be there.'

He bowed with a graceful ease surprising in a man of his virile appearance.

'I live for that moment. Your servant, mademoiselle, and, believe me, an admirer determined to applaud you to the echo.' As he straightened up, he added in an undertone: 'You need not look so, pretty child. One would swear you had met with an ogre. I do not eat little girls, I promise you, or not in the way you seem to think.'

He turned on his heel and vanished into the crowd. Marianne brushed her forehead with a trembling hand. It was damp with sweat and she drew out her handkerchief and endeavoured to mop it furtively. It was a relief to know herself safe for the present, but it had been a close thing.

'Come, what are you about?' Talleyrand's voice spoke reproachfully at her elbow. 'Dussek is already at the piano and will begin to play in a moment. It will be your turn next. Let me take you to a seat by Madame de Périgord. She is asking for you.'

He had taken her hand with his cold, aristocratic courtesy to lead her through the rows of chairs where most of the guests were already seated. As they went, he observed suddenly:

'This is, indeed, a small world. And you will agree, I think. Did you expect to meet an old friend here tonight, eh?'

'No indeed, your Highness,' Marianne said with sincerity, wondering unhappily what Beaufort could have told him. 'M. Beaufort told you—'

'That he was well acquainted with your family in England, thus confirming my own thoughts as to your origin. He seems to be a great admirer of yours.'

Hypocrite, Marianne thought furiously. *The miserable hypocrite! He is not above singing my praises if it will help him to learn more.* But aloud she asked: 'May I ask your Highness where you met Jason Beaufort?'

Talleyrand laughed. 'Oh, a long time ago. When I was in America, I was on terms with his father, a perfect gentleman and a man of some substance. At that time, young Jason was only an imp of mischief dreaming of nothing but ships and the sea. He spent his time making boats out of anything that came to hand, even the washing baskets! But their house at Old Creek Town was a place of great beauty.'

'Was?'

'It burned down, shortly after Robert Beaufort's death, which was as peculiar in its way as the fire. Ruin followed and the culprit, if culprit there was, was never discovered. Yes – an odd story. But then, surely you must know it as well as I, eh?'

Marianne lowered her eyes to hide her confusion.

'I was too young to know much of what was said in the drawing room at home. And M. Beaufort was not such a frequent visitor. I, at least, saw very little of him.'

'I'm sorry for your sake. He is a remarkable young man and I am very fond of him. He has worked hard to restore his shattered fortunes and he will succeed. He is one of those who build empires in the teeth of wind and tide. Did you know that a few months ago his vessel went to the bottom with a full load of cotton, everything he possessed in this world and the company's cargo he was carrying? Well, by some magic he has managed to acquire another ship and is at present seeking a cargo for the voyage back to Charleston. Admirable, is it not?'

They had by now reached the front row of the audience and, Marianne thought, not before time or she would have thrown prudence to the wind and said exactly what she thought. She was only too well aware of what magic this 'admirable' young man had employed to repair his shattered fortune. A game of cards and the hopeless passion of a gamester. But as she took her place, still quivering with suppressed anger, on a low stool beside the young countess's chair, she decided to put off any further examination of Jason Beaufort's actions until later, much later, by which time she would know what it was he wanted of her. For the present, the Czech pianist's long pale hands were already moving over the keyboard. It was time to be silent. The stillness spread to her heart and mind for, to Marianne, the soothing power of music never failed. She had to abandon herself totally to it in order to win through to that state of grace which must be hers in a moment. She closed her eyes. The artist began to play.

Two hours later, with a black cloak flung over her thin dress and pattens on her feet, Marianne left the house by means of a French window and, crossing the terrace, set off across the empty garden. It had stopped snowing but a thick blanket of white lay over everything, stretching like a huge carpet over the grass to the distant line of trees, turning shrubs and statues into strange white ghosts that loomed up out of the darkness. Marianne did not know whether to be afraid of the dark or of the elements. She set out boldly across the white expanse, hurrying to leave the patches of light thrown from the tall windows of the house. The temperature had risen with the snow. The cold was not so fierce. It was not long before Marianne reached the far end of the grounds and, turning to her left, approached the little octagonal summer-house. A little light filtered from behind the drawn curtains. Jason Beaufort was waiting for her.

He was seated in the circular parlour, warming his hands at the fire which was always kept laid and which he must have set light to on arrival. Marianne was struck by his stern profile outlined against the golden glow of the flames. For the first time, she saw a kind of beauty in it but as quickly dismissed the thought. It was out of keeping with the interview about to take place.

She went forward, closing the glass door behind her. Her pattens clattered on the tiled floor of black, white and grey marble but Jason did not turn his head. Without looking at her, he pointed to a chair on the other side of the hearth.

She threw back the hood of her cloak on to her shoulders and obeyed him mechanically. The light fell on her small, proud head with its crown of shining curls but still he did not look at her. Instead, he stared intently into the glowing heart of the fire and began to hum the air which Marianne had sung a little while before. He sang tunefully, in a deep pleasant voice but Marianne had not come just to hear him sing.

'Well?' she said impatiently.

'Are you in such a hurry? Tell me, what is the name of this song? I like it.'

'It is an old song, called 'Plaisir d'Amour'. It is a setting by Martini of a poem of Florian. Does that satisfy you?' Marianne said snappishly.

Jason turned for the first time and looked at her. His eyes were as calm as the sea on a fair day. He shrugged.

'Don't be so aggressive,' he told her quietly. 'We came here to talk, not to argue. I've lost all desire to quarrel with you – supposing I ever had any.'

Marianne laughed shortly. 'A miracle!' she said. 'To what do we owe it?'

He stirred impatiently. 'Don't nag. It makes you sound hideous, like a shrew! Can't you see you're breaking the spell?'

'The spell?'

'Yes,' he said bitterly, 'the spell you put on me just now, when I heard you sing. For a moment, hearing your voice, I was in paradise. So warm, and pure! For me, it was—' he fell into a momentary dream, his eyes fixed on some distance a long way beyond the dainty rustic artificialities of the woodwork.

Marianne looked at him in surprise, holding her breath and flattered, in spite of her dislike, by his obvious sincerity. But, coming abruptly back to earth, Jason only said harshly:

'No – nothing. I beg your pardon. You could not understand.'

'Am I so stupid?' she said, disappointed, but with a gentleness that surprised herself.

The American smiled suddenly, his strange, crooked smile. His deep blue eyes danced.

'Still more curious than hostile, mm? You are still very much a woman, Marianne. But, after all, I wonder whether you'd be very flattered if I told you your voice reminded me of another that I loved to hear as a child.'

'Why not?'

'Because it belonged to my nurse, Deborah – a magnificent black slave from Angola—'

Seeing Marianne spring indignantly to her feet, her cheeks on fire and her eyes flashing, he laughed and went on: 'Just as I thought. You are not flattered. But you are wrong, Deborah's voice was wonderful, like dark velvet – oh, the devil's in it! Didn't they teach you as a child that curiosity killed the cat?'

'That is enough!' Marianne cried, shaking with anger. 'Have the goodness to tell me, once and for all, the reason for this interview and let us make an end. What have you to tell me?'

He too had risen and came towards her.

'A question first, if I may. Why did you run away from England?'

'Are you unaware of what took place at Selton Hall on my wedding night?'

'No – but—'

'Then, how dare you ask me why I fled,' Marianne cried passionately, 'when you must know quite well that on that night, I killed my husband and his cousin and set fire to the house! You know it so well in fact that you gave chase with the firm intention of delivering me up to the law.'

'I? Gave chase? I meant to deliver you up to the law?' Beaufort echoed with such evident bewilderment that Marianne began to feel a trifle foolish. However, she did let this deter her.

'Yes, you! I heard you talking, one night on the quay at Plymouth! You were with a little man in black and you said that at all events I could not get far and that the gallows awaited me!'

'What? Were you there? The devil, Marianne, have you some magic potion to make you invisible?'

'It does not matter. Did you say it or not?'

Jason was laughing now with real amusement. 'I certainly did! But just as certainly it does you no good to listen at keyholes, even when there aren't any. You little fool, I wasn't talking about you! That night I still knew nothing of your exploits!'

'Then who?'

'A wretched creature called Nell Woodbury, a trull from the back streets of London who killed my best topman and robbed him – one of the only two saved from the wreck of the *Savannah Belle*. It was she I was after. She had been traced to Plymouth where she was trying to get on board a vessel bound for the West Indies. And I found her.'

'And she —'

'Hanged,' Beaufort said shortly. 'She deserved nothing better. I would have killed her with my bare hands had she been let off. But enough of that. You have reminded me of something I should prefer to forget. And we were talking about you. What do you mean to do now?'

'Now?'

'Yes, now,' he said impatiently. 'Do you intend to remain here in this house? Dancing attendance on a feather-brained beauty – until, that is, my most serene friend should happen to notice that you are ravishing?'

Always the same assumption! Marianne's ill humour came flooding back. Could no one think of her in any light but that of Talleyrand's prospective mistress?

'What do you take me for —' she began.

'For a delightful girl with no more sense than I have in my little finger! My exquisite child, you have a genius for getting yourself into impossible situations. To tell the truth, you remind me of a little scatter-brain white seagull setting out blindly to cross the ocean taking it for nothing more than a creek and without the first idea what to do about it. I am telling you that if you stay here, sooner or later you will fall victim to that old lecher Talleyrand.'

'And I tell you I shall not! You spoke, just now, of my voice. It is to that I look for my escape. I am taking lessons every day and my teacher has promised that I shall sing, and triumph, in all the great theatres of Europe. He says I can become the greatest singer of the age!'

Beaufort shrugged.

'The theatre? Is it in the theatre you hope to find a place and a future worthy of you?' Jason's voice hardened. 'If you had the voice of the archangel Gabriel himself, I would beg you to remember who you are. The daughter of the Marquis d'Asselnat treading the boards! Are you mad, indeed, or merely half-witted?'

He was growing really angry now. Marianne saw the knuckles whiten below his lace cuffs and his hawk-like face harden unbelievably.

'Neither mad, nor half-witted,' Marianne raged at him. 'I want to be free. Free, do you hear? Don't you understand that Marianne d'Asselnat is no more, that she is dead, that she died one night last autumn – and you killed her! How can you come here now and talk about my name and family? Did you think of that the night you played for me at cards, like a mere chattel, a slave to be disposed of at will? You cared little enough that night for the Marquis d'Asselnat, who died for his beliefs and for his king. You treated his daughter with no more respect than any sailor's drab!'

There were tears of rage and misery in her eyes and Jason recoiled before the violence of her attack. He had paled under his tan and was looking at her grief-stricken face with a kind of helpless pain.

'I did not know,' he said in a low voice. 'I swear to you, by my mother's memory, that I did not know. How could I have done?'

'Know what?'

'What you were like. I had never met you. What did I know of you? Your name, your family —'

'My fortune!' Marianne snapped viciously.

'Your fortune, to be sure. But Francis Cranmere and his friends I did know, and the lovely Ivy in particular. I knew them to be rotten to the core, utterly vicious and corrupt, without principle and without honour, wholly given over to the pleasures of sport, gaming and foolish wagers. How was I to guess that you were not the faithful copy of Ivy St Albans, a girl of noble birth and apparent purity, who was yet capable of giving herself to two complete strangers in a single night simply to get some money for her precious Francis? Francis was to marry you, why should you be any different? Birds of a feather, after all! And it seemed to me, Marianne, that you could not be other than Cranmere because you had consented to marry him, and because your friends had given you to him, knowing quite well what he was —'

'My friends?' Marianne said sadly. 'Never for one moment would Aunt Ellis have believed that the son of the one man she ever loved could be a worthless libertine. And she died, a week before my marriage. I was alone, in the power of a man who wanted only my money and you had no pity for me, you robbed me faster than he would have done!'

'It was not I who robbed you. It was he. I did not prompt him to stake your fortune.'

'But neither did you stop him! No, when he had nothing left to stake, you thought of me.'

'No! No, I swear to you! The idea came from Francis, it was his own suggestion to make you the stake in a final attempt to recover all.'

'And you agreed, naturally.'

'Why not? Since he had the effrontery to offer me your kisses and your person, he must know you would agree. Understand me, Marianne, I thought you as vicious as he was. Hadn't I heard him, a few days before your marriage, laughing and promising to lend you to Lord Moira when he himself had rubbed off some of your delicious bloom. And adding that he was confident of success with you? But had I known you, Marianne, I should never have agreed to play with him. I swear to you.'

'You swear too much,' Marianne said wearily. 'I do not ask you to – and I do not believe you. You saw me during the ceremony. Did I really look to you like a girl who would give herself to anyone?'

'No, you did not. But a woman's face may be deceptive, and – you were so beautiful. So very beautiful –'

Marianne gave a hard, contemptuous little laugh. 'I see. And the opportunity too was beautiful, was it not? It was so easy! You wanted me and you could have me with my own husband's blessing!'

Jason turned and walked slowly to the hearth. Marianne could not see his face but she saw the hands clasped behind his back tighten nervously.

In the few minutes silence which fell between them, Marianne was able to take stock of what he had just told her. The ignominy of Francis's offering her to his friend, even before their marriage, perhaps even in return for money. Ivy, prostituting herself so that her lover might live in luxury. Into what a sink had she fallen, and how little compunction she felt now for the death of those two! They had not deserved to live. Suddenly Jason spoke fiercely, still with his back to her.

'I admit it. I did want you, wanted you more than I thought I could want anything again! Wanted you so much that I was ready, in return for just one night of love, to give up the fortune I had won against all hope and of which I stood in such desperate need. Had I lost, I had lost everything – and you would have had your wedding night as though nothing had happened, though a little late maybe, and afterwards been handed over graciously to Lord Moira! But for a little while, you were more to me than the whole world, more than my own future, more than fortune! You were my fortune – and I would have been fool enough to give it all back to you in return for the joy of holding you for a few hours in my arms.'

Marianne was stirred despite her anger by the depth of passion in his voice. Silence fell once more inside the pretty room. In the hearth, a log split asunder and collapsed in a pool of red embers. The American stood very still but it seemed to Marianne that his broad shoulders drooped and bowed, as though under the force of some strong feeling. For a moment, she was tempted to go to him and try and find out how much sincerity was in his words, but she was too distrustful, too much on her guard against men's wiles. And this man was the architect of all her wretchedness. She could not forget that. It was time to make an end.

'Is that all you have to say to me?' she said with a sigh.

'No. I have not yet done.'

He swung round and came to her. Marianne could discern in his features no trace of the violence of a moment before. He was grave but calm.

'Marianne,' he said quietly, 'try and hear me out without losing your temper. I am sincere, I beg you to believe that. You should not, you cannot stay here. No, don't speak. I know what I am saying. If I am here tonight at all, it is solely because of you.'

'Because of me?'

'Yes. I have sought you all the way from England. I learned at Plymouth that you had gone to France and so I came.'

'How did you find me? You had me followed, is that it?' She thought suddenly of the black cab.

'By no means. I have some connections – among others at the Ministry of Police. Maillocheau, citizen Fouché's secretary, has some obligation to me. Your description was enough – especially since you arrived in company with so remarkable a man as the renowned Surcouf – and by the by, I'm still not sure how you managed to befriend the King of the Corsairs. It is not given to everyone to lead the sea tiger on a leash.'

The atmosphere relaxed. Despite herself, Marianne smiled, remembering her friend of a day. She had thought of him more than once and always with a kind of tenderness that belonged to someone she could have loved. But she would not let Beaufort use him to get the better of her and dismissed the Corsair with a wave of her hand.

'So,' she said, 'you sought me, you have found me and you are trying to persuade me to leave this house. May I ask where you would have me go?'

Again, there was silence, inhabited by the living presence of the fire. The scent of burning pine logs filled the room with warm, peppery fragrance. In spite of herself, Marianne found her eyes captured and held by the American's blue ones. She stood and faced him, like a sparrow mesmerized by a bird of prey – only the falcon's claws were, all at once, oddly gentle on her shoulders. She made no move to shake them off.

With a movement too quick and light for Marianne to be aware what he was doing, Jason unfastened the satin ribbons holding the black cloak and slipped it off her shoulders. The heavy dark folds sank down to the ground, and the slender green form, released, seemed to shoot up before him like a slim fountain from a black rock. He contemplated her for a moment and Marianne stood, riveted by that sparkling gaze, not daring to move. It seemed to her, though why she should have such a strange idea she could not have said, that if she moved at all or said a word something rare and precious would be broken. In the end, it was he who sighed and spoke first.

'You are too beautiful,' he said sadly. 'It is not right for anyone to be so beautiful. It is perilous – yes, perilous. While you stay here, you will be in danger. You must leave this house, this land – or else, sooner or later, you will suffer for it. Sirens are not made to tread earthly roads. They are daughters of the sea and their happiness can come only from the sea – and I have never met anyone who was so much like a siren as you! Come with me to the sea, Marianne –'

Drawn by the depths of the green eyes looking into his and by the freshness of the lips slightly parted to reveal moist, shining teeth, and mastered perhaps by a passion beyond his control, he made a move to draw her to him. But Marianne recoiled with an instinctive fear from the threatened kiss. The spell was broken. The sparrow shook out its feathers.

'This is the second time,' she said coldly, 'that you have offered to take me away. Why should you imagine I am more likely to agree now than on my wedding night?'

'Because you are alone and friendless, a prey for all dangers and all snares. Do you think you can go on with this fugitive life, hiding under borrowed names, at the mercy of anyone who cares to blackmail or betray you? What I am offering you is a free life in a new land, my own. I do not even ask you to be mine – merely to come with me. I have a ship –'

'I know!' Marianne cried. 'And I know too how you came by it. Do you think I could ever forget that? No, Jason Beaufort, that memory will burn within me as long as I live, as cruel as the hatred –'

'I am not asking you to forget,' Beaufort said impatiently. 'I am asking you to come with me, to let me save you. I swear you are in danger here.'

'France and England are at war. The English law will not come for me here.'

'It is not that! You are in danger from something far worse than the English law.'

'What kind of danger?'

'I cannot tell you. But it is serious.'

'If you want me to believe you, you must tell me what it is.'

'I cannot. It is not possible –'

'Then I am not interested. Nor am I interested in your warnings. Besides, supposing I am in danger, why are you so anxious to save me?'

'Perhaps because I have never been able to bear to see a work of art destroyed, and you are the loveliest of all – or, maybe just because I want very much to give you back the equivalent of what I took from you. Come with me, Marianne, I swear – I promise you, by all I hold most sacred, that you will not regret it.'

Abruptly, Marianne turned her back on him. Folding her arms, she began to walk up and down, struggling against the insidious feeling of peace invading her, against a curious longing to listen to this man and believe him, trying to whip up her anger once again.

'It is all too easy, I must say! According to you, it is enough to explain a little and say you're sorry to wipe out everything! Then all you have to do is hold out your hand magnanimously and say: "Come with me, I wish to make amends" and I will be ready to follow you blindly. Yes – I must say, it would be too easy! But you should have thought of all this before you robbed me and degraded me. Now, it is too late, do you hear, too late! I would rather live in wretchedness, like a hunted criminal, I would rather die a thousand deaths than take the least thing from you! Can't you understand that I hate you?'

She spat the last words in his face and had the bitter satisfaction of seeing him whiten. She triumphed in it as though at a victory, vaguely hoping for some sign of weakness which would put him altogether at her mercy and allow her to crush him. But this man of iron did not know how to weaken. He merely shrugged and turned slowly to pick up the big, many-caped black cloak which lay on a chair and throw it over his arm. When he looked at her again, his face was once more expressionless. The warm light had gone out of his eyes.

'You have understood nothing, and learned nothing, even now, have you?' he said grimly. 'You still think of yourself as the queen of a besieged empire. You think that things and men should bow to your wishes and merely thank you politely when you kick them like a naughty child. I fear you may soon find yourself cruelly disappointed – more cruelly even than in the past. But you are your own mistress. Farewell, then, Marianne Mallerousse, do as you like. But should you –'

'I shall not!' Marianne broke in, stiff with pride and anger. But he seemed not to hear and went on calmly:

'But should you change your mind – or wish to know the land I'm offering you for your home, a land of sunshine where the cotton grows and the natives sing, where you can hold up your head as a free woman, remember I remain in Paris for some little time yet, at the Hôtel de l'Empire in the rue Cerutti. I shall be waiting –'

'I shall not come!'

'You may – think about it, Marianne. Anger is a bad counsellor and you are in real danger. I desire only your peace and happiness, do not forget that.'

The black cloak swirled as he flung it round his shoulders. He went swiftly to the door. Marianne did not move. She remained quite still by the fire but just as, with one last look, he was about to leave her, she stopped him.

'One thing more! Was – was Selton completely destroyed?'

Now it was Jason Beaufort's turn to be cruel, to feel the need to give back hurt for hurt to her who stood like a rigid, diaphanous statue in her shimmering draperies, and see those stony green eyes falter, however little.

'No,' he said harshly. 'There was quite enough left for me to get a good price for it. And to enable me to get a good, fast vessel.'

Suffering in her turn, Marianne closed her eyes so that he should not see her tears. She wished that not one stone of the house that she had loved had been left standing.

'Go – go quickly.'

She did not see the move he made towards her, or his look of angry pain, nor did she hear him sigh. She only heard him say:

'Have the courage to look things in the face – and do not stupidly refuse what is your due.'

She did not open her eyes until a blast of freezing cold air made her shiver. The French door was swinging gently open to the empty night. A gust of wind swirled into the summer-house, raising the ashes in the hearth. Marianne bent slowly to pick up her cloak and wrapped it round her shoulders, huddling into its comforting warmth as though for refuge. Outside, Jason Beaufort was striding swiftly towards the lighted house, his great black cloak flying in the wind like the sails of the Flying Dutchman.

Marianne felt icy cold. She wished he had not gone, that he was still there to talk to her about that unknown country, full of sunshine and plaintive singing, a land where she could be a different person without ceasing to be herself. She ran to the door and opened her mouth to call him back – but no, she could not do it. She could not go with a man who had bought her for a night like some creature of the streets, a man who had coldly robbed her to repair his own fortunes. She could not go aboard the ship Selton had paid for. For a moment, she had been tempted, but it was over. She would go on the way she had chosen and if it proved stony, so much the worse.

Yet, one thought still nagged at her mind. Why had he said she was in danger? Why had he urged her to flee? To that, there was no answer but as she too made her way back to the house, her memory kept repeating like a refrain: 'Hôtel de l'Empire, rue Cerutti – Hôtel de l'Empire, rue Cerutti –' A funny thing, memory.

The five words of the address still haunted Marianne's memory when she returned to her room a few minutes later, but by dint of repeating them to herself, she had unconsciously adapted them to a melody by Paesiello that lingered in the back of her mind, making a sort of refrain.

At this late hour, the Hôtel was silent. Most of the guests had left, as soon as the supper was over, but in the salons, where the flowers were already bending their heads under the influence of the heat of the candles, several game tables had been set up. The whist had taken over the elegant rooms, and there reigned that curious quality of silence born of held breaths, ill-contained emotions, and spirits captivated by the events of the game. All these people with tense faces seemed to sacrifice to some mysterious rite that made their eyes sharper, their mouths tighter. Indifferent to the valets who circulated noiselessly between the tables carrying flutes of Champagne on silver trays, they could only see the brightly coloured cards that they regularly knocked down on the green carpets of the tables. Apart from the obligatory phrases, all that could be heard was the rustling of gold passing from hand to hand, and Marianne turned away from this spectacle, glimpsed in the crack of a door, with a sort of horror. She hated gambling by instinct, but especially since the night of Selton she had regarded it as her personal enemy. So, it was with a kind of satisfaction that she noted Jason's absence. It seemed to her that she could not have thought of him without horror if she had discovered him sitting with those passionate men and women. All in all, the girl honestly admitted to herself that in him lay the only reason which had impelled her to glance at the salons. But the American had had to leave the Hôtel immediately after their separation.

Leaving the stifling and somewhat equivocal atmosphere of the first floor, her room seemed to Marianne a haven of peace and quiet. The fire was blazing merrily in the fireplace decorated with Christmas roses and the bed, open, offered the freshness of its immaculate linen sheets. Turning her back to her writing table, on which, this night, the pen would remain dry and the paper blank - there was no question of telling Fouché about her meeting with the American and, for once, the minister would have to be satisfied with the reports as far as the party was concerned – Marianne began to undress.

With a sigh of relief, she untied the dress, whose glaucous muslins softened on the blue and pink carpet. The frothy linen followed, then, raising her arms, the girl untied the ribbons of her headdress and began to fiddle with ardour in the clever scaffolding of curls and braids which had cost Fanny a good hour of effort. The heavy silky mass fell on her naked back like a warm and soft fur and Marianne sighed again but this time with a kind of luxuriance.

She must have been very tired because it seemed to her that a sigh echoed hers, a sigh that came from who knows where and that was probably only a breath of wind in the fireplace. In a hurry to get to bed, Marianne disdained the charming image reflected in her mirror and, putting on her nightgown, she slipped into the sheets, blew out the candle on her bedside table and finally lay down with a third sigh.

She barely had time to close her eyes. Something was happening under her bed, but before she had time to wonder, a dark shape rose and fell on the bed, which screamed under the extra weight. Panic-stricken to find herself prisoner of two arms, incontestably male, and not knowing too much what happened to her, Marianne gave a muffled cry. A trembling hand was hastily placed over her mouth.

'Don't scream!' whispered a breathless voice against her cheek. I mean you no harm ... on the contrary! I just ... I only want to love you for now as I have loved you in dreams for nights and nights.

For fear of hurting him, no doubt, the hand did not press very hard and Marianne had little difficulty in getting rid of it. She now knew who she was dealing with, and in her indignation had immediately driven out fear. Her assailant was none other than the gentle, shy Monsieur Fercoc.

'You again!' she breathed angrily. 'But are you mad? Will you ... please, get out of here and leave me in peace!'

'No! Oh, no! I will not leave you! I have you, I want you and I will have you! It would be too unfair all the same!'

'Unfair? And why please? Oh, stop pulling my hair.'

Indeed, by seizing the young girl in his arms, Fercoc had, at the same time, imprisoned the long hair that painfully pulled the head of his prisoner. All gallantry abolished; the professor took advantage of it to cover her with voracious kisses on the throat of Marianne while explaining in words interspersed that there was no reason that she did not grant him the same favours as to 'this big devil of American' with whom she had locked herself up so long in the pavilion of the garden.

'You are ridiculous,' scolded Marianne while defending herself as well as possible against his caresses.

She had the feeling that she too was ridiculous, thrown as she was in a grotesque battle against a rampaging sheep.

'I was ... but I won't be again! I want you too much! Marianne ... Marianne! I looked at you just now ... when you were undressing! I was under the bed. And I thought I was going crazy!'

A supple blow on the back had half released Marianne, a well applied slap came to conclude the ardent confidences of the tutor.

'What a repulsive character you are! When I think that I thought you were nice, that I felt pity for you.'

'I don't want your pity, I want you ...'

'You have already said that! But, as I don't want you ... at any price,' said Marianne, valiantly resuming the fight for her light nightclothes, which the maniac was trying to tear off ... 'I order you one last time to leave me, or I'll scream! Oh! ...'

The fine batiste had just yielded. Deprived of this frail rampart, Marianne understood that she was going to be delivered without defence or almost to the undertaking of her tenacious lover. She discovered, at the same time, that under its delicate appearance, it was much more vigorous than it appeared there. It was perhaps the unchained desire which gave him this nervous force, but Marianne realised it would be difficult to resist for much longer. The tiredness of the day, joined to the nervous tension of the evening, was cruelly felt. Nevertheless, the rage which possessed her still supported her. Never let it be said that she would be the passive prey of men who owed their victory only to their superior force!

As he grabbed her wrists to spread her arms, she mustered all her energy to keep him away from her as long as possible.

'I'll scream!' she threatened.

In the red light of the dying fire, Mr. Fercoc's gentle, kindly face took on a devilish expression that Marianne found quite frightening. She no longer recognized her peaceful companion of the past days.

'Scream as much as you want,' he declared to her while redoubling his efforts to finally overcome her last resistance. 'Nobody will hear you. When His Serene Highness and his friends play whist, the Hôtel could collapse on them and they would still be playing in the rubble. As for the valets, they are almost all in bed at this hour ...'

Marianne gave a muffled groan of despair. At the same moment, her door opened. As if they had only waited for Fercoc's last words to bring them inside, two gigantic footmen appeared. Without showing any more emotion than a well-regulated machine, one of them approached, grabbed the tutor by his clothes and, pulling him off the bed as easily as if he had weighed nothing, they carried him off at arm's length, wriggling and spitting like an angry cat. The door closed on them. But the other valet had remained in the room.

Too stunned and, it must be said, too relieved to be angry, Marianne had only the reflex to wrap herself hastily in her sheets. Then, all dignity restored, she addressed a frozen smile to the man who looked at her without saying anything.

'You have saved me,' she said, trying to suppress the humiliation she felt at owing this rescue to valets. 'I want to thank you for that. But how did you know I needed help?'

'Nothing Madmoiselle does escape us,' replied the valet in a sullen tone. 'It's orders!'

'Whose orders? From the Prince?' she asked.

'Orders Madmoiselle!'

Marianne did not insist. She understood that the author of such solicitous orders must be outside the Hôtel Matignon. She looked more attentively at her saviour. Of course, she had already seen this impersonal face with heavy and expressionless features, but she did not know the name of this man, one of the many valets of the house. Besides, it didn't matter much. He had rid her of the cumbersome Fercoc, he was entitled to all her gratitude. She was about to repeat this to him, in a hurry to see him withdraw and let her sleep but he did not leave her the time.

'There are other orders,' he said.

'Other orders? Which ones?'

'That Mademoiselle should get up, get dressed and follow me. I will wait in the corridor when Mademoiselle is ready.'

'Follow you? At this hour? But go where?' she asked.

On impulse, Marianne, thus invited to leave her bed, had instead sunk deeper under her covers. The valet was not concerned.

'Mademoiselle must follow me without question, just as I, in certain circumstances, must ask Mademoiselle to accompany me to a certain place. But, let Mademoiselle be reassured,' he hastened to add, seeing a gleam of fear light up in her green eyes as she peered at him over the sheets, 'she will be back here well before daybreak!

'But, at last, I will be seen to come out! If His Highness asks questions ...'

'His Highness is playing,' said the man in the same even tone. 'He won't notice anything! And there are still many vehicles in the courtyard. The gate is still open! But Mademoiselle must hurry! I'm waiting for you!'

He was about to leave, perhaps to cut short any further protests, but Marianne held out her hand to delay him.

'You are the police, aren't you? What is your name?'

The man hesitated for a moment. But for the first time, Marianne thought she saw an amused glint in his colourless eyes.

'Basvin, at your service!'

And this time he went out to let the girl change into some clothes.

When she crossed the threshold of the Hôtel de Juigné, some twenty minutes later, Marianne was not surprised. She suspected, as she left the Rue de Varenne, that it was there that Basvin was leading her. She shouldn't be surprised by anything where Fouché was involved. On the other hand, she felt her bad mood return when a bailiff in slippers installed her in a cold antechamber whose stove, for economy measures no doubt, had been extinguished hours ago.

Wrapped in a thick hooded mantle, her feet in fur-lined boots and her hands in a muff of petit-gris, Marianne, sat on a hard bench in a corner of the large, bare, damp and dark chamber, was soon shivering. Moreover, she was falling asleep and did not understand why Basvin had dragged her here in the first place. Couldn't this interview have waited until the next day?

When, after a quarter of an hour, the pseudo-valet came to fetch her to introduce her at last into the minister's office, she was quite angry.

'It is about time!' she launched in a vengeful tone while rushing in the narrow office which she already knew.

Wrapped in an infinite number of flannels, camisoles, shawls and woollens of all kinds, not always of an ideal cleanliness moreover, the feet in large tapestry slippers due doubtless to the diligent needle of his duchess, and a large cotton cap pulled down to his eyebrows, Monsieur le Duc of Otranto, sternly looked at her from the bottom of an armchair in which, normally he moved at ease but for the present hour, seemed to have all the difficulties of the world to contain all this overcrowding of clothing.

In front of Fouché, in a beautiful blue and gold Sèvres cup, he warmed his yellow hands, around a smoking greenish herbal tea. And Marianne understood why she had waited all this time: All this apparatus of defence against the cold had indeed required a quarter of an hour! But, as it did not incite respect, the girl attacked him with confidence.

'Couldn't what you had to say to me wait until it was at least daylight, Minister? I was dragged from my bed, thrown into a carriage, dragged here without a word of explanation. Yet, if I am not mistaken, you were at the reception of the Prince of Benevento last night? Couldn't you speak to me for a moment? I have always heard that one is never so isolated as in a crowd!'

Perhaps to give himself another moment of reflection, Fouché drank a little of his herbal tea, made a face, added sugar, drank again and finally put his cup down with a sigh.

'Sit down, stop shouting and listen to me. It is not for pleasure that, sick as you see me, I dragged myself to this office to receive you. I too was in my bed and, believe me, I was comfortable there. But if you had stayed alone in yours, we wouldn't be here, you and I!'

Mechanically, Marianne sat down on one of the terrible stiff chairs she had remembered.

'What does that mean?" she said without understanding.

'That I had given precise orders concerning you. If you received a man in your room, he was to be removed at once and you were to be brought here without delay.

'And why?

'To hear this: I did not put you where you are to make love with anyone.'

'Me? Make love?' protested Marianne in disgust.

'Let me continue. I repeat: with anyone. You are in the Rue de Varenne for a very precise purpose and, if you want to know the bottom of my thinking, there is only one man, only one, whom I would authorize to receive ... uh, intimately: it is the dear prince!'

At once Marianne was up, red of anger until the root of her hair.

'Thus, you dare to say this to my face? You have sent me to the prince only with the aim of making me his mistress? This story of espionage was only a pretext.'

'By no means! But do you want to tell me if there is a better way to find out about someone's doings than to share a "pillow" with him? In this respect and, as long as one knows the vice-grand elector, your beauty encouraged all hopes. But are you going to fall in love with a lousy tutor?'

'However, I have not fallen in love with anyone! That is nonsense! If your henchman has even an ounce of honesty, he'll tell you that by dragging Monsieur Fercoc out of my chamber he'd put an end to a real battle.'

A coughing fit cut him off. Under his nightcap, the pale face of Fouché became brick red. Hastily he opened a file, drew a vial, a spoon and swallowed a large spoonful of a thick syrup. Marianne took advantage of this pharmaceutical interlude to catch her breath. When the minister regained his voice, he admitted:

'Indeed, he told me that you seemed to be defending yourself, but *les jeux de l'amour* are sometimes more rigourous than one imagines, and I know women ...'

It was Marianne's turn to blush. Hastily, she exclaimed:

'There was no question of *les jeux de l'amour* at least for me. This boy had hidden under my bed while I was away. He came out when I was in bed and about to fall asleep. So, I was assaulted ... and I don't see why it was necessary to drag me here in the middle of the night to be lectured on morality ... well, on your personal morality!

For the first time, Fouché risked a thin smile.

'Well, I admit for this time: You were victim the of your charm. It is a misunderstanding. But, even so, I am not dissatisfied with the meeting: at least its allowed me to specify your certain directives of which I would be happy to see you taking account in the future.'

'What do you mean by that?'

'No lover ... except the prince!' whispered Fouché who had joined the end of his fingers and contemplated them with attention, which allowed him to ignore the indignant glance of his inquisitor.

'Not even the prince!' Corrected Marianne with a sharp voice. 'Useless to keep illusions in this respect, Monsieur le Duc. The prince is full of grace towards me, but his attention is elsewhere!'

'The Duchess of Courlande, I know, but that does not hinder! The duchess is approaching the half-century ... and you are not twenty years old! Doesn't our friend like you? I thought I saw the opposite! And you even managed to charm the aggressive Madame de Périgord, which is a real accomplishment!'

'I believe, indeed, that his serene Highness likes me,' said Marianne gravely. 'But that is not the question. Even if the prince were in love with me, I would not give myself to him.'

'Why not?'

'The simplest reason of all: I don't love him. And I have promised myself that I will only ever be with a man I love.

'How romantic!' laughed Fouché. 'And you love no one?'

'No one at all!'

'Not even ... that American with whom you were locked up for so long in the pavilion at the end of the garden?'

Marianne shuddered. Did he know that too? It seemed as futile as it was ridiculous to try to hide anything from the Minister of Police! The thought gave her an unpleasant feeling: as though she were living in a sort of window lit from all sides, without shadows and without possible sanctuary … At all hours, in all places, Fouché had eyes and ears working for him … And without her really being aware of it, the girl's face dropped.

'Especially that American!' she answered at last in a voice so altered that she was frightened. 'It is not a question of love between us … but of an old account, the settlement of which will perhaps come one day … and which does not concern you at all!'

When she finished speaking, Marianne had a small feeling of guilt for the first time, as though she'd caught herself in a lie. She meant what she said, however, and there was nothing in her words that was not true … yet it was as if, deep inside herself, there was a niggling doubt! It was unpleasant for her to talk to this man about Jason Beaufort. That he was an enemy was one thing, but he belonged no less to her secret universe, to that past which no one had the right to touch. Even if he had been the instrument of her ruin, Jason belonged to the setting in Selton's time. And Fouché had nothing to do with Selton.

He didn't ask her anything else. Painfully, he extracted himself from his armchair, tightening his shawls and flannels around his thin person.

'Very well,' he said, 'I won't ask you any questions about it. But if you were to hide something important from me concerning your mission … be sure that I would sooner or later be informed! This, then, would cost you much more than it is worth. I hope you understand that?'

'Indeed,' said Marianne coldly. 'And I repeat: what happens between Monsieur Beaufort and me is our own business!'

'Perfect! In that case, we will both go back to our respective beds. I wish you a good night, Mademoiselle Mallerousse!'

He intentionally stressed the name, but Marianne disdained the slight threat that the tone implied. She had nothing to reproach herself for. She was not hiding anything … except the conversation she had recently had with the Prince, but in all situations in life, one must take a side. Marianne had chosen that of the tranquillity, which she badly needed to carry out her future projects. She made a bow.

'Goodnight, Monsieur le Ministre!'

Outside, she found the valet-police officer Basvin and then, in the courtyard, the carriage that had brought them. For a long time, they drove in silence. Marianne was no longer sleepy, but the interview she had just had with Fouché left her thinking. It was no longer possible for her to ignore or minimize the close surveillance of which she was the object. However, Fouché had not spoken to her about the infamous black carriage.

Marianne, in her anger, had forgotten it for a moment. But it was obvious that Fouché did not forget anything. In this case, it was undoubtedly necessary to conclude that not only did he know the existence of this car, but also that he was most certainly its master.

It was Basvin who first broke the silence:

'I owe you an apology, Mademoiselle,' he said softly. 'It seems that I was mistaken. Will Mademoiselle forgive me?

'You have done your job,' replied Marianne with slight disdain. 'I can't blame you. Especially since you got me out of a difficult situation. May I ask what you did with that unfortunate Fercoc?'

The policeman smiled.

'We simply put him back in his bed and told him not to move ... and we made him understand that it would be prudent for him to stay away from Mademoiselle, especially if he cares for her.'

'And ... if it is discovered that we have gone out? What will we say?'

'We won't say anything! It will not have been noticed.'

Indeed, when the car crossed the gate of the Hôtel Matignon, all the other carriages that had been waiting there when they left still there. Nothing had changed, neither in the deserted street nor in the illuminated Hôtel. The false valet jumped to the ground, helped Marianne to get off and then took off the large dark coat with which he had covered his livery.

'It remains for me to wish good night to Mademoiselle,' he said while bowing. 'Then to give her my farewells. I leave the service of the prince tomorrow.'

'You leave?' said Marianne surprised. 'But why?'

'I have business elsewhere ... It may be that we will meet again; under different circumstances. Anyway, that Mademoiselle ...'

'Is it still necessary, in this case, to use the third person?'

'No, I don't think so ... but I thank you for pointing it out. Good luck, Mademoiselle Mallerousse. And rest assured that in this Hôtel you will remain as carefully protected as ever.

Protected ... or guarded? Both, no doubt, Marianne thought as she watched him walk away towards the outbuildings. In any case, the transformation that had taken place, in a second, in this man was curious. His heavy features had come to life, his dull eyes had suddenly taken on a glow, his very attitude had changed. And she wondered how many of Fouché's men were living in this house, and under what disguises. How many also in Paris and in the enormous Empire? They formed a strange world, secret and silent, whose deep ramifications extended as far as the eye could see, a world of which she herself was a part despite herself and which seemed to cover all classes of society. Wasn't it said that the empress Joséphine herself had sometimes informed the police? And over all this reigned, as much and perhaps more than the Corsican, the worrying character of whom, just now, she had surprised at such a ridiculous aspect. But no ridiculousness could kill the fear that inspired Fouché.

While dreaming thus, Marianne entered the Hôtel and, passing in front of one of the half-opened doors of the living rooms, threw a glance at the interior. Nothing had moved, neither things nor beings. It was as if time had stopped for a moment. The demon of the game had not yet let go of his followers.

CHAPTER ELEVEN
The Night at Butard

The town berlin belonging to the Prince of Benevento sped as swiftly as the rough-shod greys could draw it along the promenade de Longchamp, deserted at this late hour. It was eight o'clock in the evening. In summer, the promenade would have been crowded with horses and carriages for some hours yet but the dark, the cold and the snow had long since driven Parisians indoors, the bourgeois to their supper and cards, the fashionable world to the large parties which took place almost every night at this time of the year. Yesterday, it had been the Prince de Cambacérès's, tonight, it was the Duc de Cadore, who had replaced Talleyrand as Foreign Minister. This, thought Marianne, was no doubt the reason why Talleyrand was sitting beside her in the berlin rather than dressing for the duke's ball.

Ensconced in the mulberry-coloured cushions which matched the paintwork on the great wheels of the carriage, she stared out indifferently at the snow-covered landscape. Longchamp was quite familiar to her now from many drives with the princess and little Charlotte and she did not greatly care to know where she was being taken. Talleyrand had told her that morning:

'Tonight, I mean to take you to the house of a very good friend of mine, and a great lover of music. I want you to be beautiful. Not that that will be difficult but I should like to see you in pink.'

It was the first time the prince had expressed any preference with regard to her clothes and Marianne was surprised, especially since, until that moment, she had believed his taste to incline rather towards cold colours, like blue and green, and she had no pink dress.

'You shall have one tonight,' the prince assured her and sure enough, later in the day a gown had arrived from Leroy which, though extremely simple, Marianne thought perfect. The dress was made of very pale pink satin, frosted with silver but with no other decoration. With it went a great hooded cloak of the same stuff, quilted and bordered with ermine, and a matching muff. The effect, on her, was stupendous, as was proved to her by the smile of satisfaction bestowed on her by the prince as she came down to meet him.

'I believe,' he told her, 'that tonight will be another triumph for you – perhaps your greatest triumph of all –'

Marianne's voice had certainly earned her a very flattering degree of success at private parties but it was a success which bore no relation with what she hoped to meet with in the theatre. She had the good sense to realize that what she had achieved so far was simply a fashionable success, and by its very nature fleeting. For some time, too, she had been feeling less confident of herself, and had worked with less enthusiasm at her singing. In addition, there was the persistent black cab always on her heels wherever she went. It was beginning to haunt her, like some inescapable omen of disaster. She had thought once or twice of going out on foot to see if anyone approached her but she had not dared, held back by a fear which she could not have explained. What was more serious was that, although she had mentioned it in her report, Fouché had made no comment and now Marianne did not know what to think. The prince had not mentioned it, either. It was all very bewildering. It was in her mind to go and see Fouché in the morning.

It was eight days now since the scene with Jason Beaufort and in spite of her expressed determination to forget him, Marianne had not yet succeeded in doing so. Whenever she thought of the American, it was with such a host of contradictory feelings that she felt quite lost. Anger predominated, and resentment, all the more bitter because she had been tempted to accept his offer. She was still too young to remain unaffected by the magic of certain words. Jason had awakened in her a desire for this new life he had described for her, a free life in a new world full of sunshine and warmth. Perhaps he really meant it when he said he wanted to give back a little of what he had taken from her? And, with that thought, Marianne was sometimes on the point of going to him. One morning, when she was out doing some errands for the princess, she even asked the coachman to drive down the rue Cerutti. She had seen the Hôtel de l'Empire at number twenty-seven, a building of some elegance with a number of vehicles outside it, and for an instant she had been tempted to stop the carriage and get out, to ask for this strange man whom she hated but who fascinated her –

But then she changed her mind. Why should she believe Beaufort's word? He had robbed her of everything, had dared to barter her love and modesty. Who could say if, once they were at sea, he would respect his promise and not claim the shameful rights which he believed were his? And how much more when they were together at the other side of the world! After all, what reason could he have for saving her and from what? What was this danger with which he threatened her if not some imaginary bogey intended purely and simply to make her fall more readily into his snare? Only that morning, Marianne had received a short, unsigned note.

'I am here for another week. To find me after that, you should inquire of my friend Paterson, the American Consul at Nantes. Think again, I urge you, and come with me. Time is short —'

Marianne had merely shrugged and tossed the note into the fire. Today, she did not want to believe Jason Beaufort.

The berlin crossed the Seine and Marianne put her face to the window, rubbing a clear patch on the misted glass with the tip of one gloved finger.

'Are we going out of Paris?' she asked. 'Is it much farther?'

In the dimness of the coach, she could see little of her companion, though she could smell the faint scent of verbena. Since leaving the rue de Varennes, he had seemed to be asleep.

'No, not much farther – the village we are going to is called La Celle Saint Cloud. The friend we are to visit has a most delightful châteaux there. It is a charming house, one of the prettiest I know. The king used it formerly as a hunting lodge —'

It was rare for Talleyrand to be so lyrical. Marianne's curiosity was aroused. It was very strange, this former hunting lodge, tucked away in a village that, however close now, was certainly well out in the country. Until now, Talleyrand had taken her mostly to fashionable Parisian hostesses such as Madame de la Laval, Dorothée de Périgord, and the ladies of Bellegarde. But this was quite an expedition.

'Will there be much company?' she asked with assumed indifference. 'Who will be there?'

The prince coughed as though pondering his reply but when he spoke his drawling voice was as smooth as glass.

'No indeed, there will not be much company. Before we get there, my dear child, there are one or two things I must tell you. This is no great party. The friend to whom I am taking you is called simply Monsieur Denis —'

Marianne raised one eyebrow in surprise.

'Monsieur Denis? Denis de —'

'Nothing. He is – a bourgeois, very rich and extremely able and also a very old friend from a time when things were – difficult. He is also an unhappy man suffering from a recent cruel bereavement. To some extent, the visit on which I am taking you is one of charity.'

'Dressed like a princess, and in a ball gown at that, to the house of a man in mourning? Surely, I ought to be more soberly dressed?'

'Mourning is in the heart, my dear child, not in the apparel. In the darkness which surrounds him, M. Denis needs to see the dawn. It was my wish that you should be that dawn.'

Something rather too unctuous in the prince's tone increased

Marianne's already awakened curiosity. He sounded over enthusiastic and not wholly sincere. Who was this bourgeois person who owned a former hunting lodge and who one visited dressed as though for a ball? She was immediately agog to know more.

'I wonder that your Highness should take so much trouble for a man so far removed from him. Is he really an old friend?'

'Very old,' Talleyrand said quite seriously. 'You would be surprised how many bourgeois I number among my acquaintance, and even among my friends. There are a good many even in the Imperial Court, although dressed up, I grant you, in high-sounding titles.'

'Then why has this M. Denis none?'

'Because such things have no interest for him. He has no need to be count or marquis. He is – himself, and that is enough. Tell me, Mademoiselle Mallerousse, I hope you are not shocked at the thought of singing for a bourgeois?'

She sensed the mocking smile in the shadow of the carriage.

'Of course not,' she murmured. 'I only hope he is not one of those former members of the Convention, a regicide – '

'He would not be my friend,' Talleyrand interrupted her with some severity. 'You may rest easy on that score.'

Under the cover of the fur rug wrapped about their knees, the prince's hand sought Marianne's and held it gently. Lowering his voice to a more confiding tone, he added:

'You will discover that people in this country sometimes do funny things, but never without a reason. What I ask of you this evening is a personal service, a favour, if you like. This man's name is not a noble one, but his heart is and his grief deserving of your sympathies – to the extent of forgetting to mention it to our friend Fouché, eh? He need not know of this visit – '

Marianne's brief uneasiness subsided but curiosity remained, sharper than ever. Although it made little difference to her who she sang for, having promised the prince to do so when it was his wish, she was now impatient to arrive and see what kind of a man this M. Denis could be for the vice grand elector of the Empire to hold him in such regard.

'I am sorry,' she said gently. 'I will be pleased to sing for your poor friend.'

'Thank you.'

The berlin was now climbing quite a steep hill. The horses had slowed down considerably but Lambert, the coachman, was holding them with a sure hand so that they did not slip. The glass in the windows was misting up again and in the well-padded interior of the carriage silence fell again as each relapsed into their own thoughts. Marianne remembered suddenly that as they left the house, she had not noticed whether the intolerable black cab was still there but then forgot about it again and her mind turned instead to the mysterious M. Denis. She was glad she was not obliged to mention him in the tiresome daily reports which it was still her painful task to write although, thanks to Talleyrand, they had become a mere formality. But why had Fouché said nothing in reply about the black cab? Unless it belonged to him. After all, why not?

White against the black background of the forest, the pavilion of Butard seemed to be dreaming on the shores of the frozen lake which spread below its terrace. Soft golden light came from its tall windows to lie in bright splashes on the frozen snow. Its low pediment decorated with a relief of a hunting scene loomed out of the night and the woods like an enchanted place. It may have been her sharpened curiosity which made her expect wonders, but Marianne was captivated by it at once.

She scarcely saw the footman in dark livery who lowered the steps for her when the carriage had passed through the gates into the circular forecourt, and she made her way to the open doorway like one in a dream. She stepped into a small entrance hall, decked with flowers and pleasantly warm from a good fire burning in the wide hearth. A staircase vanished into shadows above. But Marianne had no time to look about her very closely. Before her, the footman was opening the door into a blue and white salon with a domed ceiling surrounded by a frieze of cupids playing among the leaves.

The pretty, delicate lacquered furnishings belonged to the previous century. They were upholstered in blue and white striped silk and gave the impression that their chief purpose was as a foil to the huge bunches of iris and pink tulips that were cunningly arranged on all sides. A large baroque mirror over the fireplace gave back a reflection of the room in the light of tall, pink scented candles. Bow windows looked out across the balcony to the frozen lake and causeway running across it. Marianne's eyes had gone straight to the lovely old harpsichord that stood by one of the windows. The wooden floor, covered by a big Beauvais carpet, creaked softly under the pressure of Talleyrand's stick and limping steps. The room was quite empty. But then a door opened and a man appeared.

Thinking that this must be the mysterious M. Denis, Marianne looked at him with interest. He was of medium height, fair and far from good-looking with sharp features and brown eyes that squinted slightly. But his face looked open and intelligent with a naturally kindly expression that appealed to Marianne although she was a trifle taken aback by the bright green clothes for a man supposedly in mourning.

He held out his hand, smiling, and came quickly to meet the new arrivals.

'A positively military punctuality, I declare! How do you do, my dear prince, and so this is the young lady.'

'Yes indeed, my dear Duroc, this is Mademoiselle Mallerousse whose matchless voice you have often heard me praise. Is – M. Denis not yet here?'

'No, not yet,' answered the man addressed as Duroc, 'but he will not be long. In the meantime, I have ordered a light supper for you. I thought you would be cold after your long journey.'

He led Marianne with the utmost politeness to a mauve velvet sofa near the fire and helped her off with her cloak. Slightly overawed by the extreme elegance of her surroundings and also by the unmistakably military bearing of this stranger with the bourgeois name, Marianne submitted in silence. Her confusion at his frankly admiring glances made her drop her eyes so that she missed the glance which he exchanged with Talleyrand. The prince declined to part with his furred overcoat.

'No thank you. Mademoiselle Mallerousse will be glad to warm herself but I must be off.'

Marianne, who was warming her hands at the fire, started.

'What! Is your highness leaving me?'

He crossed over to her and taking one of her hands in both his, dropped a swift kiss upon it.

'I am not leaving, my child, I am entrusting you. I must go back. My old friend the Baroness de Staël has been given permission to travel to America with her son. She passes through Paris tonight. I wish to say goodbye to her and see her off on her journey to Morlaix where her ship is already waiting. But have no fear. My friend Duroc will look after you like a father and when you have finished charming our poor friend, he will see you taken home in his own carriage.'

'I hope you do not doubt that,' Duroc said with a warm smile, 'and that I do not frighten you, mademoiselle?'

'No – no, not at all,' Marianne replied returning his smile with an effort. She thought he seemed very nice but she was bewildered. Why had Talleyrand not told her he would not be staying with her? He had never behaved in such a way before. However, with his usual subtlety, he must have realized what was going through the girl's head because he leaned on his stick and bent down towards her.

'I feared to alarm you and startle your timidity before you had seen this reassuring fellow! To tell you the whole truth, I wish your voice to be a surprise for my friend Denis. When you hear his carriage outside, then start to sing – but don't tell him that I am responsible for this pretty surprise.'

'But – why not?' Marianne said bewilderedly. 'If you think it an agreeable surprise, then he must be grateful to you –'

'Exactly. I do not want his gratitude – or not now. He shall know the truth but not just yet. For the present, I want no other feelings, however slight, to interfere with the pure joy that he will have in finding you.'

Marianne understood less and less but she was highly intrigued. What a strange, complicated, mysterious man the prince seemed to be. And why should he think it necessary to speak to her in this rather over-emphatic way, that was so unlike his usual manner? She was grateful to Duroc when, in his own way, he expressed her feelings.

'You have some funny ideas, sometimes, prince. But you would not be yourself if it were not so. Have a safe journey.'

Watching her temporary host go with Talleyrand into the hall, Marianne wondered what could be this Duroc's position in M. Denis' household. Was he a relation? Or merely a friend? Was he perhaps the brother of the lady for whom the mysterious bourgeois was in mourning? No, the green suit made it equally unlikely that he was the dead woman's brother. A cousin perhaps, or a childhood friend entrusted with the running of the house – no, certain mannerisms, a way of holding his head, even the way he walked, the tread of a man more used to boots than pumps, made it certain he was a soldier. Duroc's return interrupted Marianne's musings. He was accompanied by a superior servant of some kind dressed in black and pushing before him a small table on which a collation was set out. Under his powdered wig, the man's round pink face reflected all the grave solemnity becoming in the servant of a great house. He bowed to Marianne with a touch of condescension which astounded her. This Denis must undoubtedly be some frightful upstart, puffed up with conceit in his luxurious way of life, if even his servants felt entitled to give themselves airs. Like master, like men! M. Denis must be quite intolerable! However, Duroc was saying:

'Put that table in front of mademoiselle, Constant, and then leave us.'

'Am I to serve your – '

'No, no, that will do.' Duroc cut him short hurriedly. 'We will serve ourselves, I tell you – '

The butler retired with dignity but Marianne had not missed the unfinished address and wondered what title he had been on the point of giving Duroc. It seemed to her that, since the mysterious Denis had not yet arrived, she might take advantage of his absence to try and find out a little more about him. She gratefully accepted a cup of soup but refused any other refreshment.

'Should I not be singing when M. Denis comes in? He cannot find me at table.'

'That is so. But it will be enough to begin when we hear the carriage.'

Marianne glanced at the harpsichord.

'Must I accompany myself?'

'No – no of course not. What am I thinking of? Wait one moment.'

He was showing signs of increasing nervousness. Marianne sipped her soup and smiled inwardly. All things considered, the adventure was proving enjoyable and she was more and more curious to set eyes on this odd bourgeois whose arrival spread such panic in his household. Duroc returned a few moments later accompanied by a thin, austere looking young man with long hair and a dark complexion. Not glancing at Marianne, the young man picked up the roll of music she had brought with her and sat down at the harpsichord. Duroc returned to his guest, looking considerably relieved.

'There, now we are ready. You may give M. Hassani any instructions you wish, but do not look for a reply. He is a mute,' he added in a low voice with a glance at the pianist.

A mute, now? Marianne began to wonder suddenly whether this M. Denis did not bear a false name, hiding something else. The owner of an ill-gotten fortune, perhaps, living luxuriously but discreetly deep in the woods, away from the prying eyes of Fouché's men, or else some noble stranger conspiring against the régime . Fouché had certainly implied that there were some doubts in high places as to Talleyrand's loyalty. There were suggestions that if he had not yet betrayed the Emperor, it would not be long before he did. This simple but unlikely name of M. Denis was almost certainly a cloak for some dangerous character, an agent of the Tsar perhaps, or even of England?

'What do you mean to sing first?' Duroc asked.

'An air by Paer – one I am very fond of.'

'M. Denis will be delighted. He too likes Paer who is, as you probably know, conductor of the court orchestra.'

'Has M. Denis been long in France?' Marianne asked the question point blank but with apparent casualness.

Duroc stared. 'Er – for some time, yes. Why do you ask?'

The sound of a carriage in the gravelled court outside released Marianne from the necessity of a reply which she might have found awkward to make. Instantly, Duroc was on his feet while Marianne hurried over to take up her position by the instrument, her back to the door. The impassive Hassani was already playing the opening bars as Duroc hastened out to the vestibule. All at once, Marianne found herself in the grip of an attack of terrible stage fright. Her hands were icy cold and she had to clasp them tightly to keep them from trembling while an unpleasant shiver ran down her spine. She cast a look of such desperate appeal at the expressionless pianist that he glanced back at her sternly. From outside, came the sound of voices, footsteps -- she had to take the plunge or else ruin Talleyrand's great surprise.

Hassani's stern gaze became imperative. Marianne opened her mouth and was wholly astonished to hear her own voice come out, sounding as warm and relaxed as though the terrible fright had not gripped her throat at all.

'Oh joy comes ever slowly,

But fleeteth fast away,
While youth is sad and lonely,
And lives but for a day—'

As she sang, Marianne was aware of a quick step in the tiled hall, a step which stopped short in the doorway of the room. After that, she heard nothing more but she had a piercing sense of someone there, watching her – the strange thing was that, far from making her uncomfortable, his presence seemed to her to release her from some unconscious anxiety, that it was friendly and reassuring. Her fright had flown away as though by magic and Marianne's voice soared forth with a warmth and fullness such as she had never known. Once again, music had come to her rescue. Its power over her was never failing, always fresh and constantly renewed. She let it carry her away, fearless and unresisting, knowing that the love between her and her music was real. There could be no betrayal here. The final words of the song fell like a sigh from the young lips:

'… false flattering hopes are lost
And love alone remains…'

It ended and silence fell. Hassani, eyes lowered, let his hands slip down on to his knees and Marianne felt the spirit go out of her. Feeling suddenly horribly nervous, she dared not turn her head to the fire where she knew someone was standing. A voice spoke brusquely:
'Excellent. Sing again, mademoiselle. Do you know "Plaisir d'Amour"?'
She looked at him at last. She saw a man of slightly less than average height, and rather fat without being in any way gross or heavy. He was leaning on the mantlepiece, dressed in a black coat, black stock and white kerseymere pantaloons covered, she saw to her astonishment, with black marks that were undoubtedly ink stains. She could even see where he had wiped his pen on them. They ended in knee boots armed with small silver spurs. M. Denis's hands and feet were small and neat but it was his face which held Marianne's attention. She had never seen one like it. In colour, a very pale ivory, it had the classic beauty of a roman mask. His black hair, worn short and straight, fell over his forehead, emphasizing the dark blue, rather deep-set eyes. Those eyes were not easy to meet but their expression was unforgettable. In his hand, M. Denis held a gold and tortoiseshell snuff box whose principal use seemed to be to distribute snuff liberally over his person and everything around him.
'Well?' he said.
Marianne reddened, conscious that she had been staring at him in a way that was scarcely polite and turned her eyes away hastily.
'I do know it, indeed.'

She began to sing the well-known tune with a degree of feeling that was beyond her control. Something was happening in the inmost depths of her being, something she did not understand but which made her identify with the music with a passionate intensity of which she would never have believed herself capable. But now, as she sang, she was not afraid to look at M. Denis. She had never felt drawn to any man as she did to him and, unable to hide the feelings which her mobile face betrayed with absolute honesty, she kept her green eyes firmly fixed on the stranger's blue ones so that the words of love in the song seemed to be meant for him alone.

'As long as these slow waters glide
Downstream by the meadow's side,
I will love you…'

But as the plaintive words of the lament fell from her lips, she saw M. Denis slowly abandon his indolent posture, put away the snuff box with an impatient air and gradually draw nearer. His eyes, too, never left her face. He was looking at her intently, looking at her as no man before had ever dared to look at her. And it seemed to her that if that look were suddenly removed, in that instant she would cease to live. Her eyes filled with tears. She could feel her heart beating under the frosted satin of her dress, so strongly that it seemed it must burst. She was happy, troubled and frightened all at once, but she knew that she could go on singing all night long only for the pleasure of having him look at her like that.

When the last note died away, Marianne and M. Denis stood face to face. Still without taking his eyes off her, he snapped his fingers sharply.

'Go, Duroc. And you too, Hassani.'

The friend and the pianist vanished instantly but Marianne had no thought of protest. It was quite natural, in the order of things. In a few minutes this stranger with the ridiculous name had become for her more important than anything in the world and Marianne tried in vain to find a name for the feeling, urgent and primitive, which overwhelmed her. It was as though she had never lived for anything but this moment. Now, she did not even want to know who this man was, whether he was really called Denis, or whether he was some noble, perhaps dangerous person. No, he was there, and all was well.

She stood with her back against the harpsichord, gripping it with cold hands, her bosom rising and falling as she watched him come closer, and closer still. He smiled at her and she felt her heart melt before the charm of that smile.

'When I was a child,' he said confidingly, 'I often wondered what it was Ulysses heard, tied to the mast of his ship, while his companions' ears were stopped with wax. He begged them to untie him so that he might throw himself in the water and swim to the sirens' voices. I know now what he felt.'

The sirens. Jason Beaufort too had likened her to the sirens – what was it he had said? Marianne could not remember exactly. Besides, was there still a Jason Beaufort somewhere? Had he ever existed? Had she herself ever lived before this minute or had she just been born?

Despite his French name, the strange Monsieur Denis must be a foreigner. He had a slight accent which made her think of Italy. For an instant the thought that he was a foreign conspirator revived but Marianne dismissed it as of no importance. He could be what he liked. She knew already that he had become the most important thing in her life. The great emptiness which had brought her to the brink of accepting the future held out to her by Jason Beaufort was there no more.

Very gently, M. Denis took Marianne's hands and held them in his own, which were warm and firm. He was shocked to find how cold they were.

'You're frozen! Come close to the fire –'

He made her sit on the sofa, then placed himself beside her and drew the table towards them.

'You will eat something?'

'No – please, truly.'

'Don't tell me you aren't hungry. At your age one is always hungry. I used to eat – here, a little of this quail pâté, a thimbleful of Chambertin – Chambertin is the king of wines. I never drink anything else. No? This is absurd! You must prefer champagne. Now, a little champagne?'

'I – that is – I have never drunk it,' Marianne said anxiously, watching him fill a crystal glass with sparkling golden wine.

'Then now if ever is the time to begin!' M. Denis told her gaily. 'You will like it. There is not a woman in the world who does not like champagne! It puts a sparkle in the eyes – although,' he added leaning a little closer, 'it is true that yours need no such artifice. I have seen many emeralds not so bright.'

He poured the wine for her as he spoke with the dexterity and attentiveness of a lover. A little nervously, Marianne set her lips to the glass, then she smiled. The wine was cold, sparkling and fragrant – altogether marvellous! Her host was watching her out of the corner of his eye and smiling.

'Well?'

'It is wonderful! May I have a little more?'

'Indeed, you may!'

He laughed and refilled her glass. Then he began to eat hungrily and Marianne found herself following his example. All at once the room had become a very warm, cosy place. No sound came from outside. All was muffled by the snow. The two of them might have been alone together in an enchanted palace, or in a warm, hollow shell lost in some immense, petrified forest. Marianne had never felt so happy and contented. She drained her glass and smiled at M. Denis. How nice and gay he was! It crossed her mind that he was in fact rather too gay for a widower, but then perhaps he might not have loved his wife as much as people thought. Or maybe the music had done him good, or – oh, after all, it did not really matter. The champagne inclined Marianne to optimism. Fatigue and nervousness were all forgotten. Her head was full of wild ideas. She wanted to laugh, without knowing why, to sing – even to dance!

'A little more champagne?' M. Denis asked. He had been watching her with a half-smile.

'Yes please! I – I should never have believed it could be so good!'

He let her drink half of it then gently took the glass away and moved closer to her.

'That's enough for the present. Tell me your name.'

The sudden intimacy in his voice seemed perfectly natural to Marianne. In a short time, they had become such good friends.

'Marianne. My name is Marianne Ma—'

'No. I want only your first name. The rest I shall learn later if I wish. But a dream should have one name and it is long since I addressed anything so pretty – you are beautiful, Marianne. Your voice enthralled me, but I am enchanted by your beauty.'

'Really?' she said happily. 'Do you really like me? In that case, you must tell me your name. Monsieur Denis is frightful.'

'I know. Call me Charles! You like Charles?'

'I don't care! I shall like it because it is yours!'

He had taken her hand and began kissing it softly, moving upwards gradually to the wrist, and then the arm and then the shoulder putting aside the short, pink sleeve to reach its curve. The caress sent a wave of surprising happiness through Marianne. She gave a long shivering sigh and closed her eyes. Not for anything in the world would she have pushed him away, perhaps because she had known half unconsciously, from their first glance, that such a moment would come. The champagne had put just enough warmth into her blood to deaden the repugnance she had felt for men ever since that first unhappy encounter with Jean Le Dru. Besides, Charles was not really a man, he was a dream – a dream from which she had no desire to awake. She did not even wish to speak, only to listen to the awakening of her own body to feelings which made her long for more than kisses.

When he slid his arm beneath her waist and laid her back gently on the cushions of the small sofa, she sighed deeply and opened her eyes to see Charles's face very close to hers but closed them again quickly as their lips touched. He kissed her gently, his lips only just brushing hers in the faintest of caresses, kindling the fire in her blood with exquisite slowness. Her heart was beating as though it would burst her breast and she lay panting in Charles's arms, avid for yet more kisses and caresses.

His mouth against hers, he whispered:

'You want me? Say – truly?'

Her eyelids flickered, *yes*, and she slid her arms round his neck to draw him closer.

'There is too much light —' she whispered.

'Come.'

His arm went round her, holding close and drawing her to her feet to lead her across the room to where a small door was almost concealed in the panelling. The room beyond was small and blue and smelled of jasmine but though the bed was turned down, its whiteness was scarcely discernible in the light of the fire crackling in the grate which was the only illumination in the small chamber clearly made for love.

Marianne flinched instinctively at the sight of the bed but Charles stopped her mouth with such a burning kiss that she almost fainted in his arms. Leading her gently to the fire, he sat on a low chair and took her on his knees like a child. He unfastened the beautiful pink dress, murmuring to her all the while in Italian, charming, tender words of love and covering with kisses first her neck and shoulders and then, as his caressing hands softly put aside the lace shift, her breasts. There was such gentleness in his touch and in his words that Marianne very soon forgot all modesty or shame in the sheer pleasure of hearing his voice telling her she was beautiful.

At last, he carried her, naked and trembling, to the bed and laid her tenderly between the scented sheets where, in a moment or two, he came to join her. When, two hours later, she fell asleep in Charles's arms, relaxed and happy, Marianne thought with a contented sigh how little comparison there was between what had just happened to her and her unpleasant experience in the barn at Kerivoas. It was more than simply that she loved Charles while Jean Le Dru had meant almost nothing to her apart from her need of him. This man, to whom she had given herself so spontaneously, had really become her lover in every sense of the word. It was tonight that she had really ceased to be a girl. Charles's love and not the sailor's clumsy haste had made her blossom into a woman. She knew now what it meant to belong to someone. Nothing and no one could ever divide her now from the man who had given her true knowledge of love and of herself.

'I love you, Charles,' she had murmured sleepily into his neck as her eyelids dropped shut. 'I belong to you for always. Wherever you go, whatever may happen to you, I will follow, I will love you —'

He raised himself on his elbow and made her look at him.

'One should not say such things, *carissima mia* – we never know what may be hidden behind the closed door to the future. I could die tomorrow.'

'Then I should die also – and we should still be together. You cannot know how much you have given me tonight – there's no help for it now. I belong to you – and you alone, kiss me, Charles, kiss me hard –'

Then he had caught her to him once more, so violently that she half cried out, and had made love to her again.

'It is you who have given all and you who gives thanks – *mio dolce amore,*' he murmured afterwards. 'You are right. Nothing and no one can undo this night. Sleep now, it is late.'

She settled obediently into the crook of his arm and closed her eyes. It was all right; everything was simple now. She loved him. He loved her. Who could prevent them being together always? He was a widower and, for the first time since that night at Selton Hall, Marianne remembered that she too was widowed.

Whether that blissful sleep was long or short, Marianne never knew but it seemed only a moment later when she woke suddenly. Charles was already sitting up in bed and in the dim light she could see Duroc murmuring something in his ear.

'What is it?' she asked sleepily. 'Is it already so late?'

'No. Be quiet. It is only three o'clock but I must go. Have the horses put to, Duroc. I'm coming.'

He was already leaping out of bed. Marianne clung to him with the feeling that her heart was being torn out.

'Why are you leaving me? Why must you go so soon? What is happening?'

Gently, patiently, he took her in his arms and kissed her eyes.

'Nothing is the matter. But I have a busy life, my heart, and not an easy one. Urgent business summons me to Paris and you must let me go.'

But still she did not let him go. This sudden departure in the middle of the night terrified her. It seemed to her she understood the reason all too well.

'Charles, I beg you – tell me the truth! You are a conspirator, aren't you?'

He stared at her in astonishment and then began to laugh, gently unfastening the arms linked round his neck.

'Since you have guessed, it is hopeless to deny it – it's true, I do conspire. But there is nothing you can do about it, so now, be a good girl –'

Kneeling among the ravaged bedclothes with the silky mass of her hair tumbled about her, she watched him with a feeling of desperation as he dressed quickly. She had not been wrong. Charles led a dangerous, fugitive life, and she could only accept it. Their love might not be easy in this land ruled by a tyrant but she would wait for him and if he had to flee, then she would fly with him.

'Promise me,' she said in a soft, loving voice, 'that if you are in danger, you will tell me. I will come to you in hell, if need be.'

He was tying his neckcloth in front of the tall cheval glass which stood in one corner but he turned and gave her a penetrating glance. Kneeling like that on the crumpled silken sheets, her skin gleaming like soft gold in the rich night of her hair, she was as bewitchingly beautiful as any pagan statuette.

'I promise,' he said gravely. Then, with sudden harshness: 'Get back into bed.'

Instead of obeying him, she stretched sensuously, like a cat.

'Why? It's too hot —'

The drowsy fire had begun to burn up brightly once more. In an instant, Charles was on Marianne.

'Because I have to go – and because you tempt me still, she-devil! Quick! Into bed with you!'

Half angry, half in fun, he began bundling her up in the sheets, wrapping her firmly in the blue covers until only her face peeped out, deaf to her cries of protest. Then, laughing, he kissed her.

'There! Now, be good. You can go home whenever you like. A carriage will be waiting.'

'But, when shall I see you again —'

'Soon, I promise you.'

'You don't even know —'

'What? Who you are? Or where you live? It does not matter. Duroc found you. He will find you again. Goodbye *mio dolce amore*. Don't catch cold, because of your voice - I love you.'

He got up and went quickly to the door and opened it. Marianne called after him.

'Charles!'

'Yes?'

'Take care of yourself, please —'

He only smiled at her, blew her a kiss and then he was gone. And not until then did it occur to Marianne that she did not know the first thing about him.

She waited, listening for the sound of carriage wheels, then after they had disappeared into the night, she sighed deeply. Now, she was truly alone.

She fought her way out of the cocoon of sheets into which he had bundled her and got up. She was no longer sleepy and felt no desire to remain longer in the house which, now that Charles had gone, seemed unfamiliar, almost hostile. The pink dress lay like a crumpled dawn cloud on the carpet. Marianne picked it up and hugged it to her with a surge of gratitude. She could never forget now, that it was in this dress he had loved her.

She saw her reflection in the tall mirror and could not repress a start of surprise. She saw herself from head to foot, but did not recognize what she saw. That woman with the dark-ringed eyes, the mouth still swollen from kisses, the provocative limbs, was that herself? She ran her hand slowly, experimentally over the thighs which Charles had caressed, realizing in some obscure fashion that the still innocent girl she had been when she came there was gone forever. She was a woman now, she thought with a sense of triumph, a woman in full possession of her powers and the thought made her glad because the change had come about through him and for him.

A light scratching at the door cut short her meditations and sent her scuttling for the reassuring shelter of the bedclothes.

'Come in,' she said.

Duroc's head appeared round a crack in the door.

'Forgive me for disturbing you but I wish for your instructions. Until what hour would you care to sleep?'

'I am not sleepy any more,' Marianne assured him. 'In fact, I should be happy to return to Paris at once.'

'But – it is still the middle of the night. And very cold!'

'I do not mind that. And it is best I should return. I do not know what his highness will think at my coming home so late. He will never believe I have been singing all this time –'

'Indeed no, but–' Duroc added with a quiet smile, 'I think that Monsieur de Talleyrand was prepared for you to return late, even very late. I will order something warming for you and have the horses put to.'

As she sat in the brougham that was ferrying her back to Paris, Marianne was still wondering why Talleyrand should have been so certain she would come home very late. Had he thought that Charles would ask her to sing for much longer than he had done? Or – or had the cunning mind of the Limping Devil foreseen what would happen? Had he foreseen how deeply his friend would be drawn to her and how completely Marianne on her side would be won by him? Had he known that they would fall in love? Had he, in introducing her to Charles Denis, meant to give him simply the pleasure of her voice, or Marianne herself? With such a man, anything was possible, but as the horses carried her onwards at a steady pace, she sent a warm, grateful thought out to the wily diplomat. She owed him the most beautiful night of her life, her first real love, because now, with the passing of time and the events which had taken place between, Marianne was able to see her brief infatuation for Francis Cranmere in its true light, a romantic schoolgirl illusion, the normal attraction of a very young girl for any good-looking man. She would never forget that it was Talleyrand who, deliberately or not, had thrown her into Charles's arms.

But now, she was in a hurry to be back. She would question the prince, even if it meant being disrespectful. He must tell her everything he knew about Charles Denis. In her new-found love, Marianne identified herself completely with the man she loved. She wanted to live his life, even or especially if that life was dangerous. All this, Talleyrand must tell her or else she would apply to Dorothée who was surely bound to have heard at least something about the strange Monsieur Denis.

It was freezing hard now and the carriage windows were thickly frosted over but wrapped in her coat and plenty of rugs tucked carefully round her by kind Monsieur Duroc, and a footwarmer under her toes, Marianne felt wonderfully happy and comfortable. Duroc had begged her pardon for being unable to escort her himself and deluged the coachman with instructions, not to go too fast, take care the horses did not slip, make quite certain the young lady reached home safely, and a host of other things. Consequently, the man was driving with great caution, due probably to the steepness of the slope they were descending.

Somewhere over the fields, a church clock struck five. It was answered by the sound of bells ringing for masses. There must be a convent somewhere nearby. After a few minutes driving on level ground, the carriage slowed down and stopped. Marianne leaned forward in surprise, and rubbing a clear patch on the glass, she saw a broad band of water a little way off. They had come to the river Seine. Suddenly, the door opened and the coachman looked in.

'You will have to get out here, Madame,' he said. 'We have to take the ferry.'

'The ferry? What ferry? We took no ferry when I came?'

'Because you came by the bridge of St Cloud. But they've been rebuilding it for two years now and when it freezes as hard as this it is not safe. Better to take the ferry. This is Suresnes.'

Looking beyond the coachman's swaddled figure, Marianne could see a big barge with a lighted lantern on it waiting a little way off. But it looked quite empty and the air which came in through the open door was so bitterly cold that she shivered and huddled deeper in her rugs.

'It is much too early,' she said irritably. 'No one will take us across at this hour. Let us go back and take the bridge.'

'Not worth it, Madame. The ferryman will take us, I promise you. It's early yet but he's already got people waiting on the other side. Folk come every morning to hear mass with the trappists of Mont-Valérien. So if you'll be so good as to get out. It's best the carriage should be as light as possible to go on board.'

'Very well, if I must,' Marianne sighed, putting aside her rugs regretfully. She gathered up her skirts and taking the hand the coachman offered with an injunction 'to take care and not slip' she jumped lightly to the ground.

At the same instant, a black cloth was flung over her head.

CHAPTER TWELVE
The Riders of the Shadows

Marianne screamed but a hand was clapped roughly over her mouth outside the cloth and she quickly realized that all resistance would be useless. Terrified and half-suffocated, she felt arms round her knees and shoulders as she was lifted off the ground. A slight rolling movement told her that her kidnappers had boarded the ferry. A masterful voice spoke.

'Make it a little quicker, if you please. It's damnably cold. The horses will be freezing on the other bank.'

There was another sound, as of a bag of money being thrown, followed by muffled, obsequious thanks and she guessed that the coachman had been paid. Certainly, the coach did not come aboard. There was a noise of metal shod wheels on the pebbled shore, a noise which soon faded and disappeared. Then there was nothing but the slap of water against the side of the boat.

Marianne was flung down on the bare planks of the deck but a strong arm still held her firmly pressed against an unknown chest. Marianne fought desperately against imminent suffocation and driving panic. Who were these men, and what did they want with her? Were they merely carrying her over to the other side or – she felt sick at the thought of the black water she had glimpsed briefly. She wriggled, trying to loosen the choking folds of cloth but the arm only clutched her more tightly.

'Lie still, little fool,' ordered the same commanding voice. 'Or I'll throw you in the water –'

The fact that he should threaten her with it meant that he did not mean to do away with her at once. Ever so slightly reassured, Marianne tried to fight down the feeling of suffocation but she failed. The material, a cloak it might be, was too thick to let even a breath of air reach her lips. She was being slowly suffocated.

'I can't breathe,' she managed to gasp. 'For pity's sake –'

'Take off the cloak,' a fresh voice advised. 'In any case, we are here—'

The thud of the barge striking the banks came just as the cloak was loosened round her head. It was only just in time. Half-fainting, Marianne gulped instinctively at the icy air while a heavily gloved hand slapped her sharply to revive her.

'She's fainted,' said the man with the harsh voice critically.

'A faint may be worse than it looks,' the other answered.

Both voices sounded cultivated. They certainly did not belong to ordinary highway robbers Marianne thought, her mind still working automatically. She opened her eyes and saw two men in black masks bending over her. They wore round hats and voluminous riding cloaks. They were now on the other side of the river and just underneath the trees of the Boulogne, which at this point came close down to the bank, she could see two other horsemen waiting beside a carriage she recognized all too readily.

'The black cab,' she said faintly.

One of the masked men laughed. 'So she had noticed it! You were right, she is much more dangerous than she seemed. Come now, we must be off.'

'One moment. Just because she is dangerous, we must make sure of her. Letting her breathe is one thing—'

'But what have I done?' Marianne protested as the second man was binding her hands swiftly with a silk scarf. 'Where are you taking me? And why?'

This was ridiculous! Anger was now beginning to overcome her fear, reviving her instinct of self-preservation.

'That, mademoiselle, you will be told when we reach our destination,' the man answered. 'For the present, you will best keep silent. We should not like to have to kill a woman—'

She was suddenly aware of the long-barrelled duelling pistol gleaming in the man's gloved hand, the muzzle pressed close to her left breast. The threat was serious.

'I'll be quiet,' she breathed.

'Good. Now, if you will excuse me—'

Another scarf was bound across her eyes, so tightly that no ray of light showed through. After this, her kidnappers took an arm each and guided her to the carriage. She felt other hands reach out to her from inside, and pull her up the steps. The door slammed. Marianne found herself sitting on a seat that was not uncomfortable. She could hear someone breathing beside her and guessed that this was the person who had helped her into the carriage. Outside, she heard someone say:

'The muff! There, by the water. We cannot leave it there. The chief said: "Leave no traces."'

'Why not? They might think she was drowned.'

'Leaving her muff carefully on the opposite side! Fool!'

A few seconds later, the door opened again and she felt someone push her bound hands into the muff. The man sitting beside her spoke for the first time and she repressed a shudder. His voice was like steel, hard and merciless. 'Such care for a renegade!'

'Our job is to take her, not to judge her,' the first man said firmly. 'If she is guilty, she will die, but she need not suffer unnecessarily. We have to get her to the chief in one piece!'

The door banged to and the carriage moved off, speeding to a gallop as it plunged into the thickets of the wood. Marianne could hear the four horsemen galloping behind. She wondered who was this chief to whom they were taking her.

The journey in the carriage was comparatively brief but it was followed by a much longer one on foot. Two of Marianne's captors seized her arms and half carried her along. The way seemed endless. And it felt to Marianne as though she were being dragged down a fearful, slippery and evil-smelling slope. The air was cold and dank as though at the bottom of a tunnel and a smell of rottenness assailed her nostrils. No light was visible below the bandage over her eyes, although the rubbing against the cushions of the coach had loosened it a little. Neither of her companions had spoken since leaving the river bank and Marianne found herself moving in a wholly dark and silent world. Only the strength of the hands holding her upright and the sound of men breathing told her she had not been spirited away by ghosts. From time to time, in the course of this nightmare journey, she heard the sound of a cat yowling or the trickle of running water somewhere. Her feet in the pink satin slippers were like ice and bruised unmercifully as she stumbled blindly along the stony path. She would have fallen had not the phantom riders held her up. Her blood congealed with terror and there was a tight ache in her throat. This hideous adventure, coming so soon after leaving the enchanted pavilion where she had known such happiness, was like a nightmare from which she knew that there was no awakening. She was like a trapped bird flinging herself against the bars of her cage but only succeeding in hurting herself.

A door banged suddenly. They had entered what must be a lighted passage because Marianne could see a yellow gleam of light. Then came some kind of muddy court or garden, followed by some crumbling steps. Someone whistled three times, then knocked twice on a door. It became suddenly warm. Marianne felt a floor beneath her feet. A smell of cabbage soup and sour wine filled her nostrils. At last, the bandage was taken from her eyes.

She looked about her fearfully. Five men stood around her wearing black masks and dressed in black, but with a certain elegance. There were two more, evil-looking fellows in dirty smocks and oilcloth caps. The figures stood out grimly against the background of a wretched wine shop, lit by two smoking lamps. The walls shone with grease and sweat, there were rickety tables, chairs losing their stuffing and, in one corner, an ancient trunk covered with moth-eaten fabric. Only the glasses and the row of bottles that stood on a shelf looked clean and new. But most of all, the prisoner was struck by the appearance of an extraordinary old woman who rose up suddenly out of the shadows, leaning on a cane. She was so bent and broken that she looked at least a hundred and on her powdered hair she wore a massive lace cap, torn and filthy, in the fashion of twenty years before, as was the greyish muslin fichu crossed on her breast. Her stained gown must once have been a handsome violet silk and a great golden cross gleamed on her bosom. The old woman's face was so criss-crossed and veined with wrinkles that it resembled the bark of some ancient tree, but although her sharp nose all but met her chin, the eyes very nearly as green as Marianne's own, were bright and young like new leaves on an old withered trunk.

This ancient creature dragged her rheumaticky limbs painfully up to Marianne and looked her up and down with a wicked grin.

'Fine game, baron! Very fine game—' she cackled. 'Satin and ermine, mark you! To say nothing of what's underneath! Do you really want to send all this to the bottom of the Seine with a stone around its neck? Do you know what a waste it is?'

A trickle of cold sweat ran down Marianne's back at the fearful sound of the old woman's cackling laugh. But the man she had addressed as baron, who seemed to be the leader of the band, merely shrugged.

'The court will decide. I carry out my orders, Fanchon-Fleur-de-Lys. I've had trouble enough laying hands on her. She never went out but by day and with a good escort. Until tonight's little affair.'

'We need not regret that,' another broke in swiftly and Marianne recognized the voice of the man who had been with her in the carriage. 'We were able to confirm what we suspected that she was meant for him. We took her on the road from Butard. And God knows we waited long enough! He must have found her to his liking.'

Once again, Marianne's hackles rose at the cackling laughter of the old woman with the curious name.

'I've had enough of this!' She burst out suddenly. 'More than enough! Tell me, once and for all what you want with me! Kill me if you insist, but do it quickly! Or else let me go!'

Her protests ended in a cry of pain as the old woman struck her sharply across the knuckles with the knob of her cane.

'That will do!' she snapped shrilly. 'Speak when you are spoken to! Otherwise, keep silent – or I might forget myself and kill you myself! And I'd be sorry afterwards because if the court will listen to me, my beauty, they'll give you into my keeping and I'll take good care of you. I have a little house at Ranelagh where I entertain some gentlemen of substance. Your favours would fetch a high price! An imperial whore! I hope he's a good lover, at least?'

'Who? What do you mean?' Marianne said in a choked voice.

'Why him, of course, the Corsican ogre! You must not be so modest. In the profession I have in mind for you, it will be something to be proud of –'

Marianne decided the old woman must be mad. What was she talking about? What was this about an ogre? In her bewilderment, she was even able to ignore the creature's sordid threats. Nothing made any sense.

'You are mad,' she said with a pitying shrug.

'Mad, am I? You wait –'

She raised her cane again but the Baron intervened.

'That's enough! I have already told you, Fanchon, it is not for us to judge. Leave her alone. We will go down now.'

'Maybe,' the old woman muttered obstinately, 'but I'll speak to the chevalier. She'll see then if I'm mad! I'll tan the hussy's hide for her before I put her to work –'

'Must you really let this woman insult me?' Marianne cried angrily.

There was a moment's silence, broken only by the sniggering of the two men in overalls. The baron took his prisoner by the arms.

'No,' he said sternly, 'you are right. Come – you Requin, open the trap – and meanwhile, let Pisse-Vinaigre outside make sure we have not been followed.'

One of the rough looking men went to the back of the room and, grasping a large iron ring, lifted a trap-door leading apparently to the cellar. The other went outside. The baron untied Marianne's wrists.

'The trap-door is only wide enough for one,' he said briefly. 'You would fall otherwise.'

She gave him a pale smile of thanks and rubbed her sore wrists gently to restore the circulation to her frozen hands.

'You are very kind,' she said bitterly.

The man's eyes studied her closely through the slits in his mask.

'And you,' he retorted, after a moment, 'are braver than I thought. I prefer that.'

As he thrust her not unkindly towards the trap-door, Marianne thought that he was quite wrong. She was not as brave as he believed, in fact she was half dead with fright but not for anything in the world would she have shown her fear. Her pride kept her upright, her chin held high before these unknown men beneath whose masks she divined aristocrats like herself, men of her own class, even if by some absurd series of misunderstandings, she had become their prisoner, though accused of what or why she did not know. In a way, she even felt a kind of impatience to find herself confronted with this mysterious court to which they kept referring, in order to find out at last why they had captured her and why they threatened her like this.

They went down a wooden staircase into the cellar in almost total darkness, illumined only by the candle held by one of the masked riders. The cellar was like any other, filled with barrels, bottles and a strong smell of wine. But in one corner underneath a rack which was moved with surprising ease, there appeared another trap-door, opening this time on to stone steps.

For all her show of courage, Marianne felt herself trembling as she made her way down into the bowels of the earth. She shuddered at the memory of the threats she had heard. A horrible idea came to her that perhaps these silent men were really leading her to her grave. From the anguish of her heart, she sent out one desperate thought to Charles. He had promised her that they would meet again soon, he might be thinking of her at that very moment, unaware that she was perhaps being torn from him forever. She saw all the cruel irony of a fate which opened the gates of death to her at the very moment when she had discovered love and happiness. No, it was too stupid! Marianne swore silently to fight for her life to the very end if only she might yet see Charles again.

About two dozen steep steps had echoed under their feet when they came at last into a huge, decaying crypt with semi-circular arches. A fierce draught blew through it, making the torches which the riders had brought with them from the first cellar stream out wildly. Their booted feet rang ominously in the tomb-like vault.

The crypt was cut in two by a large black curtain. A gleam of light showed from behind it. Before Marianne had time to wonder what was there, it was thrust aside and a man appeared. He was of medium height with short, crisp, slightly greying hair but of his face nothing was visible except a long, pale nose, owing to his mask and to his thick, black beard. The man's neck and shoulders indicated the strength of a bull, but the eyes which shone through the slits in his mask sparkled so gaily that Marianne found it hard to believe her own. His hands clasped behind his back, displaying the pair of long pistols thrust through his belt, the newcomer strolled up to the prisoner, stared at her closely for a moment and then burst out laughing, which was certainly the last thing Marianne had been expecting.

'S'blood! What a beauty!' He began but his smile changed to a frown as the baron gave an exclamation of annoyance then stepped forward and murmured something in his ear.

'Very well, if you insist! But I don't like it, Saint-Hubert, I don't like it at all. However, let's get on with it—'

The curtain was pushed aside completely to reveal a long table covered with a scarlet cloth, behind which four men sat facing them with an empty place in the middle for their leader. The bearded man sat down. Six candles stood on the table and these he lighted, revealing the faces of his companions who were also masked and sat as still as stone. But Marianne found her eyes drawn instantly to one of them. All too well she knew that strong, sardonic mouth, that rosy scar that ran up under his mask and in that instant, she knew why she had been kidnapped. One of her judges was Baron Hervé de Kérivoas, otherwise Morvan, the wrecker, the man whom Fouché had so incautiously allowed to escape. She had no eyes for any of the others. One only concerned her: the man she knew as her implacable enemy.

He did not move as she came in. There was no tightening of his features, no exclamation, but the eyes that fastened on the girl's face were bright with hatred. Marianne's only response was a slight scornful movement of her shoulders. She was not really afraid of Morvan. There was something unbalanced about him which made him weak, vulnerable perhaps. It remained to be seen what metal her other judges were made of. The four riders surrounded Marianne and marched her up to the table. All five remained standing and the leader's deep voice rang out.

'We are here,' he said solemnly, 'to hear and pass judgement on this woman who stands accused by one of our brethren of treachery, treason and intelligence with the enemy. Riders of the Shadows, are you ready to listen and pass judgement fairly and with justice?'

'We are,' judges and guards answered in unison.

'But I am not ready!' Marianne cried boldly. 'I am not ready to be judged by strangers for what crime I know not. By what law, by what right do you sit in judgement on me? And what wrong have I done you?'

'You shall know that,' the leader told her, 'when you have heard the accusation.'

'Not before I know with whom I have to deal. One who accuses should have the courage to do so openly, and a judge to pass sentence in broad daylight. I see nothing here but a dark, shadowy cellar and blind moles buried in the earth. My face is not hidden! Dare to show yours if you are really what you claim to be, if not true judges, at least real men!'

Some instinct, deep within her, drove her to defy these men. She found some comfort in it and even a kind of enjoyment.

'Silence!' one of the judges ordered. 'You need not know who we are. You only wish to see our faces the better to denounce us!'

'I understood,' Marianne observed with a disdainful smile, 'that I was not to leave here alive? Are you afraid of me? Afraid of one woman, a prisoner, alone amongst so many. Is that the truth?'

'By all the Gods, I will not have it said that a chit of a girl accused me of being afraid!' the leader cried. He tore off his mask and threw it down before him, revealing a bluff, joyous countenance which had clearly seen more than fifty summers. 'And she is right! What have we to fear from her? I am the chevalier de Bruslart. Are you ready to answer me now?'

It was a name Marianne had heard more than once. The man's reputation was high in England for courage and loyalty. Sworn enemy of Napoleon, he had for years successfully eluded the unremitting efforts of Fouché and his men to capture him. His presence here was some assurance to Marianne that, if he were really the leader of these men, then at least she would receive something approaching a fair trial. She pointed to Morvan.

'You may ask this gentleman also to remove his mask. I am too well acquainted with Monsieur de Kerivoas – or perhaps here too he prefers the name of Morvan?'

Slowly Morvan removed his mask, revealing his mutilated face. He rose to his feet and seemed to Marianne enormous in this shadowy place.

'Insolence will not save you, Marianne d'Asselnat. I accuse you of having deceived me, of pretending to be what you were not by means of stolen jewels, of causing the death of one of my men and, last of all, of loosing Fouché's bloodhounds on my trail. Thanks to you, my band is decimated, myself in flight and –'

'I had no part in what has befallen you,' Marianne interrupted him quietly, 'and my jewels are my own. But suppose we were to mention your own activities which are my best excuse for anything I may have done. I accuse you of lighting false fires on the shore to draw unhappy vessels to destruction on the rocks on stormy nights, of robbing corpses and doing to death the injured. I accuse you of being that worst of all human fiends, a wrecker! If I deceived you, it was to save my life. That is my legitimate defence. If these men are, as I think, faithful subjects of the king, they should hold you in abhorrence!'

Bruslart's great fist slammed down on the red table.

'Silence! What we may think concerns only ourselves. We are not here to settle a quarrel but to pass judgement on your actions, madame. Answer me. Your name is Marianne-Élisabeth d'Asselnat de Villeneuve as you told this man?' He indicated Morvan. 'But you are living in Paris under the name of Marianne Mallerousse, a name given you by Nicolas Mallerousse, one of Fouché's most active agents. And you have been employed of late as reader to Madame Grand.'

'To her most serene highness the Princess of Benevento,' Marianne corrected him proudly. 'You should have thought of that before you kidnapped me. Do you think that when my absence is noted in the morning there will be no search made?'

'No danger of that! The prince will receive word this morning, by a very short discreetly worded note, that you have found such favour with – the person you know of, that your presence is desired for some time longer in that charming woodland retreat where you spent the night.'

Marianne acknowledged a hit, fighting down the pain she felt at this cynical reminder of the blissful hours she had spent there. Then another thought came to her. Fouché, who always knew everything, who had agents everywhere, surely he would learn of his star's sudden disappearance! Perhaps he knew already that she had been taken to La Celle St Cloud, although there was no reason why he should be watching the house of someone of no particular importance. But there was also a possibility that Talleyrand, deceived by the letter, would arrange for Fouché to learn of what, in his eyes, would after all be no more than an amorous escapade.

The chevalier's cold voice interrupted the somewhat melancholy trend of her thought .

'Will you tell me, yes or no, whether you are indeed Marianne d'Asselnat?'

'Since you know I am,' Marianne said rebelliously, 'why do you ask? Are we in a court of justice? Are you a real judge?'

'So, you admit your name and rank – you admit them and yet –'

Bruslart paused. His bearded face twisted with sudden fury as he roared:

'– and yet, you, the daughter of a noble house, the daughter of two martyrs who died for their king, you have not feared to associate with the vilest rabble of this monstrous régime, you have dared to meddle with Fouché's police, to become an informer – and worse!'

So, he knew it all. In spite of herself, Marianne felt a red flush of shame sweep over her face. She understood that for these silent men whose eyes were fixed on her like so many daggers, that was her greatest crime, that she had seemed to come to terms with the régime of the hated Bonaparte. It troubled her like an unfair stigma. Could she make them see that they were wrong, that appearances alone were against her?

'Monsieur,' she said in a low voice, 'that I came to this country, that I have seemed to accept its laws and conditions, was because I had no choice. I did so to save my life. I can explain in detail, if you are willing to listen. But which of you has never tried to save his life at the cost of a lie? Which of you has never taken refuge in a borrowed name and character in such times as these?'

'We have lied,' acknowledged one of the judges who was still masked, 'and we have worn borrowed characters, but we have never betrayed our own people or compounded with the enemy.'

'I have never betrayed my own people!' Marianne cried passionately. 'It is my own people who have betrayed me. I was alone and helpless and I asked for help and assistance from one close to King Louis, and he rejected me without mercy, abandoning me knowingly to the worst of fates! But I have never compounded with Bonaparte's régime! I was brought up in England, brought up to hate him and I recognize his power no more than you. Whatever he made me suffer, I never betrayed the man I knew as Morvan. As for the tyrant who reigns here, I swear on my mother's grave, that I have always execrated –'

Before she could finish, one of the riders, the one who had been addressed as the Baron de Saint-Hubert, had rounded on her, his arm raised and his eyes alight with such a murderous fury that Marianne recoiled instinctively with a cry of terror.

'Renegade! Perjurer! Blasphemer! You should be burned alive for what you have just dared to say, for daring to soil your mother's memory with a lie! You serve to die in torment! Miserable creature! You dare to say you hate Napoleon?'

Saint-Hubert's hand fell heavily on Marianne's arm. He flung her violently to her knees and held her there.

'You dare to say? Dare you say it again?'

Marianne was white with shock but even now she refused to give way to her fear.

'Yes –' she whispered. 'I do dare!'

Without releasing his hold on her arm, Saint-Hubert dealt her a ringing blow to the head which sent her sprawling on the ground.

'You filthy little vagabond! So frightened for your skin you'll swear to anything! But your lies shall not save you, do you hear? So you hate Napoleon, do you? Did you hate him so much, tonight, at Butard?'

'At – Butard?' Marianne echoed dazedly.

'Yes, at Butard! At the delightful nest he keeps for his amours and where you spent the night! Or perhaps you were not in his bed? It was not he who made love to you, eh?'

Marianne's head reeled. Everything seemed suddenly to have gone mad, the world was falling to pieces about her ears. In her horror, she began to scream:

'No! No! It's not true! You are lying! The man I saw is called Charles Denis! An ordinary bourgeois.'

'Will you not cease your lies? And to think that I admired your courage, that I was ready to speak for you, perhaps to help you!'

Mad with rage, the baron was about to strike again but Bruslart sprang forward suddenly and tore the terrified girl from his friend's grip and thrust her behind his own broad back.

'Enough, Baron de Saint-Hubert!' he said grimly. 'I am no murderer, or persecutor of women! The girl is too frightened to know what she is saying.'

'Say rather she's making a mockery of us all, chevalier! Leave her to me, I'll make her talk. Creatures of her kind deserve no pity.'

'And I say enough! There is something here I do not understand –'

He turned to where Marianne lay half unconscious, face downwards on the ground. He helped her up and made her sit on a low stool. Marianne's head was ringing like a cathedral bell. She struggled unsuccessfully to collect her thoughts but decided that she must be going mad. What did these men mean? Of course, that was it. They were mad – or else she was the victim of some terrible misunderstanding. Charles! – Charles! Of God! How could they confuse him with the adventurer who held all Europe under his heel? He was so kind and gentle! They did not know him. They could not know him. He was just an ordinary man – God, how her head hurt!

Marianne became aware of the rim of a glass pressed to her lips.

'Drink this,' the chevalier ordered. 'Then we will try and get to the bottom of this.'

'Charles!' she moaned. 'Charles Denis. You cannot know –'

'Drink, I tell you. You are green.'

She drank. The wine was strong and heady. Its warmth ran quickly through her chilled body, reviving a little spark of life. Pushing the glass away with her hand, she stared at the chevalier with such a lost expression that he nodded with a trace of pity.

'So young and yet so depraved?' he murmured under his breath.

'There is no age in women's depravity!' There was no pity in Morvan's voice.

'I have asked you to let me sort this out, Monsieur the Wrecker,' Bruslart retorted, without looking round. 'Stand back a little, gentlemen, you are upsetting her.'

The Baron de Saint-Hubert gave a sardonic crack of laughter.

'One of these days, chevalier, your incorrigible weakness for women will make you do something stupid. I am not sure that day has not come.'

'If it has come, then I am old enough to see that without your help. For the present, I should like to question this one without interruptions from you.'

'Very well, question her! But we are here. We are listening.'

The Riders of the Shadows withdrew to the far end of the chamber, a black wall against the grey wall of the crypt. Marianne and Bruslart were left alone by the table.

'Last night,' he began patiently, 'you were taken to the pavilion of Butard at Le Celle St Cloud?'

'That was the name I was told, certainly.'

'Who took you there?'

'The Prince of Benevento. He told me the house belonged to a friend of his, a bourgeois named Monsieur Charles Denis, a man who had recently suffered a cruel bereavement. My singing was to be a comfort to him.'

'And you were not surprised that such a man as Talleyrand should take the trouble to escort you, in person, to the house of a mere bourgeois?'

'Yes. But the prince told me that they were friends of long standing. I thought – I thought the prince might have known him perhaps in the Revolution, or that the name might be a cloak for some foreign conspirator –'

'We will come to that later. Who met you at Butard? A servant?'

'No. I think he was a friend of M. Denis. He was called Duroc. And I saw a manservant as well.'

'A manservant by the name of Constant, was it?'

'Yes – yes, I think so!'

The chevalier's deep voice became suddenly very gentle. He bent over Marianne and looked hard into her eyes.

'This M. Denis – you love him?'

'Yes! Yes, I love him. I think I loved him from the very first. I saw him and then—'

'And then,' Bruslart finished for her quietly, 'you found yourself in his arms. He attracted you, hypnotised you, bewitched you – they say he can talk love like no one else and write it better still.'

Marianne stared at him wide eyed.

'But then – you know him? He is a man who leads a secret life, is he not, a conspirator, like yourself? I knew he was in danger!'

For the first time, Bruslart smiled briefly.

'Yes, I know him. As for secrecy, it may well be, for it is true that he is often in danger. Shall I show you your Monsieur Denis?'

'Yes – yes, of course. Is he here?' she cried, carried away by a sudden wonderful hope.

'He is everywhere,' the chevalier said with a shrug. 'Here, look here.'

Taking a gold coin from his pocket he placed it in Marianne's hand. She stared at it in bewilderment.

'The face,' Bruslart persisted. 'Don't you recognize it?'

Marianne looked. A wave of colour mounted her face. She stood up, mechanically, staring with eyes grown suddenly huge at the fine profile stamped on the gold, a profile she recognized only too well.

'Charles!' she stammered helplessly.

'No,' the chevalier corrected her grimly. 'Napoleon! It was to him that old fox Talleyrand delivered you tonight, you little fool.'

The gold coin slipped from Marianne's fingers and rolled away over the ancient flagstones. She felt the floor heave under her feet. The walls were performing a wild dance around her. Marianne gave one cry and fell headlong, like a felled sapling.

When she came to herself again, she was lying on some straw in a dark place lit by a flickering brazier. A strange individual holding a candle was bending over her sympathetically. With his pointed face, receding hair, large ears and bristling whiskers, he looked like a mouse wearing a goatee. His black eyes, which were round and very bright, strengthened this resemblance. When he saw Marianne open her eyes, he gave a broad smile which split his face in two.

'Ah, that's right! We're coming round! Are we feeling better?'

Marianne made an effort to sit up and managed to prop herself on one elbow, though not without a groan. Her head ached horribly and her body felt bruised, as though she had been beaten.

'I – yes, thank you. I do feel a little better. But what happened to me? Where are we?'

The stranger with the large ears set his candle down on the ground and sat himself beside her, arms clasped about his skinny knees, carefully lifting the skirts of his coat before he did so. His blue coat and nut-brown pantaloons were of good cloth and well cut. They must have been elegant before the prison – there was no other name for the place in which they were, a kind of cavern shut off by iron bars – had worked irreparable harm on the tasteful garments.

'As to what has happened to you,' he said calmly, 'I cannot tell you. The chevalier de Bruslart, who uses these cellars as a meeting place when he is in Paris, brought you in a short while ago with the help of some of his friends. I believe I gathered that you were to take up residence in this charming spot while the gentlemen examined your case further. They did not seem able to agree. One was for putting you in the Seine to cool off, with a good, big stone, but the chevalier, a true gentleman indeed, declared roundly that he would kill anyone who despatched you without his express permission. As for our present place of residence –' the little man made an all-embracing gesture taking in the rough-hewn chalky cavern around them – 'I am able to inform you, gracious lady, that we are in the old quarries of Chaillot which have been disused now for many years. If it were not for these bars, I could show you the old lime kiln still in very good order.'

'Quarries?' Marianne said, 'I was in some kind of crypt when I fainted.'

'It opens off these quarries. It is all that is left of the old convent of the Dames de la Visitation where the gentle Louise de la Vallière once sought refuge from the adulterous passions of Louis XIV, where Bossuet pronounced his funeral oration over Henrietta of England, where –'

This singular individual was clearly a most cultivated person but just at that moment French history was very far from Marianne's thoughts. She was amazed, and even a little disappointed, to find herself still alive. How much simpler it would all have been if the Riders of the Shadows had killed her while she was unconscious! Then there would not have been this waking with its train of heartache and bitter memories. If only they had thrown her straight into the Seine when they took her from her carriage! She would have had her moment of agony and nameless horror but it would have been comparatively brief and by now it would have been all over. She would be dead, taking with her the sweet and wonderful memory of the night she had just passed. She would have died with Charles's kisses warm on her lips, in the full, dazzling glory of love's dawn. She could have kept that, at least. But now, now that she had learned who he was and knew herself to have been no more than a plaything for an emperor's whim, now her whole life was in ruins indeed.

She had believed that when he took her in his arms, Charles had been mastered by the same attraction, had suffered the same irresistible revelation as she had herself. But no, she had merely served to distract a selfish man who, for the sake of establishing a dynasty, had just cast down from the throne the woman he had placed there, the companion of his youth, the wife whom the Pope himself had crowned in Notre Dame with such splendid ceremony that day in December. Marianne had given herself gladly to Charles Denis because that Charles Denis had needed love and tenderness but it made her sick with grief and horror to think that she had been simply a toy for Napoleon.

She understood it all now: the care with which Talleyrand had taken her there and also what the minister, at present out of favour, hoped to gain from making this handsome present to his master.

She understood the flurry caused by the so-called M. Denis's arrival and also the slight Mediterranean accent, and the Italian words of love. The Corsican! It was to the Corsican that she had given herself so trustingly, on the spur of the moment, simply because she had been drawn to him as she had never been to any man before. The memory of their kisses and caresses which, only a few hours before, had been so sweet now burned her life like a red-hot iron. Utterly overcome with shame, she buried her head in her drawn-up knees and began to cry as though her heart would break.

A gentle, clumsy hand pushed aside the tumbled hair that hung over her face and began mopping her tear-stained cheeks with a handkerchief that smelled strongly of iris and a brotherly arm was put round her shoulders.

'There, there, you must not cry like that! You're not dead yet! And if you'll take my word for it, you aren't going to die. The chevalier de Bruslart has never killed a woman yet and if he decides to protect you —'

'I don't care if he does kill me!' Marianne cried miserably. 'I ask nothing better! Let him kill me and let me have done with this stupid life once and for all!'

'You want to die? You? With that face, those eyes —'

'If you dare tell me I am beautiful, I shall scream!' Marianne burst out passionately. 'I wish I were ugly, hideous, deformed! Then I should not be where I am! Then I should have been no one's wretched plaything! You cannot know what they have done to me, how I have been degraded, ruined, dishonoured —'

The words were pouring out now in a broken, incoherent stream as her control gave way at last. But the little man with the big ears did not seem to care. He got up and going to a pitcher of water which stood in one corner, dipped his handkerchief in it and set himself conscientiously to cleaning up his companion's dirty, tear-stained face. The cold water had a calming effect on Marianne. In a little while, she fell silent and let him wash her like a baby.

'There,' he said with satisfaction when the sobs and crying had dwindled to no more than some slight hiccupping. 'It does you good to cry but, my dear child, when you are my age, which must be about twice yours, you will know that there is nothing in the world to compare with simply being alive and that for someone who looks like you to say they want to die is not merely a wicked sin, it also shows extreme bad taste and ingratitude. You may have much to complain of in this base world but you must agree with me that Dame Nature has shown herself more than generous towards you even if you have suffered a bit just recently. There's nothing more comforting, when things seem to be going wrong, than to confide in someone. So tell your troubles to Uncle Arcadius. He knows some wonderful ways of getting out of the most hopeless situations!'

'Uncle Arcadius?' Marianne said in astonishment.

'Oh the devil! Have I omitted to present myself? That would be an unpardonable lapse of manners!'

He was on his feet in an instant, and, whirling round, favoured his companion with a bow in the best swash-buckling tradition. The only thing lacking was a feathered hat.

'The viscomte Arcadius de Jolival, at your service, former revolutionary out of step with the times, very present and genuine admirer of his glorious majesty the Emperor Napoleon, artist and man of letters – and a Greek Prince into the bargain!'

'A Greek Prince?' Marianne said, stunned by this flow of speech from the little man. She could not help being diverted by it and he had succeeded in distracting her from her own sorrows.

'My mother was a Comnène. Through her, I am related, though distantly it's true, to the wife of the governor of Paris, the talented Duchess of Abrantes – very distantly, perhaps I should say.'

Marianne recalled suddenly the little dark woman, looking so elegant in the set of enormous rubies, whom she had seen chatting to Countess Metternich in Talleyrand's salon. It was extraordinary how all these French people seemed to know one another. In Paris, one could discover common acquaintances even in a dungeon. Trying to shake off the numbness which chilled her to the heart, she too rose and went to hold her hands out to the warmth of the brazier. Her head still ached but her back felt less painful now. She noticed that this strange little man had declared himself roundly for the Emperor but could she, in all honesty, blame him for that when she had herself fallen a victim so quickly to the pretended Charles Denis?

'What are you doing here?' she asked suddenly. 'Is it because of your sympathies for – the régime?'

Arcadius de Jolival shrugged.

'If Bruslart set out to imprison everyone who sympathized with the régime, as you put it, he'd need somewhere a great deal bigger than the quarries of Chaillot. Ten provinces would not be enough. No, I am here for debt!'

'For debt? To whom?'

'To the Dame Desormeaux, known as Fanchon-Fleur-de-lys. I dare say you must have met that remarkable lady on the upper floors of this desirable paradise?'

'That horrible old woman in rags? You owe her money?' Marianne cried, feeling more and more bewildered.

'Well, yes.'

Jolival settled himself more comfortably and smoothed out a crease in his pantaloons before continuing in a conversational tone:

'You must not take Fanchon's rags too seriously. She dresses as occasion demands. Believe me, I've seen her dressed like an empress.'

'She is horrible!'

'Morally, I grant you. One could not find worse, but, physically, she was once a great beauty. Do you know how she got her name?'

'How should I know?' Marianne said with a shrug. 'I saw her only a short time ago for the first time.'

'She's had her ups and downs. In her prime, Fanchon was as beautiful as a lily and was done the honours of the Parc-aux-Cerfs. She was one of the does that great huntsman and man of taste, King Louis XV, pursued. She even had a daughter by him, Manette, as lovely as her mother and, even from the first, lavishly endowed. But Fanchon's ambitions for her daughter had no end. She had her brought up like a princess which, in part, she was, under a false name – and in this very convent of which we occupy the ruins. Meanwhile, her mother was indulging in a host of activities which were all highly lucrative but frowned on by good society to such an extent that one fine morning, she found herself kneeling before the Paris executioner and having a fleur-de-lys branded on her right shoulder. But far from being ashamed of it, she actually boasted. After all, she knew all about fleurs-de-lys from the king's bed. At all events, it was that flower which enabled her to survive the Revolution without a scratch and even to enlarge what was already the beginning of a pretty fortune. Unfortunately, Manette, having being brought up as a great lady and serving in the household of another great lady, found it quite natural to act as a great lady to the end. On the day her daughter's head fell, Fanchon swore war to the death on the Revolution and all that followed from it. To this day, the king has no more faithful a servant and, naturally, she hates the Emperor to the same extent.'

'It is a strange story,' Marianne said, having listened to it with the same rapt attention she had been used to give to her beloved novels. 'But where do your debts come in?'

'Among other worldly goods, Fanchon owns an illegal gaming house, attached, incidentally, to a house of ill fame. I lost everything I possessed there, as well as a good deal I did not. I'd literally nothing left but my shirt, and only that by some last remaining shred of modesty. But Fanchon had me taken out by her men and clapped in here and here I stay until I pay her what I owe her.'

This did not appear to disturb him unduly and Marianne, distracted from her own troubles in spite of herself, could not help smiling.

'But if she keeps you prisoner here, how can she ever expect you to pay?'

'Oh, that's quite simple,' Arcadius said with an apologetic grin. 'It's marriage she wants!'

'She wants – to marry you?' Marianne exclaimed with horror.

'No, not quite that. She has a niece, much uglier than herself though rather younger. It is this frightful hag I have had the misfortune to please. I do not leave here until the ring is on my finger.'

The misfortunes of the 'Greek Prince' had worked a miracle. Marianne found herself wanting to laugh and instantly her grief seemed lessened. She was discovering that a companion in trouble, especially one like this, was the best of all comforts because he was the kind of person who took even the worst disasters philosophically.

'And – have you been here long?' she asked.

'Five days. But I can hold out a bit longer – especially with such pleasant company. The gentle Philomène is really rather too plain!'

There was a silence, employed by the man of letters in cleaning his nails with a piece of straw. Then, looking up, he saw that Marianne, who was still standing by the brazier, had lapsed once more into her own bitter thoughts. He coughed.

'Ahem – if I might – why don't you come and sit here by me and tell me your story. I can have some quite good ideas, I promise you, and besides, it's a relief to share one's burden. I have an idea that your young shoulders are carrying one that's much too heavy for them. Come here – I – I really should like to help you.'

Quite suddenly, he had dropped his careless pose and slightly ironical tone. Marianne saw on his comical face nothing but immense kindness and real sympathy. She moved slowly to sit by him on the straw.

'Thank you,' she said in a small voice. 'You are right. I'll tell you all about it.'

When Marianne had finished her story, she saw that Arcadius was looking at her with eyes that shone with admiration. He had not said a word all the time that she had been speaking except for occasional sympathetic noises at the most tragical parts, but when at last she sighed and fell silent, all he said was:

'You spent more than half the night with the Emperor – and yet you wish you were dead?'

Marianne was left speechless. For him to be a warm admirer of the usurper was one thing but that he should regard what had happened to her as the most wonderful good fortune, seemed to her rather excessive.

'You think I should be glad to have been made a pastime for the master of the hour?'

'I think chiefly that you have a very wrong idea of what has happened to you. It is not so easy to attract Napoleon.'

'And you think—'

'That you attracted him as much as he appealed to you? I'd lay my life on it. To begin with, you possess the thing above all others that he adores: a fine voice. Remember, he kept la Grassini for months when she was as stupid as an owl, and even when he still loved Joséphine. And, besides that – but haven't you forbidden me to speak of your beauty? I think you know nothing of the man you love! And yet, he is worth knowing.'

Marianne was beginning to find this conversation quite surprisingly enjoyable but it was rudely interrupted. Candlelight wavered on the chalky walls of the passage that opened off their prison cave and they stopped talking abruptly. Dragging footsteps sounded and a moment later Fanchon-Fleur-de-lys appeared leaning on her cane. After her came the man they had called Requin, who carried a large parcel under his arm. Opening the gate in the bars with a large key, he stood back to allow the old woman to enter and then followed himself.

Fanchon hobbled forward to the brazier and gazed at the two prisoners malevolently. She pointed with her cane to Marianne.

'Get up,' she ordered. 'And take your clothes off!'

Marianne did not move. 'You cannot be serious?' she said.

'I am so serious that unless you do as you're told at once, you shall taste my stick and Requin shall wield it. Now! Take off those things! Such garments were not made to be dragged in the dirt and I can sell them for a good price. Ho, don't worry,' she sneered, 'I have brought you others. It is no part of my plan for you to freeze to death.'

'And did the chevalier order you to take her clothes?' Arcadius interrupted. 'It would surprise me. If I were you, my lady, I would go and ask him first—'

'To do that, little gentleman, I should have to gallop after him. He was obliged to set off in haste for Normandy with the Riders. A friend of his, a lady, is in peril at Valognes. In such matters he does not need telling twice! He will be away for several days and, in the meantime, has entrusted this little ewe-lamb to my tender care. He wants her back unharmed so that he can come to a decision about her. And I shall make sure she's returned unharmed because it is my hope he'll give her to me. But come now, quickly—'

Requin had dropped the bundle of clothes on Marianne's knees. She stared unhappily at the three people round her.

'Leave her alone,' Arcadius said angrily. 'What an old miser you are! You'd shave an egg, wouldn't you, Fanchon?'

'And you'd better keep quiet yourself, my little fellow, or Requin will teach you to mind your manners. He's a head taller than you are. You'd come out of it badly,' the old woman retorted, brandishing her cane.

'Please,' Marianne broke in. 'It is no good. I will give her my clothes. All I ask is to be allowed to change in peace.'

Neither Fanchon nor Requin moved. The man actually came and stood directly before Marianne, his hands in his pockets and a gleam in his eyes.

'If that man does not go away,' Marianne said sharply, 'I shall complain to the chevalier!'

She had scored a hit. The threat worked. Apparently Bruslart had left strong instructions regarding her. She did not relish staying in this underground dungeon until he should return but at least it would give her some respite and from her point of view, to gain time was all important. Talleyrand might institute a search for her. For the present, the only thing that mattered was that the chevalier de Bruslart had ordered that no harm should come to her. She meant to use that precious knowledge for all it was worth. Moreover, Fanchon-Fleur-de-Lys instantly proved her right.

'Out, Requin!' she ordered.

The man growled but obeyed and Arcadius turned his face to the wall while Marianne hurriedly took off her pink dress and cloak, although it made her sad to do so. In a moment, the fairy tale dress was clutched in the old woman's skinny grasp and Marianne, with an assumption of indifference, put on the thick skirt and bodice and the heavy woollen stockings which had been brought for her and wrapped herself in the big black shawl.

The clothes were not new or particularly clean but they were warm and all things considered rather more suitable for living in a quarry filled with nothing but straw and chalk dust.

Fanchon, satisfied with her loot, was now ready to go back upstairs but before leaving the cave she had something more to say.

'You'll get some food later, at the same time as this stubborn mule here! Still nothing to say to me, then, eh, handsome? Philomène is getting impatient, you know.'

'Then let her. I am not yet ready to become one of the family.'

'Think, my lad, think carefully! If within a week you have not decided, Philomène may be a widow before she's a wife! My patience has limits.'

'Precisely,' Arcadius retorted smoothly, 'and mine has not.'

When the old woman and her bodyguard had gone, Marianne's new friend returned to her side and began piling up armfuls of straw to make a more comfortable bed.

'You should lie down and try to sleep,' he said kindly. 'I have no means of knowing the time because that gracious lady had my watch off me long ago but it cannot be long till daylight. Not that we'll see it, of course, but at least we shall be left in peace. Our charming Fanchon's little cabaret, The Iron Man, is almost deserted by day. By night, on the other hand, there is generally plenty going on. Go to sleep, you are so pale and there are shadows round your eyes. Besides, there's nothing else you can do.'

Marianne accepted the improvised bed which her companion had made for her while he went over to the brazier and threw on some logs of which there were fortunately a good supply in one corner. Curled up in her shawl, she watched him gratefully. He had been friendly and restored her courage, but above all, he was there. Marianne dared not think what her feelings would have been had she been left all alone in the dark in the depths of this abandoned quarry, a prey to all the phantoms of terror and despair. Now, she would be able to sleep a little and seek, in rest, an answer to all the questions which just at present she did not want to ask. How could she face admitting to herself, without the risk of going out of her mind, that she was thoroughly in love with the very man who, ever since childhood, she had learned to fear and hate above all others? She was utterly exhausted. Her mind refused to function. She must sleep and sleep might bring her counsel. Tomorrow, she would seek some way of escape.

PART III

The Eagle and The Nightingale

CHAPTER THIRTEEN
Greece, Rome and Carthage
Seek an Ally

Marianne woke from a fitful sleep broken by nightmares, shivering with fever in spite of all the straw which the kindly, anxious Arcadius had heaped over her. Her throat hurt and in a little while she had begun to cough.

'You have certainly caught cold,' her new friend lamented. 'You were frozen when they brought you here. You need proper care!'

Consequently, when the bearer of their food, Requin, arrived, Arcadius set up a vigorous demand for tisanes, blankets and a soothing draught for the cough.

'I've no orders,' the man said roughly. 'Makes no difference to me if she catches her death!'

'But Fanchon will make a difference to you if anything happens to her, for the excellent reason that she will have to answer for her to the chevalier. If you have no orders, then go and get some!'

Requin dragged away reluctantly, without hurrying, but returned much more quickly carrying a heap of old blankets which he dropped carelessly on top of Marianne. After that he took a flask from his pocket.

'Medicine,' he said.

'I asked for a hot tisane!'

'It's coming—'

He stood for a moment apparently engaged in some kind of inner struggle. At length with a massive sigh, he took out a second flask and handed it to Arcadius with the agonized look of one parting from a beloved friend.

'Rum,' he growled.

Arcadius held the flask up to the light and laughed.

'It's not full! Helped yourself to your share, have you? Well, I'll say nothing if you'll bring me everything I want for her.'

'Let her die,' the other muttered in an ugly voice.

'You said that before. It is of no interest to me. Now, be off with you, and do what I ask, or I shall tell Fanchon!'

Like a mother, Arcadius de Jolival set himself to make the invalid swallow a little of the medicine. Then he wrapped her snugly in the blankets. She let him do it. Her mind was a blank and she was tired to death, yet on the verge of tears. She had been ill so little in her life that she had no resources of patience or endurance with which to face this sudden weakness. Her illness only increased her longing to escape and get out of this cavern that was so depressingly like a tomb. She did not want to die there, like a rat in a hole. The moment of despair which had prostrated her the night before had vanished and nothing was left but the commanding instinct of self-preservation.

With the fever, her brain worked more frantically than ever. She cast about desperately for some source of salvation, because although she had gathered that Bruslart did not mean to kill her, she was much less sure of Morvan. He was determined not to let her escape his vengeance even if he had to stand up to the chevalier himself. Unless, that was, he would consider himself sufficiently revenged were old Fanchon to succeed in reducing Marianne to the kind of ignoble slavery she had threatened. For the present, Morvan had gone with Bruslart and the other Riders of the Shadows, but he would return and who could tell whether he would not by that time have succeeded in persuading the chevalier that she must die? He had a substantial ally in the Baron de Saint-Hubert whose contempt for Marianne was overwhelming. Day after day, while the prisoner pined in her dungeon, they could be pleading their cause, wearing down Bruslart's resistance. The more she thought of it, the more Marianne was convinced that it would come down to a choice between the Seine and the house at Ranelagh. She had to escape first. But how?

'Stop worrying your head so,' Jolival's voice broke soothingly into her thoughts. 'You think too much, my dear. The man whose regard you won last night is all powerful, surely he will seek you out?'

'If he wished for me tonight, I would have a chance, but he did not conceal from me that it might be several days before he could send for me again. Supposing he ever does—'

'You underestimate yourself. I am sure he thinks of you.'

'You are a kind friend. You are trying to comfort me but is it possible that for him I was anything more than a moment's pleasure? Is there no other woman in his life? I heard in the Prince of Benevento's house of a certain Polish countess—'

'Walewska? It is true, she loved him passionately. She gave up everything to follow him – and it was even the fact that she was pregnant that determined him to give up Joséphine.'

'You see,' Marianne sighed.

'Countess Walewska has left him. Not very long ago, but she has left.'

'Because he must remarry and because she would not suffer! Why should I be more fortunate than she? They called her his 'Polish wife' – and she is young, lovely, noble – and yet he let her go. What can I hope for more than this one night?'

This time, Arcadius de Jolival had no answer. *He knows,* Marianne thought, *that I am right but he does not like to admit it. He fears that I shall give way to despair.*

A desperate fit of coughing almost choked her. Jolival hastily made her drink some medicine and then tried to get her to drink a little of the soup which Requin had brought. But Marianne was not hungry. The mere smell of the food, which was certainly not very appetizing, made her feel sick.

'I'm thirsty,' she said. 'Just dreadfully thirsty.'

He nodded anxiously and made her drink a little water which he had warmed slightly over the brazier, then he wrapped the covers well around her and sat down beside her bed to wait. As she lay there in the silence and exhaustion of the fever, Marianne thought for the first time of Jason Beaufort. She was sorry now that she had not accepted his offer. Dazzled by the glittering, unreal prospect of a brilliant future in the theatre, she had refused to understand his warning. And yet, he had been right. The danger he had foretold had come to pass and now there was nothing he could do for her. When Bruslart and his band returned, the American would be already on the high seas. To be sure, he had spoken of a friend, a man called Paterson, the American consul at Nantes, but to the prisoner in the quarries of Chaillot, Nantes was as far away as Mars. Marianne closed her eyes and tried to force herself not to think. Thinking was painful, it only increased her fever and she wanted desperately to be better.

Hour upon unending hour, days and nights blending into one another with nothing to tell them apart. Hours that were like days, even weeks. Time dragged so slowly, broken for Marianne into periods of tense, anxious waking and heavy sleep from which she would sometimes wake trembling and drenched with sweat from the grip of a nightmare. During all this time, Arcadius's friendship and concern were inexhaustible. He did not spare himself in his efforts to make the invalid take a little food, making her swallow the endless potions and tisanes which he demanded from Requin. Once a day, old Fanchon came to see how matters stood. There was no solicitude or pity in her manner, nothing but the cold calculation of a horse dealer who sees his stock in trade likely to perish.

'She watches over you like a market gardener when the frost is on his lettuces,' Arcadius would say, attempting to laugh. But his laughter quickly died away, unable to withstand the oppressive atmosphere of the cavern. At other times, the prisoner's wants were supplied by Requin who was as gruff and unapproachable as ever. Even if she had possessed any money, Marianne would not have risked trying to bribe him. He served Fanchon-Fleur-de-Lys like a dog and was not the kind of watchdog to be won over by a bone.

And yet, little by little, she recovered. The bouts of coughing became further apart, the fever diminished and her cracked voice recovered normal tones. There came a time when Marianne was able to smile at her faithful companion:

'I think I'm better – but for you I am sure that I could never have recovered.'

'You are very young. I have merely helped nature. You would have got over it very well without me.'

She shook her head and looked thoughtful for a moment.

'No,' she murmured. 'Because if you had not been here, I should have had no wish to live.'

For the first time since her capture, she fell into a real sleep of the kind that is more restorative than any medicine on earth. She was dreaming that the black cab was taking her back to a Butard of fantasy, shining like a great star under a dazzling blanket of snow, when an unusual sound made her start up wide awake. She sat up and saw that Arcadius, in his own corner, was also awake and listening. Their eyes met in the gloom.

'What is it?' Marianne whispered.

'It sounded like a fall of rock. Listen! There it is again. It comes from somewhere back in the quarry.'

Jolival had already explained to Marianne that the passage outside their prison cave ended a little further on in a blank wall.

Now they could hear a scratching sound followed by a muffled but unmistakable oath. Arcadius was on his feet in an instant. There was a glimmer of candlelight in the passage, wavering on the chalky walls as it came nearer. By now, Marianne, too, had got nervously to her feet and moved closer to her companion. Someone was coming, beyond a doubt, but who could it be, and where had they come from?

'They must have dug through the wall,' Jolival said in a whisper. 'It's easy enough to pierce the chalk with good tools. But who —'

He did not finish. The light was coming nearer. They heard cautious footsteps, light but real. A shadow loomed up along the wall and, despite herself, Marianne pressed closer to Arcadius. Then, suddenly, she bit back a cry of amazement. Even in the distorting light of the candle he held, she recognized the features and the mop of red hair belonging to Gracchus-Hannibal Pioche, the errand boy who had warned her about the black cab. A sigh of relief escaped her.

'He is a friend,' she said to Jolival.

Gracchus-Hannibal had already spotted the barred recess, illumined faintly by the brazier. He made his way close up to the bars and his anxious face broke into a broad grin.

'So I've found you at last, Mademoiselle Marianne! You've certainly given me a run for it.'

'What? Have you been looking for me? How did you know I had disappeared?'

Her hopes rose suddenly. If the humble Gracchus had had his suspicions, then surely such a remarkable man as Talleyrand could not have failed to have them too.

'Oh, that's easy! The black cab followed you and I followed the black cab. Daytimes, at least. I mostly sleep at night.'

'The devil!' Arcadius broke in. 'You must have a strong pair of legs to follow a cab —'

'They never go very fast in Paris, especially when they are following someone. But it's true, I have got strong legs. Where was I? Oh, – one morning, a week ago, it was, when I went to find the cab, it wasn't there. Nor did I see you go out. That struck me as odd. So I got into conversation with Joris, the porter at the Hôtel Talleyrand. I swept away the snow on the pavement outside, and so we got talking. I went back later to give him a hand and took a bottle with me. There's nothing like a bottle for making a man's tongue wag. In two days, I'd become his bosom pal! He told me you'd gone out one night with the prince and not come back. There was even some rumour going about the house that you'd been taken up by someone very grand. But that cab's being gone worried me – especially since I knew where it lived and I'd seen the man who was inside it several times going in and out of a bar called the Iron Man. That didn't seem to fit at all with any tale about a grand person. And so, I started making inquiries.'

'But how did you get here?' Marianne said filled with admiration for the young man's shrewdness.

Gracchus-Hannibal laughed.

'I've known the old quarries a long time. Used to play here as a kid with me pals and had some rare old times before the people from the Iron Man blocked up this gallery which runs into the old crypt of the Visitation. There were a good many hid here during the Terror, as there were in the quarries at Montmartre. But I know them all, like the back of my hand.'

'But this passage is a dead end,' Jolival broke in. 'How did you get into it without going through the crypt? I thought I heard some kind of avalanche.'

'It was a bit like that. Beyond the dead end, the galleries run on for quite a way but the main right bank sewer joins up with them and that runs into the Seine quite close to here. Besides, they're not all that well built. There are cracks and I heard voices last night. That gave me the idea of looking here. I came back with a pickaxe – and here I am! And am I glad to see you still alive, Mam'zelle Marianne! To be quite honest, I'd been none too sure –'

'Why? Do you know these people –?'

Gracchus shrugged and gave Marianne a pitying look.

'The old woman with the fleur-de-lys? Is there anyone in Paris doesn't know her! Or 'aint scared to death of her! I think she frightens even Citizen Fouché! At any rate, he needs to pay his men well enough to show their noses in the rue des Bonshommes after sunset! They don't like going near the Homme-de-Fer either, or its twin in the boulevard du Temple, the Épie-Scié. And those that do, generally vanish without trace. And both those places belong to Desormeaux. Oh, she's a character, all right! A sort of queen of the underworld!'

Marianne had been listening to the boy's words with undisguised fascination but Jolival was beginning to show signs of impatience.

'This is all very well, my lad,' he said at last, 'but I don't suppose you've come all this way just to sing Fanchon's praises? You'd be better employed getting us out of here! I suppose this hole you've dug is big enough to let a young lady through?'

'The hole, yes,' Gracchus said. 'But how am I going to get you out from behind those bars? Those aren't just a little bit of wire! Look at them – thick as a baby's wrist!'

'Look here, my lad, if you don't put a brake on your enthusiasm for our prison and our jailors, I shall personally insert my adult arm between these baby ones and push your face in! Can't you see the young lady is ill and must be got out of here as soon as possible?'

'Oh, don't be hard on him,' Marianne begged. 'I am sure he will find a way.'

'Why would I have taken all this trouble else?' Gracchus-Hannibal replied in a surly voice. 'All the same, there's nothing to be done tonight. It's too late. It can't be far off five o'clock, though it don't feel like it. And I'll have to get hold of some proper tools. A good file might do – unless we try and get out one or two of the bars –'

'Or knock down the wall!' Arcadius scoffed. 'It seems that you're no locksmith. Find me some good locksmith's tools and come back tomorrow night, if you can. You are right, it's too late now.'

Marianne did her best to hide her disappointment. When she saw the boy appear, she had thought that freedom was within her reach, but now they had to wait another whole day. Gracchus-Hannibal was scratching his head under the blue cap.

'Locksmith's tools?' he said. 'Yes, it could be – but where from?'

'Listen,' Marianne said suddenly as an idea occurred to her. 'If you need help, there may be someone who can give it – at least, if he is still in Paris.'

'Tell us, mam'zelle.'

'Go to the Hôtel de l'Empire and ask for Monsieur Jason Beaufort, he is an American. Will you remember that? Jason Beaufort.'

The boy pulled paper and pencil out of his cap. 'Wait a moment,' he said. 'I'll put it down. There – that's it. What shall I tell him?'

'That you come from Marianne – that she needs help. Then tell him where I am.'

'And if he's gone?'

'Then say nothing to anyone,' she said sadly. 'Just come and tell me, that's all.'

'You don't want me to tell them in the rue de Varennes?'

'No! No – not at present. We'll see if M. Beaufort has gone –'

Marianne could not have said what made her call on Beaufort for help. He had wounded her deeply and even now she did not altogether trust him. But he represented her one chance of escaping from the trouble which had dogged her ever since her marriage to Francis Cranmere. Only with Beaufort did the word "escape" bear its full meaning. If she succeeded in escaping with him, when his ship left the coast of France it would break all the chains that bound her. No more Fouché, no more reports, no more Talleyrand with his cunning plots, his brilliant ideas and his subtle diplomacy. Above all, and more than all, she would put an ocean like an impassable barrier between herself and the man she could not help loving. She could have devoted her life to Charles Denis, but what was the love of a mere girl like herself to Napoleon I, Emperor of the French? In a week, less perhaps, he would have forgotten her, might indeed have done so already. By now, all his thoughts would surely have turned to that arch-duchess of Austria he meant to marry. It was better to go away and never see him again rather than risk yielding a second time. And then, over there, she would try and get over it.

To keep her spirits up, she told herself that she would accept from Beaufort only such aid as she was obliged to and that she would try and support herself by singing. There must be theatres in that far away country, and concert halls –

'You mean to go to America?' Jolival's voice spoke quietly beside her.

Marianne came down to earth and saw that Gracchus-Hannibal had gone. From the far end of the passage, came the sound of stones being moved. He must be making a rough attempt to cover the hole by which he had entered.

'I think it is the best thing I can do,' she answered.

'Maybe. You do not wish to see him again?'

'No. It is best for me, and still more for him. I must not see him again at any price.'

'Why?'

The brief question shook Marianne. It forced her to reply as simply, to give the real reason for her longing to escape and it came home to her more sharply as she said it.

'Because I'm afraid,' she said in a low voice.

'You are afraid,' Jolival finished for her calmly, 'because you realize that you love Napoleon as much as Charles Denis, perhaps more. Whatever you may think, a halo of glory never does any harm to one we love – even if our politics are not quite the same. The glory is still there. And – do you think you will forget more easily if you put an ocean between you?'

'I hope so! Someone, I can't remember who, once said that the greatest victory in love was flight.'

Arcadius de Jolival roared with laughter.

'Look no further. He said it. Napoleon has a great belief in the merits of flight where love is concerned. It still remains to be seen whether there is any truth in that pretty phrase. I promise you, he has not often tried it.'

'Well, I shall! You see, Arcadius, I should suffer too much if I stayed. He is to remarry again soon, is he not?'

'What then? A marriage of convenience, a dynastic marriage? No such union ever kept a man from his true love.'

'But I am not his true love! I am only a brief interlude in his life. Can't you understand that?'

'Even so. With his help you might become in a few days what you have dreamed of being, a great singer. But you prefer to set off, like Christopher Columbus, to discover America. It may be as well, but remember what I say, even at the other end of the world, you will not forget the Emperor.'

'The Emperor …'

For the first time, she realized the splendour of that title. The man she loved bore the loftiest of all crowns. He was the greatest warrior of any age since Caesar and Alexander. Nearly all Europe bowed before him. As though it were child's play, he had won victory after victory, conquered vast territories. As though it were child's play, he had conquered her, had made her bow beneath a love too great for her romantic little soul, a love without even the legendary wings to help her bear the crushing weight of history.

When she spoke, her voice was drained of all expression.

'Why do you think that I shall not forget him?'

Jolival sighed gustily, stretched and settled himself back on the straw. He gave a great yawn and then said placidly:

'Because it is not possible. I've tried.'

The hours that followed were, for Marianne, the most agonizing she had ever lived. The absence of a clock made itself cruelly felt because time seemed to her endless when she had no means of measuring it. Jolival did try asking Requin when he brought their one meal of the day but all he got for answer was:

'What difference does it make to you?'

They were forced, therefore, to rely on guess-work. Jolival attempted to soothe his companion's nerves by observing that darkness fell early in winter but nothing and no one could calm Marianne's nerves. So many obstacles lay between her and freedom. Would Beaufort be still there even? Would the boy manage to come back at all or would he be so overcome by the difficulties before him that he would abandon the whole plan altogether? A host of possibilities, each more desperate than the last, occurred to Marianne's fevered mind. There were times when she actually believed she must have dreamed that Gracchus-Hannibal Pioche was there. But for Jolival and his imperturbable calm, she would never have been able to control herself. But the man of letters appeared so calm and relaxed that it was almost irritating. Marianne would have preferred him to share her terrors and her cloudy suppositions instead of simply peacefully awaiting the outcome of events. But then, she reflected, he had little to fear beyond a disagreeable marriage.

Marianne had just returned for the hundredth time to striding up and down their prison when a whisper from Arcadius stopped her in her tracks.

'Someone's coming!' he said. 'Our red-headed saviour can't be far off – if my calculations are correct, it must be getting on for nine o'clock.'

Someone was certainly approaching but not from the dead end of the passage. The figure who rose suddenly before Marianne's horrified eyes was that of Morvan. He was enveloped in a great black cloak with drops of water shining wetly on it and his scarred face was without its mask. Marianne could not hold back a cry of terror as he loomed up out of the shadows and her terror was increased at the thought that any moment, they might hear Gracchus's pick working away at the loose stones in the wall. The Riders of the Shadows would have no mercy on a lad who to them would be no more than a spy and therefore a potential danger. Marianne's eyes sought Jolival's and read in them the reflection of her own thoughts. He was already standing close beside the bars and suddenly he spoke in a voice much louder than his normal tones.

'It seems we have a visitor! We certainly looked for none, or not of this quality!'

Marianne understood at once that by talking so loudly he hoped to make Gracchus, supposing he were already on the other side of the wall, hear and be on his guard and she too spoke as loudly as she could.

'I take no pleasure in such a visit. What is your business here, sir plunderer of wrecks?'

Morvan's twisted lips curved in an unpleasant smile.

'To see how you are, my beauty! In truth, since we were obliged to part so abruptly, I have thought of you almost constantly – and talked of you too!

Your ears must have been burning, we have argued so much about you, the chevalier, the baron and myself—'

'I do not know what you may have said and I do not wish to know, or not from you. The chevalier de Bruslart will no doubt repeat to me the gist of your remarks and from him they are more likely to come correctly.'

Morvan scowled and drew back a pace.

'Do you have to shout like that? I am not deaf! You are almost bursting my eardrums!'

'I am sorry,' Marianne said without lowering her voice. 'But I have been ill and my voice is only audible if I shout.'

'Shout as much as you like, before long you will shout to another tune! This little journey was quite providential. Our dear chevalier has always had an eye for a pretty woman and he was showing signs of quite unnecessary kindness and clemency towards you. He is a simple, tender-hearted soul in whom the old principles of chivalry are still regrettably alive. Fortunately, I had plenty of time to provide him with some detailed information concerning you which, I think, has prevailed upon him.'

Marianne felt her heart quake. It had happened exactly as she had feared. Morvan had turned the chevalier against her. No doubt he had come now to give himself the gruesome pleasure of informing her of her imminent death. But not for anything in the world would she have shown this man the gnawing fear within her. Instead, she turned her back on him with a disdainful shrug.

'My congratulations, if you have succeeded in persuading the chevalier de Bruslart to abandon his sacred principles and murder a defenceless woman in cold blood. You should have made yourself a career in diplomacy! It would have been more honourable than your chosen occupation – although less lucrative perhaps!'

Her words caught Morvan on the raw. He made an angry movement as though he would have thrown himself against the bars but then thought better of it. When he spoke, his voice was light enough but his smile was evil.

'Who mentioned murder? That principle is one of which the chevalier de Bruslart admits no compromise but none the less, you shall be punished as you deserve. I have managed to persuade him to hand you over to our dear Fanchon who seems to take in my view a quite excessive interest in you. She will find you employment for which you are well fitted. And she will also be grateful to the man who can renounce his own vengeance for her profit, and his own.'

'I wonder at the chevalier's scruples,' Marianne retorted, sick at heart, 'that he spares a woman's life and yet dishonours her in a baser fashion!'

'Dishonours? A fine word, coming from you! The chevalier's scruples yielded somewhat after I had told him of your exploits in my barn with that spy of Bonaparte's who was your so-called servant -- and also that I found you on the shore clad in the most rudimentary fashion and attempting to seduce two of my men. One of whom, moreover, you murdered not long afterwards. No, after this very circumstantial account, the chevalier had no more hesitation. Especially since he hopes to be your first customer.'

Speechless with horror at this display of cruelty and duplicity, Marianne could find no answer. In her disgust she even forgot Gracchus and his danger but Arcadius Jolival intervened.

'I think that will do, monsieur,' he said his fingers playing nervously with his moustache. 'You have played your foul part to perfection and now I must ask you to leave this lady in peace. As to the worth of Bruslart's scruples, if he accepts the base assertions of a wrecker, I can say nothing, but I can tell you what you are at once. You are a first-class scoundrel!'

Morvan's face paled and Marianne saw his jaw tighten. But before he could reply, the chevalier's voice called from the hollow crypt nearby.

'Ho there! Kerivoas! Come here and leave the prisoners alone. We'll settle that afterwards. For the present, we have more urgent business.'

The distant gleam of torchlight was now dancing on the walls and there was a hum of voices not far off. Morvan, who had seemed about to hurl himself bodily at the bars, stopped short and turned on his heel with a shrug.

'I'll come back later to slice off those big ears of yours, little man! Don't worry, you'll lose nothing by waiting.'

He went away to join the others and Marianne went disconsolately back to her straw bed where she sat down with her arms around her knees and her head with its long, tumbled mane of hair resting on her arms.

'This is the end,' she murmured. 'We are finished. And if that poor boy comes now, he will be finished with us.'

'Be patient. We shouted loud enough to warn him! He may be on the other side of the wall —'

'What should he wait for? He cannot get near us! The conspirators are still in the crypt and we cannot tell how long they will be there - 'you can hear them —'

'Ssh! Listen!' Jolival said sharply. He went and pressed himself up against the bars as near as possible to the confused voices coming from the crypt.

'They are having a meeting,' he whispered.

'And - can you make out anything?'

He nodded and touched his big ears with a meaning smile. Marianne was silent, watching her companion's mobile features as they grew at first grave and then thoroughly alarmed. She heard a gruff voice which she recognized as belonging to the chevalier de Bruslart but was unable to make out a word of what he said. The leader of the band was speaking. He seemed to be explaining something. From time to time, another voice would interrupt but the main burden always returned to Bruslart. And, gradually, the look on Jolival's face became so tragic that Marianne laid her hand on his arm and whispered urgently: 'What is it? You are frightening me! Are they talking about us?'

He shook his head and muttered swiftly under his breath:

'No – in fact, they are going away. Be patient a little longer.'

He listened again but the council seemed to be breaking up. There was a noise of seats being scraped on the floor and a clatter of booted feet. All the voices began speaking at once, then Bruslart's rose above the rest.

'To horse, gentlemen! For God and for the King! Tonight, at last, fortune is with us!'

This time, it was beyond a doubt. They were going. The footsteps died away, the voices faded and the lights vanished. In a few moments, Marianne and Arcadius found themselves once more alone with the heavy silence and the dim, ruddy light of their dungeon. Jolival left his post by the bars and went over to the brazier. Marianne saw that he was avoiding her eyes.

'You heard what they were saying?' she asked.

He nodded affirmatively but did not open his mouth. He seemed to be deep in thought. However, Marianne was too anxious to inspect his silence.

'Where are they going?' she asked with a touch of irritation. 'Why is fortune on their side tonight? What are they going to do?'

Jolival looked at her at last. His mouse-like face, usually so cheerful, was overcast as though by some distressing thought. He seemed to hesitate for a moment then, as Marianne came and clutched his arm anxiously, he said at last:

'I am in two minds whether to tell you but whether or not they are successful you will hear anyway. They have learned from one of their spies in the palace that the Emperor goes tonight to Malmaison. The former Empress is unwell. She has also learned that the Emperor's choice of a wife has fallen definitely on the Austrian arch-duchess and the news has affected her badly. The Emperor's decision to go was taken only an hour ago.'

'And?' Marianne felt her heart beat faster at the mention of the word 'Emperor', only to contract painfully at the news of his impending marriage.

'And they mean to carry out the old plan of Cadoudal and Hyde de Neuville, the old plan which ever since the Consulate, Bruslart has always failed to carry off. They will set a trap for Napoleon when he leaves Malmaison, probably very late, stop his carriage, overcome his guard and then carry him off and –'

'Kill him!' Marianne almost screamed.

'Bruslart said no. He wants only to carry off the Emperor, get him across the channel and deliver him bound hand and foot to England – unless he will consent to fight a duel. A duel with Napoleon has always been the chevalier's great dream.'

'Is he mad?'

'No. He is a paladin, in his way. He believes only in fair fight and you could say that he only became a conspirator because there was nothing else for him to do and because there was no longer a royalist army. But Bruslart might be killed in such a duel or, if there is not one, the others may force the chevalier's hand. The stake is high, this time, and there are some, I know – your friend Morvan among them – who want Napoleon's head at all costs.'

'Why?'

Jolival chuckled cynically.

'It's very simple. The Duke of Medina-Coeli, the richest of all the Grandees of Spain, has offered half his vast fortune to whoever kills Napoleon and brings proof of his death.'

In the silence that followed, Marianne was able to gauge the depth of her feelings. Her heart was beating uncontrollably. She was trembling in every limb but she forced herself to be calm.

'Why did they say fortune was with them?'

'Because the journey was decided very quickly. There will be only a small escort to avoid attracting attention. And tonight, the conspirators number twenty-five at least.'

'But Fouché? Fouché knows all, sees all. Can Fouché not prevent this plot like all the others?'

'Fouché will be taken by surprise. Besides which, it must be admitted that for some time now Fouché seems to have been relaxing his care a little. Deliberately, no doubt, because he is a man who does nothing without a reason. My dear child – it is very possible that in a short while we shall have the great honour of sharing our dungeon with his majesty our Emperor and King, which will give me both the greatest possible joy and at the same time the utmost regret.'

Marianne bravely thrust away the sweet yet agonizing picture he conjured up of her love, in fetters, joining her in her dungeon.

'But we have to stop it! We must! I know Morvan. He will not let Bruslart bring him here. In the dark, in a struggle, a pistol shot is soon fired. Oh my God! I must go to him! I cannot stand by and see him murdered. Not him! These villains are going to kill him! I tell you, they are going to kill him!'

She had flung herself blindly on the bars, gripping them with both hands and trying to shake them loose by sheer force but they did not so much as quiver. The rusty iron skinned her hands but she did not feel the pain, any more than she saw the prison around her. What she saw was a road at night, in the snow, a carriage halted, perhaps overturned, the horses struggling in the grip of masked men, figures stretched out in the snow which was already turning red, an unarmed man held by the conspirators

275

and Morvan laughing evilly as he held a pistol to the head of that man, the man she loved.

'I won't let them,' she screamed desperately, resisting with all her strength Jolival's attempts to prise her away from her lacerating grip on the bars. 'I won't let them kill him! I love him! Napoleon!'

In the confusion of her mind, she cried aloud for the first time the name which had haunted her ever since she had learned the truth and which she had murmured to herself many times in her fever. Arcadius had to gag her with his hand to silence her, and with a supreme effort he managed at last to tear her away from the bars.

'You will rouse the whole rat's nest!' he scolded. 'Have you forgotten we are waiting for someone?'

It was true. She had forgotten Gracchus-Hannibal Pioche. But her hysterical panic was over in an instant and Marianne crumpled on to the ground, put her head in her hands and wept.

'He will not come now. He must have heard those men and realized that there was no chance tonight. Even supposing he came at all —'

'And why shouldn't he have come?' Jolival said roughly. 'Myself, I trust that lad! He's got honest eyes. He'll do all he can to get you out of here.'

'Maybe. But not tonight. He won't come back tonight. And, oh my God, the Riders must be on the road to Malmaison by now —'

As though to shut out the sound of galloping hoof-beats ringing in her head Marianne put her hands over her ears and closed her eyes. Never in her whole life had she so longed for oblivion in that moment. Consequently, she did not see Arcadius go quickly to the bars and grip them in his turn as, from the depths of the underground cavern, came the sound of a stone falling. It was followed by another.

In a flash, Arcadius was on her shaking her unmercifully by the shoulders.

'Listen! Only listen! He's coming! He is breaking down the wall again.'

Marianne jerked upright, eyes wide, and gripping Arcadius's hand in her own, she listened with all her soul. It was true, someone was coming down the blind passage. Hardly daring to breathe, she followed the boy's progress. There was the sound of someone running and all at once, she saw Gracchus-Hannibal burst out of the passage. Hard on his heels was the much taller figure of a man and, the next moment, Jason Beaufort's large frame was towering on the other side of the bars. Marianne gave a cry of joy.

'You! God be praised, you have come! You had not left!'

She saw the blue eyes laughing in his tanned face and felt her cold hands folded in the American's warm ones as he reached through the bars to hold and clasp them.

'Not quite!' he said gaily. 'I leave tomorrow but no power on earth would have prevented me from getting you out of this new pickle you've got yourself into, you little fool! Come now, don't cry. We'll have you out of there in a trice. Look there,' he added, turning to Gracchus-Hannibal who, armed with a file almost bigger than himself was bravely attacking one of the bars with Arcadius's help, explaining as he worked that they had been forced to wait for the conspirators to go away.

'I was up top,' he said, 'and Monsieur Beaufort down below.'

'Hurry!' Marianne begged. 'We must get out of here quickly! Or, no —'

Another thought came to her. What did her own fate matter if Napoleon were safe?

'Leave us here and go and warn him!'

'Warn who?' Beaufort exclaimed in surprise. 'You are madder than I thought. Let us get on with our work.'

'No, please, listen to me – it is too important.'

She explained in a few short sentences the plot that was afoot and the Emperor's mortal danger. He listened with a frown, not pausing in his work but when she had finished, he threw down the file with an exasperated shrug.

'We are not leaving here without you. Much as I admire Napoleon, I will not leave you any longer in the hands of these savages. Especially if they come back thwarted. We'll not do it that way, kid.' The last part of this speech was addressed to Gracchus-Hannibal who was bending to pick up the file. Glancing at Arcadius, Jason went on abruptly: 'If you shout, can they hear you up there?'

'Yes. I've summoned the lackeys in this charming hotel before now by bellowing like a bull at need.'

'Then shout, my friend, shout as loud as you can, but get your jailer down here! I'll take care of the rest. Go on now, and do your best!'

Jolival opened his mouth and let out a sustained yell of such power that Marianne jumped. Beaufort, meanwhile, hid out of sight round the corner of the blind passage. His lean, muscular form, moulded into some kind of seaman's sweater and tight black breeches, merged so completely into the shadows of the passage that after a moment even Marianne could not see him. She did not understand what he meant to do but Arcadius was still yelling with complete conviction. She would never have believed that he could own such a powerful voice. It rolled among the dripping vaults until the whole place rang with it. When at last he stopped for breath, they could hear the sound of running footsteps followed by the angry voice of Requin.

'What's up with you, yelling yer 'ead of like that? I'll make you shut up!'

As the ruffian came in sight, Jolival flung himself on the ground and began rolling about like someone writhing in extreme agony, shouting once more at the top of his voice.

'Hurry,' Marianne cried urgently, having finally understood what was happening. 'He's ill! I don't know what's the matter.'

Requin swore violently as he struggled to open the gate. Before he could do so, Jason was on him. With a spring like a wild beast, the American leapt for his back and bore him down beneath his weight, at the same time locking his left arm under the man's chin, abruptly choking him. Requin gave a strangled gasp and lost consciousness. Jason gave him a swinging blow with his fist for good measure then, taking possession of the bunch of keys, he opened the gate and made straight for Marianne, sweeping her up in his arms like a feather.

'Let's get out of here,' he said kicking aside the recumbent Requin who blocked his way. 'Stow that behind bars and lock him in, then give me the key. We'll drop it in the sewer. This rat will be coming round in ten minutes and we must make the most of them.'

'What if we was to strangle him?' Gracchus-Hannibal suggested sweetly. 'It'd be no great loss and make things easier for us.'

Jason laughed.

'I should have done so a moment ago, but as I didn't, let him be. I can't kill an unconscious man.'

Still carrying Marianne, who had slid her arms instinctively round his neck, he made for the hole in the wall. He had to put her down to pass through it because the crack was only a small one. Behind him came Arcadius, endeavouring to recover some of the spring in legs rusty with captivity. Gracchus-Hannibal brought up the rear, taking the trouble to put back the displaced stones when he had passed through.

'You never know,' he remarked prudently.

Jolival laughed.

'Are you hoping to have business here again?' he said clapping the boy affectionately on the back. 'You certainly came to our rescue, son, and I hope one day that I'll be able to repay you. I owe you more than my life!'

'Go on,' the boy muttered awkwardly, 'it wasn't worth mentioning.'

'You think not? I think so!' Jolival said meaningfully.

On the other side of the wall was a short passage and then the sewer. Marianne's nostrils were filled with the foul stench. Jason had taken her up in his arms again, remarking that in a moment they would have to go through the water and there was no need for two of them to get wet.

For a short distance, they followed the narrow ledge which ran alongside the black waters. Arcadius went first to light the way, armed with a torch which he had thrust into the brazier before leaving the prison, but following directions given him by the American. The cold, which had been not unbearable in the underground caverns, grew more biting as they went towards the outside world, but Marianne did not feel it. Clinging to Jason's neck, she no longer felt any of her old loathing and distrust of him. What he had done that night had wiped out at one go all the accumulated hatred and bitterness she thought she had felt for him and instead, there was a warm feeling of trust which made her for a moment forget her terrors. If it had not been for the threat hanging over the man she loved, she would have felt a simple, almost child-like happiness in the feeling of being carried in those strong arms.

Jason had now plunged into the evil-smelling water right up to his waist and was holding her as high as he could to keep her above the stream. She saw his tanned seaman's face close to her own, with its fierce profile and the stern lips with their mocking twist. From time to time, he looked at her and smiled as if to encourage her, with a gentleness that relaxed all his features. In spite of the unpleasant stench all around them, he still gave off a faint agreeable scent of tobacco, of good leather and eau-de-Cologne which Marianne found comforting.

'Be brave,' he said at last. 'We're nearly there.'

Then they were out in the main sewer and he was able to get up again on to the narrow footway. A strong current of icy air blew in on them from a black opening beyond which gleamed the river. Jason set Marianne gently on her feet and bent to take the torch from Arcadius's chilled fingers and help him climb on to the ledge. Young Gracchus was up already. A few more steps and they were out in the open. Jolival breathed in with rapture.

'Ah! How good it is!' he said joyfully. 'I had not realized how much I missed the air of Paris!'

He was soaking wet and frozen and his teeth were chattering, but he did not seem to notice it.

Marianne, however, had no time to waste on savouring the joys of her recovered freedom. Time was short. The Riders of the Shadows had a long start and if by ill luck the Emperor should leave Malmaison too early – she dared not frame the rest of her thoughts in words but clung to Jason's arm.

'Can you find me a carriage! Quickly – very quickly.'

'I have one waiting a little way off, at the quai de Billy, near the place de la Conférence. [7]Where do you want to go?'

'I must go to Malmaison, of course!'

He made a movement of protest.

'Not that again! The Emperor is well guarded. It will take more than a few fanatics to put him in danger. I mean to take you somewhere safe – and dry! And tomorrow, I will take you away—'

'Tomorrow, yes, I will go with you, but tonight, I implore you to let me save him! I know – I can feel that he is in danger.'

She felt the American's wet arm stiffen under her hand. He drew himself up and his eyes moved away from her to the darkly moving waters of the Seine.

---

[7] The present place de l'Alma.

'He—' he said with a rather bitter emphasis, 'how you speak of him! I thought you hated him?'

'I do not hate him anymore. No more than I hate you any more now. You have acted like a friend, a true friend and that wipes out everything. Tomorrow, I tell you I will go with you because I shall have nothing more to do here and because I am tired of being continually in what you call all kinds of impossible scrapes. Perhaps, in your country, I may find peace.'

'I shall do everything in the world to help you,' he said gently. 'If it is in my power, you shall be happy.'

'Then if you really want my happiness,' she said eagerly, 'do as I ask you, Jason. Let me go to Malmaison. But quickly, I implore you, quickly! We are wasting so much time and every minute counts.'

A tremor ran through him when she spoke his name for the first time and Marianne's woman's intuition told her she had touched him. She was about to return to the attack when he suddenly bent over her and laying his hands on her shoulders, looked deep into her eyes.

'Tomorrow,' he said earnestly, 'you will go with me? You promise?'

'Yes. I promise.'

'Come then. I will take you there myself. We'll drive the horses into the ground, if need be, but we'll get there. Follow us, gentlemen. We'll talk as we go. There are dry clothes in the carriage.'

His voice rang suddenly joyful. Seizing Marianne by the hand, he ran with her along the dark river bank. Arcadius and young Pioche followed hard on their heels without further questions. They passed the buildings of the soap works and then those of the Depot des Marbres and then, as they came to the Place de la Conférence the shape of a carriage rose before them against the faint light of a lantern hung outside the shed where the fire-wagon was kept. It was then Arcadius leaned towards the boy who was running steadily beside him. He was chilled to the bone in his wet clothes but had lost none of his usual good humour for all that.

'Your name is really Gracchus-Hannibal?'

'Yes, monsieur, why?'

'Because my name is Arcadius!' was the apparently illogical answer. 'Do you know that together we represent Athens, Rome and Carthage? My boy, we have just created an alliance that not even the maddest historian ever dreamed of. And when you add to that the collaboration of America, you must admit the world has never seen a league like ours.'

'Yes, monsieur,' Gracchus-Hannibal said meekly, making no attempt to understand. 'But perhaps we'd better hurry on a bit. They're waving to us—'

'Quite right,' Arcadius said cheerfully. 'We have still to set the seal on our glory by saving the new Caesar! And a Corsican Caesar into the bargain!'

CHAPTER FOURTEEN
Malmaison

Once past the vineyards of La Côte de St-Cloud, the road to Malmaison stretched on, dreary and all but deserted and bounded on either side only by waste ground and disused quarries. The snow had dwindled to a few isolated patches, like spilt milk on the dark landscape. Shortly before the bridge, they had come down the route de la Reine to the Boulogne crossroads and there they had parted from Gracchus-Hannibal who declared his intention of going to spend the night with his grandmother, a washerwoman in the route de la Révolte.

'Come and see me tomorrow at my hotel,' Jason Beaufort had called down to him from the box. 'We must have a talk together, you and I. About eleven.'

'Very well monsieur! I'll be there.'

He was about to leap out with a cheery goodnight to those whose saviour he had been when Marianne suddenly pulled him back and kissed him warmly on both cheeks.

'Thank you, Gracchus. We are friends forever now.'

The darkness hid the deep blush which spread over the boy's face but as they moved on, Marianne heard him singing at the top of his voice.

'I know not whence this feeling comes
That grips me when I look at you --'

'Amazing!' Jolival remarked. 'He sings Mozart though he surely does not know it!'

The man of letters was settled comfortably in the carriage beside Marianne, but while she was tense with anxiety and trying vainly to control her fears, Arcadius was thoroughly enjoying the comfort of the vehicle and dry clothes he had found there. Beaufort's forethought had provided some for young Gracchus also. Marianne had been obliged to bury her head in the cushions while her companions changed, which was by no means easy owing to the fact that Beaufort had not delayed an instant for such formality.

Regardless of his wet clothes, Jason had climbed onto the box and settled himself beside the coachman. He had merely emptied his boots and wrapped himself in a great black cloak, remarking that there had been many worse times at sea. From time to time, Marianne could hear his clipped voice telling the coachman to press his horses harder.

Even so, it seemed to Marianne that they were barely moving. She sat, tense and strained, watching the trees go by. They had in fact come to a broken wooded stretch where it was difficult to go fast. Suddenly, Marianne turned to her companions.

'Did you manage to hear where they meant to attack the Emperor's carriage?'

Jolival nodded. 'They meant to hide at a place called Fond-Louvet,' he said 'not far from the Châteaux de Rueil—'

'Near where the Empress lives? They are bold.'

'The Châteaux de Rueil is not Malmaison, my dear child. It belongs to Marshal Massena, Duke of Rivoli, but the Marshal has just been made Prince of Essling and Thourars and has gone to visit his new lands. Besides, Massena is loyal to the dethroned Empress and has no wish to be involved in any of the Emperor's marriage plans. He prefers to be away at such a time.'

Marianne regarded her companion curiously.

'How do you know all this? To hear you, one would think you were familiar with the court?'

'And seeing my splendid appearance, you find that hard to believe, I daresay,' he said with a comical grin. 'My dear Marianne, you cannot imagine how much gossip one picks up in gaming houses. I am one of the best-informed people in Paris, don't forget that.'

'Then, if that is so, answer me one question. How are we going to get into Malmaison and obtain a hearing?'

'To be quite frank with you, that's just what I was thinking. One doesn't just walk into Malmaison. Perhaps we should have thought of that earlier.'

'We must get in, Arcadius. We must warn the Emperor. Is the châteaux well-guarded?'

'Like an imperial palace,' Jolival said gloomily. He shrugged. 'A detachment of the guard stationed at Rueil in the former barracks of the Swiss Guard are generally responsible for the former Empress's safety. I don't think we'll find it easy to persuade them to let us see Joséphine, especially when we look like this!'

'Shall we be there soon?'

Arcadius leaned out of the window and glanced at the high wall past which the carriage was travelling at that moment.

'We are nearly there already,' he said as he threw himself back into his seat. 'This is the wall of the Châteaux de Rueil. Malmaison is a little farther along, on the left.'

'But then – we must have gone right past the place where they are waiting for the Emperor? But we saw nothing?'

'Did you think they would show themselves? What an innocent you are. They are waiting off the road in an old quarry and they will not come out until the moment is right. But don't imagine they have missed our passing. The only thing to fear will be the watch they must have placed between the gates of Malmaison and Fond-Louvet.'

Suddenly, the carriage picked up speed. They were passing a pair of great gilded gates flanked by lodges with triangular pediments and square pilasters. Great bronze lanterns suspended from wrought-iron brackets shone on the golden lances of the gates and on the tricolor sentry boxes, by which were soldiers dressed in buff uniforms with green fronts and tall black shakos with yellow cockades.

'The Corsican Tirailleurs!' Jolival said. 'There is a world of affection in the choice of that régime nt.'

Marianne said nothing. For the first time, this reference to Joséphine, haloed in the great love Napoleon had born her, awoke her jealousy. It was true Joséphine must be suffering now, seeing herself put aside to make room for another, but had not the best part of the Emperor's heart been hers? Compared with those long years lived side by side, Marianne thought bitterly that the hours at Butard were pitifully short.

At the end of a broad avenue, she had caught a glimpse of a small, lighted châteaux. A berlin stood outside, a berlin and a number of horsemen dressed in red and green with flowing cloaks and tall red-plumed busbies. Jolival had clutched her arm in an excited grip.

'You saw? The Emperor is still there!'

'That is his carriage, are you sure?' Marianne asked.

'Those were certainly the mounted chasseurs of the Imperial Guard. I don't know who else they could be waiting for. They are fine lads, Prince Eugène's cavalry. They are not many but I wonder if we should not let them deal with the conspirators.'

'Are you mad? They are a dozen at the most –'

'But equal to thirty! Never mind, you are right. A surprise attack can come suddenly – ah, and I think we too have come.'

The carriage was indeed slowing down. Some little way past the gates of the châteaux the road made a slight bend and there they could leave the carriage without risk of being seen. Jason sprang down from the box to open the door and help Marianne out. They stood in a road enclosed between high walls overhung with trees. The bare branches were etched as though in Indian ink against a sky that was hardly lighter, while the sides of the road and the tops of the walls were lightly outlined in snow.

'We must be quick,' the American said, leading her to the left-hand wall. 'The Emperor's coach is still outside but it is not far off midnight and he will surely be leaving soon.'

'Why did you come past the châteaux? You should have stopped before—'

'So that the watch which the conspirators will certainly have posted could oversee our movements? One can tell you are not used to this kind of thing. Now, we have to get inside—'

Marianne thought privately that he, apparently, was quite used to this kind of thing but she said nothing and only asked: 'How are we going to do that? Do you think the guards will let us past?'

She saw the American's white teeth gleam for an instant in the darkness and heard his stifled laugh.

'We shan't try. It would be so much waste of time. You, sweet Marianne, are going to show me how a well-brought up young lady can climb walls. After that, we can only pray to God we don't meet a patrol before we reach the house -- at which point we can relax and get ourselves arrested.'

'Arrested! What do you mean?'

'That the only way of attracting the Emperor's attention will be to make as much noise as possible. Once outside the châteaux we'll kick up such a rumpus that someone is bound to ask questions. Those splendid horsemen kicking their heels in the snow so quietly will be only too delighted to have it out with us.'

It was wholly insane but, as put by Jason, the audacious plan sounded simplicity itself. After all, all that Marianne wanted to do was warn Napoleon of the danger lying in wait for him. After that, she did not care if they did send them to prison, her and Beaufort -- even to St. Lazare.

'You are wonderful!' she said and meant it. 'Let's go!'

'Excuse me,' Jolival's voice said politely, 'but what is my part in all this?'

'The ladder, my friend. If you feel strong enough to bear me. After that, keep our coachman company. It will be best to have someone on watch outside.'

'By the by, the coachman, are you sure of him?'

'As sure as one can be of anyone who has been well paid. It was young Pioche who found him for me. He's as deaf as a post. I'm afraid you won't have a very chatty time, Jolival, although he can lip-read quite well. But we've wasted enough time. Quick now. And I'd as soon he didn't see us get over the wall. He might start wondering.'

Without answering, Arcadius set his back against the wall, clasped his hands and waited. Setting the toe of his boot in the clasped hand, Jason moved with cat-like agility. The next instant he was sitting astride the top of the wall.

'Now you, Marianne,' he called softly. 'Unless you'd rather let me go alone?'

'Not for all the tea in China!'

Her ascent was a matter of infinitely less ease than his had been. Weakened by her recent illness and hampered by her dress, she found herself a lot less agile than she had been in those days when she used to climb the great trees of Selton like a squirrel. But she was also lighter than the American and, half pushed by Jolival and half pulled by Jason from above, she found herself on top of the wall at last.

'If we have not returned in two hours,' the American called down to Arcadius in a low voice, 'go back to Paris. Where do you live?'

'Nowhere. I had been evicted from my lodgings when Fanchon-Fleur-de-Lys took me under her wing.'

'Then go and wait for me in my room at the Hôtel de l'Empire. The coachman has been paid.'

'One way or another,' Jolival muttered, 'you'd better get out. I prefer to wait. Good luck!'

For answer, Jason jumped down into the park and held out his arms to Marianne.

'Jump! Don't be afraid, I'll catch you.'

She closed her eyes, took a deep breath and jumped. She landed in Beaufort's arms and, for a second, before he let her slip gently to the ground, he held her against him, perhaps to feel for a moment longer the kiss of her loose hair against his face.

'Marianne,' he whispered in a voice he could not altogether control, 'you will go with me tomorrow, truly?'

She freed herself, not roughly, but with some impatience.

'I had already told you so. And now is not the time to talk of that. We must run! He may be leaving –'

All her agony of mind was in those words. The park was well wooded at this point and a thick belt of trees hid the châteaux. Only a few lights shone twinkling between the trunks of the leafless oaks.

'Make as little noise as you can,' Jason breathed.

Hand in hand, like two lost children, they began to run towards the pin-points of light that showed where the châteaux lay. Wet branches smacked their faces and their feet sank deeply into a slush of rotten leaves and melted snow. Marianne's were soon frozen but she was unconscious alike of the icy water and the scratching branches.

The curtain of trees thinned out and Marianne and Jason came out abruptly into the open. Before them, rose the châteaux, gleaming white under its steep tiled roofs. In the centre of the building, a glazed entry porch was lit up like a huge lantern. The coach was still there but a curt command had just sent the troop of chasseurs into the saddle.

'The Emperor is coming out,' Jason breathed. 'Quickly –'

Between them and the house lay a large garden in the English style, laid out in lawns and flower beds. Even as Jason spoke, they could see figures moving in the porch, one of which made Marianne's heart beat faster. That grey form in the midst of all the colourful dresses and resplendent uniforms, that must be him.

But scarcely had the two of them left the heavy shadow of the trees and started running towards the brilliantly lit châteaux than a command came sharply from behind them.

'Halt! Halt or we fire!'

At the same time, the dogs began barking furiously behind the châteaux.

Marianne turned and saw some soldiers who must have been patrolling along the edge of the wood and recognized the yellow plumes of the Corsican tirailleurs. She let out a wail of despair. They were still a long way from the house. She gripped Jason's hand tightly. Ahead of them, the horses were stamping restlessly.

Lackeys in powdered wigs were opening the doors of the berlin. There were people outside, men and women muffled in thick cloaks.

'Run!' She gasped. 'Never mind if they fire!'

'Marianne, this is madness!'

She did not listen to him. She was already racing forward. Jason followed.

They had hesitated barely an instant. With one accord, they began to run on. Behind them they could hear the click of weapons being cocked.

'Halt!' The voice commanded once again. 'Stop, by thunder, will you!'

There was a shot, quickly followed by another. Marianne felt fear in the pit of her stomach and commended her soul to God. She saw nothing but the lighted châteaux coming rapidly nearer. She felt nothing but Jason's hand supporting her. The horsemen around the berlin had dismounted hurriedly and now formed a barrier blocking their way. At the top of his voice, that powerful voice which could rise above the storm on board his ship, Jason shouted:

'The Emperor! Save the Emperor!'

More shots rang out but hampered perhaps by the darkness and by the speed at which their quarry moved, the riflemen fired raggedly. Even so, one bullet must have hit Jason because he gave a muffled curse and let his hand slip from Marianne's. But the chasseurs were already surrounding them. Rough hands seized them and they were subjected to a barrage of questions:

'Who are you? What do you want? Are you conspirators?'

'The Emperor,' Marianne gasped. 'For the love of heaven, take us to the Emperor – he is in danger.'

'A woman? What are you doing here? How did you get in?'

This time it was the officer in command of the troop, a splendid tall fellow, moustaches bristling under the plumed fur busby. He was already dividing Marianne from her wounded companion but she had eyes only for the brilliant group of men and women rushing excitedly out of the porch, all talking at once. A man had emerged from their midst, a man in a grey coat holding a wide cocked hat under his arm. At the sound of his curt voice, Marianne's heart almost stopped beating for happiness.

'Captain Trobriant! What is going on there?'

The handsome chasseur had no time to reply. He was still coming smartly to attention, when Marianne wriggled away and flung herself headlong at the Emperor's feet.

'Sire, for pity's sake, listen to me! They mean to kill you! There are men lying in wait for you at Fond-Louvet! There are many of them and your escort is small.'

A low growl of disapproval gave Marianne a clear notion of what the chasseurs of the Guard thought of their own worth. However, Napoleon's eyes had widened a little at the sight of the dirty, dishevelled woman in her tattered, mud-stained garments raising to his face a pair of luminous green eyes he knew.

'What's this? You – and in this condition?' He said, unable to conceal his surprise. 'Where have you sprung from?'

Before Marianne could answer, a tall, fair young woman, in a dress and cloak of violet-coloured velvet sewn with seed pearls, with a simple diadem on her golden hair, broke in.

'Sire, be careful,' she said nervously. 'This woman may be dangerous – or mad!'

Napoleon gave a brief smile which never reached his eyes but in which Marianne, desperate and overawed, saw Charles Denis restored to her for an instant.

'No, no, Hortense, I know her. She is not mad in the least. As for being dangerous –'

'The man who came with her is unconscious, sire,' Captain Trobriant volunteered. 'He is wounded. One of the shots must have hit him.'

'Jason! He is hurt! Oh God –'

Marianne would have sprung to her feet in terror and run to him but the Emperor's iron hand held her fast.

'One moment,' he said sternly. 'Who is this man?'

'Jason Beaufort, an American, sire. He rescued me and brought me here to warn you. He is a brave man. Have his hurts seen to, I implore you, and do not send him to prison.'

'As to that, we shall see. For the present –'

'Sire,' the young woman he had addressed as Hortense spoke again, 'is it necessary to continue this out here? It is very cold –'

'A Queen of Holland feels the cold here!' The Emperor scoffed. 'Whoever saw the like?'

'Maybe, but my mother wishes to see this woman. She is very anxious.

You know how sensitive she has always been to rumours of conspiracy.'

'Very well, we'll go in. Duroc, look after this American the heavens have dropped on us and send a patrol to see what is going on at Fond-Louvet. Make it a strong one!' He turned to Marianne. 'How many are these men?'

'About thirty, I think.'

Marianne saw Duroc, her host of Butard, detach himself from the group of ladies and uniformed men but now he was dressed in splendid blue with gold braid. He too, threw her a glance of stupefaction, but it was only for an instant, then he turned and went to Jason who was being supported in the arms of two chasseurs.

'This way,' Napoleon said guiding Marianne none too gently into a marble floored entrance hall adorned with antique busts. The brilliant crowd of onlookers parted before them, out of respect for the Emperor, and from obvious disgust at his companion. Marianne, her mind in a ferment, could only think that they must make a strange couple. But she heard his voice whisper in her ear.

'Take care you'll make no allusion to the other night. I will not have the Emp – her caused the slightest pain. I have given her enough already.'

Marianne's heart throbbed with a sudden ache of mingled jealousy and pain. The curt words, the hard grip on her arm all told her that her estimate of her own part in the life of the supposed Charles Denis had been all too correct. She was a plaything, a passing fancy, a momentary distraction, soon forgotten – while she felt her love for him keener than ever. He was treating her almost as a criminal when she had risked her life to save him, when Jason had been shot by his guards. She asked nothing now except to be allowed to go away. She would go with Jason whenever he decided. She knew that she could never live in the same land with him, close to him, without the right even to be near him.

'Your garden is full of odd surprises, Joséphine,' he said with assumed lightness, 'look what I have found! The guards found this young person who merely seems to have climbed your wall in company with an American, who has been wounded by a shot.'

Brought back to earth by Napoleon's voice, Marianne saw that she was in a long room decorated in pale green, a music room to judge by its furnishings. A rather plump woman dressed in white cashmere and a great deal of filmy lace was reclining on a sofa done up in light red silk with black trimmings like the rest of the room.

'Bonaparte, please, do not make a joke of it. They told me of a conspiracy –' said the woman, who was none other than the former Empress herself.

She held out trembling hands to him. He took them and gripped them warmly.

'If there is a conspiracy, we shall soon know all about it. Don't upset yourself. Nothing will happen. Which reminds me,' he turned to Marianne who stood speechless, hardly daring to breathe, 'can you tell me who is their leader?'

'Yes, sire. The chevalier de Bruslart.'

'Him again!' Joséphine cried and the Emperor frowned.

'Come here, Mademoiselle, and tell us what you know. Here, sit here —'

She pointed to a low chair but Marianne did not even see it. She was fascinated by the still lovely woman with her pale, transparent skin, heavy mahogany coloured hair and huge Creole eyes, at present red with weeping. But all this was nothing without the truly inimitable grace which made Joséphine someone quite exceptional. Every glance, every look on her face showed her love for the husband who had rejected her so that Marianne forgot her jealousy and felt drawn to her by a sympathy as spontaneous as it was unconscious. Both of them loved the same man, both feared for him. That was a much stronger bond between them than the distant tie of blood by which they were united.

'Come,' the former Empress said again. 'Come and sit here.'

Marianne made a faultless court curtsey. 'Madame,' she murmured, 'I dare not. Your Majesty sees how I am dressed – and the harm I might do to these pretty chairs.'

'No matter,' Joséphine cried airily with the sudden playfulness which was so much a part of her charming, unpredictable nature. 'I want to talk to you, I want to find out who you are! The truth is, you are a mystery to me. You are certainly dressed like a vagabond but your curtsey is like a great lady's and your voice goes with it. Who are you?'

'Just a second,' Napoleon broke in. 'Here's another! It seems the conspirators were not the only ones on the road.'

It was indeed Duroc once more, accompanied this time by a thin figure muffled in a furred driving coat in whom Marianne was disconcerted to recognize Fouché. The Minister of Police was paler than ever except for a somewhat red and swollen nose due partly to the cold outside and partly to a magnificent cold in the head which thickened his voice and obliged him to be constantly using his handkerchief. The two men halted side by side and bowed. The Grand Marshal of the Palace spoke first.

'There was indeed a conspiracy, Sire. I found his Grace the Duke of Otranto on the spot, very busy unravelling it.'

'I see.' The Emperor stood with his hands behind his back regarding his two officials in turn. 'How is it, Fouché, that I was not warned?'

'I was not warned myself, sire, until the last moment. But, as your majesty sees, I left my bed at once although my state of health should have kept me there – besides, your majesty's accusation is unjust. You were warned, sire. Is that not Mademoiselle Mallerousse I see there, beside her majesty the Empress? She is one of my most loyal and valued agents.'

Marianne opened her mouth but no words came. Fouché's presence of mind was stupefying. That he should dare to claim the credit for what she had done and take it all to himself, when, but for Gracchus-Hannibal Pioche, she might have stayed in the underground cavern of Chaillot forever!

But Napoleon's blue eye was turned on her and she felt her heart shrink at its hardness.

'One of Fouché's agents, eh? That's news – what have you to say to that, Duroc?'

The words were a threat. The Duc de Frioul reddened and groped for a reply but Fouché gave him no time. Smiling, very much at his ease, he dabbed delicately at his nose and purred. 'Indeed yes, one of the best. I even christened her The Star. Mademoiselle Mallerousse is at present reader to the Princess of Benevento. A charming girl! Utterly devoted to your majesty as your majesty no doubt – er, appreciates.'

The Emperor made an angry movement.

'Talleyrand, now?' He turned to Marianne who was terrified by this sudden anger. 'It seems to me, mademoiselle, that there are some explanations you must give me. I had heard of a Demoiselle Mallerousse, a pupil of Gossec's, with a charming voice, but nothing more! I perceive now that your talents are not confined to singing – that you have more than one string to your bow. You are a consummate actress certainly – a great artist, truly! A very great artist! It is true that to be a star with Fouché requires a variety of talents – and a heart to match!'

His voice shook with anger and the harsh Corsican accent became more striking. He was striding furiously up and down the music room as he launched this flood of bitter insults at Marianne's head. Joséphine uttered an alarmed protest.

'Bonaparte! Don't forget she may have saved your life!'

The frenzied pacing stopped short and Marianne was crushed beneath a glance so heavy with contempt she felt the tears come into her eyes.

'That is so! I will see to it that you are rewarded, mademoiselle, according to your deserts! His Grace the Duke of Otranto will arrange for a proper sum –'

'No! No – not that!'

This was more than Marianne could bear. It had been cruel enough to be compelled to give up her dream of love and make up her mind to go away from him forever. No one could ask her to endure his contempt as well, to let him treat her like some low servant, a common spy! She was willing to go but not to let him spoil the wonderful memory of their night of love. That, at least, she meant to keep intact to feed her dreams on for the rest of her life. In her indignation, she had sprung to her feet and now stood facing Napoleon, the tears rolling down her scratched and dirty face but with her head held high and her green eyes flashing defiance at the angry Caesar.

'If I tried to save your life, sire, it was not to have you throw money in my face as though I were a servant you had dismissed – it was for love of you! And because I am indeed your servant, though not as you would have it! Is it a crime that I have worked for your police? I do not think I am the only one to do that!' She hurried on regardless of the mortified looks of Joséphine who had herself supplied the inquisitive Minister of Police with information about her husband's actions on more than one occasion. 'But I did so,' Marianne went on, too well away for Fouché's warning glance to stop her now, 'I did so only because I was forced to do it. Because I had no choice –'

'Why not?'

The abruptness of the question and the harsh voice in which it was uttered made Marianne's heart miss a beat. He was observing her ruthlessly. This was the end. She had lost him now forever. If that was so, she might as well complete the ruin with her own hands and tell him everything. Afterwards, he could do with her what he liked, throw her into prison, send her back to the gallows in England – what did it matter! She slid wretchedly to her knees.

'Sire,' she said in a low voice, 'let me tell you the whole story and then you can judge fairly –'

Fouché, anxious at the turn events were taking, made an attempt to intervene.

'All this is ridiculous,' he began but a sharp, 'Silence!' from the Emperor cut him short. Marianne went on.

'My name is Marianne d'Asselnat de Villeneuve. My parents died under the guillotine and I was brought up in England by my aunt, Lady Selton. A few months ago, I was married to a man whom I believed then, I loved. It was a terrible mistake. On the very night of my wedding, my husband, Francis Cranmere, staked everything I possessed at cards and lost. He staked my honour also. And so – I killed him!'

'Killed him?' Joséphine's horrified exclamation was not altogether unadmiring.

'Yes, madame – killed him in a duel. I know it may seem strange for a woman to fight a duel, but I was brought up like a boy – and had no one left but myself to defend my name and my honour. My aunt had died a week earlier. After that, I was obliged to flee. I had to leave England where I had nothing to look forward to but the hangman's noose. I managed to make my way to France by means of a smuggling vessel – and there, to save me from the laws against returning émigrés, his grace the Duke of Otranto offered me a post as reader to Madame de Talleyrand and at the same time –'

'To render some small services to himself!' The Emperor finished for her. 'It does not surprise me. Never do anything for nothing, do you Fouché? I think you had better tell me how you came to be offering your protection to an émigrée returning to the country illegally.'

Fouché's faint sigh of relief had not escaped Marianne. 'It is very simple, sire,' he began. 'It happened this way—'

'Later, later—'

The Emperor had resumed his pacing up and down but much more slowly now. With his hands clasped behind him and his head sunk forward on his chest, he seemed to be thinking. The kindly Joséphine took advantage of this to raise Marianne from her knees and make her sit down once more. She wiped the girl's tear-drenched eyes with her own handkerchief and, calling her daughter Hortense who, alone of her entourage, had been present at the scene, asked her to send for a warm drink for Marianne.

'Tell them to prepare a bath and dry clothes, and a room – I am keeping Mam'zelle d'Asselnat with me!'

'Your majesty is very kind,' Marianne said with a sad little smile, 'but I should prefer to go. I should like to rejoin my wounded companion. We were to leave together, tomorrow, for America. His ship waits for him at Nantes.'

'You will do as you are told, mademoiselle,' Napoleon told her shortly. 'Your fate, I think, is not in your own hands. We have not yet done with you. Before you leave for America, you shall have some more explaining to do.'

Explain what, my God? Marianne thought. What a fool she had been to plunge into this wasp's nest in order to save him, or rather, to see him, even for an instant, because she still hoped for something, though for what she could not have said. Perhaps for some return of the other night's tenderness? No, that hard, clipped voice told her all too clearly that she had never meant anything real to him. He was cold and heartless! But then, why did he have to have such a hold on her?

'I am your majesty's to command,' she murmured with death in her heart. 'Command me, sire, and I will obey.'

'I should hope so. Accept the clothes and hot water her majesty is good enough to offer you, but hurry! You must be ready to go with me to Paris within the hour.'

'Sire,' Fouché offered graciously, 'I can easily take charge of Mademoiselle. I am returning to Paris and I can set her down in the rue de Varenne.'

His willingness to oblige earned the Duke of Otranto a swift, angry glare.

'When I need your advice, Fouché, I shall ask for it. Off you go, mademoiselle, and be quick.'

'May I at least know what has become of my companion?' she asked with a measure of determination.

'In the Emperor's presence, Mademoiselle,' Napoleon retorted, 'you need concern yourself with no one but yourself. Matters are already sufficiently black for you. Do not make them worse.'

But it would take much more than Napoleon's anger to make Marianne desert a friend.

JULIETTE BENZONI

'Sire,' she said in a tired voice, 'even one under sentence of death has the right to care of a friend. Jason Beaufort was hurt trying to save you and –'

'And in your view, my behaviour is thoroughly ungrateful? Don't worry, Mademoiselle, your American friend is not seriously hurt. A ball in the arm, and I daresay not the first. Captain Trobriant is at this moment looking for the carriage he says he left on the road. After which, he will go quietly back to Paris.'

'In that case, I want to see him!'

Napoleon's fist smashed down on a fragile lemonwood table with such force that it broke beneath the blow.

'Who dares to say "I want" to me! Enough! You will see this man only with my permission and when I think fit! Fouché, since you are so keen on acting as escort, you may see to this Beaufort –'

The Minister of Police bowed and with an ironical glance, accompanied by a discreet shrug of the shoulders, he took leave and withdrew.

She watched him as he went through the door, round-shouldered and beaten. It was a sight that should have given her pleasure but the man whose anger she had just witnessed was too far removed from the charming Charles Denis. She understood now why they called him the Corsican ogre! But, for all her present fury, Marianne could not pretend to herself that she did not like that masterful tone.

Joséphine had watched this scene without interfering. But when Fouché had gone she rose and took Marianne's arm where she stood rooted to the spot.

'Obey, child. One must never cross the Emperor – whatever his commands.'

Marianne's eyes, still flaming with revolt, met Joséphine's sad, gentle ones. Despite her own love for Napoleon, she could not help feeling drawn to this lonely woman who was so kind to her and seemed to give no thought of the strangeness of her situation. She did her best to smile and then, bending quickly, placed her lips on the pale hand of the dethroned Empress.

'I obey you, madame.'

The Emperor gave no sign of hearing this final piece of defiance. He stood with his back to the two women, staring out of the window and twisting the fringe of a gleaming watered silk curtain nervously between his fingers. Without another word, Marianne dropped a curtsey to Joséphine and followed the maid summoned by Queen Hortense. As she went, she wondered if there would ever come a time when she would be able to choose her own clothes and not be obliged to borrow from all and sundry.

Half an hour later, wearing a dress and coat belonging to Madame de Rémusat, the former Empress's lady-in-waiting who was almost the same size as herself, Marianne took her place with drooping head and heavy heart in the Imperial berlin. She was not even conscious of the amazing honour done her. For her, it meant nothing because she cared not whether the ill-humoured little man who sat next to her were Emperor or not. Since he did not love her, she would a hundred times have preferred any stranger. The burning memories of Butard lay between them a source of hideous anguish now, which only increased her pain and wretchedness. The man she loved had changed suddenly into some kind of judge, as icy and indifferent as justice itself. Any fears she might have of the journey which lay ahead were because she knew what power this ruthless man possessed to make her suffer.

She had said her thanks and farewells to Joséphine and the gentle Creole had made her promise to come and visit her again while, at the same time, casting an appealing glance at the Emperor, which he pretended not to see. But even this evidence of kindness had failed to comfort Marianne. This, she did not doubt, was the last stage in her ordeal. Tomorrow, she would try and find Jason and go away with him at last. But for tonight, she did not even wonder what Napoleon meant to do with her.

Just before the door closed, Duroc's head was poked into the carriage.

'To – the Trianon, sire?'

'Don't be a fool! Not the Trianon, or Saint-Cloud. To the Tuileries! And send a messenger ahead to say I'm coming!'

'As your majesty commands.'

The door banged shut and the coach moved off towards the lighted gate. All around were the rhythmic hoofbeats of the escort of chasseurs. Marianne had noted that, in suggesting the Emperor's possible destination, Duroc had taken good care to say nothing about Butard. That was no doubt a name which must never, never be uttered again. It could not be other than highly disagreeable to the Master of Europe even to remember what had passed between himself and one of Fouché's spies.

Once through the gate amid the clatter of arms being presented, the road stretched before them. Marianne closed her eyes, partly to hold back the tears that would come and partly to breathe in the smell of Spanish jasmine and snuff which filled the carriage. The green velvet cushions were impregnated with it and she breathed in almost furtively, like a thief, because it alone had power to conjure up the sweet, tormenting memories she so longed to forget. Even the smell of him was a tiny fragment of happiness.

Suddenly, she heard him speak.

'This American, what is he to you? Your lover?'

She answered, without looking at him, trying to hide her pain.

'Only a friend – a faithful friend. Tonight, he rescued me from the prison where I had been held ever since —' her voice died away. Then, all at once her fighting instinct revived, she felt the need to give back blow for blow and turned on him. 'You have asked me a great many questions about my past life, sire, why have you not asked what I have been doing this past week and more?

'No need. I know.'

'You know? How?'

'While you were being cleaned up, I asked a few questions. I am grieved at what has happened – but that is beside the point. Where did you meet this American?'

Marianne was revolted by the monstrous egotism this persistence revealed. She flung the words at him like a challenge, unable to control herself longer.

'He was the man to whom Francis Cranmere lost all that I had brought him – myself included!'

'So, I was right. He is your lover.

'Because you suppose me capable of fulfilling such a bargain? Because you think it possible that when someone comes to a young girl on her wedding night and says: "Your husband is not coming I am going to take his place. I won you at cards", she will instantly open her arms and her bed to him? I believe I told you I had killed Lord Cranmere.'

'But you have not, to my knowledge, killed Jason Beaufort?'

'He had already gone. I threw him out. It was only long afterwards that I met him again – here, in fact, in the house of the Prince of Benevento. Oh – anyway, does all this really matter? How can my life interest you, past, present or future? You have an Empire, subjects, as many women as you want –'

It gave her a kind of awful joy to hurl the inmost feelings of her heart in wild confusion at the feet of this unfeeling man before whom all trembled. Only she was not afraid because not even if the fancy took him to put her to death could he hurt her more than he had done already. She actively enjoyed trying to provoke him and make him angry. Yet, oddly enough, Napoleon did not seem to have heard. His splendid profile was turned away, towards the road and he murmured absently, as though thinking aloud:

'I'd like to know who that devil Talleyrand doesn't know in this world.'

Then, before the choking Marianne could say another word, he turned to her suddenly.

'You know,' he said in a voice full of laughter, 'that it is treason to argue with the Emperor?'

'Argue? Me? – I –'

'Unless you wish to be punished as you deserve, you'd better hurry up and beg my pardon.'

With a quick movement he snapped down the blinds. But, not until Napoleon's lips sought her own, did Marianne realize that he had taken her in his arms.

CHAPTER FIFTEEN
Once a Merveilleuse ...

Marianne lay with her head hanging slightly over the edge of the bed, gazing up at the shining bronze gilt eagle with outstretched wings which, high above, surmounted the crown on the great, circular baldachin. In spite of the exhausting and fantastic adventures of the night, and the long love-making which had followed, she was not sleepy. She would sleep later; she was not quite sure when but she did know very well that she would never sleep in this impressive bed. The great curtains of purple velvet fringed with gold, the winged victories, their bronze feet treading globes of lapis-lazuli, even the dais on which the imperial bed was placed, all helped to make her feel that she might as well be sleeping on the throne of France itself. It was simultaneously impressive, flattering and – rather funny. Napoleon, accustomed to it, slept with his head resting on Marianne's shoulder. The glow from a night light of silver gilt threw a gentleness over his wilful features, relaxed now in sleep, bringing back a little of the child he had once been. Overcome by a vast tenderness, Marianne could not take her eyes off him. She wanted to savour this night's happiness to the last drop.

Between the bed and the windows opposite, the great carpeted expanse was dotted with a series of strange islands, her own clothes, ripped off impatiently and scattered to the winds, and his, which he was in the habit of leaving where they dropped as he got out of them. Outside, the freezing night was almost over and the regular footsteps of the sentries reminded Marianne that she was in the Tuileries. But the room in the apartment on the first floor which had belonged to the unhappy Louis XVI, was warm and safe, still vibrant with their kisses and their words and sounds of love. How he had loved her, in those two hours from the time when he had led her in by the small, private door leading directly to his apartment! It was as though he could never have enough of her. He had made her promise she would never leave him, that she would stay with him, and be all his own. And when, timidly, she had mentioned his approaching marriage of which everyone was talking, he had roared with laughter.

'I'm marrying a brood mare!' he had told her crudely, like the soldier he was. 'I need an heir for my throne – but you, you will give me what no other woman can ever give me.'

She had discovered then how hard it was to love an Emperor. Jealousy, the need she had to know everything about him brought a host of questions to her lips which she dared not ask aloud. How could she speak to him of all those women whose names she had heard linked with his? How could she speak of the Polish countess who had gone away to the snows of her own country to give birth to his child? She sensed that he would not endure curiosity from her. So many things that would be possible with an ordinary man were not so with him.

When the thought of that unknown woman he was to marry had made her pensive, Napoleon had drawn her into his arms again, softly and slowly caressing her bare skin with that intimate knowledge which never failed to arouse her. Then, with her heart beating wildly, she had forgotten everything but the furious pumping of her blood, and he had crushed her to him hard.

'I love you and only you,' he told her fiercely. 'That must be enough for you.'

'It will be enough as long as you go on loving me. But I fear it may not be possible. If I must return to my place with Madame de Talleyrand –'

'Impossibility is a bugbear for cowards and a refuge for fools! As for going back to that old cow! I have better things in store for you – my sweet, beautiful – wonderful singing bird!'

He had said no more because at that point neither of them had been able to hold out any longer against the demands of their bodies and beyond that point there was no room for anything but silence. And now he was asleep, leaving her to enjoy these moments of warm, full happiness all by herself, counting them out as a miser counts his treasure. She knew she could not stay here in the palace, that soon she would have to go but she did not even begin to wonder where to. She left everything to him, he was all powerful and he was the man she had chosen for her master. Whatever he decided would be right.

A clock from a nearby church struck seven. From the palace courtyard came sharp commands, the click of heels, the clatter of horses hoofs on cobblestones, the distant call of a trumpet. Marianne sighed. The fantastic night which had begun in the quarries of Chaillot and ended, by the strange twist of fate, in the imperial bed, was over.

The door was opened softly. A man entered on tiptoe. Quickly, Marianne pulled the sheet up to her chin. It was Constant, the Emperor's valet, and the man she had already seen that night at Butard. In one hand, he carried a branch of lighted candles, in the other a small tray on which were two steaming cups. Both these, he set down on a small side table, then quickly gathered up the scattered garments and placed them carefully on a chair according to their owners. Marianne watched from between half closed lids that quick, familiar certainty of his movements. Not until he had finished did he approach the bed.

'Sire,' he said loudly, 'it is seven o'clock. I have the honour to wake your majesty.'

As though he had only been waiting for the signal, Napoleon stirred, sat up and gave a light yawn.

'Already?' he said. 'A short night, Constant. What is the weather like?'

'Much warmer, sire, than yesterday. It is raining. May I ask how your majesty is feeling?'

'Wonderful! Ah, tea! Come on, lazy-bones, wake up –'

The concluding remarks were addressed to Marianne who had been covering her embarrassment by pretending sleep. Seizing her by the shoulders, Napoleon shook her vigorously and bundled her up in the sheets, laughing like a child at the same time.

'Come on! Open your eyes! Here, drink this! I always begin the day with a cup of tea or orange! Give it to her, Constant.'

The valet obeyed with a smile after first greeting Marianne pleasantly with: 'I hope madame has slept well?'

She thanked him with a smile and then carried the steaming beverage to her lips before remarking wickedly:

'I did not know that you had English habits, sire?'

'And you know them, don't you? The English have some good ones, you know. One must be their enemy, as I am, to admit it honestly. Any news, Constant?'

'The lady sent for by your majesty awaits your majesty's pleasure in the ante-chamber.'

'Ah, splendid! Take her into my office and ask her to wait. I'm coming. Give me my dressing-gown and slippers and find one for this young lady. Quick now!'

As Constant withdrew, Napoleon leapt out of bed regardless of his nakedness and ripped away the sheet which Marianne had drawn up under her arms.

'Let me look at you a moment more before I go off to work! You know you are lovely enough to damn an Emperor? I cannot make you an Empress, alas, but I shall make you a queen, a queen of beauty and of talent – I'll lay my empire at your feet.'

He filled both hands with the sumptuous mass of hair that fell around her, cradling her face in it. He swept her joyously into his arms and hugged her, then, just as suddenly, dropped her back on to the bed and heaped the sheets and covers over her.

'Now cover yourself, siren! Not even Constant is privileged to see my treasures.'

By the time the valet returned, the Emperor was dressed in trousers and a white flannel dressing-gown and was putting on his slippers.

'Your majesty has not put on a neckcloth?' Constant said, earning himself a black look from his master who, however, merely replied:

'My bath in fifteen minutes. Tell Corvisart that I am quite well and have no need of him this morning. See that mademoiselle has everything she needs. I am going to see Madame Hamelin.'

Marianne had no time to ask any questions about this early morning visitor. Napoleon had gone. Instead, she got up and made her way into the Emperor's dressing room, thrown open to her by Constant. As though it were perfectly natural, he gave her everything she might need, including a large bottle of eau-de-Cologne.

'His majesty gets through vast quantities of it,' he observed with a smile. Marianne thought she liked this confidential servant. He had a frank, open face, immediately likeable, the face of one belonging to the north. On the other hand, she also had the feeling that Constant liked her, a feeling partly due to the many little attentions he showed her without in the least appearing to do so.

When, after ten minutes or so, Napoleon returned, she was already dressed in the soft blue woollen gown given her by Madame de Rémusat.

'Bravo!' he cried. 'I like women who don't dawdle over their toilet. You'd make a good soldier! Come now, I'm going to present you to the lady I've decided shall have charge of you until I find you a house worthy of you.'

'Is she this – Madame Hamelin?' Marianne said with a slight hesitation. 'I know the name and I believe I may already have seen the lady.'

'You will certainly have seen her at Talleyrand's. She is a great friend of his but the only difference is that I trust her, which is more than I do our dear Prince of Benevento. His house is no place for the woman I love.'

'Is she then a very virtuous lady?' Marianne hazarded, thinking of Madame Fouché and seeing herself already shut up in a household of grim respectability.

Napoleon's shout of laughter reassured her instantly.

'She, Fortunée? She has been called the giddiest creature in France. Oh, no, she is by no means a prude. She was one of the most spectacular *merveilleuses* in the time of the Directory and since then has lost count of the number of her lovers. But though her virtue may be only a distant memory, she has other much more solid and reliable qualities, such as an honest, sincere heart, unfailing loyalty and a strong belief in friendship. Do you know, she even went on her knees to beg me not to divorce my wife? Yes, she's a good friend. Her house, her belongings and her sharp tongue are always at the service of those she likes – and I want her to like you. You will never find a better bastion against the malice of the fashionable world, which she knows as no one else does. Besides which, she lives in a delightful house not far from Montmartre, and sufficiently discreet for nocturnal visitors to pass unnoticed and to make it possible to hide someone there.'

'Hide someone? Who is to hide there –'

'You, *mio dolce amore!* I have decided to hide you until the time, don't worry, it will not be long, when you shall burst on the world. Didn't I tell you I wanted to put Paris, Rome, Milan and Brussels at your feet. No. No questions. You'll see. Now come.'

The Emperor's office was a plain room, dominated by tall mahogany book-cases. Marianne remembered the woman waiting there at once. How could she ever forget that dark, fascinating creole face? Fortunée Hamelin's style of beauty was frankly exotic and, at thirty-four, she was still a remarkably attractive woman with magnificent black hair, teeth that were very white and pointed, and red lips with a very slight thickness that betrayed perhaps a touch of African blood. With all this went an island grace which only Joséphine could rival. The one came from Martinique, the other from Saint Domingo but they had always been firm friends. Marianne liked Madame Hamelin's steady, smiling eyes and even the strong scent of roses which enveloped her like a cloud.

As soon as Marianne appeared, looking somewhat stiff and uncomfortable, Fortunée leapt up from the little green and gold striped satin sofa on which she had been sitting amid a great mass of furs, and came forward eagerly to embrace her, exclaiming as she did so in her musical creole voice:

'My dear, dear girl, you cannot conceive how happy it makes me to take you under my wing. For ages I've been longing to steal you from that great stupid princess! How did you manage to dig her out, sire? Our dear Talleyrand watched over her like Jason with the Golden Fleece –'

'To be honest, it was not so very hard. The old rogue was hoist with his own petard! But I shall not prevent you telling him that I have given her into your keeping – on condition he keeps his mouth shut. I don't want her talked of for the moment. He will have to make up some story when he knows what has become of her.' Napoleon smiled wickedly. 'I have an idea,' he went on, 'he must be beginning to feel a little anxious about her! Now, run away both of you. It is nearly time for my levee. Your carriage is at the side gate, Fortunée?'

'Yes, sire. It is waiting.'

'Excellent. I'll come to your house tonight, about eleven. Now be off with you. As for you, my singing bird, take care of yourself but think only of me.'

He was in a hurry now, fiddling nervously with the heaps of papers and portfolios in red Morocco which littered his enormous desk. But Marianne herself was too lost in thought to feel offended. Madame Hamelin's reference to the Golden Fleece had reminded her of the companion of her adventures and the recollection was not a pleasant one. He had been hurt, he might be waiting for her and she would have to break the word she had given him. It was an uncomfortable thought. But then, she was so happy. She could not help preferring that slight sense of guilt to the regret that would have been hers had she left France. Jason would soon forget the girl he had won at cards in one night's madness.

Napoleon tweaked her ear. 'You might at least kiss me instead of standing there dreaming,' he reproached her. 'The time will go slowly for me, until tonight. But I must send you away.'

Fortunée had gone discreetly to look out of a window but even so Marianne was conscious of her presence and gave herself to his embrace with some timidity. Napoleon, though still in his dressing-gown, was Emperor once more. She slipped from his arms and swept him a deep curtsey.

'Your majesty's to command and, more than ever, his faithful servant.'

He laughed. 'I love you when you put on your court airs,' he told her. Then, in a different voice, he called out; 'Roustan!'

On the instant, the Mameluke appeared, dressed in a splendid costume of red velvet embroidered with gold and a white turban. He was a Georgian of great size, formally sold as a slave by the Turks and brought home by General Bonaparte with a hundred others from his Egyptian campaign. Although he slept each night across the emperor's door, he had been married for two years to the daughter of an usher at the palace, Alexandrine Douville. No one could have had a more peaceable nature but Roustan, with his brown skin, his turban and his great, curved scimitar, was an impressive figure, although it was his exotic character which most impressed Marianne.

Napoleon now told him to conduct the two ladies to their carriage and, with a final curtsey, Marianne and Fortunée left the imperial presence.

As they went down the little private staircase behind Roustan, Madame Hamelin slipped her arm through her new friend's, enveloping her in the scent of roses.

'I predict that you will be all the rage,' she said gaily, 'that is unless his majesty enjoys playing sultan and keeps you shut up too long. Are you fond of men?'

'I – I am of one man,' Marianne said in astonishment.

Fortunée Hamelin laughed. She had a warm, open, infectious laugh that showed a gleam of sharp, white teeth between her red lips.

'No, no, you don't understand! You do not love a man; you love the Emperor! You might as well say you love the Pantheon or the new Arc de

Triomphe at the Carroussel!'

'You think it is the same thing? I don't. He is not so imposing, you know. He is—' She paused, hunting for the word that would best express her happiness but, finding nothing strong enough, she simply sighed: 'He is wonderful!'

'I know that,' the Creole exclaimed. 'And I know too, how attractive he can make himself; when he wishes to take the trouble, that is, because when he cares to be disagreeable—'

'Can he be?' Marianne cried, genuinely astonished.

'You wait until you have heard him tell a woman in the middle of a ball room: "Your dress is dirty! Why do you always wear the same gown? I have seen this one twenty times!" '

'Oh no! It cannot be true!'

'Oh yes, it is, and if you want me to tell you what I really think, it is that which makes his charm. What woman is there who is truly a woman who does not long to know what this boorish Emperor with his eagle look and boyish smile is like in bed? What woman hasn't at some time or other dreamed of playing Omphale to his Hercules?'

'Even – you?' Marianne asked a trifle wickedly. But Fortunée answered with perfect sincerity.

'Yes, I admit it – for a while at least. I got over it very quickly.'

'Why was that?'

Once again that irresistible laugh rang through the palace corridors and out to the steps.

'Because I am too fond of men! And believe me, I have good reason. As for his majesty the Emperor and King, I think that what I have given him is worth as much as love.'

'What is that? Friendship.'

'I wish,' the other woman said in a voice grown suddenly thoughtful, 'I wish I could be really his friend! Besides, he knows I am fond of him – and more than that, that I admire him. Yes,' she added with sudden fervour, 'I admire him more than anyone in the world! I am not sure, if, in my heart of hearts, God does not take second place to him.'

The sun was just rising, painting the Venetian horses on the new Arc de Triomphe a delicate pink. It was going to be a lovely day.

Madame Hamelin lived in the rue de la Tour d'Auvergne, between the former barrière de Porcherons and the new barrière des Martyrs, cut in the wall of the Fermiers Généraux, in a charming house with a courtyard at the front and a garden at the back where, before the Revolution, the Countess de Genlis had brought up the children of the Duke d'Orléans. For neighbour, she had the inspector of the Imperial Hunts and opposite, a dancer from the Opéra, Margueritte Vadé de l'Isle, the mistress of a financier. The house itself had been built in the previous century and recalled the clean lines of the

Petit Trianon, although with substantial outbuildings and while the wintry garden was silent and melancholy, there was a fountain singing in a pool in the courtyard. Marianne liked it at once, and especially because the sloping street lay a little out of the common way. Even at this hour of the morning, with servants going to and fro about their work and the cries from the streets as Paris woke once more, there was something quiet and restful about Fortunée's white-walled house which made her feel much happier than all the luxurious splendours of the Hôtel Matignon.

Fortunée conducted her guest to a delightful room done up in pink and white pekin silk with a bedstead of pale wood hung with full white muslin curtains. This room, which was close to her own, belonged to her daughter Léontine, then away boarding at Madame Campan's famous school for girls at St-Germain. And suddenly, Marianne realized that the Creole's vagueness was only apparent and that she was, on the contrary, a person of great energy. In no time at all, Marianne found herself presented in succession with a flowing robe of lace and batiste, a pair of green velvet mules, a lady's maid all to herself (all these being possessions of Léontine Hamelin) and a substantial breakfast. To this last, she was very soon sitting down by a good bright fire in company with her hostess, who had also shed her walking dress. Marianne was amused to see that the former *merveilleuse*, who had once dared to appear in public in the Champs-Élysées stark naked underneath her muslin gown, happily reverted to her old ways in the privacy of her own apartments. Her filmy draperies, in spite of an abundance of delicately coloured ribbons, did little to conceal her perfect figure and served, in fact, to bring out something of the primitive, southern quality of her dark beauty.

The two young women set to with enthusiasm to consume new bread, butter, preserves and fresh fruit, washed down with quantities of tea drunk very hot and strong with milk in the English fashion, all served on an exquisite pink service of exotic pattern. When they had eaten, Fortunée sighed contentedly.

'Now,' she said, 'let us talk. What would you like to do now? Bathe? Sleep? Read? For myself, I mean to write a note to Monsieur de Talleyrand to let him know what has become of you.'

'If you please,' Marianne broke in earnestly, 'there is something which seems to me still more urgent. One of my friends, the man who rescued me yesterday from the quarries of Chaillot, was hurt. He is an American, a sea captain and a most remarkable man, and I do not know what has become of him. The Emperor—'

'—Who, like most Corsicans is subject to terrible fits of jealousy, refused to answer your question! But tell me about this American. I have always adored people from his country because I was born not far away myself. There is a breath of adventure and eccentricity about them I find fascinating.

Besides, the Emperor has told me very little about what has happened to you. It sounds just like a novel. You must tell me all about it, for I adore novels!'

'So do I,' Marianne said with a smile. 'But I did not enjoy this one very much.'

Fortunée's eyes sparkled as she listened with rapt attention to all that had happened since the evening of twenty-first of January when Marianne had left the house in the rue de Varennes to go to Butard. Marianne told her about Bruslart and Morvan, of whose fate she was still ignorant, about her friend Jolival, who must also be in some anxiety on her account, about Gracchus-Hannibal Pioche and, finally, about Jason Beaufort in whose company she should have been setting out for America that very day.

'I would have gone with him without hesitation,' she finished, 'if the Emperor had not made me promise to stay.'

'You would really have gone with him – even after what happened last night at the Tuileries?'

Marianne thought for a moment and then sighed.

'Yes. If I had not been made to promise that I would remain, if I had not been assured that I was needed, I should have gone today without a moment's hesitation.'

'But – why?'

'Because I love him. Now that I know who he is and what must happen in the months ahead, this – this marriage to the archduchess, I am frightened of being hurt. Whatever he may say or do, I know I shall be hurt because I can't help being jealous of her. That is why it would have been better for me to go, even more after those hours of love. Then I should have taken away with me a wonderful memory. And even at this moment, while I am talking to you, I am still sorry I have stayed because I am afraid of what lies in store for me. I even wonder if it would not be better to go against his will. I don't even know what he means to do with me, what kind of life I shall have!'

'In your place, I should trust him and have a little patience. As for running away, you cannot do that,' Fortunée said seriously. 'He would not let you go. He would have you pursued, caught, brought back to him willy-nilly. Napoleon has never let go anything he wanted. You belong to him! And, sooner or later, you must be prepared for him to bring you suffering, even if it is not by his own will. It is no easy task to love a man like that. But if you take it on, you will have to do all you can to make the best of it and not suffer more than you can help. That was why I asked you, just now, if you liked men. With more than one to think about, their power to make us suffer is that much less. For myself, I'd rather make two men happy than one miserable.'

'Love more than one man?' Marianne exclaimed, genuinely shocked. 'But I could never do that!'

Fortunée rose, stretched her long, supple golden body in its white gauzes and bestowed on Marianne a smile part-friendly and part-quizzical.

'You are too young to understand. We'll talk about it again another time. But now, write a few lines quickly to your American and invite him to come and call on you. Where does he stay?'

'At the Hôtel de l'Empire in the rue Cerutti.'

'Not very far. I'll send a man round at once. Here, there are writing materials on this table.'

A few minutes later, the side gate banged behind Fortunée's messenger and Marianne went to perform a toilet somewhat more complete than that which had been possible at the Tuileries. Without being altogether willing to admit it, she was glad to think of seeing Jason again with Jolival and Gracchus, whom she had asked him to bring with him. All three had now assumed a special place in her heart because they had shown her what true friendship could be. Once the letter had been written and entrusted to a servant, Fortunée had asked her suddenly whether Jason was in love with her and Marianne had answered quite sincerely:

'No, not really. He believes he owes me a great debt and being an honest fellow, I see that now, he wants to give back what he has taken from me. He'll be disappointed that I do not go with him but nothing more.'

'Has he never claimed – your part in your husband's wager?'

'Oh no. Oh, I think he finds me attractive, but there is nothing in it. He is a strange person, you know. What he loves more than anything is the sea, his ship and his crew. There is not much room for love in such a life.'

Fortunée had not insisted. She had merely shrugged and smiled indulgently. But when, an hour later, the doorbell rang announcing a visitor, she reappeared in the salon, fully dressed, as though by magic. Clearly, the American had piqued her curiosity. But it was not Jason who appeared. As the two young women came in through one door, Arcadius de Jolival was making his entrance through the other. He was dressed like a fashion plate, radiating elegance and cheerfulness. Marianne stared at him with a mixture of amusement and disappointment as he made a bow with all the elaborate grace of a past age.

'You behold me, ladies, bursting with pride and happiness at the privilege of laying my homage at your charming feet!'

'Fortunée was looking at the new arrival with frank curiosity. 'Who is it?' she asked.

'My Greek prince of whom I told you, Arcadius de Jolival,' Marianne replied absently. 'But where is Jason, my friend? Why is he not with you?'

The happy smile faded from Jolival's face.

'But he is, my dear child, he is! Only, in the form of a letter which I have here. I could not persuade him to come. He said it could do no good. And as I left to accompany your servant, madame, he was on the point of setting out for Nantes.'

'He has gone? Without seeing me, without saying goodbye?'

The sudden break in Marianne's voice brought Fortunée's observant eyes upon her. It suggested something very like distress. Arcadius came forward slowly, taking a letter from inside his snuff brown coat and slipped it into Marianne's hand.

'I think he says goodbye in this,' he said gently. 'He believed there was no more for him to do here. His ship and his business called for him.'

'But, his wound?'

'A small matter for a man like him. The Emperor sent him his personal physician this morning with expressions of his gratitude – and a memento. Besides, there is nothing like sea air for an invalid. Wounds are well known to heal far quicker at sea than on land. That, at least is the opinion of the Emperor's physician. He expressed it more than once. But–' the man of letters spoke with some hesitation, 'did you, then, still mean to go with him?'

'N-no–' Marianne said doubtfully. 'No, of course not! That cannot be now.'

She had not missed the reference to the imperial physician. Certainly Napoleon left nothing to chance.

'Well then. Read his letter, it will certainly tell you more than I can.'

Quickly, Marianne broke the black seal with its simple device of a ship in full sail, unfolded the paper and read the few words Jason had written in a large, bold hand.

'Why did you not tell me what you were to him? It might have stopped me making a fool of myself. I realize it is not possible for you to come and live in my country. But did you really, honestly, wish to? I wish you all the happiness in the world, but if, someday, that happiness seems to you to leave a bitter taste, then remember me – and that I owe a debt to you – for the danger of which I told you is not yet past. But it is true that in future you will have a much better defence than any I could give you. Be happy. Jason.'

Marianne held out the letter to Fortunée with trembling fingers. But a cloud had come over her happiness less on account of this new mention of the mysterious danger which hung over her than because he had gone making no attempt to see her, giving her no chance to explain, or even to ask his forgiveness, and tell him of her gratitude and friendship. The sharpness of her disappointment took her by surprise. God alone knew what she had been hoping for. Perhaps that Jason's wound would oblige him to stay longer in Paris so that they might have had time to see one another, to talk and get to know each other better. It would have made her so happy to establish their hitherto stormy relationship on a basis of real friendship. But then, she dared say, Jason did not want her friendship maybe because she was the Emperor's mistress and had not told him of it. The tone of his letter suggested that his masculine pride was injured. He could not have known how much he had come to matter to Marianne, to be someone dear whose absence could be a source of grief.

She looked up and met Jolival's eye and it seemed to her that she read some pity in it. But just at that moment in her life, pity was one thing she could not endure. She threw up her chin, gripped her hands tightly together and forced herself to smile and speak of something else, no matter what, so long as it hid her feelings.

'You are looking splendid,' she said to fill the silence which had fallen. 'What has happened to you? But please, won't you sit down?'

Jolival sat, carefully smoothing the pale blue pantaloons over his bony knees where they fitted snugly into his elegantly pointed boots.

'Our friend Beaufort lent me a little money with which I was able to recover my wardrobe and my room on the Montagne Sainte Geneviève. But none the less, I shall have to find some situation by which to earn my living. Gaming has few attractions for me and besides, I am not anxious to come up against Fanchon-Fleur-de-Lys and her Philomène a second time.'

'Do you think we have anything more to fear from her?' Marianne asked with sudden horror at mention of the dreadful old woman and remembering the danger of which Jason had still spoken.

'For the present I do not think so. So long as we do not venture into her territorial waters, she will not sail into ours. And I cannot see that we should have much to do at the Épie-Scié or the Homme de Fer. Besides, Bruslart and Saint-Hubert managed to escape but the rest of the conspirators were arrested. Our friend Morvan is under lock and key. And I think there was a raid on the cabaret in the rue des Bonshommes, although Fanchon is certainly too clever to be caught like that.'

At this point, Fortunée, who had finished reading the letter and had for a moment or two been looking rather pensive, gave it back to her friend.

'What is this danger he speaks of?'

'Truly, I do not know. He has always talked of it and then said he can tell me no more in my own interests. But, apart from that, what do you think of his letter?'

'If this man does not love you, I'll be hanged,' Madame Hamelin answered simply. 'For myself, I am very sorry he has gone. I should have liked to meet him.'

'What for?'

'Shall we say —' the Creole gave her teasing smile, 'I like his handwriting. I have always told you I was fond of men. Something tells me this one is a man. Should he come back, you must present him to me without fail.' She turned to Jolival. 'But did he say anything to you about this mysterious danger?'

'Yes,' said the man of letters. 'I know what it is but it is best that Marianne should not. One never knows. It may never come to anything. So why worry? Forget it. And, should our American come back one day, I shall make it my personal business to present him to you, gracious lady!' he finished gallantly.

Deliberately rejecting the possible notion of Jason and Fortunée's becoming one day attached to one another, Marianne launched into a grandiose account of what she hoped to do for those who had helped her and promised Jolival to do what she could on his behalf. She would speak to the Emperor, who would certainly find some employment for the varied talents of such an inveterate idler.

'I wish I could do something for you,' he said with a sigh. 'Have you given up the idea of a singing career?'

'It is not for me to say,' she answered blushing with mingled pleasure and embarrassment at this proclamation of her dependence.

'Well, if you should come back to it, remember me. I have all the makings of a quite outstanding impressario.'

Meanwhile, since it was by now almost dinner time, Fortunée invited Jolival to share it with herself and her new friend. She had a fondness for original characters and he had taken her fancy. In spite of the shadow thrown on Marianne's spirits by Jason's departure, the meal was a very cheerful one. Fortunée and Arcadius occupied themselves in thinking up a host of plans for their young friend, nearly all of which were centred on the theatre. Fortunée, like all Creoles, adored the theatre and music and her delight at finding out that Marianne was the possessor of an exceptional voice was almost child-like.

'The Emperor must let her sing!' she cried, filling Jolival's glass up with champagne for the fifth time. 'If necessary, I shall tell him myself.'

Marianne scarcely listened. It was as though all this did not concern her. She was still dazed by this sudden turn her life had taken. She was not yet used to the idea that a power quite out of the ordinary had taken charge of her life. Everyone was saying what she ought to do but surely, she herself had some say in the matter. While the others talked, she was making her own decision.

I will sing, she told herself fiercely. *I will sing and he will have to let me! That is the one thing that would make it possible for me to live in his shadow without too much suffering. He has his glory – I shall have mine!*

Late that afternoon, she was surprised when they received a visit from Talleyrand himself. Dressed with his usual dark elegance and leaning on his gold-headed cane, the prince bowed over Madame Hamelin's hand and then kissed Marianne on the forehead with a fatherly warmth that took her by surprise.

'Nice to see you again, my child,' he said, for all the world as though they had parted the night before. 'The princess sends you her warmest regards and Madame de Périgord, who has been very anxious on your account, commands me to tell you how glad she is to know that you are safe and sound.'

'My lord,' Marianne said in some confusion, 'your highness is too kind, I feared you might be offended –'

'How? By seeing our lovely bird spread its wings and fly away into the sky to sing? But, my dear, it is what I have always wished. Why do you think I took you to – Monsieur Denis? I had foreseen, and am delighted by, everything that has happened, except of course the interlude at Chaillot! Let us keep your friendship, that is all we ask. And while I think of it, my dear friend,' he added turning to Fortunée, 'have your people take out the boxes which are in my carriage. The princess insisted that this child must have all her things at once.'

Marianne's cheeks flushed with happiness. 'There is no end to the princess's goodness, my lord!' she exclaimed. 'Will your highness be so good as to convey to her my gratitude and also that I remain her servant as in the past?'

'I will tell her. Did you know, my dear, that I had a letter from Casimir this morning? He sends you a host of compliments.'

'Could he not have sent them to me directly,' Fortunée said tartly, half jesting, half angry, 'or are the Dutch women keeping him so busy that he has no time to write to me?'

'Believe me, he is far more occupied with money than with women.'

Casimir de Montrond, Talleyrand's closest friend, was also Fortunée's favourite of all her lovers. Attractive, witty, and as wicked as sin but a great lord to his fingertips, he was a born gambler with an inordinate love of money and had a finger in a host of financial pies, not all of which would have had the approval of the authorities. Fortunée adored this scapegrace who Talleyrand had nicknamed 'Hell's Infant Jesus', but, as a faithful subject of the Emperor, she had made no protest when he exiled her turbulent lover to Anvers on the grounds that virtue was impossible with him at court.

'The truth is,' she explained to Marianne a little later when Talleyrand had departed after a brief visit, 'that poor Casimir was unlucky. At the end of last year, there was a duel in the rue Cerutti. The fight took place at dawn in Queen Hortense's garden. Charles de Flahut and Augustue de Colbert crossed swords over her *beaux yeux* and Casimir got drawn in because he lived nearby. Napoleon could not take it out on Hortense or Flahaut and so he satisfied himself with sending Augustue de Colbert to get himself killed in Spain and despatching Montrond to Anvers with orders not to stir.'

'Wasn't that rather harsh?'

'I told you the Emperor was not easy. But I must admit that was not the whole of it. Before that, in the summer, that wretch Casimir went to Cauterets where the Duchess of Abrantes was weeping because Metternich had left her and, so they say, helped to console her somewhat. On the whole,

Napoleon acted wisely. And, in one way, he was doing Montrond a service because otherwise he might have been mixed up in the Abrantes scandal as well.'

'What scandal?'

'My dear, where have you been?'

'In the quarries of Chaillot, as you know quite well.'

'Oh, yes, of course! So you were! Well, you must know that last month, after Count Marescalchi's ball, Junot, who everyone knows deceives his wife quite shockingly, threw a frightful scene in the course of which he half killed her with a pair of scissors in a fit of jealousy. If Madame de Metternich had not intervened, I really think he would have killed her. The Emperor was furious. He sent Junot back to Spain and his wife with him, to force them to make it up. To my mind, he would have done as well to punish that cat Caroline as well!'

'Caroline?'

'Her sister, Madame Murat, Grand Duchess of Berg and Queen of Naples for the last year and a half. A gorgeous, dimpled blonde, as pink and luscious as a bon-bon – and the greatest bitch ever born! It was she who told Junot about poor Laure d'Abrantes – when he had actually been her own lover!'

This brief glimpse into the habits of the great ones of the court, made Marianne open her eyes wide, much to Fortunée's delight.

'You had no idea such things went on, I daresay? But, while I am about it, let me give you some advice. Love the Emperor as much as you like, but take care with his noble family. Apart from his mother, the inaccessible Madame Laetitia, who remains as stiff-necked and Corsican as ever, and Lucien, who has chosen exile for love, the others have made themselves into a kind of nest of vipers, a collection of people as arrogant and greedy and as vain as peacocks and altogether, to my way of thinking, not fit to be with. Avoid them like the plague, for they will hate you as much as the Emperor loves you.'

Marianne took good note of her advice but she had no desire to come to blows with the imperial family, or even to be known to them. She wanted to love Napoleon in the shadows, without drawing attention to herself, because it was only away from the light and noise of the crowd that such a love as theirs could blossom fully.

As the day wore on, her mood became more and more abstracted, so that she listened to Fortunée's gossip with only half an ear. Her eyes kept going back more frequently to the bronze gilt clock with its representation of the sleeping Psyche. Never had she been so glad to see night fall because the night would bring him back to her. A fever began to run in her veins when she thought of the hours of love ahead. Already, she had so much to tell him! And yet the hours seemed to go more and more slowly.

Fortunée, having barred her doors to all her friends on the excuse of a headache, had yawned at least thirty times before ten o'clock sounded from the church of Notre-Dame-de-Lorette.[8] The last stroke had just died away when they heard the rumble of a carriage. It slowed down and entered the gates which the porter had been told to leave open, then stopped in the deliberately darkened courtyard. Marianne ran to the window with her heart beating wildly while Fortunée rose intending to withdraw to her own room. But she had no time. In an instant, Napoleon was there.

'Don't run away, Madame,' he said as his hostess sank into a curtsey at the door of the salon. 'I have only a moment —'

Flinging his hat on to a sofa, he caught Marianne into his arms and kissed her while she protested:

'What, only a moment?'

'An Emperor cannot often do as he likes, *mio dolce amore*. I have to go back to the Tuileries. There are important despatches waiting for me and someone I must see, so I have not much time. But there were a number of things I had to tell you which would not wait. This first.'

From a pocket in his coat, he drew a roll of papers sealed with a great red seal which he placed in her hands.

'I promised you a house,' he said smiling. 'I am giving you this one. I think you will like it.'

Marianne unrolled the papers but before she had read more than the first words of the deed the colour fled from her face. There were tears in her eyes as she flung herself into his arms.

'Thank you – oh, thank you!' she gasped, hugging to her breast the wonderful deeds which told her that the Hôtel d'Asselnat in the rue de Lille, her family's house where her parents had been arrested and where she herself had been found abandoned by the Abbé de Chazay, was now her own.

Gently, Napoleon stroked the heavy crown of dark hair.

'Don't cry. More than anything, I want you to be happy. I have already given orders. Tomorrow morning, Percier and Fontaine will go to the rue de Lille to begin on the necessary repairs, for the house has stood empty since 1793. Fortunée will go with you and you can order it all as you like. There now, don't cry. I have something else to tell you,' he added with affectionate roughness.

She made an effort and dried her eyes.

'I am not crying —'

'Liar! Never mind, I shall go on. Tomorrow, Gossec will come here. He

---

[8] Not the present church, which dates only from 1836. When the old church of Notre-Dame-de-Lorette was destroyed, its name was given to the Chapel of St-Jean-Port-Latine at the Cimetière Des porcherons.

has orders to prepare you for an audition with the director of the Opéra. Within a month, all Paris shall acclaim a new idol. Maria Stella. You have a wonderful voice and it shall be your glory!'

'Maria Stella?' she was too surprised now to feel any wish to cry.

'That is the name I have chosen for you. You cannot appear in the theatre under your real name and as for your adopted one of Mallerousse, that is hideous. Besides, the public will dote on an Italian. You can have no idea of the snobbery of Parisians! They may not take readily to one of their own country women, but an Italian will be sure of their support. So there you are, established as a singer from Italy. Where should you prefer? Venice, Rome, Florence?'

He offered a choice of cities as easily as a choice of gowns.

'Venice!' Marianne cried rapturously. 'I should so love to know Venice.'

'You shall go there! You shall sing in Venice, my whole empire will be fighting for you – so, we'll give you a Venetian passport.'

Vast prospects were suddenly opening up before Marianne, but these prospects involved so many separations. Yet they were inevitable separations. When he could not have her with him, it would be better for her to travel, to be far away. And with her music, everything would be easy.

'Maria Stella!' she murmured as though engraving her new name on her mind.

'It was not I who gave you that name, it was Fouché, star you were, and star you shall remain – but in a very different sky. One more thing. A great singer needs someone to be a kind of impressario for her, to deal with contracts, arrange her programme and protect her against unwelcome intruders. I think I have found what you need. What do you say to the little man with the big ears we found kicking his heels on the road outside Malmaison last night in company with a deaf coachman? I have had a suitable report on him during the day. He seems an odd fellow, but I think he'll do the business. And, if I have understood correctly, you owe him something–'

'But–' Marianne was almost speechless. 'How do you know all this? In so short a time?'

'Didn't you know? I have excellent police. And Fouché stands in some need of forgiveness.' He smiled so wickedly that Marianne could not help laughing. Dazed by the unexpected avalanche which had fallen on her, she had sunk on to a sofa but now he bent forward quickly and tweaked her ear to draw her back to him.

'Happy?'

'How could I help it? I don't know what to say. All this is so sudden, so unexpected – it's almost frightening!'

'I told you I had a heap of things to tell you. Now kiss me and then get some sleep. You need it. And there's nothing like a good night's rest after a deal of excitement. I must go.'

Urgent to be gone now, he kissed her somewhat absently, picked up his hat and was striding to the door when, just as he reached it, he stopped and clapped his hand impatiently to his forehead.

'Fool that I am! I nearly forgot!'

Turning back to Marianne who still stood rooted to the spot, he put into her hands a large green Morocco jewel case, stamped with the imperial arms, which he produced as though by magic from yet another of his enormous pockets.

'Here,' he said. 'Wear these on the night of your first appearance! Then I shall know you are thinking of me.'

As though in a dream, Marianne opened the case. Lying on a bed of black velvet, gleaming and flashing in the candlelight, was a fabulous set of emeralds and diamonds. Not even at Talleyrand's had she ever seen anything so splendid. But when she looked up with dazzled eyes, she saw that Napoleon was already back at the door.

'Don't tell me they won't suit you. They are the same green as your eyes. Goodbye, my heart.'

When, a little later, Madame Hamelin, growing anxious at the continued silence in the salon, entered cautiously, she found Marianne sitting on the floor by the fire with her hands fll of documents and a cascade of fabulous jewels on her knees, crying as though her heart would break.

CHAPTER SIXTEEN
The Phantom of the Rue de Lille

In the grey, rain-swept light of a new day, beneath a sky that held no promise of sunshine, the great entrance portico framed by delapidated walls, with here and there a stone missing, presented a dismal sight. Dead weeds sprouted from the gaps in the stonework where their seed had been carried by the wind and the paving stones before the door with its sad, flaking green paint gaped to make way for a mass of brown and soggy vegetation.

Marianne stood leaning on Fortunée's arm and her eyes behind the heavy veil which hid her face filled with tears as she looked at the old house where her life had begun, from which her father and mother had gone out hand in hand to meet their deaths. She had wanted to visit it alone, before the architects took possession of it, because it seemed to her that she alone had the right to break the silence which had enveloped the Hôtel d'Asselnat for so many years. She wanted to see it in all its loneliness and neglect, before the magic wand was waved that would give it a new life, but she found now that this neglect was painful to her. So much lay behind it.

But for the Terror, all her youth would have been passed in this splendid old dwelling, its noble proportions and the cracked stone trophies over the porch still telling of the splendours of the reign of the Sun King, or else in the old Châteaux in Auvergne which now she might never see. Instead, she would have a different life, but would it be any happier? Who could tell what Marianne d'Asselnat de Villeneuve might have been at this moment if – but there was no end to it.

Behind her, Marianne heard Arcadius de Jolival telling the coachman to wait. She walked a few steps towards the house, strangely unwilling to make use of the keys which had been handed to her on waking. Opposite the silent entrance, a splendid, luxurious mansion was just awaking to a spate of furious activity contrasting strongly with its neglected neighbour. The staff were going about their morning tasks, and the place was alive with servants sweeping out courtyards and pavements, polishing brass and beating carpets. People were coming and going, many of them men in army uniform on foot or on horseback, entering or leaving a vast forecourt at the far end of which rose an impressive building in the Egyptian style. Seeing Marianne turn to look, disturbed by the noise breaking in on her thoughts, Arcadius frowned.

'You're going to have noisy neighbours, when they are in Paris, at least. That is the Hôtel de Beauharnais. Prince Eugène , the Viceroy of Italy is there at present. And yesterday, 29 January 1810, there was a ball and a reception. Prince Eugène likes entertaining and the Emperor was there. But it means hard work for the servants this morning. That's why they are so busy. But when he is back in Milan it will be quieter. The Emperor is very fond of him,' he added knowing that this would be the best way of soothing his young friend's irritation. He was quite right. She smiled.

'Oh well, if the Emperor is fond of him. Come, shall we go in? It is freezing out here!'

She proffered the great keys which she had been carrying in her muff. Arcadius took them and went up to the little postern gate beside the main one.

'It will probably be very stiff,' he said, 'if this gate has not been opened for years, the wood frame will have warped and we'll probably have trouble from rusty hinges.'

He inserted the key and leaned against the door, prepared to push with all his strength as he tried to turn it. But the key turned smoothly in the lock and the door opened without the least; resistance.

'Someone seems to have taken the trouble of oiling the lock,' he said in surprise. 'And the door opens as though it were used every day. Who can come here?'

'I don't know,' Marianne answered in some alarm. Let's go in.'

The forecourt lay before them in all its desolation. Ahead, framed in moss-grown outbuildings, the noble, classical facade displayed black windows with broken panes and stonework smeared with green stains and chipped, here and there, by bullet holes. A number of steps were missing from the imposing perron and the stone lions which had formerly guarded it lay headless among the weeds in the courtyard. The ground was strewn with debris of all kinds and over on the right some blackened walls and pillars told of the beginnings of a fire, probably the same the Abbé de Chazay had put out before he fled. A riot of vegetation had sprung up everywhere, as though trying to draw a veil over the poor, gutted house. A thin trail of ivy had begun climbing tentatively up the carved oak door, as though nature were trying to comfort the mutilated stones with this fragile ornament. A black cat sprang suddenly through the twisted ironwork of the cellar grille and streaked away to disappear through the gaping doorway of an old stable.

Like a good, superstitious Creole, Fortunée Hamelin shivered and clutched Marianne's arm a little tighter. She sighed.

'Percier and Fontaine will have their work cut out. What a ruin! I am beginning to think the Emperor has given you an odd present!'

'But none that could have given me greater pleasure,' Marianne said fiercely. 'Even the emeralds are nothing besides this sick old house.'

'It is not as bad as that,' Arcadius said comfortingly. 'With a little care and work all this can soon be repaired. The damage is more superficial than really serious. Let's look inside.'

He gave his hand to Marianne to help her up the few wobbly steps that remained of the perron and then returned to perform the same service for Madame Hamelin who followed.

The carved door opened as easily as the one in the street had done. Arcadius frowned.

'Who troubles to look after the locks in a ruined house?' he mumbled. But Marianne was not listening. She stepped forward with a thudding heart into the huge, deserted entrance hall. Not a stick of furniture remained. The coloured marble which had clothed the walls and surrounded the doors lay shattered on the cracked black marble floor. The exquisitely painted doors had been torn from their hinges, allowing the eye to penetrate unhindered into the recesses of the house where everything showed the same traces of blind vandalism.

In the dining room with its tattered hangings, the bare sideboards, tall cabinets and furnishings too heavy to be carried away showed shattered panels rotten with damp. The mutilated remnants of King Louis XIV's profile still showed on a large cartouche above the red marble fireplace, and the grate was full of ashes in which were small bright scraps of gilt bronze from the furniture burnt there.

In the salon which came next, the ravages were still more terrible. Not one piece of furniture was left standing. The once exquisitely polished harpsichord lay in a heap of rubbish, among which one carved foot and a few ivory keys were still distinguishable. The pale silk hangings were only filthy, blackened rags hanging from bits of wood that still showed traces of gilding. Only the scrolled panelling – but suddenly Marianne gave a start. Her eyes widened, staring. Over the mantelpiece, lonely, splendid and wholly unexpected, the portrait of a man reigned over this scene of devastation. It was a fine piece of work. The face beneath the powdered hair was dark, with proud features and fierce, brooding eyes. He stood, hand on hip, proud and arrogant in his handsome colonel's uniform, against the smoky background of some battle scene. The painter's model must have been a man of rare charm and Fortunée, coming up behind Marianne, exclaimed in wonder.

'Oh—! What a splendid man!'

'It is my father,' Marianne said tonelessly.

All three stood motionless, their feet in the dust, their eyes riveted on the portrait which gazed back at them mockingly, with eyes that were extraordinarily alive. For Marianne, there was great poignancy in this confrontation. Until this moment, her father had been to her only a rather faded miniature in a frame of seed pearls, the picture of an elegant, sardonically smiling man, a little world-weary, almost effete, whom she had regarded with the same kind of vague fondness she might have felt for any attractive portrait or for the hero of a novel. But the arrogant young soldier portrayed here touched her in the deepest fibres of her being, because in each of those bold features she recognized herself. He was so like her. The high cheek-bones, the challenging look in those mocking, slightly upward curving eyes, the wide, sensual mouth, betraying the stubbornness of that strong, square jaw. He was all at once very close to her, this father she had never really known.

It was Jolival who broke the spell.

'You are his daughter all right,' he said pensively. 'He cannot have been much older than you when that picture was painted. I have never seen a man more handsome, or more virile. But who could have hung it there? Look—' Jolival brushed the gilded frame with one pale kid-gloved finger, 'not a speck of dust! While everything else—'

An expressive movement of his arm embraced the desolation around them. Then he paused, his arm still in mid-air, as from somewhere upstairs a floorboard cracked sharply, as though under someone's feet.

'But – is there someone here?' Marianne said softly.

'I'll go and see,' Arcadius told her.

He ran quickly to the staircase, whose broad sweep could be seen through a gaping doorway and leapt up two at a time with the lightness of a dancer. Left alone in the salon, the two women looked at one another, neither anxious to break the silence. Marianne had a strange feeling that this empty, desolate house where the one portrait hung in state, was none the less alive, with a dim, underground life of its own. She was torn between two contradictory urges, to sit down right there on the dusty ground and wait for what God knew what or to run away, and shut fast the doors that had opened with such suspicious ease and never return. The thought that very soon workmen would come and break the silence of this peculiar shrine with all their clamour troubled her, as though there was something wrong about it. And yet, no one had more right than she to cross this threshold, and to awaken the sleeping echoes of the old house. The house to which, even yesterday, she had not given a thought had now become part of her flesh and she knew that she could never tear it from her again without leaving a wound. Her eyes returned to those of the portrait which seemed to follow her wherever she went and she spoke to it, a silent, earnest prayer from her heart.

'Is it your wish, tell me, is it your wish that I should come back here, to our house? Already, I love it so! I will restore it to its past splendours, and once again you shall preside over a setting worthy of you.'

Then, as though the house were trying to answer her, the one remaining whole window in the room, its fastening perhaps broken or ill-latched, was caught suddenly by a gust of wind and flew open. Marianne moved across to shut it and in doing so saw that it gave, like the rest, on to a small garden laid out around a green and stagnant pool. Beside the pool a stone cupid with a blackened nose stood dreaming with his arms around a large dolphin that had long since ceased to spout water. And just at that very moment, the rain-filled clouds parted to make way for a pale, timid ray of sunshine which caressed the cupid's cheek, revealing his enigmatic smile. And, without quite knowing why, Marianne felt comforted and accepted. Just then, Arcadius came back.

'There's no one there. It must have been a rat.'

'Or just the woodwork creaking,' Fortunée added, shivering in her furs. 'It is so dank in here! Are you sure you want to live here, Marianne?'

'Quite sure,' Marianne answered on a note of sudden happiness, 'and the sooner the better. I shall ask the architects to work as quickly as possible! I think they will be here soon.'

For the first time, she had spoken out loud, as though officially taking possession of the silence. The warm notes of her voice rang through the empty rooms triumphantly. She smiled at Fortunée.

'Let's go,' she said. 'You are almost dead with cold. It's as draughty here as in the street.'

'You don't want to see upstairs,' Jolival said. 'I can tell you, there is nothing there. Apart from the walls, which could not be stolen, and the charred remains in the fireplaces, absolutely nothing is left.'

'Then I had rather not see. It is too sad. I want this house to find its soul again –'

She stopped, her eyes on the portrait, with the sensation of having said something foolish. The soul of the house was there, before her, smiling arrogantly against an apocalyptic background. What she had to do was to restore its body, by re-creating the past.

Outside, they could hear the horses blowing and stamping on the cobblestones. The cry of a water carrier rang out, waking the echoes of what had been formerly the rue de Bourbon. It was the voice of life, of the here and now which held so much appeal for Marianne. With Napoleon's love to protect her, she would live here as sole mistress, free to act as she pleased. Free! It was a fine word when, at that very moment, she might have been buried alive in the heart of the English countryside by the will of a tyrannical husband, with boredom and regret her only companions. For the first time, it occurred to her that after all she might have been lucky.

Slipping her arm affectionately through Fortunée's, she walked back with her to the hall, though not without one last affectionate look of farewell at the handsome portrait.

'Come,' she said gaily. 'Let's go and have a big, scalding hot cup of coffee. That's the only thing I really want at present. Close the doors carefully, my friend, won't you?'

The "Greek prince" grinned. 'Don't worry,' he said. 'It would be too bad if so much as a single draught escaped.'

In a cheerful mood, they left the house, re-entered the carriage and were driven back to Madame Hamelin's.

Charles Percier and Leonard Fontaine might have been called the heavenly twins of decoration under the Empire. For years, they had worked together in such close collaboration that beside them, Castor and Pollux, Orestes and Pylades might have seemed mortal enemies. They had met first in the studios of their common master, Peyre, but then, when Percier won the Grand Prix de Rome in 1785 and Fontaine the second Grand Prix in 1786, they came together again beneath the umbrella pines of the Villa Medici and had remained together ever since. Between them, they had undertaken to re-design Paris in the Napoleonic style, and there was nothing good of Percier's that did not show the hand of Fontaine and no proper Fontaine without a touch of Percier. And being the same age, within a year or two, one born in Paris the other at Pontois, they were generally regarded in everyday life as inseparable brethren.

It was this pair, so eminently representative of French art under the Empire who, late that afternoon, stepped through the doors of Fortunée's salon. That salon had never been so empty of company, but since this was Napoleon's wish, that amiable lady uttered no word of protest. Except for Gossec, not a soul had crossed her threshold all that day.

The two architects, after bowing politely to the ladies, gave Marianne to understand that they had paid a preliminary visit to the house in the rue de Lille earlier that afternoon.

'His majesty the Emperor,' Charles Percier added, 'has intimated to us that the work should be so carried out that you, mademoiselle, may take possession of your house with the least possible delay. We have therefore no time to waste. To be sure, the house has suffered a good deal of damage.'

'But we feel,' Fontaine went on, 'that we shall very soon be able to remove all traces of the ravages worked by time and men.'

'We have therefore,' Percier took him up, 'taken the liberty of bringing along with us some designs we happened to have by us, simply one or two ideas sketched for our own pleasure, but which seem perfectly suited to this old house.'

Marianne's eyes, which throughout this well-orchestrated dialogue had been swivelling between the two men, from the short Percier to the tall Fontaine, came to rest at last on the roll of papers which the first named was already unfurling on a table. She caught a glimpse of roman style furnishing, Pompeian friezes, alabaster figures, gilded eagles, swans and victories.

'Gentlemen,' she said quietly, taking some pains to stress the slight foreign accent with which she spoke French so as to lend substance to her supposed Venetian origin, 'can you answer me one question?'

'What is that?'

'Are there in existence any plans indicating what the Hôtel d'Asselnat was like before the Revolution?'

The two architects looked at one another with barely concealed alarm. They had known they were to work for an Italian singer, as yet unknown, but destined for great fame, a singer who was quite certainly the Emperor's latest fancy. They were expecting a creature of whims and caprices who might not be easy to please and this start to the interview seemed to prove them right. Percier cleared his throat with a little cough.

'For the outside, no doubt we can find plans, but for the interior – but why should you wish to have these plans, mademoiselle?'

Marianne understood perfectly the meaning behind the question. Why should a daughter of Italy be interested in the original appearance of a house in France? She smiled encouragingly.

'Because I should like my house, as far as possible, restored to the state in which it was before the troubles. All this you have shown me is very fine, very attractive, but it is not what I desire. I want the house to be as it was and nothing more.'

Percier and Fontaine raised their arms to heaven in unison, as though performing a well-drilled ballet.

'In the style of Louis XIV or Louis XV? But, mademoiselle, permit me to remind you that is no longer the fashion,' Fontaine said reproachfully. 'No one has anything like that nowadays, it is quite outdated, not at all the thing. His majesty the Emperor himself—'

'His majesty will wish first and foremost for me to have what I want,' Marianne interrupted sweetly. 'I realize of course that it will not be possible to reconstruct the interior decorations exactly as they were, since we do not know what that was like. But I think it will do very well if you will carry out everything to suit the style of the house and, especially, the portrait which is in the salon.'

There was a silence so complete that Fortunée stirred in her chair.

'The portrait?' said Fontaine. 'Which portrait—'

'But, the portrait of—' Marianne stopped short. She had been on the point of saying: 'The portrait of my father', but the singer Maria Stella could have no connection with the family of d'Asselnat. She drew a deep breath and then continued hurriedly: 'A magnificent portrait of a man which I and my friends saw this morning hanging over the fireplace in the salon. A man dressed in the uniform of an officer of the old king's —'

'Mademoiselle,' the two architects answered in unison, 'I can assure you that we saw no portrait —'

'But, I am not going out of my mind!' Marianne cried losing patience. She could not understand why these two men refused to discuss the portrait. She turned in desperation to Madame Hamelin.

'Oh really, my dear, you saw it too —?'

'Yes,' Fortunée said uneasily, 'I saw it. And do you really say, gentlemen, that there was no portrait in the salon? I can see it now: a very handsome man of noble bearing, wearing a colonel's uniform.'

'We give you our word, madame,' Percier assured her, 'that we saw no portrait. Had it been otherwise we should certainly have mentioned it at once. A single portrait left in a devastated house would have been remarkable enough!'

'And yet it was there,' Marianne persisted stubbornly.

'It was there, certainly.' Jolival's voice spoke from behind her. 'But just as certainly, it is not there now.'

Arcadius had been missing all afternoon but now, as he walked farther into the room, Percier and Fontaine, who had been beginning to wonder if they had fallen among lunatics, breathed again and turned gratefully to this unlooked-for rescuer. But Arcadius, as amiable and unconcerned as ever, was kissing the fingers of the mistress of the house and Marianne.

'We can only imagine someone has taken it,' he remarked lightly. 'Well, gentlemen, have you reached an agreement with the -- signorina Maria Stella —'

'Er -- that is -- not yet. This business of the portrait —'

'Forget it,' Marianne said tersely. She had realized that Jolival did not wish to speak of it before strangers. Now, much as she had liked these two in the beginning, she had only one wish, to see the back of them and be left alone with her friends. With this view, she forced herself to smile and say lightly but firmly:

'Remember only one thing. That my desire to see the house look as it used to do remains unaltered.'

'In the style of the last century?' Fontaine murmured with comical dismay. 'Are you quite determined on that?'

'Quite determined. I want nothing else. Do your best to make the Hôtel d'Asselnat look as it used to do, gentlemen, and I shall be eternally grateful to you.'

There was nothing more to add. The two men withdrew, assuring her they would do their best. Barely had they gone downstairs before Marianne fell on Arcadius.

'My father's portrait, what do you know about it?'

'That it is no longer where we saw it, my poor child. I went back to the rue de Lille without saying anything to you, after the architects had gone in fact, I watched them leave, I wanted to go over the house from top to bottom because there were a number of things which struck me as odd, those well-oiled locks among other things. It was then I noticed that the portrait had disappeared.'

'But, then what can have happened to it? This is ridiculous! It's unbelievable!'

Marianne was bitterly disappointed. It seemed to her that now she had really lost the father she had never known and had discovered that morning with such joy. This sudden disappearance was very cruel.

'I should not have left it. I was so incredibly lucky to find it, I should have taken it with me, at once. But how could I have guessed that someone would come and move it. For that must be what happened, surely? It has been stolen!'

She was walking up and down the room unhappily as she spoke, wringing her hands together. Arcadius, though outwardly calm, never took his eyes off her.

'Stolen? Perhaps —'

'What do you mean, perhaps?'

'Don't be cross. I am merely thinking that whoever put it in the salon has simply taken it away again. You see, instead of trying to find out who took the portrait, I think we should do better to try and find out who put it there in the midst of all that wreckage. Because it is my belief that when we know that, we shall also know who has the portrait now.'

Marianne said nothing. What Jolival said was true. Instead of grieving, she began to think. She remembered the brightness of the canvas and the frame, how meticulously clean they were in contrast to the squalor around them. There was some mystery there.

'Would you like me to inform the Minister of Police?' Fortunée suggested. 'He will make inquiries, discreet ones if you like, but I'll be prepared to swear that he will find your portrait before very long.'

'No – thank you, I would rather not.'

What, above all, she would rather not see was the astute Fouché dabbling in something which concerned her so closely. She felt that by putting Fouché's men with their dirty fingers on the trail of her father's disappearing image, she would be in some way soiling the beauty of that image which she had so briefly recovered.

'No —' she said again, 'truly I would rather not.' She added: 'I prefer to try and find out myself.'

In that moment her mind was made up.

'Jolival, my dear,' she said calmly, 'tonight, we will go back to the rue de

Lille, as unobtrusively as possible.'

'Go back to the rue de Lille tonight,' Fortunée protested. 'You cannot mean it? What for?'

'It would seem that there is a ghost in the old house. Don't ghosts prefer the night time?'

'You think someone comes there?'

'Or hides there.'

An idea was growing in her mind as she spoke. Or rather, a memory which was becoming clearer with every moment. Of a few remarks she had heard as a child. More than once, Aunt Ellis had told her of her adventures as a tiny baby, how the Abbé de Chazay had found her, left all alone in the house after her parents had been taken away. At that time, the Abbé himself had been living in the rue de Lille, in one of those secret hiding places which had been constructed in a great many aristocratic houses in town and country to hide refractory priests. 'That must be it!' she said, finishing her thoughts aloud, 'someone must be hiding in the house.'

'It is impossible,' Jolival answered. 'I have been everywhere, I tell you, from top to bottom.'

But he listened very attentively when she told him the story of the Abbé de Chazay. Unfortunately, she did not know where this hiding place lay. It might be in the cellars, the attic or behind the panelling in one of the rooms. The Abbé himself, whether intentionally or from sheer absentmindedness, had never told her precisely.

'In that case, we may search for a very long time. Some of these hiding places were completely impossible to discover, except by a stroke of luck. We shall have to sound out the walls and ceilings.'

'At all events, no one could live long in one of those hiding places without outside help,' Marianne said. 'They would need food and fresh air and all the other necessities of life.'

Fortunée, who was lying on a blue watered-silk chaise longue, sighed and stretched, then began rearranging the folds of her red cashmere gown, yawning widely as she did so.

'You don't think perhaps you two are romancing a little?' she said. 'I think the house has been empty for so long that some poor homeless wretch must have been living in it, and our going in like that, followed by the architects, must have disturbed him, that is all.'

'And the portrait?' Marianne said seriously.

'He must have found it in the house, perhaps in the attics or hidden away in some odd corner, which would explain why it escaped when everything else was wrecked. Because it was the only pretty thing left, he used it to adorn his desert and when we invaded his domain today, he simply went away and took with him what he had come to regard as his own property. I sincerely believe, Marianne, that if you want to get your picture back the only sensible thing to do is to tell Fouché. It can't be easy to wander about Paris with a canvas that size under one's arm. Would you like me to send for him? We are reasonably good friends.'

It began to look as though the charming Fortunée had good friends everywhere, but once again, Marianne refused. Against all the evidence, some instinct was telling her that there was some other explanation, and that the eminently simple and rational theory put forward by her friend was not the right one. She had been conscious of a presence in the house, which she had at first put down to the magnetic power of the portrait, but now she realized that there was something else. She recalled the footfalls they had heard upstairs. Arcadius had decided it must have been a rat, but was it? She could not help thinking that there was some mystery about her ancestral home and she meant to get to the bottom of it, but she would do so alone. Or at least, with only Arcadius to help her. She turned to him now.

'I mean what I said. Will you come with me tonight and see what is going on in my house?'

'Why ask?' Jolival shrugged. 'For one thing, not for anything in the world could I allow you to go alone into that morgue, but for another – I must admit that this peculiar business intrigues me too. We'll leave here at ten o'clock, if that suits you.'

Fortunée sighed. 'And much good may it do you! My dear child, you do seem to be inordinately fond of adventures. For myself, I shall stay quietly at home, with your permission. Firstly, because I have not the slightest desire to go and freeze to death in an empty house, and secondly because someone must be here to warn the Emperor, in case you are running into another of those traps you seem to have a knack of finding. And I dread to think what he will do to me if anything should happen to you!' she finished with comical alarm.

The remainder of the evening passed in supping and afterwards in making ready for the intended expedition. For a moment, it did occur to Marianne to think of the mysterious danger against which Jason Beaufort had warned her but she rejected the idea at once. Why should she expect any danger? Surely no one could have foreseen that Napoleon would give her back the house which had been her parent's? No, the Hôtel d'Asselnat could be in no way connected with the American's fears.

But Marianne was not fated to go adventuring with Arcadius that night. The clock had just struck a quarter to ten and she had already risen from her chair to go and put on some more suitable clothes for what lay ahead, when Fortunée's black servant Jonas appeared to announce with his invariable solemnity that 'Monsigneur le Duc de Frioul' requested admittance. Absorbed in their own conversation, neither Marianne, nor Fortunée, nor Arcadius had heard the carriage arrive. They gazed at one another blankly but Fortunée recovered herself at once.

'Show him in,' she said to Jonas. 'The dear duke must be bringing word from the Tuileries.'

The Grand Marshal of the palace was doing better than that.

Hardly had he entered the room and kissed Fortunée's hand before he said gaily to Marianne:

'I come in search of you, mademoiselle. The Emperor is asking for you.'

'Truly? Oh, I am coming, I am coming at once —'

She was so happy to be going to him that evening when she had been given no reason to hope for it, that for a second she forgot the business of the missing picture. In her haste to go to Napoleon, she hurried away to put on a pretty dress of green velvet braided with silver with a deeply scooped out neckline and short sleeves trimmed with a froth of lace, snatched up a pair of long white gloves and flung on a great cloak of the same velvet, cut like a flowing domino with a hood trimmed with grey fox. She loved these things and blew a kiss with her fingertips at the radiantly joyful reflection in her mirror before running down to the salon where Duroc was calmly drinking coffee with Fortunée and Arcadius. He was talking at the same time and, as he was talking about the Emperor, Marianne paused in the doorway to listen to the end of what he was saying.

' — and when he had seen the finished column in the place Vendôme, the Emperor went on to inspect the Ourcq Canal. He is never still for a moment!'

'Was he pleased?' Madame Hamelin asked.

'With these works, yes, but the war in Spain remains his greatest anxiety. Things are going badly there. The men are sick, the Emperor's brother, King Joseph, lacks imagination, the marshals are weary and jealous of one another, while the *guerilleros* harry the army and are helped by the local population, who are both hostile and cruel. And then Wellington's English are firmly established in the country.'

'How many men have we there?' Arcadius asked in a grave voice.

'Nearly eighty thousand. Soult has replaced Jourdan as Major General. King Joseph has Sebastiani, Victor and Mortier under him, while Suchet and Augereau are occupying Aragon and Catalonia. At this moment, Massena and Junot are joining forces with Ney and Montbrun ready to march into Portugal —'

Marianne's entry cut short Duroc's military disquisition. He looked up, smiled and set down his empty cup.

'Let us go, then, if you are ready. If I let myself be drawn into army talk, we shall be here all night.'

'All the same, I wish you could go on! It was very interesting.'

'Not for two pretty women. Besides, the Emperor does not like to be kept waiting.'

Marianne felt a brief stab of remorse when she met Jolival's eye and remembered their planned expedition. But after all, there was no danger in the house.

'Another time,' she told him with a smile. 'I am ready, my lord duke.'

Jolival gave her a sidelong smile while continuing to stir the spoon gravely in his blue Sèvres cup.

'But of course,' he said. 'There is no hurry.'

When the impassive Roustan opened the door of the Emperor's office for Marianne, Napoleon was sitting working at his big desk and did not look up, even when the door was shut. Marianne looked at him in astonishment, uncertain how she should react. The wind was completely taken out of her sails. She had come to him in happy haste, borne up on the wave of joy which the mere thought of her lover awoke in her. She had thought to find him in his own room, or at least waiting for her impatiently. She came, expecting to throw herself into arms wide open to receive her. She had come, in short, hurrying to meet the man she loved – and found the Emperor.

Hiding her disappointment as best she could, she let her knees give and, sinking into a deep curtsey, waited with bent head.

'Get up and sit down, mademoiselle. I will be with you in a moment.'

Oh, that terse, cold, impersonal voice. Marianne's heart contracted as she moved to sit down on the little yellow sofa placed in front of the desk at right angles to the fire where she had seen Fortunée for the first time. There, she sat quite still, not daring to move, practically holding her breath. The silence was so complete that the swift scratching of the imperial pen across the paper seemed to her to make a shattering noise. Napoleon went on writing, eyes down, amid an improbable pile of red folders, open and closed. The room was strewn with papers. A sheaf of rolled up maps stood in a corner. For the first time, Marianne saw him in uniform. For the first time, the thought came to her of the vast armies he commanded.

He was wearing his favourite olive-green uniform of a colonel of the chasseur of the Guard but instead of the high uniform boots he wore white silk stockings and silver buckled shoes. As usual, his white Kerseymere breeches were ink stained and showed the marks of his pen. Across his white waistcoat lay the purple ribbon of the Légion d'Honneur, but what struck Marianne most of all were the locks of short brown hair plastered to his forehead by beads of sweat from the heat with which he worked. In spite of her disappointment, in spite of her vague feeling of anxiety, she was suddenly overwhelmed by a warm rush of tenderness. She was suddenly so sharply conscious of her love that she had to make an effort not to throw her arms about his neck. But, certainly an emperor was not a man like any other. The impulses which would have been so sweet and natural with an ordinary mortal, must be held until it suited his pleasure. No, Marianne thought with childish regret, truly it was not easy to love one of the giants of history.

Suddenly, the "giant" threw down his pen and looked up. The eyes that met hers were as cold as steel.

'So, mademoiselle,' he said abruptly, 'it seems you dislike the style of my times? From what I hear, you wish to revert to the splendours of the past century?'

For a moment, surprise left her speechless. This was the last thing she had been expecting. But anger soon restored her voice. Did Napoleon, by any chance, mean to dictate every single act of her life, even her likes and dislikes? All the same, well knowing it was dangerous to cross swords with him, she forced herself to be calm and even managed to smile. After all, it was rather funny. Here she came running to him, all throbbing with love, and he was talking about decoration. The thing that seemed to vex him most was her apparent lack of enthusiasm for the style he had adopted as his own.

'I have never said I did not like your style, sire,' she said sweetly. 'I merely expressed a wish that the Hôtel d'Asselnat should look once more as it used to do—'

'What makes you think that when I gave it to you, I desired such a resurrection? The house I gave you must be that of a famous Italian singer, belonging wholly to the present régime . There can be no question of turning it into a temple for your ancestors. Do you forget that you are no longer Marianne d'Asselnat?'

Oh, the tone was merciless and cutting! Why did there have to be two such contradictory natures to this man? Why, oh why did Marianne have to love him so desperately? She rose, white to the lips, and shaking with distress.

'Whatever name it may please your majesty to call me by, it cannot make me other than I am. I have killed a man for the honour of my name, sire, and you will not prevent my feeling for my parents the love and respect which is their due. For myself, if I belong to you, body and soul, which you cannot for an instant doubt, I alone belong to you. My family is my own.'

'And mine too, remember! All Frenchmen, past present and to come, belong to me, by which I mean they are my subjects. You are somewhat too apt to forget that I am the Emperor!'

'How could I forget it?' Marianne said bitterly. 'Your majesty gives me little chance! As for my parents—'

'I have no wish to prevent you mourning them, discreetly, but you must understand that I have little love for the fanatics of the old régime. I have a good mind to take that house back and give you another.'

'I want no other, sire. Your majesty may withdraw your architects if it offends them to work in an outmoded style, only leave me the house. I prefer the Hôtel d'Asselnat as it is, ruined, mutilated and pitiful, to the most sumptuous house in Paris! As for the noble subjects of the king – I thought your majesty had been one of them!'

'Do not be insolent. It will do you no good with me. The reverse, in fact. It seems to me, that you have too much pride of caste, to be a loyal subject. I hoped to find more submission and obedience in you. Know that what I value most in a woman is gentleness, a quality in which you seem to be singularly lacking!'

'The life I have led hitherto has scarcely taught me gentleness! I am deeply sorry I must offend your majesty, but I am as I am. I cannot change my nature!'

'Not even to please me?'

The tension was increasing. What game was Napoleon playing? Why this sarcasm, this attitude almost of hostility? Was he truly such a despot as to demand from her a submission that would make her blind, deaf and dumb? Was it the servile obedience of a slave in a harem that he wanted? If so, it was too bad. Marianne had fought too hard simply to preserve her dignity as a woman to bend now. Even if it meant tearing the heart out of her breast, she would not yield. Her eyes did not fall before that terrible blue gaze as, with infinite gentleness, she said:

'Not even to please you, sire! And yet, as God is my witness, I have no more earnest desire than to please your majesty.'

'You are going the wrong way about it,' he said with a sneer.

'But not at the price of my self-respect! If you had deigned, sire, to tell me that all you looked for in me was a servile creature, a mere consenting slave, going in perpetual terror of your majesty, then I should have begged you to let me leave France as I had meant to do. Because, for me, to love so is not to love at all.'

He took two steps towards her and with a quick movement untied the velvet ribbons holding her cloak. The heavy folds slid to the ground. He gazed at her for an instant, standing very straight before him. The candlelight fell softly on her beautiful shoulders and on the swell of her bare breasts, gilding them like summer fruits in their basket of white lace. Her face was very pale under the heavy helmet of midnight-coloured hair but her long green eyes were bright with bravely unshed tears. She looked, in that moment, breathtakingly lovely. He had only to make a single movement, to take her in his arms and wipe away the pain from her face. But he was in one of those tyrannical moods when no human power could have made him yield to that desire. She dared to stand up to him and that was enough to rouse in him a cruel determination to break her.

'And what if that is how I wish to be loved?' he said slowly without taking his merciless eyes off her.

'Then I do not believe you! You cannot wish for a love that is crawling, terrified, debased – not you!'

He ignored the cry of protest, in spite of all the love it held. His hand was on her breast, hot, ungentle fingers working upwards to the slender column of her neck.

'What I love in you,' he said with brutal sarcasm, 'is your matchless voice and your beauty. You are a wonderful singing bird with the body of a goddess. It is my intention to enjoy both to the full. I am not concerned with feelings. Go and wait for me in my room. Take your clothes off and get into bed. I will come to you in a moment.'

Marianne's high cheek-bones flamed suddenly as though he had hit her. She recoiled instantly, and her two hands flew to her uncovered breast. Her throat dried suddenly and her eyes burned with shame. All at once, she remembered the gossip overheard in the rue de Varennes. The story of Mademoiselle Durdesnoy whom he had dismissed without so much as a word of explanation after getting her into his bed. The episode of the little girl he was betrothed to in Marseilles, got rid of by a curt letter on the patently false excuse that she had not asked her parents for her own hand. And, finally, the well-known story of the Polish countess whom he had so maltreated that she became unconscious, of which he then took advantage to rape her and then afterwards send her back to her native Poland to bear his child. Was it possible that all this could be true? Marianne was beginning to think so. At all events, not at any price, even that of her love, would she consent to be treated so. Love did not give him the right to everything.

'Don't be too sure,' she murmured, clenching her teeth to force back her anger. 'I gave myself to you before I knew you, because, like a fool, I fell in love with you. Oh, how I loved you! I was so happy to belong to you! You could have asked anything of me because I thought you loved me a little! But I am not an eastern concubine to be caressed when the fancy takes you and then kicked out when your desire is slaked.'

Napoleon drew himself up to his full height, hands clasped behind his back. His jaw was set, his nostrils white with anger.

'You refuse to belong to me? Think carefully! That is a grave insult!'

'And yet – I do refuse,' Marianne said sadly. She felt suddenly very tired. Now there was only one thing she wanted, to escape as soon as possible from this close, quiet room into which she had come so happily a few minutes before and where, since then, she had suffered so much. She knew very well that she had just placed her whole life in jeopardy once again, that his power over her was limitless but not for anything in the world would she have accepted the degrading part that he was trying to force on her. She still loved him too much for that. In a low voice, she said: 'I refuse – more for your sake even than my own – because I want to be able to go on loving you. Besides – what pleasure would it give you to possess a senseless body, made insensible by grief?'

'Don't look for excuses. I had believed myself to possess a greater power over your senses than you grant me.'

'Because there was a love between us then which you are killing now!'

She almost screamed the words, goaded by the grief that nearly stopped her heart. Now she was trying to find the chink in his armour. He could not be this monster of ruthless pride, this utterly insensitive despot! She could still hear his words of love ringing in her ears.

Abruptly, he turned his back on her, walked over to a bookcase and stood before it, hands clasped behind his back.

'Very well,' he said curtly. 'You may withdraw.'

For a moment she hesitated. They could not part like that, quarrelling over a trifle. It was too hard! Suddenly, she wanted to run to him, tell him that she renounced everything he had given her, only so long as he would keep her with him, that he could take back the Hôtel d'Asselnat and do what he liked with it! Anything, only not to lose him, not to be cut off from the sight and sound of him – she stepped forward.

'Sire,' she began brokenly.

But then, as though the plain front of the bookcase had opened suddenly, she seemed to see before her, with terrifying clarity, the great portrait hanging on the crumbling walls. She saw the proud eyes, the arrogant smile. The daughter of such a man could not demean herself to beg for a love that was denied her. And just then she heard:

'Have you not gone?'

His back was still stubbornly towards her. Slowly, she went and picked up her green cloak and laid it over her arm, then sank into a curtsey so deep that she was almost on her knees.

'Farewell – sire,' she whispered.

Once out of the room, she walked straight ahead, like a sleepwalker, not even seeing Roustan who looked at her with big, horrified eyes, not even thinking to throw her cloak over her bare shoulders. She was dazed with grief, too numb to feel the full pain. Shock had formed a merciful cushion around her which, as it melted away, would give place to the real suffering, in all its sharpness and cruelty. She did not even think what she was going to do, what would happen now. No. Nothing mattered to her at all, nothing except this dull burning pain within her.

She went down the stairs without so much as seeing them and did not turn, even when a breathless voice called after her. Not until Duroc took the cloak from her to place it round her shoulders she aware of his presence.

'Where are you off to so fast, mademoiselle? I hope you did not mean to go out by yourself at this hour of night?'

'I? Oh, I do not know. It doesn't matter –'

'How's that? Doesn't matter?'

'I mean – I can easily walk. Don't trouble yourself.'

'Don't talk foolishness! You do not even know the way. You'd get lost – and, here, take this.'

He thrust a handkerchief into her hands but she did not use it. It wasn't until the Grand Marshal of the Palace gently wiped her cheeks that she realized that she was crying. He handed her carefully into the carriage and wrapped a fur rug round her knees, then went to give some orders to the coachman before climbing in beside her.

The coach was on its way before Marianne moved a muscle. She seemed like one thunderstruck. She huddled into the cushions like a hurt animal, seeking only silence and darkness. Her eyes looked out unseeingly at the passing spectacle of Paris by night. For a time, Duroc watched his young companion in silence but then, as the tears began again, running slowly down her cheeks while she made no move to stop them, he began trying clumsily to comfort her.

'You must not upset yourself so,' he murmured gently. 'The Emperor is often harsh, but he is not unkind. You have to understand what it means to have an empire stretching from Ushant to the Niemen and from Denmark to Gibraltar resting on the shoulders of a single man –'

The words came to Marianne as though through a fog. For her, that gigantic empire had only one meaning. It had made its master into a monster of pride and a ruthless autocrat. However, encouraged perhaps by hearing her sigh, Duroc went on:

'You see, the fifth anniversary of the coronation was celebrated two months ago and a fortnight later, the Emperor divorced his wife for the sake of assuring the crown, which still seems to him so precarious. He lives in a state of constant uneasiness because only the power of his will and his genius keeps this unlikely mosaic of peoples together. His brothers and sisters, though he has made them sovereigns, are incompetents, thinking only of their own interests and ignoring those of the Empire. Think how many victories it has taken to weld all this together since the Italian campaigns first made him Emperor of the French! Six great battles since the sun of Austerlitz, and that scarcely four years old, to say nothing of the endless fighting in Spain ... Jena, Auerstadt, Eylau, Friedland, Essling, where he lost his best friend, Marshal Lannes, and then Wagram where he defeated the man whose daughter he is now about to marry. If the Empire is to continue, there must be an heir – even if he has to sacrifice a little of his heart to achieve it, for he loved his wife. The Emperor is alone against them all, between the changeable moods of an unstable Tsar and the hatred of England, hanging like a bulldog to his coat tails. And so – when there are times when you think you could hate him, when he rouses feelings of anger and revolt in you, you must think of all that. He needs to be understood – and it is not easy.'

He fell silent, exhausted perhaps, with the effort of saying so much. But his plea, even if it found a way to Marianne's heart, only added to her grief. Understand Napoleon? She asked nothing better! But would he let her? He had driven her away, flung her back into the shadows, into the anonymous and faceless crowd of his subjects from which, for an instant, he had plucked her.

She looked at the grand Marshal who, still bent towards her, seemed to expect a reply, and nodded sadly, murmuring the thought that was in her mind.

'I wish I had the right to understand him – but he will not let me.'

Then she huddled back again in her corner and resumed her melancholy thoughts. Seeing she was not going to speak again, Duroc sighed and settling himself as comfortably as possible in his own corner, closed his eyes.

Time must have stood still. Numbed and incapable of thought, Marianne had paid no attention to the route, which was in any case one she did not know. Even so, after the passing of a period of time whose length she had no means of estimating, she did begin to feel that the journey was unusually long. She looked out of the window and saw that the carriage was now travelling through open country. The night was bright enough for her to be in no doubt on this score. She turned to her companion and spoke abruptly.

'If you please? Where are we going?'

Startled awake, the Emperor's confidant sat up with a jerk and glanced wildly at Marianne.

'I – you were saying?'

'I was asking where we were going?'

'Er – well, that is – where I was told to take you.'

This as good as told her that she would get no answer to her question. Perhaps he was cross with her for refusing to talk to him? But, in her heart of hearts, she did not greatly care. Napoleon must have decided to send her away from Paris in order to be thoroughly rid of her. They were probably taking her to some châteaux a long way away, a prison where it would be easier to forget than in Paris. And the Emperor would no doubt feel that a woman who had once received his favours could not be shut up in any common prison. But she had no illusions as to her fate, and not much interest either. Later, when she was not so tired – then she would try and see if she still had any will to fight.

The carriage passed through tall gates and entered what seemed to be a park. They drove along a paved avenue and drew up at last before a lighted entrance. Still half dazed, Marianne caught a glimpse of the pink marble columns of a vast peristyle which had been enclosed with glass windows,[9] the magnificent extent of a large, low palace surmounted by a marble balustrade, a few splendid rooms, in the best Empire style, through which she was led by a servant in a powdered wig, carrying a heavy branched candlestick. Duroc had vanished as soon as they were inside, without her even noticing. A door opened, revealing a room decorated in beige satin and deep mauve velvet. And Marianne found herself suddenly face to face with Napoleon.

He was sitting in a claw-footed armchair by the fire, watching her with a teasing smile, evidently enjoying her bewilderment as she struggled vainly to get her thoughts into some kind of order. She had a gloomy feeling that she must be going mad. She felt deathly tired, her body ached and her legs felt like jelly. It did not occur to her to curtsey, or make the least polite acknowledgment of his presence. She simply leaned back against the door post.

'I wish I understood –' she murmured.

'What? How I could be here before you? It's quite simple. Duroc had orders to take you a long way round before reaching the Trianon.'

'No – it's you I wish I understood. What, exactly, do you want of me?'

He stood up at last and came towards her and tried to take her in his arms but she resisted. Far from being angry now, he merely smiled briefly.

'A test, Marianne, a simple test. I wanted to know just what kind of woman you were. Remember, I hardly know you. You fell from the skies one night like a beautiful meteor, but you could have been any number of things: a clever adventuress, a courtesan, an agent of the princes, an unusually devoted friend of our dear Talleyrand – and you must admit the last was the most likely. Hence this test – I had to know just what you were.'

'A test that could have been the death of me –' Marianne murmured, still too shaken to feel in the least comforted.

Even so, Duroc's words were gradually coming back to her. She realized that they had made their way into her mind and that now she saw this extraordinary man with new eyes and, more important, according to his true dimensions.

'You are angry with me, aren't you? But that will pass. You must understand that I have the right to know who it is I love.'

'Because – you love me?'

'You don't doubt it for a moment,' he said softly. 'As for me, you can't imagine how many women try to get into my bed, for their own reasons. Everyone around me is trying to provide me with a mistress so as to have some kind of influence over me. Even my family! Especially my family and

[9] The columns of the Grand Trianon were glazed in at this period by the Emperor's order.

especially since I have been obliged to part from the Empress. Only a few weeks ago, my sister Pauline presented me with one of her ladies-in-waiting, a certain Madame de Mathis, a charming girl—'

'And – without success?'

He could not help laughing at that and the odd thing was that it was his laughter, so young and gay, that melted Marianne's resentment more surely than any amount of explanation.

'Oh,' he admitted, 'to be sure, to begin with. But I did not know you then. Now everything is different.'

Very gently, he laid his hands on Marianne's shoulders and drew her to him. This time, she let him do it, though with still a faint trace of rigidity. She was trying, with all her strength, to understand, to catch hold of this quick incisive mind which she admired, even while it frightened her. She knew well enough now that she had not only not stopped loving him but that, on the contrary, her love had emerged from this nightmare stronger than ever. But he had hurt her so! She felt as though she were slowly coming to life again after a long illness. She tried to smile.

'And so,' she murmured, 'have I passed my examination?'

He tightened his arms around her till they hurt.

'Admirably. You would make a worthy Corsican! Oh no, you have not the soul of a slave, you proud little aristocrat! You are not servile or self-seeking, but clean, open and upright. If you had been what at one moment I feared, you would have given in on all points, but you did not give an inch. And yet – you could not have guessed how I should react. You do not know me either. But I love you, Marianne, you can be sure of that, for all these and many other reasons.'

'Not just my voice and my person?'

'Idiot!'

Then, at last, she gave in. Suddenly, her nerve broke. Shuddering, she pressed herself against him and with her head on his shoulder she began to cry in great tearing sobs, like a little girl who has been punished and forgiven. The tears eased her and tenderly, with patience, Napoleon waited until she should be calm again, holding her with most brotherly gentleness. Still cradling her close, he led her over to a small sofa and sat her down. When her tears had died away a little, he began murmuring in Italian, the fond words she had loved so much that first time. Little by little, his kisses and caresses calmed her. After a while, she freed herself from the arms that held her and sat up, wiping her eyes with Duroc's handkerchief which he had put into her hand earlier.

'Forgive me,' she said unsteadily. 'I am very stupid—'

'Perhaps, if you really think so – but you are so lovely not even tears can make you ugly.'

He went over to a large silver-gilt wine cooler standing on a small table with some clear glasses and a small cold supper, took out a bottle of champagne and filled two glasses. Then he brought one to Marianne.

'Now, we must set the seal of our reconciliation. We will begin again from the beginning. Only this time, we know who we are and why we love one another. Drink, *mio dolce amore*, to our happiness.'

They drank, gazing into one another's eyes, and then Marianne let her head fall on to the back of the sofa with a little sigh. For the first time, she looked around her at the exquisite fabrics, the gilt bronze and satinwood furnishings, all these strange and magnificent surroundings. What had he told her a moment ago? That this was the Trianon?

'Why here?' she asked. 'Why this journey, all this comedy?'

'There too I have an excellent reason. I am going to give myself a little holiday – comparatively speaking. I remain here a week – and I am keeping you with me.'

'A week?'

'Yes. Do you think it's too long? Don't worry, you will have plenty of time afterwards for your audition with the Director of the Opéra. You are engaged in advance. Rehearsals begin on your return. As for your house –'

He paused and Marianne held her breath, not daring to interrupt. What was he going to say? Surely their stupid argument was not going to begin all over again after all? He looked at her, smiling and then, dropping a light kiss on the fingertips he had taken in his own, he finished calmly:

'As for your house, Percier and Fontaine do not need you to carry out their work. Don't worry, they have orders to act strictly in accordance with your wishes. Does that make you happy?'

For answer, she offered her lips and dared for the first time to say the words.

'I love you.'

'You've taken your time about saying it –' he observed between kisses.

Much later in the night, a log falling in the fire woke Marianne from a light doze. Lifting herself up on the pillows, she flung back the heavy mass of hair out of her eyes and leaned on her elbow to look at her lover as he slept. He had gone into sleep in an instant after their lovemaking, and now he lay across the bed as naked as a Greek warrior on the field of battle … For the first time, Marianne was struck by the perfection of his body.

Stretched out like that, he looked taller than he really was.[10] The firm muscles showed through the smooth, ivory-coloured skin in the manner of some ancient marble. Napoleon's chest and shoulders were broad, almost hairless, and his arms and legs modelled on the strictest canons. He had

---

[10] His actual height was about 5' 6".

excellent hands and took the greatest care of them, as of all his person. Marianne laid her face softly against his shoulder, stroking it with her cheek and breathing in the faint smell of eau-de-Cologne and Spanish Jasmin, softly taking care not to wake him.

A great Venetian mirror over the fireplace gave her back their two reflections. She saw herself, pink in the soft candle-light, half shrouded in the gleaming wave of her hair and was pleased with what she saw. It made her glad and triumphant because if she was beautiful tonight, it was for him, and because of him. Happiness had given her a glow which she had never had before, and which filled her at the same time with joy and humbleness. There, in that quiet room that still throbbed to their caresses, Marianne offered to the man she loved a more total and absolute submission than any he had asked of her earlier, a submission which she herself perhaps would deny him when daylight came again.

'I'll give you all the love you want,' she whispered softly, 'I'll love you with all my heart, and all my strength – but I will always speak the truth to you. You can ask anything of me, my love, any suffering and sacrifice, anything except lies and servility –'

The fire in the hearth was almost dead. The room which had been warm a moment before was growing chilly. Marianne got up quickly, and opening the white and gold rail that enclosed the bed, ran on bare feet to the hearth and stirred up the glowing embers. Then, piling on a few more logs, she waited for them to catch and burn up again.

She glanced at her naked image in the mirror and smiled to think of the picture she would present should any of the four men who, according to etiquette, slept in the ante-chamber dare to open the door.[11]

Faithful Constant also slept in a little room close by, ever ready to answer a ring at the bell, and then there was the impressive Roustan, barring the door with his great, sleepy body.

Marianne stood on tiptoe and leaned forward to examine the new woman she had become. It was something to be the mistress of an emperor! No doubt, the servants and officials, like the Grand Marshal of the Palace, would treat her with the greatest respect during her brief stay here, a stay which might well be unique because the new Empress –

She thrust back the unpleasant thought as hard as she could. She had suffered enough for one night. And now, she was going to have him all to herself for a whole week. In a way, she would be Empress herself and she meant to extract every last ounce of happiness from those few days. She did not mean to waste a single second.

She walked with her light step back to the bed and pulled up the covers

---

[11] A page, an aide-de-camp, a sergeant, and a corporal of the Imperial Mews.

softly over the sleeping man. Then with infinite caution, she slipped in beside him, and cuddled up close to him, drawing his warmth into her own shivering body. He turned in sleep and put his arm around her, murmuring something indistinct. With a happy sigh she pressed close against his chest and fell asleep, satisfied with the pact she had concluded with herself and with the sleeping master of Europe.

CHAPTER SEVENTEEN
Brief Happiness

The Grand Trianon, a huge, shimmering, translucent soap bubble of crystal and rose-coloured marble set amongst immemorial trees, unreal and splendid as a dream ship anchored to the shores of heaven, was covered in the early hours of the morning by a soft silent mantle of snow. Far more than the remote splendours of the Tuileries or the rather sophisticated charm of le Butard, it came to stand in Marianne's mind first as an ideal and then, afterwards, as the symbol of paradise lost.

She very soon discovered, however, that Napoleon had his own peculiar ideas of what he called a holiday. When the first ray of cold, wintry sunshine struck through the windows of the Imperial bedchamber, which faced East, like all the private rooms the Emperor had set aside for his own use in the Palace, she found that she was alone in the big bed and that Napoleon was nowhere to be seen. The fire was blazing cheerfully in the hearth, and a frothy lace wrapper lay over the back of a chair but there was no-one else in the room.

Alarmed in case Constant or some other servant should come in, Marianne hastily slipped on the night-gown she had left unused the night before. It was the property of the Emperor's sister, Pauline Borghese, who frequently resided at the nearby Petit Trianon. Next, she put on the wrapper, thrust her feet into a pair of pink velvet slippers and throwing back the heavy black masses of her hair, ran to the window like a happy child. As if in her honour, the park was dressed in an immaculate white splendour, enfolding the Palace within a casket of silence. It was as if heaven had decided to cut off the Trianon from the rest of the world and halt the vast machine of Empire at the gilded gates of the park.

All mine! she thought joyfully. *I am going to have him all to myself for a week.*

Thinking that he might be at his toilet, she turned and made quickly for the adjoining dressing room. Just then Constant came out, calm and smiling as ever, and bowed respectfully.

'May I assist mademoiselle?'

'Where is the Emperor? Is he already dressing?'

Constant smiled and, taking a large enamelled watch from his waistcoat pocket, studied it gravely.

'It is nearly nine o'clock, mademoiselle. The Emperor has been at work for more than an hour.'

'At work? But I thought ...?'

'That he was here for a rest? That is so indeed, but mademoiselle is not yet familiar with the Emperor's idea of a rest. It means simply that he will work a little less. Has mademoiselle never heard his favourite description of himself: "I was born and made for work—"?'

'No,' Marianne said, feeling somewhat disconcerted. 'But then, what shall I do meanwhile?'

'Breakfast is served at ten o'clock. Mademoiselle will have ample time to dress. Afterwards, the Emperor is accustomed to set aside some time for what he calls "recreation". Here he very often takes a walk. After that, he returns to his desk again until six o'clock, when he will dine and then spend the evening in a variety of ways.'

'Good God!' Marianne said weakly. 'How dreadful!'

'It is, indeed, rather taxing. But the Emperor may relax his rule somewhat in honour of mademoiselle. I should add that on Tuesday and Fridays, his majesty generally presides over his Council of State – but this is Wednesday and, by God's grace, the Trianon!'

'And it has been snowing and Paris is a long way away!' Marianne cried so impetuously that the faithful valet's eyes twinkled. 'I hope the Council of State will stay where it is until next Friday.'

'We may always hope. But at all events, mademoiselle need have no anxiety. The Emperor will not allow her to be bored or disappointed with her stay.'

In fact, for a creature like Marianne, bubbling over with youth and vitality, it was wonderful, tyrannous, absurd, agonizing and incredibly exciting all at once. She was discovering Napoleon as he really was and also that daily life with him, even when hemmed in by protocol and etiquette, was a continual adventure. The very first meal she had alone with him was a startling revelation.

She had been slightly puzzled when, as he opened the door for her, Constant had murmured in her ear:

'Mademoiselle would be advised to waste no time at the table in contemplating his majesty, especially if mademoiselle should be at all hungry, or she may be in some danger of rising from the table without having swallowed a morsel.'

But once seated, facing the Emperor across the large mahogany table, she forgot the warning. The table was laid with an exquisite blue Sèvers breakfast service and a great deal of cut glass, which went very well with the cutlery and the silver-gilt epergne. Napoleon attacked his food as though it were an English redoubt, but his eating habits were so eccentric that Marianne gazed at him in astonishment. He began with the cheese, swallowing a large slice of Brie, then, after selecting and disposing of a *timbale milanaise*, proceeded rapidly to an almond cream before finishing up by gnawing at a chicken wing à la Marengo. All that in the space of ten minutes, to the accompaniment of two glasses of Chambertin, and a shower of splashes and stains inseparable from such speed. Marianne, having practically fainted with horror at seeing him attack his chicken, had just decided that meals at the French court must be taken backwards, as in China, and was beginning at random on the almond cream, when Napoleon wiped his lips, threw his napkin down on the table, and exclaimed:

'What, not finished yet? You are a slow coach. Come along, hurry up, coffee will be here in a moment.'

Marianne was obliged to follow him with a sinking heart while Dumas, the butler, long accustomed to the vagaries of the Imperial digestion, did his best to hide a smile. The coffee, boiling hot and strong, went down Marianne's throat like a ball of fire, but her heroism earned her a beaming smile from Napoleon.

'Bravo!' he said, slipping his arm into hers. 'I too like my coffee very hot! Now go and fetch a coat and we'll go out. We must take advantage of this weather.'

In the bedroom she found Constant waiting imperturbably with a coat lined with miniver, and a hat and muff of the same fur, also borrowed from the wardrobe of the Princess Borghese, as well as a pair of pattens for the snow. As he helped her into the warm coat, Constant murmured softly:

'I did warn mademoiselle. But don't worry, when the Emperor returns to his desk I will see that a substantial collation is served to mademoiselle in here. Otherwise, since dinner will be the same as breakfast, mademoiselle would be in some danger of death by starvation.'

'And is it always like this?' Marianne sighed, calling to mind, with a good deal of admiration, the gracious figure of Joséphine who had lived this life for years on end. Then as she slipped her hands into her muff, she added in a different tone: 'Tell me, Constant, what would the Emperor's sister say if she knew I was wearing her clothes?'

'Nothing at all. Her highness would be in no way disturbed. She has so many dresses, coats and garments of all descriptions that she scarcely knows what belongs to her. The Emperor, and with some reason, has nicknamed her Our Lady of Frippery. Mademoiselle may see for herself! But hurry now, the Emperor does not like to be kept waiting.'

Marianne ran to meet Napoleon, thinking that a faithful servant was indeed a blessing of the gods. She was duly grateful for the help, at once friendly and discreet, which she received from the imperial valet. But for him, God alone knew how many mistakes she might have made!

He was waiting outside in the pillared walk, wearing a huge, frogged great-coat that made him look almost as broad as he was long, striding up and down so fast that Marianne wondered for a moment whether their walk might not turn out to be more in the nature of a military exercise. But he stopped when he saw her and tucking Marianne's arm beneath his own, said quietly: 'Come, and see how lovely it is.'

Arm in arm, they strolled across the vast, snow-covered park watched over by a still, sad population of statues. They walked beside frozen lakes where a queen had once skated, and where the bronze tritons and sea gods now turned slowly green in the loneliness of forgotten things, as uncared for as the cupid with the dolphin standing by his pool in the Hôtel d'Asselnat. The farther they went from the Trianon, the more they seemed to be entering an enchanted domain where time itself stood still.

They walked for a long time in silence, happy simply to be together, but gradually the tragic stillness of this park where everything had been created for the honour and glory of the most brilliant of all the kings of France, seemed to have an effect upon Napoleon. He stopped by the side of a great dead pool in the midst of which Apollo's chariot seemed to be striving uselessly to break free of its icy setting. Before them a long perspective of tall trees ended in the distance in a line of large and noble buildings. Marianne's hand tightened on her companion's arm.

'What is that?' She asked in a low voice, sensing instinctively that whatever it was, it belonged to the dead.

'Versailles,' he said.

Marianne caught her breath. The sun had gone in, as though unwilling to shine on the deserted dwelling of him who had taken it for his empire. The huge, empty palace slept in the grey light of a winter day, lightly shrouded in mist, while nature led the slow assault on its pure line with the relentless advance of moss-grown terraces and neglected gardens. The great spectre of departed royalty was so poignant that Marianne turned to the Emperor with eyes filled with tears. But the face she saw might have been carved from the same stone as the statues in the park.

'I can do nothing for it,' he said at last, gazing with brooding eyes on the huge, hollow monument. 'The people might rise against me if I so much as tried to restore it. The time is not yet. The people could not understand.'

'A pity. It would suit you so well —'

He thanked her with a smile and laid his hand over hers as it rested on his arm.

'I have sometimes dreamed. But one day, I too shall build a palace worthy of my power. On the hill of Chaillot probably. There are plans already. But there are still too many memories attached to this one, too many memories which the people still hate.'

Marianne said nothing. She dared not say that the imminent arrival of a niece of that martyred queen might well affect the French people more than the employment of a few hundred workmen at Versailles. Besides, she too had her memories. It was in the chapel of this palace, visible from where they stood, in the days when it seemed that Versailles must live forever, that her mother had been married. But she made no attempt to ask him to go nearer so as to see the chapel. She was too much afraid of feeling again the grief that had pierced her heart as she pushed open the door of her own ruined house. Instead, she only pressed a little closer to Napoleon and asked to go back.

In silence, as they had come, each wrapped up in their own thoughts, they made their way back to the Trianon from which a troop of mounted couriers was at that moment setting out in all directions, carrying the morning's letters. It was also time for the changing of the guard and all this gave to the palace an air of bustling activity.

But instead of returning to his desk as Constant had predicted, Napoleon led Marianne straight back to their bedroom and shut the door. Without a word, but with a desperate ardour that seemed as though it would never be quenched, he made love to her as he had never done before. It was as though he sought to draw from her young body all its reserves of fresh strength and energy to help him fight the invading shadows of the past. Perhaps he was trying in some way to combat an unacknowledged dread of the unknown Viennese in whose veins ran some of the blood of the Sun King himself.

Then, with no explanation beyond a long kiss and a brief 'See you later', he vanished, leaving her alone in the untidy room, an island of quiet in the midst of the Palace humming like a hive with military orders, the clatter and the coming and going of servants. But when, a few minutes later Constant entered gravely bearing a laden tray, Marianne had done her hair, restored some order to her clothes, and even made the bed, so embarrassed was she at what the solemn valet might think. She was very far, as yet, from having acquired the traditional shamelessness of a royal favourite.

However, this did not prevent her from devouring everything Constant set before her with the utmost enjoyment. The keen morning air and the lovemaking which followed had sharpened an already considerable appetite. When she had finished, she glanced at the valet gratefully.

'Thank you,' she said. 'That was lovely – though I doubt I shall be able to eat a mouthful at dinner.'

'I should not be so sure of that. In theory, dinner is at six, but if the Emperor takes it into his head to work later, he may well dine three or four hours after that.'

'It can't be fit to eat.'

'Not at all. The cooks have orders to keep something always ready, even if only a roast chicken. They put a fresh one on the spit every quarter of an hour, so that one is always ready when his majesty wishes to sit down.'

'And – do they get through a great many that way?'

'On one occasion, mademoiselle, we attained the figure of twenty-three,' he told her with pride. 'So mademoiselle has plenty of time in which to recover her appetite. I might add that most of those honoured with an invitation to the Imperial table are accustomed to take some precautions beforehand. If not, they are unlikely to satisfy themselves in ten minutes, especially as they are generally obliged to answer the Emperor, who talks incessantly without missing a mouthful.'

Marianne laughed. She enjoyed discovering Napoleon's little oddities, but, however surprising, she was much more inclined to find them funny than shocking. She loved him too well for that.

'Never mind, Constant,' she said. 'One does not need food when one is with the Emperor. That is enough in itself.'

The valet's broad, pale face was suddenly serious. He nodded.

'Mademoiselle says so because she truly loves the Emperor. But not everyone thinks as she does.'

'Are there really people who do not love him? Truly, I can't imagine it.'

'How could it be otherwise? He is so great, so powerful, so far above the common run of men! But he was not born to a throne and there are those who would a hundred times rather see the crown on the head of some half-witted scion of a royal house than worn by a man of genius who frightens them and makes them see themselves for what they are. Inferiority is never an agreeable sensation. There are some who avenge themselves by jealousy, hatred and ambition – he can trust no-one. His marshals are envious and think for the most part that they would have made better sovereigns than he, his family plague him constantly, his friends, or those who claim to be his friends, are for the most part only thinking of what they can get out of him – only his soldiers give him a simple, honest love. And that poor, sweet Empress who loved him and cared for him like the child she was never able to give him.'

Constant was speaking now without looking at Marianne and she realized that this was probably the first time he had spoken his thoughts aloud for a very long time. And he was doing it because he had sensed that Marianne truly loved the master he revered. When she spoke, it was so softly as to be almost a whisper.

'I know all that. The Grand Marshal said something of the kind yesterday and I have met the Empress. But what do you think of the one who is to come?'

Constant seemed to come back again to the real world. He shook his head, picked up the tray and moved a few steps towards the door as though unwilling to reply. But before opening it, he turned to Marianne and smiled rather sadly.

'What do I think, mademoiselle? Saving the respect I owe him, exactly what the grumblers of his Old Guard think as they sit round their fire. "The Tondu ought not to have sent his old woman packing! She brought him luck – and us too!"'

'The Tondu?'

'That's what they call him, and sometimes the Little Corporal, or Puss in Boots, or Père la Violette. I told you they worshipped him! They're old devils who fought their way through a good many campaigns and they are not often wrong! I'm afraid they may be right again. It wasn't an Empress from the Danube that he needed.'

That night, just as she was dropping off to sleep, her body overwhelmed by a delicious weariness, Marianne was surprised to see Napoleon leap out of bed, stark naked, as though the building were on fire. He put on his white flannel dressing gown and slippers, wound a white silk scarf about his head and, picking up a candlestick, was already making for his office when Marianne sat up amid the pillows and asked, like any young bride: 'Where are you going?'

'To work. Go to sleep!'

'Again? But what time is it?'

'Half past twelve. Go to sleep I tell you.'

'Not without you! Come here –'

She held out her arms, confident in the power her beauty had over his awakened senses. But he frowned and made as if to go. Then he seemed change his mind, put down the candle and came back to the bed. Marianne closed her eyes, but instead of kissing her parted lips he merely tweaked her ear hard.

'I have already told you, you are a dreadful siren, *mio dolce amore*, but don't abuse your power. I have just sent the Comte de Narbonne back to Munich as Ambassador with the King of Bavaria and I have important despatches to send him. Besides that, some rogues have been circulating counterfeit coins among the soldiers of one of my Irish régime nts stationed at Limoges and I forgot to deal with it –'

'State affairs, never anything but state affairs!' Marianne complained, tears starting to her eyes. 'I have so little of you to myself – and for so little time! You promised me a week.'

'And you have it. If you were the Empress, you would not have me for more than a few minutes a day, or not much more at least. I have cleared a space around us so as to be able to love you. Do not ask for more –'

'I wish I could help you – I mean, be useful to you in some way. I am nothing but an instrument of pleasure, a kind of odalisque for a busy sultan!'

He was not smiling now. Taking Marianne's head in his two hands he forced it gently back on to the pillow and then bent over her until all he could see were her wide eyes, ringed now with a faint bluish shade.

'Do you really mean that?'

'With all my heart – don't you know I am all yours?'

He kissed her, a long, passionate kiss, then muttered rapidly: 'One day, I shall remind you of those words. When I need you, I will tell you as frankly as today I tell you that I love you. But just at present, what I need is your love, your being here, your wonderful voice – and your body, of which I can never tire. Sleep now – but not too deeply. I shall wake you when I come back –'

Later, Marianne would often look back on those days at the Trianon. It was broken by the meals taken helter-skelter in the pretty room looking out over the bare, winter woods, by the long excursions on foot or on horseback in the course of which Marianne had been able to note that Napoleon was nowhere near as good a rider as herself, by long fireside talks and by the sudden bursts of passion which hurled them into one another's arms at the most unexpected moments and then left them panting and exhausted, like ship-wrecked mariners washed up on some strange shore.

During the hours Napoleon devoted to his exhausting work, Marianne also worked. On the second day, the Emperor had taken her into the music room and reminded her that before very long she would have to face the public in Paris. She had flung herself into her work with a new ardour, perhaps because she was conscious of him there, close by, and because sometimes he would slip quietly into the room to listen to her for a moment.

It was true, she had to do her studying alone, but she soon discovered in her lover an expert capable of appreciating the most obscure musical points. He was astonishingly versatile. He might have been as good a teacher as Gossec, just as he could have been a talented writer or a remarkable actor. As time went on, the admiration he inspired in his young mistress became stronger than ever. She longed desperately to be worthy of him, one day perhaps to reach those arid, inaccessible regions where he moved.

Yet perhaps conscious of the extent to which his bewitching Marianne had given herself to him, Napoleon gradually began to confide in her a little more. He would talk about certain problems, small ones perhaps, but which gave her an insight into the vastness and complexity of his task.

Each morning, she saw Fouché, her old tormentor, now become the most gallant and attentive of her admirers, appear in person to give the Emperor his daily report on all that was going on in his vast Empire. Whether in Bordeaux, in Anvers, in Spain, Italy or the smallest villages of Poland or the Palatinate, the Duke of Otranto's fantastic organization seemed, like some gigantic Hydra, to have an eye hidden everywhere. Let a grenadier be killed in a duel, an English prisoner escape from Auxonne, a ship from America dock in Morlaix with despatches or cargo from the Colonies, a new book appear, or a vagabond commit suicide, Napoleon would know it all the next day.

In this way Marianne learned, incidentally, that the Chevalier de Bruslart was still at large and the Baron de St Hubert had managed to make his way to the island of Hoedic, where he had boarded an English cutter, but she felt no great interest in the news. The only thing she wished to talk about was the one subject that no-one mentioned in her presence, that of the future Empress.

There seemed to be a conspiracy of silence on the subject of the arch-duchess. And yet, as time passed, her shadow seemed to loom ever larger over Marianne's happiness. The days were so short and passed so swiftly. But every time she tried to bring the conversation round to the arch-duchess, Napoleon side-stepped the issue with depressing skill. She sensed that he did not want to talk about his future wife to her and feared to see, in his silence, a greater interest than he cared to admit. And meanwhile, the hours flew by ever more swiftly, the wonderful hours that she so longed to hold back.

However, on the fifth day of her stay at the Trianon, something occurred which came as an unpleasant shock to Marianne and very nearly spoiled the end of her stay.

Their walk that day had been a short one. Marianne and the Emperor had intended originally to go as far as the village where Marie-Antoinette had once played at being a shepherdess, but a sudden fall of snow had forced them to turn back half-way. Soon the flakes were falling so thick and fast that in no time at all they were up to their ankles.

'Wet feet,' Napoleon said with finality, 'are the worst thing possible for the voice. You can visit the Queen's village another day. But instead – ' a gleam of mischief danced in his eyes, ' – instead, I'll promise you a first-rate snowball fight tomorrow!'

'A snowball fight?'

'Don't tell me you never played at snowballs? Or doesn't it snow in England nowadays?'

Marianne laughed. 'Indeed, it does! And snowballs might be thought a proper pastime for ordinary mortals – but for an emperor…'

'I have not always been an emperor, *carissima mia*, and my earliest battles were fought with snowballs. I got through a prodigious number of them when I was at college in Brienne. I'm a devil of a hand, you wait and see!'

Then he had slipped his arm about her waist and half-leading, half-carrying her, had set off at a gallop back to the rose-coloured palace where the lamps were already bright against the darkening sky. There, since the time set aside for 'recreation' was not yet over, the two of them had retired to the music room, where Constant brought them an English tea with buttered toast and jam which they ate in front of the fire, as Napoleon said, 'like an old married couple'. Afterwards, he asked Marianne to sit at the great gilded harp and play to him.

Napoleon was passionately fond of music. It calmed and soothed him and in his frequent periods of abstraction he liked to have it as a murmurous background to lend wings to his thoughts. Besides, the sight of Marianne seated behind the graceful instrument, her slender white arms etched against the strings, was to him an exquisite enchantment. And today, in a gown of watered silk the same green as her eyes that rippled to the light with every inclination of her body, her dark curls clustered high on her head and bound with narrow ribbons of the same subtle shade, pearl drops in her ears and more pearls, round and milky, like a huge cabochon between her breasts and joining the high waist, she was irresistible. She knew it, too, for while her hands played without effort the slight air by Cherubini, she could see dawning in her lover's eyes a look which she had learned to know. In a little while, when the last, vibrating notes had died away, he would rise without a word and take her hand to lead her to their room. A little while – and once more she would know those moments of blinding joy which only he could give her. But meanwhile the present, filled with sweet anticipation, had its own charm.

Unfortunately for Marianne, she was not allowed to enjoy it to the end. Right in the middle of her sonata, there came a timid scratching on the door which opened to make room for the furiously blushing face of a youthful page.

'What is it now?' Napoleon spoke curtly. 'Am I not to have an instant's peace? I thought I said we were not to be disturbed?'

'I – I know, sire,' stammered the wretched boy. It had obviously taken more courage on his part to enter the forbidden room than to storm an enemy redoubt. 'But – there is a courier from Madrid! With urgent despatches!'

'Despatches from Madrid invariably are,' the Emperor commented dryly. 'Oh, very well, let him come in.'

Marianne had ceased playing at the first words and now she rose hurriedly, preparing to withdraw, but Napoleon signed to her briefly to be seated. She obeyed, divining his annoyance at being disturbed and his reluctance to leave his comfortable fireside for the draughty corridors leading to his office.

The page vanished, with significant haste, to return a moment later and throw open the door to allow the entrance of a soldier so liberally plastered with mud and dust that it was impossible to see the colour of his uniform. The soldier advanced to the middle of the room and stood to attention, chin up, heels together, his shako on his arm. Marianne stared thunderstruck at a face fringed with a few days' growth of golden beard, a face she knew from the first moment, even before he fixed his eyes in a blank, military stare on the grey and gold silk covering the wall and spoke.

'Sergeant-Major Le Dru, with special despatches from his excellency the Duke of Dalmatia to his majesty the King Emperor. At your majesty's service!'

He it was, the man who had made a woman of her and to whom she owed her first, disagreeable experience of love. He had not changed much in these past two months, despite the ravages of fatigue upon his face, and yet Marianne had the feeling that she was looking at a different man. How, in so short a space of time, had Surcouf's sailor become transformed into this stony-faced soldier, the messenger of a duke? On his green jacket she noted with surprise the brand-new mark of the Légion d'Honneur. But Marianne had been long enough in France to realize the kind of magic which surrounded Napoleon. What might have seemed preposterous or absurd elsewhere was the daily bread of this strange country and the giant who ruled it. In no time at all, a ragged sailor out of an English prison hulk could become a hero of the army, galloping like a centaur from one end of Europe to the other.

Napoleon, hands clasped lightly behind his back, walked slowly round the newcomer who, stiff with pride and awe, strove desperately to overcome his weakness under this august scrutiny. Marianne sat wondering how long it would be before Le Dru's glance fell on her and what would happen then. She knew the Breton's impulsive nature too well not to fear the worst. Who could tell how he would react on seeing her? Better to slip away quietly now and disarm Napoleon's probable wrath later.

She rose, intending to make her way unobtrusively to a side door. As she did so, the Emperor stopped in front of Le Dru and put out a finger to lift the cross that glittered on his breast.

'You are a brave lad, it seems. Where did you get this?'

The soldier's set face flushed with pride.

'At Ciudad Rodrigo, sire. From Marshal Ney in person.'

'What for?'

'For – a peccadillo, sire.'

The Emperor's face lit briefly with his rare and wonderful smile. He put up his hand and tweaked the boy's ear. The young eyes filled with tears.

'I like such peccadillos,' Napoleon said, 'and I like your modesty. What is your message, my friend?'

Marianne had stayed where she was, held in spite of herself. After all, she thought, why should she run away? Her past was no secret from the Emperor now and even if Le Dru dared to attack her in his presence, he could not hurt her. Somewhere inside her, there was an irresistible curiosity, tinged perhaps with perversity, urging her to stay and watch this young man of whom at one time she had been so afraid, and towards whom she was no longer very sure what her feelings were. Quietly, she resumed her seat at the harp.

Le Dru was feverishly pulling a large sealed package from inside his jacket. His colour had faded and now he looked to Marianne to be growing paler with every second, as though about to collapse. The spasm of pain that crossed his face as he held out the despatch told her all she needed to know. She found her voice at last, experiencing a sense of excitement in thus challenging the danger.

'Sire,' she said tranquilly, 'this man can hardly stand. I am sure he must be wounded.'

At the sound of her voice, Le Dru turned to look at her. Marianne saw with some amusement the erstwhile sailor's blue eyes widen with astonishment.

'True, by thunder,' Napoleon began. 'Are you —'

The sound of the man's fall cut short his words. Le Dru had only held himself upright by a supreme effort of will but the unexpected shock of finding himself gazing full at Marianne had been too much for his overstrained nerves, and the courier from Madrid had fainted clean away at the Emperor's feet.

'Well, well,' commented his sovereign, 'if my dragoons take to swooning like green girls ...'

But even as he spoke, he was on his knees ripping open the high collar of the green dolman to give the man air. Blood spread in a widening stain across his shirt near the shoulder.

'You were right,' Napoleon said to Marianne, 'this man is wounded. Come and help me.'

She had already fetched a crystal decanter from a side table and was pouring a little water on to her handkerchief. Kneeling beside the Emperor on the carpet she began bathing Le Dru's temples, but without effect.

'He needs a cordial,' she said, 'and a doctor as well. Have we any brandy?'

'We call it cognac in this country,' Napoleon retorted. 'As for the doctor —'

He went quickly to the hearth and pulled the bell. The frightened page reappeared, his eyes growing rounder than ever with horror as he saw the man he had let in stretched unconscious on the floor.

'A doctor, at once,' the Emperor commanded. 'Also a stretcher and two footmen to see this man put to bed in the soldiers' quarters.'

'Send a wounded man out in the cold in this weather?' Marianne protested. 'Your majesty cannot be serious?'

'You may be right, though my soldiers have tough hides, you know.

Never mind. Have a room made ready for him here. Well, go on, hurry, imbecile! What are you waiting for?'

Le Dru must have been in the last stages of exhaustion. He was still deeply unconscious when the palace doctor appeared, accompanied by the servants who were to carry him to bed.

While the medical man made his brief examination, Marianne retired to an armchair and watched Napoleon break the seal on the despatches and cast a quick eye over them. She was disturbed to see him frown and look grim. The news must be bad. When he had finished reading, the Emperor crushed the thick sheet angrily in his fist.

'Incompetents!' he muttered between his teeth. 'I am surrounded by incompetents! Could there not be one person in my whole family capable of making reasonable plans, or at least of carrying mine out with disinterested greatness!'

Marianne said nothing. The words, she knew, were not addressed to her. For the moment, Napoleon had forgotten her, preoccupied as he was with the new problems raised by the despatch. He was talking to himself and to have risked a reply would inevitably have been to seek a rebuff. In any case the doctor was on his feet again.

'The man may as well be put to bed, sire,' he said. 'I will be able to attend to him more readily there.'

'See to it, then. But make sure he is fit to talk soon. I have several things to ask him.'

While the servants, acting on the doctor's instructions, were getting the unconscious Le Dru on to the stretcher, Marianne approached the Emperor who, with the letter still in his hand, was clearly about to depart for his office.

'Sire,' she said, 'have I your permission to go and inquire how the man does?'

'Are you afraid he will not be well cared for?' Napoleon sounded half angry, half in jest. 'My medical men know their job, I promise you.'

'It's not that. The reason I wish to learn how he goes on is because I know him.'

'What, another? You are as bad as Talleyrand for being intimately acquainted with half Europe! Do you mind telling me how you come to know this fellow who is sent from Spain when you yourself came straight from England?'

'I met him in England, on a stormy night in Plymouth Sound, on board the vessel belonging to Nicolas Mallerousse. He was escaping from the hulks. He had sailed under Surcouf and was with me when I was taken by the wreckers.'

Napoleon frowned. Evidently the story did not altogether convince him.

'I see,' he said sardonically. 'You are old comrades-in-arms! But what intrigues me is what your friend is doing in the dragoons? There is still fighting at sea and Surcouf needs men more than ever. And, I might add, his men are generally so devoted to him they would rather lose their right arms than leave him. So what is he doing on land? Was he seasick?'

Marianne began to wish she had not spoken. Napoleon's ironic tone boded no good and she even had a vague suspicion that he did not altogether believe her. But it was too late now to draw back. She could only go on to the end.

'He was indeed devoted to Surcouf but he loved the Emperor more,' she began cautiously, wondering how she was going to explain the episode at the Compas d'Or without provoking a storm and, still more important, without finding herself obliged to go into the mortifying happenings in the barn. It had not occurred to her that he could ask so many questions and as she paused, searching for a way to go on, she was expecting every instant to hear a dry: 'That is no explanation,' or something equally forbidding.

But to her surprise, the ominous crease vanished from the imperial brow, to be replaced by an indulgent smile.

'There are some such,' Napoleon said complacently. 'Very well, my heart, go and visit your fellow-fugitive whenever you wish, you have my permission. The page on duty, young St Géran, will take you. But don't forget what time we sup. Until then, farewell.'

A second later, to Marianne's intense relief, he was gone. She heard his quick tread fading down the corridor and could not repress a grateful sigh. It had been a near thing and she sank into a chair to recover. She was in no hurry to visit Le Dru. First, she needed time to think what she meant to say to him.

She was certainly under no obligation to go and see a person she had no cause to remember with kindness. If she made no move he might even think when he recovered consciousness that he had been under a delusion and had dreamed her sudden appearance. But the idea no sooner presented itself than Marianne rejected it. Le Dru might be a superstitious Breton, but he would hardly believe in hallucinations of that order. At least he would ask the doctor whether the woman in the green dress he had seen with the Emperor had been dream or reality. And how could she be sure that once he had learned the truth, he would not commit some folly in order to see her again? As a result of which Marianne would undoubtedly find herself compelled to furnish explanations infinitely more detailed than those she had already provided … No, her request to visit the injured man had been an inspiration. In that way she had every hope of doing away with misunderstandings and putting matters to rights with him without the Emperor suspecting anything.

Her mind made up, Marianne went to her room to fetch a large cashmere shawl in a mixture of autumnal shades from dark green to palest gold, and with this draped round her shoulders over the low-cut gown, she went in search of young St Géran to ask him to take her to the bedside of the wounded man.

The page was killing time out in the gallery, staring out with a disillusioned air at the sentries marching to and fro in the snow outside with their bearskin hats pulled well down to their eyebrows. He welcomed Marianne with eagerness.

'Do you know where the injured courier was taken?' she asked him. 'The Emperor wishes me to inquire how he does and would have you lead me to him.'

'It will be an honour, madame! He has been put in one of the small rooms upstairs.'

The boy was clearly delighted at the chance and Marianne suppressed a smile as she caught the admiration in his gaze. He could not have been more than fourteen or fifteen, but even at that age boys know beauty when they see it and Henri de St Géran had instantly constituted himself her slave. With the utmost dignity he went before her up the staircase and flung open the door of one of the rooms, then stood back for her to enter, inquiring politely if she wished him to wait for her.

'No, thank you. And I should prefer not to be disturbed.'

'As you wish, madame.'

With a lordly gesture he beckoned to the woman who sat by the bed and went out with her, closing the door behind him. Marianne was left alone with the wounded man. A deep silence reigned in the room and she hesitated a trifle nervously before going forward.

The curtains, patterned with exotic flowers, had been drawn against the early dark outside and the room was unlighted except for the glow of the fire in the hearth and the nightlight burning on a table by the bed.

The bed was placed in such a way that its occupant was unable to see the door and Marianne moved forward softly in case he should be asleep. It would scarcely be wondered at if he were after his long ride, and with his wound and the sedatives which the doctor must have given him. But then she heard a very human sound: someone sniffing hard, like a person who had been crying.

Without more hesitation, Marianne stepped up to the bed and into the pool of light thrown by the nightlight. Once there she saw that the man who had once sailed with Surcouf and was now a soldier of Napoleon was indeed crying like a baby.

At the sight of Marianne, however, Jean Le Dru stopped short and stared at her, without surprise this time but with sudden anger.

'What do you want?' he asked abruptly.

'To know how you feel – and also, perhaps, a little how we stand, you and I. Don't you think it might be time you confessed at last that you were wrong about me? And that we were both serving the same cause, you knowingly, I without yet being aware of it?'

She spoke with great gentleness, firstly because she was dealing with an injured and exhausted man, and secondly because she genuinely wished to make an end of the tragic misunderstanding which had developed between them as a result of the mischievous words of Morvan's vindictive mistress, Gwen. But the boy was determined to regard her as an enemy and no amount of sweetness in her voice could have any effect on him. He gave a short, bitter laugh.

'The same cause? When we know where you came from?'

Marianne shrugged, hugging the big, soft shawl more closely round her.

'When will you make up your mind to understand? Or are you really too stupid to accept the truth? When we met, I was escaping from the English police and you from the hulks. We were equal then. I had nothing left but my life and I did my best to keep that.'

'You seem to me to have succeeded admirably. When I asked just now who was the woman in the green dress I saw with the Emperor, no one could tell me your name but they said you were his latest love and that you were living here in this palace with him – and if I wept just now, it was for rage and helplessness because I was powerless to save him from you!'

Marianne had heard that Bretons were accounted unusually obstinate but she would never have believed they could be so to this extent. She sighed resignedly and sat down on the bottom of the bed.

'Suppose we have a little talk – if you are not too feverish.'

'I have not yet lost my reason.'

'Then try to use it. Let us take matters up from where we left off. When you denounced me and had me thrown into prison you were convinced, if I remember rightly, that I was an English spy sent here especially to bring about the downfall of the corsair, Robert Surcouf. Is that correct?'

'Correct,' Le Dru admitted unwillingly.

'I was therefore thrown into prison, only to be released through the intervention of that very Surcouf who did not seem to appreciate your part in the affair.'

'He sent me away,' the Breton said sourly. 'Sent me packing just like a felon, me, one of his best seamen who loved him more than anything in the world, except the Emperor, of course.'

'And I realize that is something you find hard to forgive me for. But afterwards, I had every chance to do what I liked with Surcouf. With you out of the way, I could carry out my supposed purpose at leisure?'

'Yes.'

'Are you trying to tell me that anything untoward has happened to the man you admire so much? I have not seen the baron since but I do know that he is at present at St Malo and threatened by no worse dangers than those he ordinarily runs at sea. So what do you think happened? Did I betray my masters and abandon my mission? Or will you finally admit that I was never a spy except in your own imagination?'

'The fact that you are here with the Emperor is the best answer to that. Beside him, even Surcouf is a poor prize! You'd be a fool to stick to the first when you could have the second!'

Marianne exclaimed angrily. She had a sudden, strong desire to slap the stubborn face which looked at her with such implacable sternness from the shadow of the bed curtains, but she controlled herself with an effort and managed to ask in a tone of the utmost detachment:

'And what, according to you, am I supposed to be doing with him? Am I to persuade him to abandon his empire and his subjects and go with me to England to live in perfect love so that, no doubt, I can hand him over duly bound and gagged to the British government? Or do you expect me to open the palace gates one dark night and let in a band of secret conspirators? Unless, of course I am hiding a dagger under my clothes –'

Sarcasm was, to all appearances, lost on Jean Le Dru. He was a Breton, solemn, obstinate and utterly without imagination. He answered roughly:

'I don't know. But I daresay you are quite capable of any of those.'

'Simply because I failed to return the sentiments you were pleased to feel for me,' Marianne finished for him calmly. 'It has not occurred to you that I too could love the Emperor as much or even more than you do, that I could be his in soul as much as in body?'

Jean Le Dru said nothing but his eyes closed for a second and Marianne could have sworn that a fresh tear slid furtively from beneath his lid.

'And yet, suppose it were so?' she persisted gently. 'Don't you think, you who serve him with such blind devotion, that he has charm and glory enough to make a woman mad about him? For that is what I am. Believe me or believe me not, Jean Le Dru, but I love Napoleon as no one, except perhaps the Empress Joséphine, has ever loved him. And, let me tell you, you are wrong once again if you think me at the peak of happiness. There is a poison in my joy. My days here can have no future to them because the future belongs to the one who comes here to marry him, the Austrian stranger who will take from me – and from you too, perhaps, a little of his heart! And you can never know how wretched I am!'

Le Dru spoke slowly, as though speech were infinitely painful to him.

'You love him – so much?' Then he added, as if to himself: 'Of course! How could it be otherwise! Even if you were the lowest of the low, you could not help it! I know he casts his spell on women almost as readily as he dominates men. No woman has been able to betray him yet and why should you be the first? No one can help but love him…'

'And yet, I know those who hate him, though it is true that they are men

...' She was silent for a moment, allowing the Breton to think his own thoughts. She knew, all her quick woman's intuition told her, that she was gaining ground and that his doubts were gradually lessening. After a few seconds, she stretched out her hand and laid it on the boy's hot, feverish one.

'Since we both love and serve the same master, can we truly not be friends, Jean Le Dru?'

'Friends? You and I?' he said slowly, as though striving to weigh the words he uttered. Then, with sudden anger: 'No! It cannot be!'

'Why not?'

'Because—' A pause, followed by an explosion. 'Because you are you. And because there has been that between us which I cannot forget! And yet, God knows I have done my best! When I entered the army, I knew it was for Spain but I was glad to go because it was a long way off and perhaps, I might not think of you when I was there. But you would not let me go, not for all the distance I travelled, not for the battles, the sun and the snow, the blood and all the horrors that I saw! You can have no idea what it is like, those frozen sierras where nothing seems to live, where one is cold and hungry and yet where death is hidden behind every rock, in every hollow – and such a death!'

Jean had forgotten Marianne. His eyes were wide open as if on a present terror. Marianne held her breath and when she spoke it was very gently, so as not to break in too suddenly on the tragic scenes she sensed were in his vision.

'Was it – so very dreadful?'

'Worse than that. The men there are savages! And worse than savages. I have seen savages in my seafaring days and none of them had faces so twisted with hatred and hideous cruelty. But these – these olive-skinned devils can make our poor fellows suffer endless tortures before they let them die. They are worse than animals! Woe betide any isolated detachments or any stragglers! They'll soon be carried off into some barn or other lonely spot by a band of leering demons, as often as not led by a priest waving a crucifix, and tortured cruelly. They even mutilate the wounded and not even dead men can be left in peace without their corpses being treated to fearful indignities. We found them all along the road, some half burned, others with their limbs lopped off, yet others nailed to trees or hung up by their feet, their eyes and nails torn out ...'

Marianne shrank with horror and put her hands before her eyes.

'For pity's sake – no more!' she cried. 'Don't say such things!'

He started at her cry and turned to look at her in vast surprise.

'Why not? They talk of us in drawing-rooms as barbarians. They say we burn villages and shoot the Spanish guerrilleros, but how can any man not give way to fury after seeing such sights? All we want is to give them back a taste of what they have done themselves, make them pay – for all that.' His voice changed suddenly as he added, quite calmly, as though making a simple statement of fact: 'There have been times in that hell when I have thought I was going mad – yet even then, I never managed to forget you. I think I even accepted it all because of you.'

'Because of me?'

'Yes, as if it were a price I had to pay.' And suddenly he turned on Marianne a pair of eyes so blue and innocent that she almost gasped. 'I know that you are far from me by birth, that you are an aristocrat, but all that counts for very little in the Emperor's armies, because there are ways of lessening the distance. Men whose fathers were innkeepers or blacksmiths have been known to rise to high rank, earn pensions and titles and marry duchesses. And however much I might pretend I had gone there to forget you; the truth was that I was hoping to become someone – someone who could address you as an equal. But now, it is all up with that – all up with everything! What can I do to compete with the Emperor? I have not even the right to be jealous of him, while as for bearing him a grudge – that I could never do.'

He turned on his side abruptly, and hid his face in his folded arm. Marianne found herself gazing in perplexity at the shirt covering one thin bony shoulder and a mop of tousled fair hair.

For a second she was unable to speak. The boy's naive and touching confession that he had done his best to hate her and only succeeded in loving her the more, and had undergone the most frightful dangers in the vague hope of one day winning her, wrung her heart. She suddenly wanted very much to be done once and for all with all misunderstandings and get back to the comradeship they had shared on board Black Fish's boat, when they were no more than escaped prisoner and fugitive. She realized that those were the only moments which had really mattered to her and that this odd, rough, unsophisticated boy was dearer to her than she knew.

As she bent over him, she heard him muttering:

'I cannot fight my Emperor – all I can do is go back there, when I am better, and hope that this time it will make an end of me.'

Tears sprang to her eyes and she put out her hand and began gently, very gently to stroke the roughened hair.

'Jean,' she said softly, 'please, don't cry! I do not wish to cause you such unhappiness. I can't bear to see you so distressed.'

'There's nothing you can do about it, is there?' he answered in a muffled voice. 'It isn't really your fault that I fell in love with you … and not your fault at all if you love the Emperor … if anyone's to blame it is myself.' He looked up suddenly and his blue, tear-drenched eyes fastened on Marianne's. 'It is true that you do love him, isn't it? That, at least, was no lie?'

'It is true – I swear it on my mother's memory and it is true that I am very nearly as wretched as you are yourself and you would do wrong to be jealous of him. I may not have the right to love him for much longer. And so – I wish we could be friends now, you and I.'

Jean sat up suddenly and, taking Marianne's two hands in his, drew her down to sit beside him on the bed. He was smiling a little wistfully but his anger had gone.

'Friends? You are sorry for me, is that it?'

'No. It is not pity. It is something else, something deeper and warmer than that. I have met many people since I saw you last, but very few have made me want their friendship. But I do want yours. I – I think I am fond of you.'

'In spite of everything that happened between us?'

Before Marianne could answer, a harsh voice spoke from behind the curtains close to her ear.

'And I should like to know precisely what it was that did happen between you.'

At the sudden appearance of Napoleon, Jean Le Dru gave a cry of alarm but strangely enough, Marianne showed no sign of shock. She stood up quickly, hugging her shawl more closely around her, and folded her arms.

'Sire,' she said boldly, 'I have learned to my cost, on more than one occasion, that listeners hear nothing to their advantage and in general miss the real sense of what they over-hear.'

'By God, madame,' the Emperor said in a voice of thunder, 'are you accusing me of listening at keyholes?'

Marianne curtseyed, smiling. This was in fact precisely what she meant, but he must be made to admit it without an outburst of wrath for which the injured man might suffer.

'Not at all, sire. I merely wished your majesty to know that if you desire any further information as to my past dealings with Jean Le Dru I shall be happy to supply it myself, later on. It would be unkind to question one so truly devoted to his Emperor, and who has suffered so much in his service. I cannot think your majesty has come here with that in view.'

'I have not. I desire to ask this man some questions ...'

The curt voice left no doubt of his intentions. Marianne sank into a deep, respectful curtsey and with a smile and a pleasant word of farewell to Jean Le Dru, left the room.

Back in her own apartment, she had little time to prepare herself for the storm she guessed was coming. This time she would not escape close questioning. She would have to tell him everything, except the episode in the barn which nothing on earth would force her to confess. And this not for her own sake alone. She was herself too much in the grip of jealousy not to feel strongly tempted to tell Napoleon frankly that Jean Le Dru had been her first lover. But there would be no enjoyment for anyone but herself in arousing the imperial jealousy and poor Le Dru would very likely have to bear the consequences. Moreover, she was under no obligation to mention an amorous incident which she only wished to forget. It was enough – but Marianne's reflections were interrupted at this point by the Emperor's return.

At first Napoleon merely threw her a glance loaded with suspicion and began striding nervously up and down the room, his hands clasped behind his back. Marianne forced herself to keep calm, and going to a chaise-longue near the fire reclined upon it in a graceful posture, arranging the shimmering folds of her dress becomingly about her ankles. Above all, she must not appear ill at ease, must not let him see the small, nagging fear within her or the unnerving effect his anger always had on her. Any moment now, he would come to a halt in front of her and fire his first question …

Almost before the thought was formulated, he was there, saying in a harsh voice:

'I imagine you are now ready to explain, madame?'

The formal address made Marianne's heart contract. No hint of softness or affection showed in the marble severity of his face – no trace of anger, either, which was infinitely more disturbing. Even so, she managed to conjure up a gentle smile.

'I thought I had already told the Emperor the circumstances of my meeting with Jean Le Dru?'

'Indeed. But your confidences did not extend to the most intriguing parts of what – er – happened between you. And it is just this which interests me.'

'And yet it is hardly worth it. It is a pathetic tale, the tale of a boy in unusual and tragic circumstances falling in love with a girl who could not return his feelings. Out of pique, perhaps, he preferred to listen to certain slanderous stories presenting her as the irreconcilable enemy of his country and of all he held most dear. The misunderstanding grew to such an extent that the time came when he denounced her as an agent of the princes and an émigrée returned to France illegally. That is more or less the whole of what happened between Jean Le Dru and myself.'

'I do not care for "more or less"! What else?'

'Nothing, except that his love changed to hatred because Surcouf, the man he worshipped most next to yourself, dismissed him for what he had done. He entered the army, was sent to Spain – and your majesty knows the rest.'

Napoleon gave a short laugh and resumed his walking up and down, although more slowly now.

'From what I saw, not an easy tale to believe! I'll take my oath that had I not come in, the fellow would have taken you in his arms. I'd like to know then what nonsense you'd have told me.'

Stung by the contempt in his voice, Marianne rose, white-faced. Her green eyes met the Emperor's, flashing a greater defiance than she knew.

'Your majesty is in error,' she retorted proudly. 'Jean Le Dru would not have taken me in his arms. It was I who would have taken him in mine!'

The ivory mask had grown so deathly pale that Marianne found herself exulting wickedly in her power to hurt him. Disregarding the menacing gesture he made, she stood her ground as the Emperor bore down on her, eyeing her relentlessly. Nor did she flinch when Napoleon caught her wrists in a grip of steel.

'*Per bacco!*' he swore. 'Do you dare—?'

'Why not? You asked for the truth, sire, and I have told it you. I was about to take him in my arms, as one would do to anyone one wished to comfort, like a mother with a child—'

'Cease this farce! Why should you comfort him?'

'For a bitter grief – the grief of a man who finds his love again only to see her in love with another, and worse than that, with the one man it is forbidden him to hate, because he worships him! Can you dare say that does not merit some comfort?'

'He has done you nothing but harm and yet you could feel such compassion for him?'

'He harmed me, yes, but I think that I did worse to him unwittingly. I want to forget the wrongs that lay between us and remember only what we suffered together and that Jean Le Dru saved my life, and more than that, when I was washed up from the sea into the hands of the wreckers.'

Napoleon was silent. Marianne could see his taut face close to hers. His fingers bruised her wrists until the pain brought tears into her eyes. He was breathing hard and she was conscious of the hot breath on her eyeballs.

'Swear to me,' he rasped into her face, 'swear to me that he has never been your lover ...'

The moment she dreaded had come and Marianne almost swooned with the anguish of it. She could not lie and yet she had to lie to him, to the man she loved more than all else. If she refused him the oath, he demanded he would banish her without mercy. Within the space of a few minutes, she would have left the Trianon, banished like a slave who had ceased to please, for she knew that he would give no quarter. Already he was growing impatient, was shaking her roughly.

'Swear, I tell you! Swear, or get out!'

No, that she could not take. They could not ask her to tear out her own heart. Mentally praying for forgiveness, she closed her eyes and with a little moan—

'I swear,' she said. 'He has never been my lover ...'

'That is not enough. Swear by the great love you say you bear me!'

The pain of her wrists made her cry out.

'For pity's sake! You're hurting me!'

'Never mind. I want the truth –'

'I swear, swear there was never anything between us – I swear it by the love I bear you!'

'Take care! If you are lying, our love will not endure …'

'I am not lying!' she cried in terror. 'I love only you … and I have never loved that boy. I feel nothing for him but pity – and a little kindness.'

Only then did the terrible fingers relax their hold.

'Good,' the Emperor merely said. He took a deep breath. 'Remember you have sworn.'

Superstitious, like all Corsicans, he attached an almost fanatical importance to oaths and feared the vengeance of fate on perjury. But the ordeal had been too much for Marianne. Once the cruel hands no longer supported her, she fell to the ground, convulsed with sobs. She was broken by the fright she had endured and also by shame that was already overwhelming her for her perjured oath.

But she had been forced to do it, as much for Napoleon himself as for the wretched Le Dru.

For an instant longer, the Emperor remained motionless, as though petrified, listening perhaps to the chaotic pounding of his own heart as it slowly returned to normal. The hand he brushed across his forehead was trembling slightly. Then, suddenly, he seemed to become aware of the desperate weeping that filled the room. He looked down and saw the girl huddled at his feet in heartbroken tears, and at the pitiful sight the demon jealousy relaxed its grip at last. Kneeling swiftly, he put his arms around her and gently raised the tear-stained face to his and began covering it with kisses.

'Forgive me – I am a brute but I cannot bear the thought of another man touching you. Don't cry now, *mio dolce amore* – It's all over now. I believe you –'

'T-truly?' she sobbed. 'Oh, you must believe me – or the grief of it would kill me. I couldn't bear it.'

He laughed suddenly, the young, light-hearted laughter that sometimes followed his worst rages.

'I will only let you die of love. Come, we must wipe out all this.'

He helped her to her feet and holding her close against him led her softly to the bed. Marianne went with him, scarcely conscious. But he was right, only love could restore them to what they had been before the arrival of the courier from Madrid. She felt the silk counterpane beneath her shoulders and closed her eyes with a sigh.

Some while later, as Marianne emerged from her happy trance, she saw Napoleon leaning on his elbow gazing earnestly at the great purple bruise that marked one of her wrists. Thinking that she could guess his thoughts, she tried to draw her hand away but he held it fast and laid his lips to the place. She expected some word of regret but all he said was:

'Promise me you will not try to see that boy again.'

'What! Are you still afraid —'

'Not in the least! But I should prefer you not to see him. Love is too strong.'

She smiled a little sadly. What a man he was, and how hard it was to understand him. When he himself was actually on the point of taking a new bride, he could still demand that his mistress break off all connection with another man whose only fault was that he loved her. She might perhaps have said something of this, when another idea came to her. Very well, it should be tit for tat. She would make a bargain with him.

'I promise,' she said sweetly, 'but on one condition —'

He stiffened at once and jerked away from her a fraction.

'A condition? What is it?'

'That you repair the hurt I inflicted without meaning to. Don't let him go back to that dreadful Spain where he will get killed for nothing, for a country he does not know and cannot understand. Send him back to Baron Surcouf. One word from you and he will certainly forgive him and take him back. Then he will have the sea again, and the life he loves, and a man he loves to serve under, and so he will more easily forget me.'

For a moment there was silence. Then Napoleon smiled. He gave Marianne's earlobe a gentle, loving little tug.

'There are times, *carissima mia*, when you make me feel ashamed, and I tell myself I do not deserve you. Of course, I promise. He shall not go back to Spain ...'

When Marianne took her seat at the supper table two hours later, she found beside her place a green leather case stamped with the imperial arms. Inside, were two wide bracelets of chased gold set with a pattern of seed pearls but when, the next day, she sought discreetly for news of Jean Le Dru, she learned that he had left the palace at dawn in a closed carriage for an unknown destination.

She experienced a momentary sadness but she was bound by her promise and, when all was said, only one thing mattered to her. The single cloud that had nearly overshadowed these few days of happiness had disappeared, leaving her free to enjoy the last hours of this wonderful gift from heaven in peace. There was so little time.

On the last evening, though she desired above all to leave him an unforgettable memory, it was all Marianne could do to smile. She felt deathly sad. For dinner, the last they would have alone together, she dressed with special care, striving to make herself more beautiful than ever. Her dress of heavy, pale-pink silk moulded every line of her body. Her neck and shoulders rose from the draped and silvered corsage as though from a huge, dew be-spangled flower, and not a single jewel broke the pure line of her throat. The high-piled curls held in place by silver ribbon showed off the graceful poise of her head. But the green eyes under their soft, sepia lashes were bright with unshed tears.

For once, the meal took longer than usual, as though Napoleon too thought to prolong these last private moments. When at last they rose from the table, he took Marianne's hand and kissed it tenderly.

'Will you sing for me tonight? Just for me?'

Her eyes said yes, and leaning on his shoulder, she went with him to the music room. Gently he seated her at the gilded harpsichord but instead of going away and sitting down, he remained standing behind her, his hands gripping her shoulders.

'Sing,' he told her softly.

Marianne could not have said what made her, in that grieving moment, choose the sad song which Marie-Antoinette had once sung, here in this very Trianon, for the handsome Swede with whom she was secretly in love.

'C'est mon ami, rendez-le moi,
J'ai son amour, il a ma foi,
J'ai son amour, il a ma foi.'

Sung by her warm voice, the words of love and regret became charged with such a poignant sadness that on the last note the melody broke and Marianne's head drooped. But the hands on her shoulders became hard and commanding.

'Don't cry,' Napoleon said. 'I forbid you to cry.'

'I – I can't help it. It's stronger than I am.'

'You have no right! I have told you; I must have a wife who will give me children. No matter whether she is pretty or ugly, so long as she can give me fine boys! I will give her that which is due to her rank, but you, you will always be my escape. No! Don't turn around! Don't look at me! I want you to trust me, as I trust you – she shall never have what I have given you and will give you again. You shall be my eyes, my ears – my star.'

Overwhelmed Marianne closed her eyes and sank back against Napoleon. The burning hands on her shoulders came to life, slowly caressing the smooth skin, moving down towards her breasts.

The little room was warm and very private. A deep silence fell, scarcely broken by Marianne's trembling sigh.

'Come,' Napoleon murmured hoarsely. 'We still have one night left.'

Early the next morning, a closed carriage left the Trianon at full gallop bearing Marianne back to Paris. This time she was alone, but to avoid any risk of a repetition of what had occurred on the way back from La Celle St-Cloud, a company of dragoons was to follow at a distance as far as the

362

bariére de Passy.

Never had Marianne's heart felt so heavy. Muffled in the big green velvet cloak she had worn on her arrival, she gazed out absently at the passing wintry landscape. The morning was very cold and grey. It was as though the world had used up all its store of joy. It made no difference that she knew nothing was at an end between Napoleon and herself. It made no difference that he had sworn to her that as the ties between them were now too strong for anything to harm them, not even the marriage of convenience which he was bound to make. Still Marianne could not help thinking that never again would things be as they had been during those few days. For an instant, her love had shone out in the broad light of freedom, now it must return to shadows and secrecy. For however strong the passion which bound her to the Emperor, in future there would always be between them the figure, vague as yet, of the wife who officially would have all and who must not be offended. And Marianne, in an agony of fear and jealousy, could not help trembling at the thought of what might happen if Marie-Louise had only a fraction of the irresistible charm of the unfortunate Marie-Antoinette. Suppose she were to resemble her ravishing aunt, that proud bewitching creature for whom so many men had been prepared to die? Suppose he were to love her? He was so easily won by women's charms.

Furiously, Marianne dashed away the tears which ran unbidden down her face. She was impatient now to return to Fortunée Hamelin and her friend Jolival. For the present, they alone were real to her. Never had she felt such a rush of warmth and affection as she did now. At the thought of Fortunée's little bright salon where, very soon, she would be sitting down to the fragrant morning coffee which Jonas made so well, Marianne felt her pain ease a little.

The coach descended the hill of St-Cloud towards the bridge. But shimmering in the mist beyond the tree and beyond the quicksilver band of the river, she saw the blue-tinged roofs of Paris topped by so many grey-white plumes from the smokey chimneys. For the first time, she was struck by the sheer size of the city. Paris lay stretched at her feet like a huge, tame animal and suddenly she had an irresistible desire to master this beautiful quiet monster, and make it cry out for her more loudly still than it would cry out for her rival when she drove for the first time through its streets.

To conquer Paris, to win first Paris and then all France and all the vast Empire, that, surely, was a task inspiring enough to soothe the bitterest regrets of the heart? In a few weeks' time, Marianne would be facing her first battle with this great and fiercely artistic city, whose seething life she could feel almost like the blood in her own veins. There was no time to waste now if she were to be prepared to face that fight.

Filled with a sudden impatience, she leaned forward and tapped on the little window to attract the coachman's attention.

'Faster!' she told him. 'I am in a hurry.'

At the bridge of St-Cloud, the rough-shod horses sprang into a gallop and at the barrière de Passy, while the dragoons vanished into the morning mist, the carriage with the imperial arms plunged hell for leather across Paris, as though already charging to the attack.

That night, a proclamation appeared on all the walls of the capital.

'A marriage will take place between his majesty the Emperor Napoleon, King of Italy, Protector of the Confederation of the Rhine, Mediator of the Swiss Confederation and her Imperial and Royal Highness the Arch-duchess Marie-Louise, daughter of His Majesty the Emperor Francis, King of Bohemia and of Hungary …'

There was no going back now. Fate was on the move, and, while Marianne was endlessly rehearsing with Gossec a melody from 'Nina, or the Lovesick Maid', Napoleon's sister Caroline Murat, Queen of Naples and Grand Duchess of Berg, and Marshall Berthier, Prince of Neuchâtel and Wagram, were already making ready for their journey to Vienna to bring back the bride.

CHAPTER EIGHTEEN
Time Returns

Marianne kicked with one small gold satin slipper at a log which had rolled out of the grate. She picked up the tongs and rearranged the smouldering logs before returning to curl up again in the big armchair at one side of the fire, and resumed her musings. It was Tuesday, the 13th March, 1810, the day on which she had moved into the Hôtel d'Asselnat, repaired in record time by one of those miracles which only the Emperor knew how to create. This was her first evening in her own home. For the first time for many weeks, Marianne was absolutely alone.

This was how she had wanted it. She would have no-one to come between herself and the ghosts of her family for this, her first acquaintance with the old house in its new dress. Tomorrow, the doors would open wide for her few friends, for Arcadius de Jolival who had taken lodgings in a house nearby, for Fortunée Hamelin with whom Marianne meant to celebrate her entry into possession worthily, for Talleyrand who, in these last weeks, had been a discreet and attentive friend, for Dorothée de Périgord, who had promised to bring the best society to call on her, and, lastly, for her teacher Gossec, who would come tomorrow as he did every morning, to help prepare her for her first contact with the public of Paris. Tomorrow, there would be all sorts of things, known and unknown, faces that would all soon be familiar. But tonight, she wanted to be alone, to listen to the silence of her house. There must be no stranger, however friendly, to disturb her first meeting with her own memories.

The servants, carefully hand-picked by Madame Hamelin, would not arrive until tomorrow. Mademoiselle Agathe, the young ladies' maid, would not be coming to take possession of the little room which had been set aside for her near Marianne's own until after eight o'clock. Only young Gracchus-Hannibal Pioche, newly promoted to the rank of coachman, was in the house, and even he had his own quarters in an outbuilding. He had orders not to disturb Marianne on any account. She had found it by no means easy to escape from the attentions of her friends. Fortunée in particular had been decidedly unwilling to leave Marianne all alone in the great house.

'I should die of fright if it were me!' she had declared roundly.

'What is there to be afraid of?' Marianne had answered. 'There I shall really be at home.'

'Yes, but remember, the portrait and the prowler comes here —'

'I think he must have gone for good now. And besides, the locks have been changed.'

It was true that all attempts to trace the mysterious visitor had been unsuccessful. There was no sign of the missing portrait of the Marquis d'Asselnat in spite of all Arcadius' investigations. A time had come when Marianne had begun to wonder if she had not really dreamed it all. If Fortunée and Arcadius had not been there also, she would have begun to doubt her own memory.

Wrapped in a long house gown of white cashmere, its high neck and long sleeves edged with ermine, Marianne looked round her at the big, bright, cosy room which tonight had become her own.

Her eye rested in turn on the soft blue-green hangings, the exquisite lacquered corner cupboards, the small chairs upholstered in a gaily flowered Aubusson, the great bed draped in changeable taffetas, and came to rest at last on a big céladon vase filled with lilac, irises, and huge tulips. The blaze of colour and freshness made her smile. Those flowers were like a presence in themselves, his presence.

They had arrived that morning, armfuls of them, brought by the gardeners of St-Cloud, and the whole house was full of them, but the best of all were in Marianne's own room. She found them better company than any human being because she was conscious of their fragrance even when she was not looking at them.

Marianne closed her eyes. Several weeks had passed since those days at the Trianon, but she was still living under their spell. And it would be much, much longer before she ceased to regret their brevity. It had been an instant of paradise which she would cherish for ever in her inmost heart, like a tiny, delicate and fragrant plant.

Marianne got up from her chair with a sigh, stretched and went across to one of the windows. On the way, her foot brushed against a newspaper that lay on the floor. It was the latest number of the *Journal de l'Empire* and Marianne was all too familiar with its contents. In it the people of France were informed by the writer, Joseph Fiévée, that on this day, the 13th of March, their future Empress had left Vienna with her household. She had already been married to the Emperor by proxy in the person of Marshal Berthier, , prince of Neuchâtel (and also of Wagram). In a few days, the Empress would be in Paris and then Marianne would no longer have the right to cross the threshold of the great bedchamber in the Tuileries, where she had been so many times since her return from the Trianon that she had finally begun to feel at home there.

When she tried to picture this unknown Marie-Louise, who would so soon become a part of the Emperor's life, Marianne still found herself shaking with an anger and jealousy all the greater because she had neither the right nor the opportunity to show them. Napoleon was marrying for purely dynastic reasons. He would listen to no arguments that went against his determination to have a son. He himself was endlessly jealous and watchful, and had questioned Marianne more than once about the real state of her relationship to Talleyrand and, even more, with Jason Beaufort, who he seemed unable to forget. But he would not have countenanced a similar display on her part, or not where his future wife was concerned. And, little by little, Marianne had come to feel an all-embracing sympathy for his divorced wife, Joséphine.

One day in the middle of February she had gone with Fortunée Hamelin to call on the ex-Empress. She had found her as melancholy as ever although apparently resigned, but when the Empress's name was mentioned, tears were never far away.

'He has given me a new châteaux,' Joséphine had said pathetically. 'The châteaux of Navarre, not far from Évreux , and says he hopes that I shall like it. But I know why, it is because he wants me to be out of Paris when she arrives – that other!'

'The Austrian!' Fortunée spoke angrily. 'The French have been quick to call her that. They have not forgotten Marie-Antoinette.'

'Oh no. But they are sorry now, and they will do their best to make the niece forget the sufferings of her aunt.'

To Marianne, Joséphine was especially kind. She seemed delighted to learn of the distant kinship between them and immediately embraced the younger woman with a quite motherly affection.

'I hope that you, at least, will remain my friend, although your mother gave her life for the late queen.'

'I hope you cannot doubt it, madame. Your majesty shall have no more faithful or loving servant than myself. Make what use of me you will.'

Joséphine smiled faintly and brushed Marianne's cheek with her finger.

'Indeed – you love him too! And I have heard that he loves you. Look after him, I beg of you, as far as you may. I foresee grief and disappointment ahead. How can this girl have been brought up as a Habsburg and to hate the victor of Austerlitz, how can she love him as I do when only six months ago, he occupied her own father's palace?'

'And yet, it is said your majesty approved this marriage?'

There had been many rumours to the effect that Joséphine had been personally concerned in the choice of her successor.

'One must choose the lesser of two evils. The Austrian was better for the Emperor than the Russian. And I shall always place the Emperor's good before my own personal satisfaction. If you love him truly, cousin, you will do the same.'

Marianne had devoted much thought to those words of Joséphine's. Had she, the newcomer, any right to raise the slightest protest to make any complaint of her own sufferings when this woman was prepared to wipe out so many years of glorious memories? Joséphine left a throne as well as a husband. The sacrifice that Marianne must make seemed very pale in comparison, though none the less cruel in her own eyes. But at least she had hope for the future in looking forward to a great career as a singer. That in itself was no small blessing.

She had been standing leaning her burning forehead on the cold glass to cool it when she started suddenly. Penetrating the mists of melancholy into which she had fallen, she had heard footsteps, stealthy, but distinct, on the small wooden staircase that led up to the attic floor.

Wide awake now, Marianne went to the door, holding her breath. She was not afraid. The sense of being at home in her own house sustained her. It occurred to her that Gracchus-Hannibal might have come into the house for some reason, though why she could not think. Besides, had it been he, she would have heard him walking about downstairs, not over her head. No, it was not Gracchus. Then she thought of the mysterious person who had been there on their first visit, of the hiding place which they had never discovered. Had the unknown prowler returned? Yet how could he have got in? He could hardly have lived in the abbe's old hiding place all these weeks without being discovered by the workmen swarming over the house. Softly, with infinite caution, Marianne opened her bedroom door. It gave on to the broad landing at the head of the great stone staircase, and she was just in time to see a glimmer of candle-light in the doorway of the main salon. This time, it was beyond a doubt. Someone was there.

Marianne glanced about her for some weapon. If this were a prowler, then she must have something to defend herself with. But there seemed to be nothing apart from a China vase or a jade statuette standing on a chest of drawers, neither of which would be of much use if it came to a fight. The mysterious visitor might be armed. Suddenly she remembered. Turning back into the room she went quickly over to a beautiful Venetian cabinet which Fortunée had found and presented to her, insisting that she absolutely must have something in the way of local colour. Opening it, she took out a long, flat, satinwood case inlaid with silver. When opened this revealed a pair of magnificent duelling pistols. Napoleon himself had given his mistress this unusual present, one of many.

'A woman like you should always have the means of self-defence to hand,' he had told her. 'I know that you can handle a gun and these may be useful to you one day. The times we live in are not so secure that a woman can be safe, alone and unarmed in her own house.'

Grasping one of these pistols firmly, Marianne loaded it and then, slipping it into the folds of her white gown, made her way back to the landing. She could still see the yellow light. It seemed to be moving about slowly, as though whoever was carrying it were looking for something. Unhesitatingly, Marianne began to walk downstairs.

Before leaving her room, she had kicked off her slippers at the foot of her bed. Now barefooted on the tiled floor, she neither felt the cold nor made the smallest noise. She was not in the least afraid. The weapon cradled in her hand put her on an equal footing with any burglar. What she felt was more a kind of exultation, and a sense of heightened curiosity like that of someone who, after living with a mystery for a long time, suddenly finds the key put into his hand. She no longer had the slightest doubt that the stranger moving about in the salon with a candle at this hour was the same person who had removed the portrait.

She reached the foot of the stairs, but although the double doors leading into the main salon stood wide open, she could see nothing beyond the candle-light, now stationary, and the restored fireplace with the last embers dying in the hearth, and the great, empty panel of yellow damask above it. By Marianne's wish nothing hung there because it seemed to her that nothing should be put in place of the vanished picture.

Thinking that the thief, if thief there was, must be going round the room, probably estimating the value of the works of art it now contained, she decided not to go in through the main door. Facing her, the smaller one leading into the Music Room was part open. From there she thought she might be able to see her nocturnal visitor without being seen. Very gently she pushed the door wider and went into the little room to which there already clung a faint fragrance of her chosen scent of tuberoses. Enough light came in from the salon next door to enable her to move about without bumping into the furniture. She saw the music she had put out ready for her lesson tomorrow on the pianoforte, stepped round the big, elaborately gilded harp and reached the door. The velvet curtain offered her a refuge from which to peep into the salon. It was all she could do to hold back an exclamation of surprise. Her visitor was a woman.

From where she stood, Marianne could see her only from the back, but there was no escaping the dress, which seemed to be grey, and the hair bundled up in an untidy knot. She was a small frail looking woman, but she carried herself as straight as a ramrod. In her hand she carried a heavy silver candlestick and she did seem to be making a circular tour of the room. She paused for a moment before the fireplace and Marianne saw her lift her arm so that the candle light fell on the empty space. She heard a short, dry laugh with such a note of mockery in it that she could no longer doubt that she was looking at the thief. But who was she, and what did she want?

A dreadful thought struck her. Suppose this woman were something to do with Fanchon-Fleur-de-lys and the crone were once more on her track? Who could say whether the rest of the gang were not also in the house and any moment the hideous creature and her two associates, the frightful Requin and the pale Pisse-Vinaigre would not suddenly appear? Already, it seemed to her that she could hear the tapping of a stick on the stone floor in the hall.

Then, suddenly, Marianne stopped thinking and sprang forward, driven by an impulse stronger than any reason. The woman had moved on beyond the fireplace and was making for a damask curtain with an air of unmistakable purpose. Marianne realized with horror that she was going to set fire to it. In a flash, she had left her hiding place and taken several strides into the room, the muzzle of her pistol levelled at the unknown. Her voice rang coldly in the silence.

'Can I help you?'

The woman swung round with a cry. Marianne saw a face of no particular age or beauty, or rather one that might perhaps have been beautiful, but for the great arrogant beak of a nose which dominated it. The skin on the fleshless face was dry and sallow and the thick, grizzled hair seemed too heavy for the little head that carried it, but the eyes, an innocent baby blue, were so round with terror as to relieve Marianne instantly of any fears she might have felt. The mysterious wanderer looked exactly like a frightened hen. Calmly, although still without lowering her weapon, Marianne walked towards her, but to her surprise the other woman backed away fearfully holding out trembling hands as though to ward off some nightmarish vision.

'Pierre!' she muttered in a shaky voice. 'Pierre, oh my God!'

'Are you unwell?' Marianne enquired pleasantly. 'And do please put down that candle before you set the house on fire.'

The woman seemed completely overcome. Still staring at Marianne with eyes almost starting out of her head, she reached out a trembling hand and let the candlestick down on the table with a clatter. Her teeth seemed to be actually chattering, and it occurred to Marianne that her behaviour was extremely odd coming from one who had appeared to harbour such violent intentions. She regarded the stranger in some perplexity convinced that she must be dealing with a mad woman.

'Will you be good enough to tell me who you are and why you are trying to set this house on fire?'

Instead of answering, the woman asked a question of her own, but in a voice that trembled so much as to be scarcely audible.

'For – for the love of heaven! Who are you?'

'The owner of this house –'

The stranger shrugged, her eyes still fixed on Marianne's face.

'You cannot be. Your name?'

'Don't you think it is rather for me to ask the questions? But I will tell you. I am called Maria Stella. I am a singer and in a few day's time, I shall appear at the Opéra. Does that satisfy you? No. Don't move –'

But ignoring the pistol still trained on her, the strange woman closed her eyes and passed a trembling hand across her brow.

'I must be mad!' she murmured. 'I must have been dreaming! I thought – but it is only some opera singer.'

The inexpressible contempt in her voice aroused Marianne's anger afresh.

'You are insufferable! For the last time, I ask you to tell me who you are and what you are doing here. There are no more portraits to steal.'

The stranger's thin lips, so pale and narrow as to be almost non-existent, curved in a disdainful smile.

'How did you know it was I?'

'It could be no-one else! Where have you put it?'

'It is no concern of yours. That portrait belongs to me. It is a family heirloom.'

'Family?' Now it was Marianne's turn to be surprised. 'What family?'

'My own, of course! I fail to see how it can interest an Italian singer, but this house belonged to my family. I say 'belongs' because you may not keep it long. It is said that Napoleon means to honour his forthcoming marriage to the niece of Marie-Antoinette by making the purchasers of émigré property disgorge it again.'

'No doubt that is why you wished to set fire to this house?'

'I could not see the house in which the Asselnats had lived and suffered become the setting for an actress's wanton revels! As for my name –'

'I will tell it you,' Marianne interrupted her, realizing at last who stood before her. 'Your name is Adélaïde d'Asselnat. And I will tell you something else as well. When I came in just now, you looked at me with a kind of terror because you were struck by a resemblance –'

'Perhaps, but that was an illusion –'

'Was it then? Look at me more closely!' Now it was Marianne's turn to seize the silver candlestick and hold it near her face. 'Look at my face, my mouth, my colouring! Go and find the picture you took away and put it beside me. You will see that I am indeed his daughter!'

'His daughter? But how —'

'His daughter, I tell you. The daughter of Pierre d'Asselnat, Marquis de Villeneuve and of Anne Selton! Maria Stella is not my real name, only a pseudonym. My name is Marianne Elizabeth d'As —'

She had no time to say more. Mademoiselle d'Asselnat must have had more than her share of excitement for one day. With a little sigh she subsided on to the salon carpet in a dead faint.

Marianne succeeded, with something of an effort, in getting the little old spinster on to one of the sofa's near the fireplace. Next, she stirred up the fire as best she could, lit some more candles to give a better light, and then made her way down to the kitchen in the basement in search of something to revive her cousin. The evening's melancholy had flown away as though by a miracle, and, all things considered, the discovery of this remarkable Adélaïde she had believed confined to the depths of Auvergne under the watchful eye of the imperial police, an eye which now seemed somewhat lacking in watchfulness, might well qualify as a miracle. She had earlier promised to plead her cousin's cause with the Emperor, but with the selfishness of all those in love, she had let it go out of her mind during the enchanted days at the Trianon. Yet now that this d'Asselnat had dropped from heaven like a dusty, grey spider, she was suddenly as happy as though she had been given a present.

As she moved about filling a tray at random with a bottle of wine, glasses, plates, a pâté which she happened to come across in the larder and a big chunk of bread, she caught herself humming the tune from 'The Vestal' which she was studying at that moment. At the same time, she was racking her brains to remember what the Duc d'Avaray and then later on Fouché had said about her turbulent relative. 'An old mad creature,' the first had called her, 'the friend of Mirabeau and La Fayette', 'a somewhat undesirable relative for one in your situation,' the second had said. From all this and from her own observations, Marianne concluded that Adélaïde was certainly no ordinary person and this pleased her.

Whatever the case, mad or not, dangerous or not, Marianne had firmly made up her mind to try and make friends with this one remaining member of her family. When she returned to the salon with her tray, she saw that the few hearty slaps she had administered to her before leaving had produced their effect. Adélaïde's eyes were open and she was sitting upright on the sofa where Marianne had left her lying down, gazing about her with the bemused expression of one who had seen a ghost. She looked up suspiciously at the pale smiling figure coming towards her.

'Are you feeling better now, cousin?' Marianne asked, putting her tray down on a small table.

Mechanically, the little spinster pushed back a lock of hair that had fallen over her eyes and stretched out her hand for the proffered glass of wine. She swallowed a full glass with an ease denoting a certain familiarity and then sighed deeply.

'Yes, I feel better now. And so, you are his daughter? You are so like him, I should not even have to ask. Except for the eyes. Pierre's eyes were black, and yours—'

'I have my mother's eyes.'

Adélaïde's thin face hardened with a look of anger.

'The Englishwoman's eyes! I know!'

'Did you – did you dislike my mother?'

'I hate the English. I never wished to know her. What need had he to seek a wife from among her hereditary enemies?'

'He loved her,' Marianne said gently. 'Does that not seem to you a sufficient reason?'

Adélaïde did not answer, but her expression told Marianne much more than any words. She guessed the tragedy of the plain girl, secretly in love with her handsome cousin only to see him one day fall in love with a girl so exquisitely lovely that there was no longer any question of fighting. She understood why Adélaïde d'Asselnat had begun to live somewhat apart from her family, why she had sought her friends among the intellectuals whose heads were full of great, revolutionary ideas. The brilliance of Versailles which had suited the young married couple so well must have been painful to this night bird who had sucked in the new ideas greedily as a thirsty traveller coming upon an unexpected spring of fresh water. But then—

'What did you do during the Terror?' Marianne asked suddenly, seized by a terrible suspicion. Surely this old maid's frustrated love would not have driven her to associate with those who had turned the ideal of a revolution into a blood bath? But there was no shadow in the candid blue eyes that looked into hers. Adélaïde shrugged.

'What could I do? I went to ground in Auvergne. Those great minds which had worked for the people's good, had become the enemies of the Convention. To Robespierre's men, I was simply an aristocrat, and hence meat for the guillotine. I had to go. My house in the Marais was given to a rope-maker from the Faubourg St-Antoine who turned it into a livery stable. And I knew that I had nothing to fear from our peasants at Villeneuve who were all devoted to the family. I had thought to end my days there, but when Bonaparte became Napoleon I, I had a mind to see just what kind of a man he was who could make victory follow at his heels like a well-trained dog. I came back to Paris—'

'To this house?'

'No. That was not possible. But I came here very often to think about – about those who were no more. That was how I came across the portrait in one of the attics. Probably your father had it put away because its warlike subject could not help but remind your mother how often France and England had been at war. I liked coming here. For all its dilapidated condition, it made me feel at home.'

'Where did you live?'

'With a friend. She died, three months ago, and I was forced to look for somewhere else. But while there, I had met someone who had a house nearby and was willing to rent me a pair of rooms –'

She broke off and, for the first time, she smiled, a smile so amazingly young and mischievous that Marianne was astounded. Suddenly, her frowsty cousin was twenty years old.

'– and now I am going to surprise you,' she went on, 'my landlady is English, she is that famous Mrs Atkins, who also tried to save the Royal Family and especially the unfortunate little King Louis XVII. But she was drawn to me by my name and her extraordinary kindness made me forget her nationality.'

'But you have been in this house? I heard you just now come down from the attic. I suppose you must know the secret hiding place?'

'Of course, I know it. It was made such a long time ago. And I used to play there as a child. The d'Asselnats have not always been the most obedient subjects and there have been troubles from time to time with the king – or with the Regent as the case might be. The hiding place was useful. I hid there when you came with those others who were with you. But I did not see your face. You wore a veil. What I suffered to think that this old house, so full of memories for me, was to belong to an actress!'

She stopped abruptly and a deep blush spread over her plain features. Marianne understood her feelings and knew a moment's anxiety. She was discovering that this woman who, a moment ago had been no more than a vague name to her, had suddenly become someone almost dear. Perhaps it was the fact that the same blood ran in both their veins, but more probably because of the strange life which Adélaïde herself had led, an unconventional life which had even taken her to prison. The two of them ought to understand one another. And , Marianne decided to have done with half-truths once and for all.

'I am not an actress,' she said gently. 'Indeed, I have never sung in public yet, except in a few private houses. The reason I have chosen to be a singer, is because I want to be free to live my life. I make my first appearance in a few days' time. Does that shock you dreadfully?'

Adélaïde thought for a moment, though the cloud which had come over her face did not lift.

'No,' she said at last. 'I think I can understand that. But it is also said that the new owner of this house is a special favourite of the Emperor's and —'

'I love him,' Marianne interrupted her firmly. 'And I am his mistress. That too, you must understand. Unless it is too difficult —'

'Well, one can at least say that you do not mince your words,' Adélaïde said when she had recovered from the shock of Marianne's announcement. 'That you should love him does not surprise me. I did myself until this senseless divorce! I cannot forgive him his arch-duchess.'

'I have been forced to forgive him. He must have an heir.'

'There were other ways he could get one. The Habsburg blood is worthless. They should know that in France. But this fool has let it go to his head! What can he hope to gain in the way of offspring by mingling his own good Corsican blood, that is pure and rich and noble, with an old strain thinned by intermarriage and hereditary weakness? What Marie-Louise brings him is the inheritance of Mad Jeanne and of Philip II. Much cause for rejoicing there! And, by the way, tell me how it is that you, a Frenchwoman, with English blood in you, are passed off as an Italian?'

Marianne sighed and poured another glass of wine for herself. She felt she needed it, if only to recover from hearing Adélaïde abusing Napoleon so freely.

'It's a long story.'

'Bah!' the old maid retorted, settling herself more comfortably. 'I've plenty of time. And if I may have a little of this pâté — I'm always hungry!' she finished up triumphantly. 'And I'm passionately fond of stories.'

As though they had known one another all their lives, the two of them sat on either side of the little table and attacked the food and Marianne's story with equal relish. Marianne herself had never felt so comfortable. She could not wait, now, to tell the whole story to this quaint old spinster whose twinkling blue eyes regarded her with such a spontaneous sympathy. The words seemed to come of their own accord and in telling Adélaïde of all that she had been through, she felt as though she were telling it to the spirits of her house as well. She was making her confession to all the past members of her family and she discovered at the same time that all the hatred and resentment she had built up suddenly left her, as though she were recovering from an illness. She had only one fear, that Adélaïde would think that she was mad. But the old lady was not without experience. When Marianne had finished, she merely patted her young cousin's hand as it lay on the table and sighed.

'And to think I thought that I had led an exciting life! If you go on at this rate, my dear child, I don't know where you might not end up! But it will be interesting to watch.'

Marianne looked up almost timidly and asked:

'You are not shocked? You do not blame me? I am afraid I may have my honour too cheap!'

'You had no choice! Besides, in all justice, it was Lady Cranmere's honour which suffered. Marianne d'Asselnat has merely followed her heart. You would not have me weep for an English honour? Especially one of such melancholy origin —'

She rose, shaking crumbs off her grey dress. Then, with a thoughtful look at Marianne, she asked:

'This American – you are quite sure you are not in love with him?'

What could Adélaïde be thinking of to ask such an apparently preposterous question? Had she not understood anything Marianne had told her, or had she some special picture of Jason? For a second, the sailor's tall figure seemed to invade the quiet room bringing with it a rush of sea air, but Marianne thrust it back.

'In love with him? How could I be? I feel friendship for him now, and a certain gratitude, but I told you I loved —'

'So you did. But too much gazing on the sun can make one blind, even to one's own heart. I don't know whether you realized it, but you have just described to me an extraordinarily attractive man, and if I were in your shoes —'

'Well?'

'Well – I think I might have paid my stupid husband's gambling debt! Just to see! He seems to know what he is about, that one – and there's no doubt but he's madly fond of you!'

At the sight of Marianne's stunned face as she sat wondering whether she could have heard right, Adélaïde suddenly burst out laughing.

'Don't look at me like that,' she exclaimed. 'One would swear you had set eyes on the devil! Let me tell you, my girl, I'm not such an old maid as you may think. Believe me, there is some good even in the most troubled times! But for the Revolution, I should still be a canoness in some aristocratic convent and no doubt bored to death! But thanks to it, I have been able to discover that virtue does not have all the charm it is cracked up to have and store up one or two fragrant memories that I may tell you about later, when we know one another better. But just remember this. There has always been hot blood in the family, and you won't be the first! And with that I'll bid you goodnight —'

Marianne could not have been more astonished if a thunderbolt had fallen on her. She was discovering that nothing she had ever thought about Adélaïde came half-way near the truth, and she would have to begin all over again. The mere fact that she had mentioned Beaufort had been enough to bring him back, tenacious and encroaching, into Marianne's mind though she still persisted in trying to drive him out again. Why? Marianne began to have strange doubts. Could she perhaps have loved the American? Oh dear, it was clear that she was still very young and there was a great deal she had to learn!

She became aware that Adélaïde was walking purposefully in the direction of the kitchen staircase and called out to stop her.

'But – where are you going?'

'Down to the cellar, child. I forgot to tell you it communicates with that of Mrs Atkins. A circumstance I discovered not long ago but one which I have found very useful ever since you changed the locks. Goodnight.'

She walked on but Marianne called after her.

'Cousin!'

It was only one word but there was a world of feeling in it. It suddenly seemed to Marianne that in Adélaïde she had rediscovered something of her Aunt Ellis and that cry was the product of her need for some of the warmth of kinship. Adélaïde paused in the doorway as though something tangible had struck her. She turned slowly, a look of strain on her face.

'Yes?'

'Why – why must you go on living with a friend when there is this house, our house? It is too big for me. I – I need someone – you! I will ask the Emperor to pardon you and then we can –'

She could not go on. There was a silence. Blue eyes and green eyes met and held one another with an intensity that was far beyond words. Was it an illusion, or was that a tear that gleamed for a moment under the older woman's lashes? She pulled out a handkerchief and blew her nose vigorously.

'I dare say I'd better move,' she muttered. 'It's dreadfully gloomy here with nothing over the fireplace.'

Patting her tottering pile of hair into place with an air of stern determination, Adélaïde turned and marched firmly in the direction of the cellar.

Left alone, Marianne gazed at her surroundings in triumph. It seemed to her that now, suddenly the old house was really itself again, that only now had the old walls begun to live and to accept their new dress. The wheel had come full circle. The house had got its soul again and Marianne a home.

Six days later, on the 19th March, the streets around the Théâtre Feydeau were crammed with carriages all turning in to deposit their elegantly dressed contents beneath the round arches of the former Théâtre de Monsieur. Women muffled in expensive furs from beneath which came the occasional gleam of jewels, heads crowned with flowers, feathers and diamonds, men in huge overcoats that concealed splendid uniforms or dark coats studded with decorations. In spite of the persistent rain which had been drenching Paris for some days, all that was most distinguished by rank or fortune in the French capital was thronging to the doors of the famous Theatre.

The choice of the Théâtre Feydeau was a late one and due particularly to the size of the auditorium which was much larger than that of the opéra in the rue de la Loi. It had also been thought that an Italian singer would find herself more at home on a stage traditionally the preserve of the Italian Comedy and then of the Opéra Comique, rather than at the Opéra where ballet was generally the chief spectacle. The dancers were notoriously averse to sharing the limelight, while the Theatre Feydeau was truly the temple of *bel canto*. If the Director of the Opéra, Picard, had felt some twinges of regret at the fabulous takings which would not come his way, he consoled himself by thinking of the trouble it would have called down on his head from the temperamental Auguste Vestris, that 'god' whom age did not mellow and who ruled as a despot over a theatre which he regarded as his own personal property.

The members of the Feydeau company, the celebrated Dugazon, the lovely Phyllis and Madame de Saint-Aubin and their male counterparts, the irresistible Elleviou and his colleagues Gavaudan, Martin, Solié and Chenard, had all displayed great deference to the imperial command and declared their willingness to welcome the singer Maria Stella whose great fame, most of it due to the efficient publicity which sprang full-grown from Fouché's fertile brain, had gone before her.

The four Parisian daily newspapers, *Le Moniteur*, the *Journal de l'Empire*, the *Gazette de France* and the *Quotidienne*, duly instructed, had all published laudatory articles about the new star of *bel canto* whom none of them had yet seen. Meanwhile, the streets of Paris became covered with bills announcing the forthcoming event at the Theatre Feydeau presenting 'for the first time in France, the celebrated Venetian diva Signorina Maria Stella, the golden voice of the peninsula'. As a result, Paris was talking quite as much about the mysterious new singer as about the new Empress still making her slow way towards France. Fashionable gossip had done the rest. The Emperor was rumoured to be wildly in love with the beautiful Maria, to have installed her secretly in an apartment in the Tuileries and to spend a fortune covering her with jewels. The magnificent preparations for the marriage went almost unnoticed: the alterations to the *salon carré* in the Tuileries for the ceremony, the overworked dressmakers and seamstresses, the endlessly drilling of troops, and even the transformations taking place on the site of the Arc de Triomphe at the Étoile, where a false arch was being erected out of scaffolding and canvas until the real one could be built. This, too, was not without set-backs caused by the carpenters going on strike for more pay every five minutes.

Marianne was both amused and terrified by all the fuss. She was well aware that on the great night, all the eyes in Paris would be on her, that her figure and her clothes would be subjected to the closest scrutiny and that the slightest weakness in her voice would be fatal. And so, she had worked to the very utmost of her strength until her friends became worried about her.

'If you wear yourself out,' said Dorothée de Périgord, who now came to the rue de Lille every day in order to encourage her friend, 'you will be too tired on Monday night to bear the fatigue and excitement of the evening.'

'Who would travel far must spare his horse,' cousin Adélaïde, who now watched over her like a mother, would remark sententiously, while every morning, Napoleon sent his personal physician Corvisart to check on her health. It was the Emperor's command that Mademoiselle Maria Stella should take care of herself.

But Marianne, scared to death, would listen to none of them. It took Gossec himself to declare that he refused to practise with her more than one hour a day and Arcadius de Jolival to take it upon himself to lock up the piano for the rest of the time before she would finally agree to take a little rest, and even then, the harp had to be shut up in the attic and the guitar in a cupboard before she could be brought to resist temptation altogether.

'I'll be a success,' she cried, 'if it kills me!'

'If you go on like this, you'll not get the chance,' retorted Fortunée Hamelin, who was constantly obliging her to swallow mysterious concoctions from her native islands, intended to sustain her, and waging a daily battle against Adélaïde who prescribed egg-nogs. 'You'll be dead first!'

The Hôtel d'Asselnat, so peaceful a few weeks before, had become a forum for the expression of everybody's opinion and filled all day long with seamstresses, bootmakers, furriers, milliners and purveyors of endless frills and fancies. Rising above the general uproar was the greedy voice of the couturier Leroy, who ordered everyone about. The great man had not slept for three nights while he was designing the clothes that Marianne was to wear on stage, and in between times had wandered about his salons with such a distracted and distant expression that three princesses, five duchesses and the wives of half a dozen marshals had practically died of rage. A fortnight from the imperial wedding day and Leroy could think of nothing but one lovely figure!

'The evening will either be my triumph, or it will not!' was all he would say, wading through miles of satin, tulle, brocade and gold thread, to the even greater confusion of the scribblers for the various journals, who one and all concluded in their article that Maria Stella would be dressed with such splendour that even the glories of the most fabulous sultanas of Golconda would pale in comparison. They claimed that she would stagger under rivers of diamonds, that she was actually to wear the crown jewels, that the Emperor had had his largest diamond, the 'Regent', mounted in a necklace for her to wear, that he had given her permission to wear a diadem like a princess and a great deal more nonsense of the same kind. Paris retailed it with all the more assurance when it was known that the Austrian Ambassador had gone anxiously to visit Fouché in private to find out how much truth there was in it all.

Meanwhile, Picard, the director of the Opéra, locked himself firmly in his office while his artists gathered round his door weeping with fury, and the performers of the Theatre Feydeau exulted as though in a personal victory. Everyone, right down to the most insignificant member of the chorus, felt immensely proud and considerably flattered to be taking part in an event of this importance.

Several times in the last few days, Marianne went to rehearse on stage, accompanied by Gossec and Arcadius, taking his role of impresario very seriously indeed. There she met Jean Elleviou, the fashionable tenor who was to sing with her in the first part of the evening. Since there had been too little time for her to learn and rehearse a whole opera, it had been decided that she would begin with a scene from Spontini's opera *The Vestal*, an elaborate Roman piece, which was one of Napoleon's favourite works. As a curtain raiser, therefore, they would sing the duet for Julia and Licinius, after which Marianne would sing Zétulbé aria from the *Calif of Baghdad* followed by a longish extract from *Pygmalion* by Cherubini. The second half of the concert was confined to Marianne alone when she would sing a number of arias from Mozart, Austrian being decidedly the coming fashion.

Everything had gone very well for Marianne. She had met with great kindness from her new colleagues and a good deal of gallantry from Elleviou, whose numerous feminine conquests left him by no means insensitive to the charms of the new star. He did his best to make her feel at home on the great stage whose dimensions had terrified her when she set foot on it for the first time.

'When the footlights are alight,' he told her, pointing to the impressive array before them, each with its own small reflector, 'you can scarcely see the audience. Besides you will not be alone on the stage for your entrance since we are to sing together.'

To help familiarize her with her surroundings, he took her on a tour of the theatre from top to bottom, showing her sets, dressing rooms, the auditorium decorated in the style of the last century in pink velvet and gilt bronze, with clusters of candles on the front of the balconies and the huge, glittering crystal chandelier. The whole of the centre of the first circle was taken up by one vast box, the Emperor's, and Marianne swore to herself that she would look nowhere else throughout the performance.

She was determined to be quite calm for this most important evening of her life. She spent most of the day in her room, resting in semi-darkness, watched over by Adélaïde, who had already taken charge of the household and herself prepared the light meals which were all that Marianne would take on the all-important day. Apart from Fortunée Hamelin, who was almost as nervous as Marianne herself, no-one was allowed near her, although three or four notes of tender encouragement had been delivered from the Tuileries.

But despite everything, even all the affectionate care of her friends, Marianne's hands were icy cold and her throat dry when she reached the theatre that night. She was trembling like a leaf in the great Pelisse of white satin lined with sable which Napoleon had given her, in spite of all the foot warmers which her maid Agathe had stuffed into the carriage. She had never been so nervous in her life.

'I can't do it,' she said again and again to Arcadius, who looked almost as pale as she in his black coat. 'I can't do it – I'm too frightened!'

'Stage fright,' he told her with a coolness he was far from feeling. 'All great artists have it. Especially for their first appearance. It will pass.'

Elleviou was waiting for Marianne at the door of her dressing room with a huge bouquet of red roses in his hands. He presented them with a bow and an encouraging smile.

'Already you are the most beautiful,' he told her in his deep voice. 'Tonight, you will also be the greatest – and we two, if you will, may perhaps be friends for life.'

'We are friends already,' she told him, and gave him her hand. 'Thank you for giving me such a comforting welcome. I needed it.'

He was a fair, good-looking man, whose figure did not betray his forty years, and although his eyes showed a somewhat disagreeable inclination to linger on her bosom, he was pleasant and kind in offering to help her past a difficult moment. His support was not something to be scorned. Moreover, Marianne had to get used to her new and rather strange surroundings, very different from anything she had known before, but in which she meant not simply to make a place for herself, but a reigning one.

The dressing room which they had given her had been transformed into a flower garden. It seemed as though there could not be a single rose, carnation or tulip left in all Paris, her friends had so conspired to outdo one another. There were huge sprays sent by Talleyrand, by Fortunée and her friend the banker Ouvrard, even, in a wild burst of unusual extravagance from Fouché, as well as from the grand marshal of the palace, and a host of others. One small bouquet bore the timid signature of M. Fercoc. Inside the great cushion of violets sent by Napoleon was another bouquet, this one made of diamonds, and with it three words which tripled it in value: 'I love you, N.'

'You see,' Arcadius told her softly. 'How can you fail to be brave with so much affection all around you? And think, he will be there. Come and see!'

While Agathe took possession of the dressing room and endeavoured to make some room among the flowers, Arcadius took Marianne by the hand and led her behind the stage curtain. Stage hands and members of the chorus were moving about in all directions, busy with last minute preparations. In the orchestra pit, the musicians were tuning their instruments and men were beginning to light the footlights. From beyond the great velvet wall, they could hear the hum of the audience.

Arcadius made a tiny crack. 'Look.'

The theatre was literally sparkling with the countless points of light from the great chandelier. All the foreign ambassadors were there and all the dignitaries of the Empire, dressed in the slightly fantastic uniforms ordained by Napoleon. Marianne's heart beat faster as she caught sight of Madame de Talleyrand in one box with a group of friends, Talleyrand himself in another surrounded by lovely ladies and Dorothée's sharp little face in a third. Prince Eugène was there, with his sister, Queen Hortense. In a low voice, Arcadius pointed out the chief of those present: Old Prince Kurakin, the Arch-Chancellor Cambacérès, the beautiful Madame Récamier, dressed in silver gauze with long pink gloves, Fortunée Hamelin, brilliant and dazzling as the bird of paradise beside the crafty-looking Ouvrard. In a box facing her sat Adélaïde d'Asselnat, resplendent in the dress of plum-coloured velvet and white satin turban which Marianne had given her. Her lorgnettes held insolently to her eyes fixing everything and everyone with a proud, imperious stare. This was her moment of glory, and her re-entry into society. A wooden-faced lackey guarded the door of her box where she sat enthroned in splendid isolation while every box around her was filled to overflowing.

'The whole Empire is here – or very nearly,' Arcadius whispered. 'And on time, too! One can see the Emperor is coming. In a little while, all these people will be in love with you!'

But Marianne's eyes had fastened on the great box, empty as yet, where Napoleon would sit with his sister Pauline and one or two of his court.

'Tomorrow,' she murmured half under her breath, overcome by a sudden sadness, 'he leaves for Compiègne to meet the new Empress. What do I care if others are in love with me. Only he matters and he is going away!'

'But he will be yours tonight!' Jolival said quickly, realizing that if Marianne gave way to melancholy she was lost. 'Run and get ready now. The orchestra is beginning the overture – quickly!'

He was right. Marianne had neither the time, nor the right to think only of herself. In this final moment, she belonged to the theatre. She had become an artist and, as such, must do her best not to disappoint those who had trusted her. Marianne d'Asselnat was gone and Maria Stella took her place. Marianne meant it to be a dazzling change.

Returning the friendly greetings which met her on all sides, she made her way back to her dressing room where Agathe stood waiting for her in the doorway holding a big bouquet of pure white camellias, lace-edged and tied with a bunch of green ribbon. She handed it to Marianne with a little bob.

'A messenger brought them.' Marianne could not help a sudden feeling of excitement as she read the little card that came with them. On it were only two words, a name, 'Jason Beaufort'. Nothing else.

So he too had been thinking of her? But how, and where? Had he come back to Paris after all? Suddenly, she wanted to go back on stage and peep through the curtains again to see if she could catch a glimpse of the American's tanned face and tall, loose-limbed figure anywhere in the audience. But it was too late now. The violins were already striking up. The chorus must be already on stage. In a moment, the curtain would go up. Marianne had just time to slip into her dress. Yet even then, as she laid the white bouquet down on her dressing table, something stirred in her, despite herself, that almost made her forget her fear. Merely with his name pinned to a few flowers, Jason had brought into that crowded, hot-house dressing room, something of his own fierce personality, a free breath of the open sea and his keen love of struggle and adventure. And Marianne discovered that no other evidence of affection had done as much for her as those few syllables.

While Agathe was putting the finishing touches to her hair and setting a few diamond stars among the thickly piled locks, Marianne remembered Adélaïde's astonishing question: *'Are you sure you're not in love with him?'*

It was ridiculous, of course she was sure! How could she hesitate for a single moment between the American and Napoleon? She was honest enough to admit the American's charm, but the Emperor was something different. Besides, he loved her with all his heart and all his power while there was absolutely nothing to show that Adélaïde's supposition was right. She had decreed, without ever seeing him, that Jason loved her but Marianne herself thought differently. The American felt guilty towards her and whatever she might have thought before, he was a man of honour. He was sincerely anxious to wipe out the wrong he had done her, that was all. None the less, Marianne admitted that she would be very glad to see him again. It would be so wonderful if he too were there tonight to share her triumph.

She was ready and the image reflected in her mirror was indeed very lovely. Leroy's much-talked-of dress was, in fact, a masterpiece of simplicity. The heavy, pearly satin with its long train lined with cloth of gold was moulded to her body like a wet sheet, only widening a little at the hem, with an effrontery which only a woman with her figure and her legs could have carried off. With its plunging neckline that showed off to the full the emeralds and diamonds Napoleon had given her, the dress undressed more than it covered her, but what might have been indecent on another became, on her, merely the height of beauty and elegance. Leroy has predicted that by the next day his salons would be besieged by a host of women all wanting a dress like it.

'But I shall not let them have it,' he had declared firmly. 'I have my reputation to think of and there is not one in a thousand could wear such a dress so regally.'

Slowly, and without taking her eyes from herself, Marianne pulled on the long, green lace gloves. Tonight, she was fascinated by her own reflection. Her beauty seemed to her like a promise of triumph. The diamond stars in her black hair flashed fire.

For a fraction of a second, she hesitated between the two bouquets that lay before her. The violets or the camellias? She was tempted to choose the latter, which would have gone better with her dress, but could she slight the flowers of the man she loved for such a reason? Quickly, with one last look at the delicate white flowers, she picked up the violets and made her way to the door while outside in the passage the stage manager was calling:

'Mademoiselle Maria Stella, on stage please!'

The duet from *The Vestal* had just finished in a storm of applause led by Napoleon himself with uncharacteristic enthusiasm. Her trembling hand clasped firmly in that of Elleviou, who was flushed with pride, Marianne made her bow with a feeling of triumph so fierce that her head seemed to spin with it. But her eyes were less on the packed house now giving them a standing ovation, than on the man in the uniform of a colonel of chasseurs sitting up there in the big, flower-filled box and smiling back at her with such love in his eyes. Next to him, was a very pretty, dark woman with a chiselled profile, his youngest and favourite sister, the Princess Pauline, and from time to time he leaned towards her as though asking her opinion.

'You've got them!' Elleviou muttered under his breath. 'Everything will be all right now. Courage! They are all yours.'

She scarcely heard him. The applause was like triumphal music filling her ears with its wonderful tempestuous sound. Was there any more intoxicating noise in the whole world? Her eyes never left the man in the box, and she looked up at him, seeing nothing else but him and dedicating all this dazzling success to him alone.

He dominated the vast black hole which had almost made her faint with terror when she came on stage so little time ago. But the panic had passed. She was herself again and not afraid any more, Elleviou was right. Nothing could touch her now.

Silence fell once more, an expectant silence that was yet more living than all the bravos that had gone before. It was as though the whole audience were holding its breath. Marianne's fingers tightened on the bouquet of violets as she began to sing the aria from the *Calif of Baghdad*. Never had her voice, trained now to cope with the most difficult tests, been so wholly at her command. It soared out across the audience, warm and flexible, containing in its pure notes all the pearls and jewels of the east, the burning scent of desert and the joyous happiness of children playing in a fountain's spray. Marianne herself, bent like a bow string towards the Emperor's box, sang for one man alone, forgetting all the others whom she carried with her along the magic pathway of her music.

Once again, it was a triumph, noisy, uproarious, indescribable. The theatre seemed to explode into frenzied applause and a sweet-smelling storm of flowers began to rain down on the stage. Across the orchestra pit, a radiant Marianne could look out on a standing audience, wild with applause.

On all sides there were cries of 'Encore! Encore!'

She took a few steps forward to the front of the stage. Her eyes left the imperial box at last and, meeting the conductor's look, she nodded to him to begin the aria again. Then she lowered her eyes while gradually the audience quietened down and the musicians resumed their instruments. Once again, the music began to spin its enticing thread.

But suddenly a movement in one of the stage boxes caught Marianne's attention. A man had just come in and instantly her eye was drawn to him. She thought for a second that it was Jason Beaufort, whom she had sought in vain among the rapt faces before her. It was not him but someone else at the sight of whom Marianne's blood seemed to freeze in her veins. He was very tall with broad shoulders encased in dark blue velvet and thick fair hair brushed in the latest style and the face above the high, white muslin cravat bore a cynical expression. He was a handsome man in spite of the thin scar that ran across one cheek from the corner of his mouth to his ear, but Marianne gazed at him with the incredulous horror belonging to those who have seen a ghost.

She wanted to cry out, to try and overcome the terror which was taking possession of her but no sound came. She felt as though she were in a bad dream, or else going mad. It could not be true. This frightful thing could not be happening to her. At one blow she saw the wonderful, delicate world she had built up for herself at the cost of so much suffering crumble to pieces at her feet. Her mouth opened, gasping for air, but the impression of nightmare became more terrifying while the audience, the imperial box with its dark red roses, the great velvet and gold curtains, the footlights and the conductor's startled face all merged into one infernal kaleidoscope. Marianne put up her hands with a small pitiful movement, trying with all her strength to push the spectre back into the darkness from which it had risen. But the spectre would not go. He was looking at her now, and he was smiling …

Marianne gave one small desperate cry and then collapsed on to the flower-studded stage while, towering above the uproar which arose all about him, her husband, Francis Cranmere, the man she had believed that she had killed, bent forward to look down on the stage and on the slender white form that lay there, twinkling with tiny stars in the stage lights. He was still smiling.

When she opened her eyes, some minutes later, Marianne saw a ring of anxious faces bending over her, against a background of flowers, and realized that she was in her dressing room. Arcadius and Adélaïde were there, Agathe was bathing her temples with something cool and Corvisart was holding her hand. Elleviou was there too and Fortunée Hamelin while, towering over them all, was the resplendent figure of the Grand Marshal Duroc, despatched no doubt by the Emperor.

Seeing her open her eyes, Fortunée immediately seized her friend's free hand.

'What happened?' she asked affectionately.

'Francis!' Marianne murmured. 'He was there – I saw him!'

'You mean – your husband? But that is impossible! He's dead.'

Feebly Marianne shook her head.

'I saw him – tall and fair, dressed in blue – in Prince Cambacérès's box.' She struggled to raise herself and her eyes met Duroc's imploringly. The grand marshal understood and disappeared at once. Marianne allowed Corvisart to push her gently back on to the cushions.

'You must calm yourself, mademoiselle. His majesty is in the gravest anxiety on your account. I must be able to reassure him.'

'The Emperor is very good,' she said faintly. 'I am ashamed to be so weak—'

'There is no need to be ashamed. How do you feel? Do you feel able to continue the concert or should we ask the public to excuse you?'

The cordial which the imperial physician had given her was gradually having its effect on Marianne. She felt a little warmth and life return to her body. Now she felt nothing beyond a general lassitude and a slight headache.

'Perhaps I can go on,' she began, a little hesitantly. It was true, she felt strong enough to return to the stage but at the same time she was afraid of the audience, of seeing again the face which had filled her with such terror. In a flash, in the moment of seeing it, she had understood why Jason Beaufort had done all he could to make her go with him and what the mysterious danger was, the precise nature of which he had always refused to divulge. He must have known that Lord Cranmere was alive. But he had wanted to spare her the knowledge. In a moment, perhaps, when Duroc had found him, Francis was going to cross the threshold of this very room and come to her. He was coming now. There were footsteps in the passage. The footsteps of more than one man.

Marianne clung desperately to Fortunée's hand.

'Don't leave me – at all costs, don't leave me!'

There was a knock. The door opened. Duroc was there but the man he brought with him was not Francis, it was Fouché. The Minister of Police looked grave and anxious. With a wave of his hand, he dismissed all those gathered about Marianne except for Fortunée, who stayed holding tightly to her friend's hand. 'I fear, mademoiselle,' he said speaking very deliberately, 'that you have been the victim of an hallucination. At the grand marshal's request, I myself went into the Prince's box. There was no one there corresponding to the description you gave.'

'But I saw him! I am not mad; I swear to you! He was dressed in blue velvet – the moment I close my eyes, I can see him still. The people in the box must have seen him!'

Fouché raised one eyebrow and made a helpless gesture.

'The Duchess of Bassano, who is in Prince Cambacérès's box thinks that the only blue habit she saw just after the interval belonged to the vicomte d'Aubecourt, a young Flemish nobleman just recently arrived in Paris.'

'Then you must find this vicomte. Francis Cranmere is an Englishman. He would not dare to come to Paris under his own name. I want to see this man.'

'Unfortunately, he cannot be found. My men are turning the theatre upside down in search of him but so far –'

He was interrupted by three quick raps on the door. Fouché went himself to open it. Outside was a man in evening dress who bowed briefly.

'There is no-one in the theatre, Minister,' he said, 'who seems able to tell us where the Vicomte d'Aubecourt can be found. He appears to have vanished into thin air during the uproar which followed mademoiselle's illness.'

There was a silence so profound it seemed that everyone had stopped breathing. Marianne was as white as a sheet.

'Nowhere to be found! Vanished!' she said at last. 'But he can't have done! He was not a ghost—'

'That is all that I can tell you,' Fouché said shortly. 'Apart from the duchess, who believed she saw him, no-one, do you hear me, no-one had seen this person. Now will you tell me what I am to tell the Emperor? His majesty is waiting!'

'The Emperor has waited long enough. Tell him, if you please, that I am at his service.'

A little unsteadily, but with determination, Marianne rose to her feet and putting aside the woollen shawl they had wrapped round her, went to her dressing table for Agathe to restore some kind of order to her hair. She forced herself not to think of the spectre which had risen from the past to appear so suddenly against the red velvet background of a stage box in a theatre. Napoleon was waiting. Nothing and no-one should ever keep her from going to him whenever he was waiting. His love was the one really good thing in the world.

One after another, her friends left the box, Duroc and Fouché first, followed by the singers and then by Arcadius, though with evident reluctance. Only Adélaïde d'Asselnat and Fortunée Hamelin remained until Marianne was ready.

A few minutes later, a storm of applause shook the old theatre to its foundations. Marianne was back on stage.

About the Author

Juliette Benzoni was born Andrée-Marguerite-Juliette Mangin on 30 October 1920 in Paris, France. She spent her childhood in Saint-Germain-des-Pres until she was almost 15 years old, when her family went to live in Saint-Mandé. She was educated at College d'Hulet, then at the Institut Catholique, where she studied philosophy, law and literature. In 1941 she married a doctor from Dijon, Maurice Gallois, and was soon mother of two children, Anne and Jean-François. In her twenties, she spent many hours in libraries, studying the history of Burgundy in Medieval times. One day she came across the legend of the Order of the Golden Fleece, which would later inspire her to write the Catherine series.

After her husband died in 1950, she went to Morocco to visit a relative of his, and ended up staying for two years, joining the editorial staff at a radio station called Radio-International. She then met Colonel André Benzoni, who in 1953 became her second husband. After her return to Paris, France, she launched into journalism, writing for several newspapers. At the beginning of the 1960s, a literary editor who had seen her make a television appearance invited her to write a historical romance in the style of Anne Golon's *Angelique*. The outcome was *Catherine: One Love is Enough* (original title, *Catherine, Il Suffit d'un Amour*), the hugely successful first entry in what was originally intended to be a five book series.

Next came another big success with the *Marianne* series, set during the Napoleonic period, beginning with *Marianne: A Star for Napoleon* (original title, *Marianne: Une Étoile Pour Napoléon*). Juliette was then asked if she would write two additional *Catherine* books, due to their sensational popularity. She agreed, and the series' seventh and final entry, *La Dame de Montsalvy*, appeared in 1979.

In 1983, the French station Antenne 2 adapted *Marianne: A Star for Napoleon* for television, directed by Marion Sarraut. This led on three years later to a television adaptation of all seven books in the *Catherine* series, again directed by Sarraut; the end result pleased Juliette far more than a substandard movie version produced in 1968.

Juliette continued to write up to her death on 7 February 2016.

For more information about Juliette and the *Catherine* books visit the official website: www.catherinedemontsalvy.ch.

Also by Juliette Benzoni